Under the Dog Star

Under the Dog Star

A Rachel Goddard Mystery

Sandra Parshall

Poisoned Pen Press

First Edition 2011

10 9 8 7 6 5 4 3 2 1

Library of Congress Catalog Card Number: 2011926958

ISBN: 9781590588789   Hardcover
        9781590588802   Trade Paperback

Poisoned Pen Press
6962 E. First Ave., Ste. 103
Scottsdale, AZ 85251
www.poisonedpenpress.com
info@poisonedpenpress.com

Printed in the United States of America

For Jerry

Acknowledgments

As always, I'm grateful to my husband, Jerry Parshall, and my friends Carol Baier and Cat Dubie for their suggestions, critiques, and encouragement. I couldn't write a book without them.

My friends in the Guppies Chapter of Sisters in Crime are a daily source of support and never fail to relieve the loneliness of the solitary writer.

Dr. Doug Lyle is an invaluable source of information, and I don't know how anyone can write a mystery novel without his Writer's Forensics Blog. If I get anything wrong, it's my fault, not Doug's.

Special thanks to Ellen Thornwall and Kim Hammond for allowing me to include their pets in this novel.

My editor, Barbara Peters, made this a better book with her insights and suggestions, and the whole crew at Poisoned Pen Press is a pleasure to work with.

Many thanks to the readers who have taken the time to tell me they enjoyed my books. You can't possibly know how sustaining your praise is in times of self-doubt.

Chapter One

In the silver moonlight, the dogs appeared as a dark mass moving down the hill and across the pasture. They headed straight toward three dozen sheep huddled on a carpet of autumn leaves under an oak.

Tom Bridger aimed his shotgun at the sky and fired.

The blast stopped the dogs for a second. The startled sheep jerked apart, turned and ran.

The largest dog broke from the pack and streaked after the sheep. The rest followed, yelping and baying.

Tom fired into the air again, and again. The dogs didn't stop until his fourth shot. They milled about in the pasture as if trying to make up their minds whether to stay or go.

Another shotgun blast decided the issue for them. They wheeled around and took off over the hill.

Lying in the dark, with Tom's space in the bed growing cold beside her, Rachel tensed at the sound of gunshots in the distance. She clutched the blanket, bunching it in both fists. She knew Tom wouldn't shoot to kill, but she also knew he was losing patience after going out night after night to protect his sheep from the feral dog pack.

At the third shot, Rachel's cat Frank stirred from his spot against her legs and dropped off the bed to hide underneath.

From his bed near the door, Tom's bulldog Billy Bob gave a low growl.

Rachel sat up, hugging her knees. A fourth, then a fifth shot rang out. She waited, but heard no more.

The feral dogs weren't Rachel's problem, weren't her responsibility, but she was a veterinarian and couldn't be indifferent to their fate. Mason County, in Virginia's Blue Ridge Mountains, had become a dumping ground for pet dogs as unemployment soared in the state and many people lost their homes. They probably thought they'd done the dogs a favor by turning them loose in a rural area, but the animals were hungry and desperate. Struggling to survive, they had formed a pack, and for the last few months they'd roamed the county, stealing eggs and killing chickens in farmyards. Lately they'd attacked a couple of lambs and a calf. If left on their own, they would starve or the farmers would exterminate them.

The ringing telephone jolted Rachel. For a moment she hesitated. She'd moved into Tom's house a month ago, but the situation still felt tentative, and she was reluctant to answer his home telephone. She had no choice, though. A call at midnight was an emergency, usually a summons from the Sheriff's Department. As chief deputy and second in command, Tom had to respond. Nobody ever summoned the aging, frail sheriff anymore when trouble arose.

Stretching across the bed, Rachel switched on the lamp and grabbed the receiver.

"Hi, is this Dr. Goddard?" a young female voice asked. "I'm sorry if I woke you up. This is Gail, the dispatcher, calling for Captain Bridger."

Rachel knew she shouldn't be surprised that every employee at the department knew she and Tom were living together, but it still made her feel as if she were doing something disreputable in this small, conservative community. "Captain Bridger's outside right now." She caught sight of Tom's cell phone on the bedside table. "And he doesn't have his phone with him. I can run out and get him, but it'll take a few minutes. Can I tell him what it's about?"

"Well, I don't have a lot of information and I'm not real sure what happened, but Dr. Hall—you know, from the hospital?—he's dead. Somebody attacked him."

Rachel gasped when she heard the name. Dr. Gordon Hall, one of Mason County's most prominent citizens, owned Tri-County General Hospital. The family's German shepherd was one of Rachel's patients. "Dr. Hall was attacked? You're sure he's dead?"

"Oh, yes, ma'am, he's definitely dead. His wife called it in, and she doesn't know how it happened. Their kids went looking for him and found him laying in the yard. She's just about going crazy, screaming and crying. I already sent a couple of deputies to secure the scene, but Captain Bridger needs to get out there."

"I'll find him and tell him right away." Rachel hung up and rushed to get dressed, yanking on jeans, sweater, shoes, raking her thick auburn hair out of her eyes with her fingers. She could imagine Dr. Hall's wife waiting for the police, probably with her children around her yet feeling suddenly alone in the world.

Billy Bob trotted after Rachel down the stairs and along the hallway. "Sorry, boy," she said at the back door. "You can't go this time. Stay."

She snatched a flashlight from a hook by the door and ran out in search of Tom.

Chapter Two

An hour later, dressed in his brown Sheriff's Department uniform, Tom leaned over the body of Dr. Gordon Hall and trained his Maglite on the man's ravaged throat. Dr. Gretchen Lauter, Mason County's medical examiner, crouched on the other side of the corpse. The victim, a tall man in his late fifties, sprawled on his back in deep shadow along the edge of the woods, several hundred feet down a slope from his house. Nothing remained of his throat but a bloody mess.

"What the hell did this?" Tom had come out here expecting to find evidence of a familiar means of murder, but now he wasn't sure he was looking at a murder at all. "An animal?"

"That's my first impression. Only an animal could cause this kind of wound. And that looks like animal hair." Dr. Lauter flicked her own flashlight to Hall's clenched right fist, resting on his chest. A few dark hairs stuck out between his fingers.

Dr. Lauter rose, the bones in her arthritic knees grinding together audibly as she struggled to straighten them. Tom held out a hand to steady her, and for once she accepted his offer of help instead of brushing it aside. Together they moved away from the body.

"Arterial spray everywhere." Tom swept his flashlight beam over the red-streaked autumn leaves on the ground. He'd arrived seconds before Dr. Lauter, and they'd come directly to the body without seeing the family first. Reaching Gordon Hall meant walking through his blood, and now they had to track through it again. Tom didn't want to carry any of it into the house when he went to talk to the widow.

They ducked under the crime scene tape and onto an expanse of well-tended grass. Dr. Lauter gestured toward the Hall family's imposing brick house, sitting at the peak of a gentle rise. Every window glowed with light. "Someone could have been looking out while it was happening," she said, "and they wouldn't have seen a thing down here."

Security floodlights attached to the house cast a yellowish tint over the patio and swimming pool, and moonlight brightened the lawn, but the illumination didn't reach the spot where Hall lay dead.

"You'd think they would have heard something, though," Tom said. "He must have been screaming, fighting—"

They stood in silence for a moment, and Tom stared down at the bright circle of his flashlight beam on the grass until the horror of Gordon Hall's last moments overwhelmed his imagination. He shoved the images to the back of his mind and asked, "Any idea what kind of animal?"

"Well, it doesn't look like a bear attack. Aside from the throat, I mean. If a bear had killed him, I'd expect to see deep claw marks on his torso, and his clothes would be ripped apart. He only has a few scratches on the front of his jacket, and they hardly even tore the fabric."

Reluctant to voice his own suspicion, Tom prodded, "So? What else could have done it?"

Dr. Lauter sighed. "I hope the autopsy proves me wrong, but right now, if I have to guess, I'd say a large dog killed him."

"Aw, god. This is what I've been afraid of, that wild pack hurting somebody." But something about this didn't seem right to Tom. "If I've got the timing of this attack on Hall figured correctly, the dogs were over on my property a few minutes later. That's five miles. They could have cut across land and jumped fences—"

"No." Dr. Lauter shook her head. "I don't think a whole pack of dogs attacked Gordon, for the same reason I don't think a bear did it. I'll have to examine him in good light, but it looks like the throat is the only severe wound. I'd guess it was a single dog—a big one, and mean as hell, but only one."

Tom's momentary relief that the feral pack wasn't responsible quickly gave way to a different kind of apprehension. "Don't the Halls have a big German shepherd? Where is it now? If it turned on its owner, it's dangerous."

"Gordon's old dog probably doesn't have enough teeth left to do this, even if he wanted to. And I can't imagine why he'd want to. Gordon doted on him as if he were a child."

"Then we're probably talking about a feral dog acting alone, maybe one that hasn't taken up with the pack," Tom said. "Or somebody's pit bull that's roaming around loose."

"Maybe those hairs in his hand can tell us what breed it was, and if there's DNA it can identify the specific animal."

"Yeah, right. Now all I have to do is search the countryside for one particular dog and do a DNA match." Tom blew out a breath. "Hell. This is going to cause a panic."

"You bet it will," Dr. Lauter said. "Well, I'll stay with the body until the techs get here and take their pictures, then I'll have him moved to the hospital morgue temporarily. Come on over after you talk to the family and we'll take a look at him together before he goes to Roanoke for autopsy."

What a way to end up, Tom thought. Dr. Hall's mutilated body would be combed over for evidence in the hospital he'd owned and run. "Try to get him moved in the next couple of hours, will you? His wife and kids don't need to have him lying dead in the yard all night."

As he climbed the slope to the house, Tom thought of Rachel, probably back in bed and asleep by now, her dark red hair splashed across her pillow. He wouldn't see her again tonight.

A couple of deputies stood on the patio, awaiting further orders after stringing up the crime scene tape. Tom scraped his boots on the grass to remove any blood he'd picked up, then nodded at Brandon Connolly, the sandy-haired young deputy who often acted as his partner. "Come on in with me, Bran."

Even before he opened the French doors from the patio to the living room, Tom could hear Vicky Hall's sobs. She sat on the couch, crying on her teenage daughter Beth's shoulder. When Tom entered, Beth looked up at him with tear-reddened eyes, a strand of her wavy brown hair stuck to one cheek. A child in need of comfort herself, she seemed helpless in the face of her mother's grief.

"Mrs. Hall, can I talk to you for a minute?" When Tom approached her, he caught the sharp odor coming from her body and breath. The smell of advanced kidney failure. While Brandon took up a position by the French doors, Tom sat in a club chair across the coffee table from the new widow. "Beth, would you get your mother a glass of water? You don't want her to get dehydrated."

"Yes, sir," the girl said in a near-whisper. She pulled away from her mother and rose, tall and slender in jeans and a sweater. Pushing her hair back behind her ears, she hurried from the room.

Tom hadn't seen Vicky Hall up close in several years, and her appearance shocked him. Although she was no more than fifty-five, she looked like a wizened old woman, bone-thin inside a blue robe, her skin a sickly yellow. Tom remembered her as energetic, always smiling, not beautiful but pretty in a bubbly way that made men run to open doors and pull out chairs for her. Her brown hair had once fallen to her shoulders in shining dark waves. Now it hung lank and dull, not so much gray as colorless. She was losing her long battle with lupus.

"I'm sorry about your husband," Tom said.

Slumped against the sofa cushions, she dabbed at her eyes with a wad of soaked tissues. "I can't believe this is happening."

He averted his gaze from that heartbreaking ruin of a face. "I need to ask you some questions. I'll make it as brief as I can."

At her nod of agreement, Tom asked, "Who found Dr. Hall?"

She twisted the tissues between her fingers, shredding wet fragments onto her robe. "Beth and Marcy," she choked out. "They ran right out when they heard what was on the answering machine."

"The answering machine?" Tom reached inside his uniform jacket and pulled a notebook and pen from his shirt pocket. "What do you mean?"

"It's all there, the sounds—" She covered her face with both hands. "Oh, god, it's horrible."

"Mrs. Hall, please," Tom said. "I know this is hard, but I have to ask you to concentrate and explain what happened. Tell me everything."

Beth appeared in the doorway, a glass of water in one hand, and paused as if reluctant to interrupt. Beside her stood her younger sister, a beautiful dusky-skinned little girl in pajamas and robe. Dark red smears stained her pink slippers.

Tom waved a hand, urging Beth to go to her mother. The younger girl remained in the doorway, chewing on her bottom lip.

Beth held the glass while her mother sipped the water. When she was more composed, Vicky told Tom, "I was getting ready for bed, and Gordon went out to walk the dog. I was in the bathroom, and I heard the bedroom phone. The answering machine picked up. When I came out, I heard Gordon's voice. Then—" A shiver shook her body. "He screamed. I grabbed the phone, but he wasn't there anymore."

Good god, Tom thought. Did they have a recording of the attack? "Where's the answering machine? I need to hear the tape."

"It's on our phone in the bedroom. Beth, honey, go get it, would you?"

"Show Brandon where it is. Let him handle it." As they left the room, Tom called after the deputy, "Don't take the tape out. Unplug the phone and bring it down here."

While they waited, he asked Vicky, "You heard the message, then sent your daughters to look for your husband?" Hadn't she stopped to think the girls might be in danger out there in the dark?

"Beth was still up, and she ran into the bedroom when she heard me screaming. Then she ran out to look for Gordon. I didn't realize Marcy had gone with her until they came back in."

"What did they tell you when they came back?"

The younger girl, Tom noticed, had disappeared into the hall when Beth and Brandon passed, but now she crept back and stood just inside the door.

"They said he was hurt," Vicky told Tom, her voice thick with tears. "I called 911. I wanted to go to him, I'm a nurse, I thought I could help, but Beth wouldn't let me. She said it was too late." Vicky couldn't control the sobs that wracked her frail body.

Tom turned his attention to Marcy. He knew she was around eleven, but she looked a couple of years younger. She was one of the Halls' three adopted children, a mixed-race girl with brown skin and curly black hair. Tom, whose Melungeon heritage showed in his dark olive skin, coal-black hair, strong nose and cheekbones, couldn't help feeling a kind of kinship with her, but he doubted she saw him as anything but a frightening adult in a uniform.

"Marcy, would you come over here and talk to me for a minute?"

She shot a wide-eyed glance at him, ducked her head, didn't move. Her rigid posture made Tom think of a trapped animal steeling itself for an attack.

"It's okay," he said. "I just need to ask you a couple of questions."

"Marcy, for heaven's sake," Vicky Hall snapped. Regaining a degree of composure, she sniffed and swiped tears from her face. "Do as you're told. Come over here."

"Mrs. Hall—" Tom caught himself. Vicky Hall was distraught. She didn't know how she sounded. Right now she might not be capable of considering how Marcy felt after seeing her father lying dead with his throat torn open. Ignoring the mother, he spoke quietly to the daughter. "Marcy, can I ask you some questions?"

She nodded without looking at him.

"Answer Captain Bridger properly," Vicky told her. "Say *Yes, sir.*"

"Yes, sir," the girl whispered.

"And speak up," Vicky said.

Tom kept his own voice gentle. "Did you see any animals down by the woods?"

Marcy started to shake her head, then glanced at her mother and murmured, "No, sir."

"Is your father's dog okay? Did he come back to the house with you?"

"Thor?" Vicky exclaimed. "Oh dear lord. I haven't even thought about him. Where is he? What happened to him? Marcy, answer me. Where is Thor?"

"I don't know."

"We'll find him," Tom said.

He heard Brandon clomping down the stairs, and he rose when the deputy returned to the living room with Beth trailing him. Brandon set the phone, the kind with a built-in answering machine, on a console table and plugged the line into a jack underneath that Beth pointed out.

"Are you sure you want to hear this again?" Tom asked Vicky.

With her lips pressed together in a grim line, she straightened her back and nodded.

Gordon Hall sounded calm at first. "Hey, honey, Thor wants to nose around for a while, so we'll stay out another fifteen or twenty minutes before we turn back. I don't want you to start worrying about us."

Vicky whimpered and buried her face in her hands. Beth rushed to the sofa and wrapped her arms around her mother. Marcy had retreated to a corner, where she stood with shoulders hunched and arms straight at her sides.

The call didn't end with Hall's message for his wife. A brief silence followed, then Hall exclaimed, "What the hell?"

His voice grew louder. "Where did you come from? What are you doing here?"

Animal snarls and barks erupted into the quiet. Gordon Hall yelled, "Shit! Get away! Get off!"

No human voice, responded.

The growling and snarling sounded like an escalating dogfight.

"Thor! Good god—He's going to kill my dog! Stop it!"

The next sounds were muffled, indistinct, as if Hall had dropped the phone into the leaves and it was kicked around in a scuffle. Gordon Hall screamed, a piercing cry of terror. The answering machine cut him off.

In the sudden silence of the living room, Tom cleared his throat. "Beth," he said, "did you hear or see another person or an animal when you went outside to look for your father?"

"No, I didn't see anything," she answered without looking at Tom. She focused all her attention on her mother.

"Was your father's dog there with him?"

"No. I don't know what happened to him."

"Well, then," Tom said, stuffing his notebook into his shirt pocket, "we'd better try to find him. He could be hurt."

Vicky moaned. "Thor wouldn't have left Gordon. That dog worships him. He would've tried to protect Gordon. He might have been hurt, but he still would have chased after—" She stood abruptly and wobbled on her feet. "We have to find him. Gordon would never forgive me if I let Thor die too."

"You stay here," Tom said. "We'll look for him."

Vicky took several deep, quavering breaths, pulling herself together. "All right. Thank you, Tom."

For the next few minutes, they searched for the shepherd, Brandon looking in the house and Tom outside. The dog wasn't there. The crime scene team had arrived, and Tom asked them to look for Hall's cell phone in the leaf litter around and under his body.

When Tom returned to the living room, another of the Halls' adopted children had appeared. David, Marcy's teenage brother, stood against a wall next to his sister, with his fists jammed into his jeans pockets. Like Marcy, he was a good-looking kid, but a sullen, watchful expression spoiled his handsome face.

The only Hall children missing were an adult son who lived in Florida and a daughter who was away at medical school.

"Were you here when it happened?" Tom asked David. "Did you go outside?"

"I was asleep," the boy mumbled. "I woke up when the cops got here."

Hadn't he been awakened by his mother's screams? Tom knew teenage boys could sleep as if drugged, but wouldn't the unfamiliar noise of a crisis in the household penetrate that fog? It seemed odd, but Tom didn't see that it mattered, so he let it go.

He told Vicky, "I've called for more deputies, and they'll look for your dog in the woods. If he's there, they'll find him. Is Thor aggressive? Has he ever bitten anybody?"

"No, never. He looks ferocious, but he's just a sweet old pet. I'm sure he tried to protect Gordon, but he's got hip dysplasia, and I don't think he could even protect himself." Vicky raised wet eyes to Tom. "We've seen that pack of wild dogs around here a couple of times. Do you think they could have ganged up on my husband and killed him?"

Tom hesitated, wondering how she could have missed the implications of what was recorded on the tape. The animal sounds hadn't been made by a whole pack of dogs. Hall hadn't screamed at a pack of dogs. First, he'd sounded surprised to find somebody, another person, on his property. Then he'd begged that person to call off a single dog. The intruder remained silent and let the animal attack. Tom glanced at Brandon, who looked back with a frown. He'd reached the same conclusions.

"The medical examiner will have to give us the exact cause of death," Tom said. "I'd rather not speculate."

But he was certain of what he'd heard—somebody had murdered Gordon Hall, using a dog as the weapon.

Chapter Three

Tom returned home at six in the morning, when Rachel was finishing her breakfast cereal at the kitchen table. Taking in his chin stubble and bloodshot eyes, she said, "You're going to get a little rest now, I hope."

"Afraid not." He leaned to kiss her, then patted Billy Bob, who had trotted into the kitchen to greet him. "I just want to shave and grab something to eat before I head back. The sheriff's coming in for a meeting about the case, and he sounded cranky as hell on the phone."

She knew she'd be wasting her breath if she argued in favor of a nap before he went back to work. "Sit down and have some coffee. I'll make you a hot breakfast."

"I'll just get some cereal. You don't have to cook for me."

"I want to, okay? Sit down before you collapse." Rachel rose, poured a mug of coffee for him, and began pulling together breakfast ingredients. While a skillet heated, she cracked a couple of eggs into a bowl and whisked them with a fork. "So, was it murder?"

"Yeah, I think it was. The weirdest one I've ever seen. It looks like somebody set a dog on him, then stood by while it killed him. Tore out his throat."

Tom's words sent a chill through Rachel. "That's horrible. Just one dog? And somebody was with it? You're sure?"

"It wasn't the feral pack, if that's what you're worried about."

Thank god. She dropped a pat of butter into the skillet and it landed with a sizzle. "Well, that's good. If anything about this could be called good."

"I think it's only a matter of time before they hurt somebody, though. You and Holly had better get moving if you want to save them."

Surprised, Rachel said, "So you've changed your mind about that?"

"I want to prevent a tragedy. After seeing what one dog did to Gordon Hall—" Tom shook his head. "I'd hate to think what a pack of them could do to a kid."

Rachel nodded. The less she said about the planned rescue operation, the less likely Tom was to withdraw his support. Pouring the eggs into the skillet, she asked, "How can you be sure someone was controlling the dog that killed Dr. Hall?"

She listened with growing horror to his description of what was on the answering machine tape. Setting his plate of eggs and toast on the table, she said, "Why kill him that way? Practically everybody in Mason County owns a gun. Shooting him would have been quicker and easier."

"I've been wondering about that," Tom said. "I think the person who did it might be hoping we'll blame the dog pack and not recognize it as a murder."

"Who could hate Dr. Hall enough to do something that vicious?"

Tom gave a humorless laugh. "Remember I told you my mother was head of the nursing staff at the hospital? Some of the stories she told about him—Believe me, there's no shortage of people with grudges against Gordon Hall."

Rachel had just stepped through the front door of Mountainview Animal Hospital when she saw Holly Turner, her young assistant, taping a new missing dog notice on the wall of the waiting area. Rachel moved closer to examine it. The poster showed a color photo of a young beagle, rising on his hind legs with an orange rubber ball in his mouth. "Oh, no. Not Jazzy. He's just a puppy."

"Poor little thing." Tears pooled in Holly's blue eyes. She was a beautiful young woman, Melungeon like Tom, with olive skin and long black hair, but when she was upset her lower lip trembled, red blotches appeared on her cheeks, and she looked years younger than nineteen.

The new poster made an even dozen notices on the wall. Purebreds and mutts, big and little, young and old, the dogs had all disappeared from their owners' yards in the past few weeks.

"I'll bet somebody's stealin' those poor dogs," Holly went on. "And they're probably sellin' them to some awful lab that's doin' experiments on them. I don't believe for one minute they're all runnin' away from home to join that wild pack. That's just crazy talk."

"I don't believe it either," Rachel said. "It's awfully suspicious that so many pets have disappeared so close together. I wish it hadn't taken so long for a pattern to emerge."

"What are we gonna do about it?" Holly blinked away her tears, her face transformed by a new focus on action.

"I don't know yet, but we can't stand by while this keeps happening. We have to do something." Right now, though, they had other dogs to worry about. "Did you hear about Dr. Hall?"

"Yeah, somebody called Joanna real early this mornin' and told her." Holly now roomed with Joanna McKendrick, owner of a horse farm where Rachel and Holly had shared a cottage until recently. "She thinks those wild dogs did it, and she thinks they're killin' all these pets too. She's goin' off to Kentucky today to deliver a horse, and she's takin' both of her dogs with her cause she doesn't think they'd be safe here. But I don't believe a bit of that. I'm real afraid people are gonna hunt the wild dogs down and kill all of them."

"Tom wants us to go ahead and start trapping them, and I agree with him. Do you have any pens ready yet at the McClure place?" Holly was creating an animal sanctuary on the property she'd inherited from an aunt, but construction had begun only a month before.

"The men just got one big section finished. The indoor shelter's not ready, but we can go ahead and put some dogs in the pens. They'll be okay until the weather turns real cold. I'm gonna move into the house with Grandma, and I'll help her take care of the animals. Let's do it. Let's start tonight."

"It won't be easy," Rachel cautioned. "They've become very wary of people. We can't expect to get more than one or two at a time, and some nights we won't catch any."

"You can do it, you and the dog warden, I know you can. And do you think you can you get Captain Bridger to do somethin' about all these pet dogs gettin' stolen?"

"I'll try, but I don't know if he'll have time right now. The Sheriff's Department may be too busy during a murder investigation."

"This is just downright crazy, you know? Pet dogs disappearin' and wild dogs runnin' loose, and now Dr. Hall gettin' killed by a dog. What's goin' on around here?"

Rachel had no answer. Something strange and frightening was happening in Mason County that nobody had put a name to yet. She scanned the missing dog posters, all of them showing happy, pampered animals. Their owners were searching for them, comforting crying children who missed their pets, offering rewards for their return. At the same time, a pack of dogs that had once been pets roamed Mason County, scrounging for food and struggling to survive after being dumped like garbage by their owners.

Rachel thought she understood dogs as well as anyone could. She doubted she would ever understand people.

Tom played the answering machine tape three times for Sheriff Toby Willingham but couldn't get him to focus on its meaning. "Can't you hear what the rest of us hear?"

Dr. Lauter and animal warden Joe Dolan, seated at the conference room table with them, looked as exasperated as Tom felt.

"All I know is, my phone started ringing before six o'clock this morning," the sheriff said from his place at the head of the table. He looked ill, his skin pasty and his hands trembling, but he'd come in to make sure Tom got something done about the feral dogs. "People want those damned animals rounded up before they kill somebody else."

"Oh, for heaven's sake, Toby," Dr. Lauter said, "how many times do we have to tell you the dog pack didn't kill Gordon Hall? Just wait and see, the state medical examiner is going to agree with me—the wounds were inflicted by a single animal."

"Look at the pictures." Tom opened a folder and began laying photos of Hall's body in front of the sheriff.

Willingham drew back and averted his eyes, his face screwed up in disgust.

Joe Dolan, a wiry young man with freckles and bright red hair, blew out a noisy breath and shook his head at the sheriff's reaction.

"Will you please look at the pictures of the victim, sir?" Tom said. "There are no wounds to support the theory that he was killed by an entire pack of animals."

"Then it was one dog that's part of the pack." Willingham shoved the photos toward Tom without looking at them.

God damn it. Tom bit back angry words and snatched up the pictures.

"That's not real likely, Sheriff," Dolan said. "One dog attacking and the rest of them just standing by. Or one dog from the pack going off by itself and doing something like this. That doesn't sound like pack behavior to me."

Willingham pointed a finger at Dolan. "Don't try to get off the hook. This is your fault, young man. If you'd stayed on top of this when people started dumping their animals here, it never would've gone this far."

Dolan's cheeks colored, his freckles disappearing in the flush of red. "I'm one person, Sheriff. I'm the whole Department of Animal Control and there's a limit to what I can do. I spend half my time getting coons and possums out of people's chimneys and garages. You want me to do more about those dogs, you'll have to get me the funding to hire a team."

"My deputies are going to be the team on this." Willingham shifted his glare to Tom. "I want this to be top priority, and I don't want you to quit until every damn one of those dogs is dead and gone."

"I've got a murder to investigate." Despite his effort to sound reasonable, Tom couldn't keep the sarcastic edge out of his voice. "You want me to put dog-catching ahead of that? I don't—"

"Wait a minute here," Dolan interrupted. "Sheriff? You want us to *kill* them? What if some of them turn out to be pets that went missing lately? How are the owners gonna feel if deputies shoot their dogs without giving them a chance to go home again?"

"They've gone wild," the sheriff said. "There's more of them every day, and they're a danger to our citizens and their livestock. We wouldn't have any debate about shooting a pet that was rabid. These dogs are every bit as dangerous." He leaned his palms on the table and pushed himself to his feet. "Get rid of them. That's an order."

The sheriff hobbled out, his shoulders stooped. Tom heard him coughing in the hallway. The old man ought to be at home in bed instead of at headquarters interfering with everybody else's work.

Dr. Lauter threw up her hands. "Honestly, Tom, I don't know how you put up with Toby. I certainly hope you plan to ignore him and treat this as a murder investigation."

"Of course I do." Tom looked across at Dolan. "You're in charge of rounding up the dogs. I'll give you whatever manpower I can spare, but it won't be the whole department."

"Just remember I'm not shooting any dogs, and I won't stand by while anybody else does."

Tom waved that aside. "We're not going to kill them. You know what Holly Turner's doing with the McClure property?"

Dolan nodded. "Sure, I helped her plan the layout. But there's only one row of pens that's ready."

"If it can hold dogs, I want you to use it."

"Another thing is, I've caught strays, but I've never had to catch a whole big bunch of dogs that are all scared of people."

Oh, great. The dogcatcher didn't know how to catch dogs. "Do it one at a time," Tom said. "Rachel will help you. And we need to find out what happened to Gordon Hall's shepherd. Until we do, at least some people are going to believe Hall's death was just a case of a dog turning on its owner."

"I think somebody stole him," Dolan said. "I think Dr. Hall got killed because somebody was trying to steal his dog."

"Somebody tried to steal Thor while Gordon was right there?" Dr. Lauter put in. "Wouldn't that be a little, well, stupid?"

"Maybe the shepherd was off-leash and the thief didn't see Dr. Hall until he tried to stop his dog from being grabbed," Dolan said. "I think all the pets that have disappeared have been stolen. The thief had his own dog with him last night, and when Hall tried to stop him, the thief sicced his dog on Hall."

Tom considered this but quickly discarded the theory. It didn't jibe with what was on the answering machine tape. To Dolan, he said, "So why are pet dogs being stolen?"

Dolan leaned forward, shoulders hunched and elbows on the table. "You want to know what I really think?"

"What?"

Dolan lowered his voice. "I think they're being sacrificed."

"Sacrificed?" Tom frowned. "What are you talking about? Sacrificed for what?"

Dolan's voice dropped further, to a whisper. "Devil worship. A satanic cult."

Tom exchanged a look with Dr. Lauter, who raised an eyebrow quizzically. He asked Dolan, "Are you serious?"

"You bet I am. Animal sacrifice is part of their worship services, their black mass. They—"

"I'll keep that in mind." Tom rose. Ushering Dr. Lauter ahead of him, he walked out before Dolan could get started again on his theory.

Devil worship. Black masses. A feral dog pack. A killer using a dog as a murder weapon. What next?

The answer waited for him in the squad room.

Lily Barker and Sergeant Dennis Murray were deep in conversation at his desk. Tom wanted to retreat before Mrs. Barker spotted him, but he didn't act quickly enough. She rose, a long red caftan rippling around her angular figure. A striking black woman in her sixties, she stood almost as tall as Tom.

"Hey, Tom," Dennis said, "Mrs. Barker wanted to talk to you about Dr. Hall's death." He pushed his chronically slipping wire-rimmed glasses back up his nose, his hand barely concealing a smirk of amusement.

"You've got some information for me?" Tom asked her. *A feeling, an intuition, a mysterious image that came to you in a dream?* The woman claimed to possess what mountain people called "the sight"—but although she'd guessed correctly in a general way about a couple of past crimes, Tom couldn't take her seriously. He didn't want to invite her back to his office.

The resignation in her slight smile told him he'd allowed his impatience to show. "I won't keep you from your work, Captain Bridger," she said, "but I felt compelled to warn you that there is a great deal more to Dr. Hall's death than might be readily apparent."

"And what would that—Wait a minute. You're connected to the Halls, aren't you? Through Raymond Porter? He's your nephew or cousin?"

"Raymond is my cousin Lucinda's son. And yes, he is Marcy and David's natural father."

Tom frowned, realizing that he hadn't considered the possible involvement of Raymond Porter in Hall's murder. David and Marcy's birth mother, a white woman named Jewel Riggs, had never married their black father. When Jewel died of a drug overdose eight or nine years ago, Gordon and Vicky Hall quickly adopted the children. Tom hadn't heard anything about their father kicking up a fuss over the adoption or trying to reclaim the kids, but that didn't mean he was happy with the arrangement.

"Where is Raymond now?" Tom asked. "Is he back in the county?"

The look Mrs. Barker gave him combined sorrow and reproach. "No, Captain, he's not here. He's in Richmond, and he was in Richmond at the time Dr. Hall was killed. You went to high school with Raymond, didn't you? If you know him at all, you know he is incapable of committing murder."

Tom and Raymond hadn't been best buds, but except for an occasional foray into drug use, Raymond had seemed like an ordinary nice guy. It was a stretch to imagine him turning a killer dog loose on somebody. But Tom knew better than to write off the nice guys. They could be the most dangerous of all.

"If Raymond happens to come visiting, tell him I'd like to see him." Tom rose. "Thanks for stopping by."

"Before you dismiss me, Captain, I'd like to tell you what brought me here today."

Tom suppressed a weary sigh. "You've got something for me?"

"Not hard cold facts, no, I'm sorry. But I feel very strongly—"

Right, Tom thought. *Here we go.*

"—that something evil is happening in Mason County." Mrs. Barker tilted her chin. "It took root under the dog star, and now it flourishes in hidden places. It must be stopped before more lives are lost."

◇◇◇

Rachel paused in the doorway of the pharmacy room and watched Dr. Jim Sullivan transfer vials and bottles from the cabinets to his leather case. Sullivan, the clinic's large animal vet, traveled to his patients instead of the other way around, and Rachel wasn't used to seeing him at the animal hospital during the work day. Lately, though, he'd been in more often, and taken an unusually large stash of supplies—surgical materials, bandages, medications.

Without looking up, Sullivan asked, "Can I help you with something, Dr. Goddard?"

As he always did, he somehow made her feel like the underling dealing with an authority figure. He was in his fifties, more than twenty years her senior, with gray hair and the leathery skin of a man who spent too much time outdoors in every kind of weather. His superior air always threw Rachel off a little. *You're the boss,* she reminded herself. She owned the clinic. Sullivan worked for her.

"Have you been seeing a higher than normal rate of illness and injury?" she asked.

"Naw, I'm just running low on everything. I've been restocking a little at a time. Didn't want to clean you out all at once."

He still didn't look at her. That was the most irritating thing about the man. Rachel couldn't recall him ever making direct eye contact with her. "If you'll give me a list," she said, "I'll order supplies especially for you."

"That's okay. I've got everything I need now." Sullivan closed the drug cabinet and locked it. He flipped open the log book and began to enter the medications he was taking.

Sullivan had his own key to the drug cabinet, and a key to the clinic's back door, because he usually came in after hours. Rachel felt uneasy about this situation, but she couldn't justify taking away his keys and forcing him to requisition supplies through her. After a fire had damaged the clinic's rear wall the previous January, and the door was replaced, she'd reluctantly handed over a key to the new lock to Sullivan. He had worked here for three decades before Rachel bought the place a year and a half ago, and he had his own way of doing things. As long as he accounted for his time and turned in the fees he collected from clients, she couldn't find fault with his work. And yet—

She pushed the thought away and said, "I was wondering if you'd help out at the animal sanctuary Holly Turner's creating. We want to get those feral dogs into the shelter, and we'll need to do a health evaluation on every animal that's brought in."

Sullivan's harsh laugh startled her. Was he laughing at her or at the very idea of what she'd proposed?

Snapping his case shut, Sullivan said, "What's the point of putting dogs like that into a shelter?"

"The point is to save their lives. I don't want them to starve to death, or end up getting shot. They can be rehabilitated. We can try to find homes for them."

He chuckled, a humorless and derisive sound, and shook his head. "Look, Dr. Goddard—"

"Rachel," she put in. "Please. Isn't it about time you started calling me Rachel?"

"I don't see that it makes any difference what I call you." His gaze flicked toward her face, skidded away. "I was about to say, most of the animals I treat are going to end up on somebody's dinner plate. I keep them healthy so they can be slaughtered and cut into pieces and cooked and eaten. I learned a long time ago not to get dewy-eyed and sentimental about any animal. Least of all a bunch of dogs that have already been ruined."

"But don't you think we should at least try—"

"You can do whatever you want to." Sullivan hefted his case and faced her, but instead of meeting her eyes he looked over her right shoulder at the wall beyond. "In my opinion, those dogs ought to be put down when they're caught. They're damaged. Nobody's going to want them, and I don't see the point of making them live in cages the rest of their lives. Sorry, but I can't be part of your rescue fantasy."

Sullivan walked out and left Rachel, her face burning, unsure whether she was embarrassed or angry.

Chapter Four

Ethan Hall didn't so much ask to see Tom as summon him to the Hall house for an audience. "I want a full accounting of what you're doing about my father's death," the Halls' oldest son said on the phone. "I'll be expecting you within the hour."

He hung up before Tom could reply. Dropping the receiver back into its cradle on his office desk, Tom gave a moment's cranky consideration to ignoring Ethan's command. The guy had always been an arrogant punk. Ethan was in his mid-twenties now, a med school dropout, and he worked as a regional rep for a medical supplies company, but he was as self-important as his physician father had been.

He was also a son whose father had just died under horrifying circumstances, so he had to be cut some slack. Tom was planning to head out to the Hall house again this morning in any case.

He pushed away from his desk and rose. It was such a mild late-September day that he left his uniform jacket hanging from a hook on the back of the office door.

The Halls' big Georgian house looked deceptively peaceful, with the mellow morning sunlight warming the red brick and reflecting off the rows of windows. Red and yellow leaves drifted down from massive oaks and maples. Tom pulled into the brick-paved parking circle next to Ethan Hall's black Lexus and climbed out of his cruiser. As he mounted the front steps, a bluejay in a tall holly next to the door gave a squawk of alarm and burst into flight.

Tom had barely touched the brass knocker when Ethan yanked the door open. He cut off Tom's greeting. "I want you to know that I hold the county officials, including the Sheriff's Department, entirely responsible for my father's death. If any of you were doing your jobs, those dogs would have been caught and disposed of months ago."

"Don't jump to conclusions," Tom said. "The dog pack didn't kill your father. Hasn't anyone told you about the answering machine tape?"

Ethan's sister Soo Jin joined him at the door, crossed her arms and regarded Tom with cold dark eyes. "Everybody says there were no other voices on the tape. Maybe it's easier for you to deny the dogs killed him—"

"Easier?" Tom shook his head. "No, I wouldn't say a murder investigation is easier than tracking down a few dogs. Look, I know you're both upset, you're trying to come to terms with your loss—"

"Don't patronize us," Soo Jin said. "We'll be watching every step you take, and we'll make sure you do what needs to be done."

"Nobody has to force me to do my job."

The two of them glared at him. Their contemptuous expressions were all they had in common. Ethan, his parents' natural son, looked like a younger version of Gordon Hall, with a boyish face, wavy brown hair and brown eyes. Soo Jin, several years younger than Ethan and now in medical school, had been adopted as a baby from a Korean orphanage. Her shining black hair fell to her shoulders around a square face with prominent cheekbones.

"Tom?" Vicky Hall called from the living room. "I'm in here."

"Do you two mind if I come in?" Tom stepped into the foyer, forcing Ethan and Soo Jin to get out of his way.

They trailed him to the living room, with Ethan hissing over Tom's shoulder, "I don't want you grilling her and upsetting her even more. She's having enough trouble coping with this."

Tom ignored him and joined Vicky Hall, who was plucking faded flowers from a vase atop a cabinet. Although she had dressed in slacks and a blouse and combed her lusterless hair back from her face, the attempt to keep up normal behavior patterns only succeeded in emphasizing her dire condition. Her clothes swallowed her skeletal body, and without a tightly cinched belt her slacks might have slid to the floor. Her hands trembled when she thrust the rejected flowers at Rayanne Stuckey, the family's housekeeper.

Rayanne, a sharp-featured woman in her early thirties with bleached blond curls, took the discarded blooms as Vicky pulled them out of the vase.

"Oh, they're all beyond saving," Vicky said. She shoved the vase itself, sloshing water and still half full of flowers, at Rayanne. "Get rid of them."

"Yes, ma'am." Rayanne struggled to grasp the big vase while holding onto the half-dozen stems already in her hands. One flower slipped from her grasp, and Tom heard her whisper, "Oh, shit." When he retrieved it and stuck it into the vase she threw a vague, distracted glance his way and didn't thank him.

Rayanne marched out of the room with a sour twist to her lips, as if she couldn't wait to dispose of her burden. Ethan and Soo Jin stationed themselves on either side of their mother, and Tom got the strong message that they were there to protect Vicky from him. For the first time Tom noticed someone whose presence puzzled him—Leo Riggs, who owned a local car repair shop, stood by the French doors with his slight shoulders hunched under a sweatshirt and his hands jammed into the pockets of grease-streaked jeans. Leo was David and Marcy's uncle, their birth mother's brother, but he was the last person Tom would expect to find in the Hall house. Leo's eyes met Tom's briefly, then shifted away.

Vicky was saying something about her husband hating the sight of half-dead flowers around the house.

Turning his attention back to her, Tom asked, "Can I speak to you privately?"

"About what?" Ethan demanded. "There's nothing you have to say to my mother that you can't say in front of me."

"Oh, Ethan, don't be ridiculous," Vicky said. "Yes, of course we can speak privately. Children, would you—No, wait, let's just go into Gordon's home office."

"Mom," Ethan protested.

At the same time, Soo Jin said, "Mother, you need someone with you when you speak to the police."

"What makes you think that?" Tom asked her. "I'm not accusing your mother of a crime. This isn't an interrogation."

Soo Jin took a breath and drew herself up as if trying to stand taller before Tom's six-feet-plus. "Then what is it, exactly? Hasn't she already told you everything she remembers?"

"Why do you want to put her through it again?" Ethan added.

"Will you two stop it?" Vicky said. "The last thing I need is all this carping. Now go away and let us talk."

Ethan and Soo Jin reacted to their mother's reprimand with the shocked expressions of kids who thought they'd been scolded unfairly. Instead of doing as she asked, the brother and sister trailed Vicky and Tom out of the living room and down the hall. Vicky led Tom into her husband's home office. He shut the door in Ethan and Soo Jin's faces.

"You'll have to excuse them." Vicky sank onto a small sofa as if coming to rest after a long, exhausting journey. Against the dark green upholstery, her skin had a pale grayish cast. "This is so hard on all of us. They're just striking out because they feel helpless, and I suppose a policeman makes a convenient target."

"Are you all right?" Tom rolled the desk chair over to the sofa and sat facing her. "Do you need to see your doctor?"

She shook her head. "I feel as if I need dialysis again already, but I just had a treatment yesterday and I'm not due again until tomorrow."

"If you need it—"

"I'll call the doctor in a little while if I don't feel better." She sat forward, clasped her bony hands in her lap, and fixed her attention on Tom. "Now. How can I help you?"

"You can start by telling me that you realize your husband wasn't killed by the feral dog pack."

"If that's the opinion of the medical experts, I believe it without question. But Gordon *was* killed by a dog, wasn't he?"

"By one dog. If the rest of the pack had been there—"

"They would have joined in. They would have torn him apart." Her voice broke on the last words.

At least one member of the Hall family had accepted the truth. "It was one dog, and someone was with it. Its owner, another person."

"Who stood by and let his dog kill my husband." A tear trickled down her right cheek.

"That's what it sounded like." Tom hoped she could hold herself together long enough to get through this interview. "It could have been an accidental encounter that went bad, but it was on your land, well inside the property line where you wouldn't expect to see other people with their dogs. I believe it was a planned attack. It was murder."

A shudder ran through Vicky, shook her thin shoulders. "Why would somebody do such a thing?"

"Do you know of anybody with a grievance against your husband? Has anything happened lately that stands out in your mind?"

"Gordon was a good man," she said. "He was generous, always trying to help people. Everybody loved him."

Was Hall's wife really as blind to his faults as she pretended? "He ran a hospital. He had lots of employees, the hospital has lots of patients. There must have been people who had disagreements with him. This isn't the time to hold anything back. Can you think of somebody he'd fired, somebody whose relative died at the hospital—"

"Oh!" Vicky pressed a hand to her mouth.

"What?" Tom said. "Do you remember something?"

"That man whose wife—She died in the hospital and her husband thinks she was mistreated."

"He thinks the hospital was responsible for her death?"

"No, no. She had cancer that had metastasized. There was no hope of saving her. But her husband claims she was tortured, if you can believe that, because she was allowed to experience pain. He's been threatening a lawsuit, and he keeps turning up wherever Gordon goes and causing a scene."

Tom frowned. "We haven't had any reports about your husband being harassed."

"No, because Gordon was too kind a person to get the poor man in trouble on top of everything else he's going through. I begged Gordon to get the police involved, but he said the husband was working out his grief and would come to terms with it eventually."

"What's his name?" Tom pulled his notebook and a pen from his shirt pocket.

"Wallace Green. Do you know him?"

"Oh, yeah, I know Wally." The man was now raising four children alone. "His wife died about six months ago. Breast cancer, wasn't it?"

"Yes. It was terribly sad." Vicky shook her head. "She was so young, and it could have been caught at an early stage if she'd seen a doctor regularly. It's a tragedy, but Gordon wasn't at fault in any way. He understood, though, that her husband needed someone to blame for her suffering at the end. With any painful death, there's always a need to make sense of it. Do you think he could have done this? Turned his dog on Gordon?"

"I'll look into it," Tom said. "Can you think of anybody else with a grudge against your husband?"

Vicky leaned back, sighed, and closed her eyes as if suddenly overcome with weariness. "I'll have to think about it. Right now I just—I'm just *feeling*, you know? It's hard to think coherently when I'm so emotional."

"I understand," Tom said. "But I do have to look into your husband's dealings with other people, personal and professional. I'd appreciate it if you'd tell your children not to stand in my way."

"I will, Tom, I'll do that, but Ethan and Soo are both convinced Gordon was killed by those wild dogs, and I don't know how long it will take for them to see the truth."

"If they loved their father, and I'm sure they did, they'll cooperate and help me find out what really happened." As they rose to leave the office, Tom asked, "By the way, what's Leo Riggs doing here?"

"Oh, he drove Rayanne to work. You know, I had no idea she was even involved with him. I wouldn't have hired her, I wouldn't have her working right here in the house, if I'd known. Now he's helping Ethan organize people to hunt down those dogs." Vicky sighed. "If Gordon were still alive, Leo Riggs wouldn't get through the door."

"Marcy and David know he's their uncle, don't they?" Tom wondered how freely the Halls communicated their contempt for Marcy and David's birth family to the kids.

"Yes, of course they know," Vicky said. "And it's not as if we have anything against Leo personally. But Marcy and David are *our* children now."

"Do you ever hear from their birth father and his family?" Their black father, their black grandparents. "Have they seen the kids since the adoption?"

"Of course not." Vicky seemed astonished that Tom had asked such a question. "It would be too confusing for them to have interaction with those people."

It wouldn't be easy to enforce a lifelong total separation when they all lived in the same small county, where everybody knew the story of the children's adoption by the Halls. But that didn't concern Tom unless it had something to do with Hall's death. His immediate problem was putting a stop to any plans Riggs had to round up his gun-toting pals for a dog hunt.

When they returned to the living room, Tom realized it was already too late to call a halt. While he and Vicky Hall talked, a dozen men had gathered on the patio, and every one of them held a rifle or shotgun.

"What's going on?" Tom demanded of Ethan.

"Oh, my lord, Ethan," Vicky exclaimed. "Who are these people? What are they doing on our patio?"

"I'm getting a search party together," Ethan said. "We're going after those dogs, since the Sheriff's Department doesn't seem interested in protecting citizens from them."

"This is not a good idea," Tom said.

"Leo and Rayanne got all their friends together to help," Ethan said. "These people don't want the same thing that happened to my father to happen to somebody in their families."

Leo Riggs, who still lurked just inside the French doors as if hesitant to venture farther into the expensively furnished room, kept his eyes focused on the carpet. When Tom glanced at Rayanne Stuckey, she dropped her gaze.

"The Sheriff's Department and the animal warden are going to deal with those dogs, probably starting tonight," Tom said. "I don't want a mob of people roaming around with guns, especially not at the same time we're—"

"A *mob?*" Ethan cut in. "That's how you describe people who are trying to protect their families from a menace that's running loose in the county?"

"Those dogs didn't kill your father, Ethan."

"Nobody's shown me any proof of that."

With some effort, Tom kept his voice level. "I want you to come into headquarters and listen to the answering machine tape. And you can read the autopsy report when we get it. It won't be pleasant, but it ought to give you the proof you need."

"If the dog pack didn't kill him," Soo Jin said, stepping forward, "then who—or what—did?"

"I'll do my best to find out. All this nonsense—" Tom waved a hand at the men milling about on the patio. "—just confuses the issue. And it's going to use up police manpower that could be put to better use elsewhere. If I have to assign deputies to make sure this bunch doesn't accidentally shoot somebody, that's fewer officers I have to investigate your father's death."

"Don't worry about baby-sitting us," Ethan said. "We don't need any deputies along to slow us down."

Tom focused on Riggs. "Don't get mixed up in this, Leo. If somebody gets hurt, it'll be on your head."

Riggs shrank back against the wall and hunched his slight shoulders, making Tom think of the Uriah Heep character out of Dickens. He couldn't see any resemblance to David and Marcy in this man's sharp features and closely cropped brown hair. "I'm not lookin' to stir up trouble, Captain. Ethan here asked me to do a favor and I couldn't rightly say no. Dr. Hall was a good man. I appreciate what him and Mrs. Hall are doin' for my sister's kids."

Tom heard Vicky's sharp inhalation.

Riggs hung his head, as if fully aware that Vicky was reacting to the reminder of their connection.

Tom pushed open the French doors and stepped onto the patio. The men gathered there all turned to face him and fell silent.

"I know you guys mean well," he told them, "but I can't allow this hunt."

He could see resistance and hostility take hold in their eyes, but no one responded.

Ethan, following him out, said, "If people allow us on their property, you have nothing to say about it."

Mumbling started among the assembled men.

"Listen to me," Tom said. "This is getting to be—"

"Hey, look!" one of the men cried. He pointed toward the woods.

Tom followed his gesture. Down at the bottom of the slope, an animal had emerged from the woods and was limping toward the house.

"Oh my god," Ethan exclaimed. "It's Thor. It's Dad's dog."

He started running, with Tom right behind him.

Chapter Five

The German shepherd cringed when Tom and Ethan approached.

"My god," Ethan said, the color draining from his face. "Look at him. What's happened to him?"

Several layers of tape bound the old dog's muzzle. Forced to breathe only through his nose, he labored to pull in enough air, his sides contracting and expanding in a ragged rhythm. In place of his collar, a length of rope dangled from his neck. Dried blood encrusted one hind leg, and Tom saw bite wounds on his neck, shoulders, and back.

"We'll figure out what happened to him later," he said. "Right now we need to cut that tape off so he can breathe and get him up to the house."

Ethan knelt and held out a hand to the dog. "Come on, boy," he coaxed.

The dog backed away.

"He's scared to death." Tom pulled out the latex gloves he always carried in a pocket and tugged them on. He didn't want to smudge any fingerprints that might be on the tape. "Take it slow."

"Hey, Thor, come on, boy," Ethan crooned. "I'll bet you're hungry, aren't you? We'll take care of you. Come on, Thor. Come to me, boy."

Thor cast longing eyes toward the house on the hill, toward safety, but he hung back, whining. Tom had to admire Ethan's patience with the dog. He coaxed Thor until the animal's rigid body began to relax. He limped forward, one inch at a time. When he was within reach Ethan closed his arms around the dog.

"Just hold him there for a minute," Tom said. He extracted his Swiss army knife from his pants pocket and stepped forward slowly. As if realizing he was being freed of the restraint, Thor stood still while Tom slit the tape and eased it off. He folded it and stuck it in his pants pocket, hoping he wasn't obliterating any fingerprints in the process.

"Let's get him home now," Tom said. The dog was too big for either of them to carry up the slope. Thor would have to walk on his own, despite his injured leg.

On the way up, with Thor limping between them, Tom pulled his cell phone from his shirt pocket and called Rachel.

By the time they reached the patio, Vicky had stepped out, along with Soo Jin, Beth, David and Marcy. "Dr. Goddard's on her way," Tom told Vicky.

She dropped to her knees before the dog and caressed his head. Thor licked her cheek. "Oh, you poor baby. I've been so worried about you."

The crowd of men on the patio stood back, guns in their hands, and watched silently.

Looking up at Tom, Vicky said, "He's so old and feeble he couldn't defend himself against that vicious dog. Just look at all these wounds."

Yeah, Tom thought, but that vicious dog didn't tape Thor's mouth shut and tie a rope around his neck.

Half an hour later, Rachel knelt beside the dog in Gordon Hall's home office, where Thor's big bed occupied a corner. While her children crowded the doorway, Vicky Hall sat on the sofa, blotting a continuous flow of tears with the handkerchief Tom had given her.

Tom crouched beside Rachel, ready to help restrain Thor if he reacted while she tended his wounds. The rope and the taped muzzle were undeniable evidence that someone had held the dog overnight and had plans for him. Memories, the kind Tom didn't like to dwell on, flooded his mind. Memories of dogs he and other deputies had confiscated from fighting operations. After every raid, Tom spent weeks trying to shake the images.

"Would somebody bring Thor a bowl of fresh drinking water, please?" Rachel asked the assembled Halls.

Young Marcy raised her hand as if responding to a teacher's request. She wheeled around and disappeared. Less than a minute later she returned, carrying a dog bowl brimming with water. She presented it to Rachel with a brief, shy smile.

"Thank you." Rachel rewarded the girl with her own warm smile as she took the bowl.

Before she began her exam, she allowed Thor to take a few laps of water, then removed the dish and set it a couple of feet away. "Let's see if he keeps that down, then he can have some more," she said. "Mrs. Hall, would you get him something to eat? Just a little to start, a quarter cup, and bring a spoon with it."

After Vicky pushed past her children in the doorway and went off to the kitchen, Rachel pulled back Thor's blood-matted hair to get a better look at his wounds. He remained still and quiet. "His skin's ripped open," Rachel told Tom, "but I don't see any deep puncture wounds. He should be okay."

Tom spoke quietly. "You know, I'm starting to think…"

When his words trailed off, Rachel prompted, "What? What are you thinking?"

Conscious of the Hall children a few feet away, Tom said, "I'll explain later. Don't let me slow you down."

Vicky brought in the canned dog food and fed tiny amounts to Thor on a spoon to distract him while Rachel treated his wounds. Tom stood back and took in the family's reactions. Marcy and Beth, standing just inside the door, grimaced as Rachel wove a needle and black suture thread in and out of the dog's torn skin, but Soo Jin craned her neck to get a better view. David leaned in the doorway, wearing a sullen teenager's scowl. Ethan stood rigid, hands jammed in his pockets, his face blank.

Her work finished, Rachel sat back on her heels and asked Vicky, "Can you look after him here? I don't want to stress him any more by moving him, but if you can't manage him here I'll take him to the animal hospital."

"I'm a nurse," Vicky said. "I can take care of him."

"Mother," Soo Jin said, "I don't want you to exhaust yourself."

"Your father loved this dog," Vicky said. "I can't help Gordon, but I can help Thor. Now all of you go find something else to occupy yourselves. Thor needs peace and quiet."

Her children reluctantly turned away, one by one. Rachel gave Vicky a bottle of antibiotics for the dog. When Tom and Rachel left the room, Vicky was sitting cross-legged on the carpet next to Thor, stroking him. Tom couldn't help wondering if she had given any of her suddenly fatherless children a fraction of the attention she lavished on her husband's pet.

In the hallway, Tom told Rachel, "I want to talk to you before you leave, but first I need to deal with that mob on the patio."

"There's a mob on the patio?" Rachel said. "Why?"

"It's a bunch of idiots with guns who think the feral dogs killed Gordon Hall. They want to hunt down the dogs and kill them."

"What?" Rachel exclaimed.

"Aw, Christ. Why didn't I keep my mouth shut?"

"I want to talk to these people. Which way is the patio?"

"Oh, no. Don't even think about it. I'll handle them."

"But I can tell them—"

"You can't tell them anything they'll want to hear, believe me. Stay out of it. All right?"

Rachel blew out an impatient sigh. "All right, all right."

When Tom opened the French doors from the living room onto the patio, the armed men greeted him with truculent silence. Ethan, looking pale and shaken, followed Tom outside and stood with the men.

"I want all of you to go home and put away your guns," Tom said. "The Sheriff's Department and the animal warden will deal with the dog pack."

The men muttered, a drone of discontent that produced no clear words Tom could make out. One man, though, spoke up. Tom knew the guy, a sharp-nosed runt named Larry Randolph who had been hauled in a few times for assault after drunken Saturday night fights with his wife. His wife inevitably came around the next morning begging for his release and claiming the fight had been entirely her fault. "All you've been doin' is actin' like it's not any kind of a problem to have a pack of wild dogs runnin' loose. If you'd been doin' your job, this boy's dad would still be alive." He gestured at Ethan.

A chorus of voices rose in agreement. Ethan looked down at his feet.

"The dogs didn't kill Dr. Hall," Tom said. "All the evidence—"

"The hell they didn't," Randolph said. "We got to protect our families, if you won't do it. I don't want my kids gettin' attacked by those dogs. We need to get rid of every last one of them."

Tom was about to answer when Rachel stepped onto the patio. "We're going to trap the dogs, starting tonight," she said.

"Rachel, go back inside," Tom said. Why couldn't she stay out of this? She had no authority that these men would recognize. "Please."

She went on, "There's a shelter being built on the old McClure property, and it's ready now to house some animals. We'll trap them and take them there."

"Then what?" one of the men asked.

"Yeah," put in another. "You gonna feed 'em and pamper them like they's somebody's housepets?"

"They *were* pets," Rachel said. "They could be again, after they're rehabilitated."

"Rehabilitated?" Randolph exclaimed. He looked around at the men, an incredulous half-smile on his face. "You hear that? She's gonna *rehabilitate* a bunch of killer dogs."

The other men responded with derisive laughter.

Tom could see Rachel winding up to fire back a hot response. He gripped her arm and spoke in a low growl. "Get back inside. You're making matters worse."

She threw an outraged look at him, but she spun and stepped back in, closing the French doors after her.

"You sure you can handle that woman of yours?" Randolph asked. The others laughed. "She'd better be careful if she's goin' out at night lookin' for them dogs. We're gonna be shootin' anything that moves."

"Did I hear you right?" Tom stepped closer, looming over the man. "Did you just threaten to shoot Dr. Goddard?"

"I said what I meant. You take it any way you want to." Jutting his chin, Randolph tried to hold his challenging posture, but he didn't have Tom's staying power. After a few seconds under Tom's glare, Randolph broke eye contact and scraped a hand over his stubbly chin.

"If anything happens to her," Tom said, "I'm coming straight for you."

"Nobody's threatening your girlfriend," Ethan said. "We just want to get rid of those animals."

"You don't know what you're doing," Tom told him. "I want you and your sister to come to headquarters and listen to that tape. I want you to talk to Dr. Lauter too. You need to accept what's really happened here. And you ought to be looking after your mother and the rest of your family instead of stirring up trouble."

Without giving Ethan a chance to answer, Tom shoved open the French doors and strode back inside.

Vicky sat on the living room couch, taking a cup of tea from Rayanne Stuckey. "Thor's fallen asleep," Vicky told Tom. "Dr. Goddard said she'd wait for you out in front. I'll call if I think of anything else you ought to know. And I promise I'll try to talk some sense into Ethan and Soo."

◇◇◇

On her way to her Range Rover Rachel kicked at the fallen leaves, sending a flurry of red and gold into the air. "Idiots." At least Tom had picked the right word to describe them. "Ignorant, stupid—"

She stopped herself, hating the sound of her own words. *Calm down. Get a grip.* Tom would handle it. He was better with people like that than she could ever hope to be.

Rachel leaned against her SUV, her face tilted toward the sun. Her SUV and Tom's cruiser were the only vehicles in the parking circle. The family cars undoubtedly occupied the outsized garage attached to the house, and none of the men on the patio had parked this close to the Halls' impressive house. All those dented cars and rusted trucks she'd seen on the shoulder of the main road must belong to them.

Bright leaves fell like a light rain from the trees and settled on the paved parking area. Except for the ridiculously large garage, the Halls' property reminded Rachel of the house where she'd grown up in Northern Virginia, the woods she had roamed on her solitary explorations. At home the foliage would just be starting to change color, the September nights would still be warm and humid, and the trees wouldn't be bare until early December. Autumn, the season when the world dies, she thought. Here in the mountains, it came too soon.

She straightened as Tom approached. "I really do wish you wouldn't be so damned bossy," she said. Then she registered his troubled expression. "What's wrong?"

He reached into his pants pockets and pulled out two plastic bags containing tape and rope. "These were on Thor's muzzle and neck when he showed up. And his collar was missing."

Rachel frowned. "Then he wasn't out in the woods by himself all night. Somebody had him."

"Maybe the same person who sicked his dog on Hall."

"Somebody used a dog to kill Dr. Hall, then stole his dog? Why would they want Thor?"

"I don't know what the connection to Hall is, I don't know why he was murdered, but I've seen dogs restrained this way, tied up with their muzzles taped. I could be way off, but I'm wondering if Thor ended up in the hands of people running dogfights. Maybe they planned to use him as a bait dog, to train the fighters."

"A bait—" For a second Rachel felt too sick to speak. "Tom. All those pet dogs that have disappeared—Do you think—"

"It's starting to make sense. If that's why they were stolen, a lot of them are probably dead already."

"But I haven't heard anything about dogfighting in Mason County." Rachel didn't want this to be true. She wanted Tom, sensible Tom who always carefully examined the evidence before making up his mind, to admit he'd jumped to an irrational conclusion. "And wouldn't you have known about it?"

Tom shook his head. "It's illegal, it's carefully hidden. It always takes a while before we hear about it."

"It's happened before?"

"Oh, yeah. Dogfighting's like some damned fungus we can't get rid of. We put a stop to it, arrest the people responsible, rescue the dogs, and a couple of years later it pops up again—usually with the same people involved."

"When did all this happen?" Rachel asked. "Why don't I know about it?"

"The last time was right before you moved here. The time before that was a year earlier. My dad broke up a dogfighting operation a week before he died. In all the years he was chief deputy, he must have raided a couple dozen dogfights."

Rachel drew a shaky breath. "This is awful. But what are you saying, exactly? That the people involved in dogfighting wanted Dr. Hall dead? Why?"

"I have no idea right now. I don't know what connection somebody like Hall might have to the kind of people who run dogfights. I only know one thing for sure—Hall was killed by a vicious dog that was under the control of a human being."

"But the feral dogs are a completely separate issue, aren't they?"

"As far as I can see," Tom said.

"Why didn't you tell those men what you're thinking, so they'll back off?"

"Because some of them might be involved. If they're not personally involved, they know people who are, and if they realize I'm suspicious, they'll spread the word. Most of them live in Rocky Branch District, and that's always where the fighting takes place."

"Oh, why doesn't that surprise me?" The mention of Rocky Branch District was enough to make Rachel shudder. "I'm doing a rabies clinic out there tomorrow, you know."

"Yeah, and I'm sending a deputy along to make sure nothing happens to you. I'm also going with you tonight to look for the ferals. You made some enemies here today, Rachel."

"Me and my big mouth."

Tom almost smiled. "You and your good intentions."

"My good intentions and my big mouth." That combination would be the end of her one day.

Chapter Six

Tom bumped along a one-lane dirt road that probably hadn't been graded in a decade, looking for a mailbox with the name Porter on it. Marcy and David's paternal grandparents—their real father's parents—had a little farm in this remote corner of Mason County. Tom had known their son Raymond in high school, had played basketball with him, but they'd never been friendly enough for Tom to visit his home.

Why weren't we friends? Tom wondered now. In a county with a tiny minority population, Raymond stood out because he was black and Tom, with his dark Melungeon skin, might as well have been black. The bigoted basketball coach didn't like having either of them on the team. Yet they had avoided each other when they weren't on the court. Maybe they'd sensed that hanging out together would double the prejudice they had to deal with every day. Or, Tom admitted to himself for the first time, as a Melungeon he knew he had a better chance of fitting in and didn't want a black friend to hold him back. Tom stuck with the team and became captain, but Raymond quit playing, got involved with Jewel Riggs, and started using drugs.

The Porters' silver mailbox, with neat black lettering, stood at the entrance to a gravel driveway. When Tom drove up to the white, one-story farmhouse, he found Lucinda Porter raking leaves into a pile in the yard. She paused and leaned on her rake, watching him approach. Like her cousin, Lily Barker, Lucinda stood tall and straight, with a dignified self-possession, but she lacked Mrs. Barker's flair for fashion. Her baggy trousers and gray cardigan looked as if they'd been pulled from her husband's closet to go with her flowered blouse.

"Hello, Mrs. Porter," Tom said as he approached her. "You probably don't remember me, but we met a long time ago—"

"I remember you, Tom." Her face, as angular and lacking in softness as Mrs. Barker's, remained solemn. "What brings you here?"

"I was wondering if Raymond has been around lately."

Her eyes told him she knew exactly what he was getting at, but she would be polite and play out the game. "Raymond is in Richmond. He has a job there. He hasn't been home to visit in several months."

Tom nodded. Dennis Murray had already checked out Raymond's alibi for the time of Gordon Hall's death, and it was solid. He'd been working late at his second job, as a valet parking attendant at a hotel. Did Raymond's mother and father have something to do with Hall's death? Tom couldn't see that happening, but he had to check it out.

"This is a nice place." He looked around, taking in the modest but perfectly maintained house, the late roses still blooming along the front porch. A stand of apple trees stretched away from the yard on one side, a fenced field occupied the other side of the property. He smiled when he saw the dozen or so sheep grazing in the field. "I raise sheep too. There always seems to be somebody willing to buy the wool."

Lucinda Porter gave him a small, patient smile. "I'm a weaver and a knitter."

The crunch of footsteps on gravel made both of them turn. Abel Porter, his face full of questions, walked briskly down the driveway toward them. "Tom Bridger, is that you?"

"Yes, sir." Tom stuck out his hand. "Good to see you again after all these years."

Abel frowned as he shook Tom's hand. He stood next to his wife, and although he was a head shorter than she was, his attitude was that of a guardian, ready to shield her from whatever unpleasantness Tom had brought to their home. "Are you here about Dr. Hall's death?"

"It's just routine," Tom said. "I have to pin down the facts and—"

"Facts like where our son was when it happened? Facts like whether we own a dog mean enough to kill a man?"

"I know Raymond was working at the time," Tom said.

"And we don't own a dog anymore," Lucinda said. "Our little border collie Sally died during the summer and we haven't had the heart to get another one."

Tom stayed silent for a moment, looking from one to the other. Lucinda's eyes might freeze him where he stood, but he sensed that Abel was simmering, holding back a scorching, bitter anger. "How long has it been since you saw your grandchildren?" he asked them.

Lucinda made a choking sound in her throat and turned away with a hand over her mouth. Abel's chin quivered. "We haven't been allowed to see little David and Marcy since the Halls took them. They told us that if we went anywhere near them—our only grandchildren, our flesh and blood—if we got anywhere near them, they'd get a restraining order on us."

The threat of legal action sounded like overkill to Tom, but it also sounded like something Gordon Hall would have done. Hall had money and influence. The Porters, with nothing but a blood kinship to those children, wouldn't have stood a chance.

"How did you feel about the adoption?"

Abel expelled a harsh laugh. "How we felt wasn't important to anybody. We couldn't fight the likes of the Halls." He took a deep breath and released it. "And we told ourselves it was for the best. The Halls could give them a lot that we never could."

Except love, Tom thought. *You could have given them love.*

"I'm sorry I bothered you folks," he said. "Next time Raymond comes home, tell him to give me a call. I'd like to see him. Not about this business. Just to catch up."

Man, that sounded lame, he thought as he walked to his car. They'd never been friends. What would they have to catch up on?

Lucinda called out behind him, "Are they safe? Our grand-children? They're not going to get hurt being in that house, are they?"

Aw, god, Tom thought, picturing the terrified, nearly mute Marcy and her sullen brother. Their grandparents had no idea how much those kids had been hurt already.

Margaret Thornwall, a dark-haired young woman in jeans and sweatshirt, stared at the missing dog posters on the waiting room wall while her exuberant white Pomeranians, Ramone and Emma, wound their leashes around her legs. "I saw these on the way in," she told Rachel, "but it never occurred to me that somebody stole all these dogs. This just scares me to death."

"Don't ever let them outside unless you're with them, and it's probably a good idea not to go far from the house when you take them out at night." Rachel scratched Ramone and Emma's heads. She had decided it was time to alert all her dog-owning clients to the danger that their pets could be snatched from their yards. Sometimes a little panic was a good thing, if it made people more careful.

"I won't let them out of my sight," Mrs. Thornwall said. She unwound the leashes from her ankles and scooped up the tiny dogs. She left with one wriggling under each arm.

As Mrs. Thornwall exited, Lily Barker entered with a cat carrier.

"Good morning," Rachel said. "Sorry I had to push your appointment back. I had an emergency outside the clinic."

"No apology is necessary." Mrs. Barker's striking face, with its strong angles and planes, seemed tight with tension.

"Is something wrong with your kittens?" Rachel asked. "I thought this was a routine first visit for them."

Mrs. Barker's brief smile looked forced. "Oh, yes, they seem to be in fine health."

Something was on the woman's mind, but with Mrs. Barker Rachel believed it was best not to inquire further. She gestured toward an exam room. "Come on in. Let me take a look at them."

While Rachel examined the young cats, Mrs. Barker stood with her back rigid and her hands clasped together as if in prayer. Any minute, Rachel thought, Mrs. Barker was going to tell her something she didn't want to hear, and it would have nothing to do with her pets. Rachel asked, "How are your other cats dealing with the new additions to the family?"

"Oh, the girls simply dote on them. It's quite heartwarming to see their mothering instincts coming to the fore."

Rachel injected vaccines into Anubis, a longhaired gray kitten with the face of a little lion, and got a screech of protest. The other kitten, Bastet, decided to beat a hasty retreat before she got stuck, and Rachel barely managed to catch the tiny brown-striped tiger as she dove off the table.

Mrs. Barker's smile seemed more natural now. "They are a handful. I'd forgotten what it's like to have kittens around."

Rachel was beginning to hope she would get through this visit without hearing one of Mrs. Barker's dire predictions or ominous warnings. Although Tom didn't believe in her psychic abilities, and Rachel normally scoffed at woo-woo, the woman had been right too many times to be dismissed automatically.

Mrs. Barker leaned forward, her intense gaze locked on Rachel, and Rachel knew she wasn't going to escape the latest revelation after all.

"I apologize for bringing this to you at your place of work," Mrs. Barker said. "Normally I would not impose this way, with a matter of a personal nature. However, I was already scheduled to see you—"

"Personal?" Rachel said, suddenly struggling to hold back a flood of apprehension. "For me? Or for Tom?"

"The captain's job entails certain risks," Mrs. Barker said, "and he is fully aware of those risks. You, however, are too often driven by your emotions, and you are not as careful as you might be. Please forgive what may sound like a judgment, I don't mean it that way at all, I am simply concerned about your safety. I implore you to take every precaution. Evil forces are at work in Mason County. They surround you, but you are unable to see them."

Oh, for pity's sake. This was over the top. But Rachel couldn't fight the deep unease this woman stirred up in her. "Are you talking about those people who don't want me to help the feral dogs?" she said. "They might try to scare me, but would they actually hurt me because I'm helping abandoned pets?"

Drawing a sharp breath, Mrs. Barker gave her a look that Rachel could only take as pity. *She thinks I'm too stupid to take care of myself.*

"My dear," Mrs. Barker said, "you are a strong young woman with a generous heart, quite admirable in many ways. But you are not invincible. Promise me, please, that you will be careful. That you will not be foolishly trusting."

Would I be foolish to trust you? Rachel made herself smile and answered, "Yes, I promise to be careful. I appreciate your concern, I really do. It's good of you to warn me."

Mrs. Barker shook her head slightly, her pitying gaze unchanged. Obviously she knew when she was getting the brush-off, and Rachel felt a little guilty. The life of a psychic in a doubting world couldn't be easy.

"I have done all I can." Mrs. Barker lifted the carrier from the floor to the table. "Thank you for taking such good care of my pets."

They didn't speak again while they wrestled the uncooperative kittens into the carrier. As Rachel opened the exam room door for Mrs. Barker, she felt compelled to say something conciliatory before letting her go. All she came up with was a restatement of what she'd already said. "I do appreciate your concern."

Mrs. Barker's piercing gaze seemed to bore deep inside Rachel. When it was withdrawn and the woman walked out of the room, Rachel felt shaken and profoundly frightened without being able to name the cause of her fear.

◇◇◇

"There used to be a creek over there." Tom raised his voice to a shout so Brandon could hear him over the roar of machinery above them. They paused in their trek up the broad bulldozed path as Tom pointed to the right. "And some houses."

"Man, what a mess," Brandon shouted back.

Tom had parked at the foot of what used to be a mountain. Now it was an open wound on the land where men used giant machines to scoop out ribbons of coal. Debris spilled down the slope in every direction. Red clay soil, boulders and stones, uprooted trees and wild rhododendrons had buried everything in their path. On the surrounding untouched hills, colorful autumn leaves fluttered in a breeze.

The sight of the ravaged landscape, with the dragline towering over all of it like a monstrous praying mantis, made Tom clench his jaw in helpless anger. Mason County had little to offer beyond its beauty, and even that was being sliced away with every pass of the earthmovers and mining machines.

Reaching the point where the scraped-bare land leveled off, Tom paused to catch his breath. This day felt endless, and he was so tired from a night without sleep that his body ached all over. Brandon, ten years younger, had been awake just as long but didn't seem bothered by the lack of rest.

Tom looked around for Wallace Green, the man who was angry because his wife had suffered in Dr. Gordon Hall's hospital. This was a relatively small surface mining operation, with no more than a dozen men on site. A single dragline excavator, its crane reaching fifteen stories into the air, moved a massive bucket along an open coal seam, breaking up the black mineral and tearing it loose with the kind of racket Tom would expect from a fifty-car pileup at high speed. Eight or nine industrial trucks brimmed with coal, and several more sat ready to be filled. The trucks would carry the coal away to a tipple, where it would be washed and dumped into rail cars for transport out of the county.

Wallace Green, tall and lanky, leaned against one of the empty trucks with his arms folded. Coal dust coated him from his hair to his boots, leaving only the area around his eyes clean behind protective goggles.

Tom waved to get his attention. Green was probably wearing earplugs, but even without them he wouldn't hear anything above the noise of the machinery. Tom moved closer, wishing with every step that he had some protection for his own ears.

Green caught sight of the deputies and pushed away from the truck, watching them approach.

Tom stuck out a hand. Green hesitated a moment, wiped his hand on his filthy jeans, and accepted the handshake. His gritty palm left black smudges on Tom's. Removing one earplug, Green angled his head to catch Tom's shouted words. "I need to ask you some questions."

"About what?" Green yelled back. "I'm workin'. I'm about to make a run to the tipple."

"This won't take long." Christ, Tom thought, why didn't I wait and go to his house tonight? Brandon grimaced as if the noise was causing physical pain. "Where were you last night, Wally?"

Green cast a worried glance toward a man in a hard-hat who stood a hundred yards away, watching them. The supervisor, Tom guessed. Bringing his gaze back to Tom, Green shouted, "Home with my kids. Why?"

"Was anybody else there? Did anybody call you on the phone?"

Green narrowed his eyes. "No. What're you gettin' at?"

"Have you heard about Gordon Hall?"

The excavator lifted its bucket off the coal seam, swung it around and dumped the coal into a truck with a rumble like thunder. Then, abruptly, the noise ceased. In the sudden silence, Tom's ears rang.

He repeated his question.

"I heard he got tore up by that pack of wild dogs." One corner of Green's lips lifted in a smirk. "What a way to go, huh? Suited him, if you ask me. But what're you talkin' to me about it for?"

"You've been making threats against Hall the last few months."

Green scowled. "Threats? I was tryin' to get the man to own up to what he done to my wife. Him and that hospital and everybody in it."

"Exactly what is it you think they did to your wife?"

"What I *think*? It's what I *know*. They let her die screamin' from the pain. They tortured her. Wouldn't do a damn thing to help her 'cause high and mighty Dr. Gordon Hall didn't like *abusing* pain medicine." As he spoke, Green grew more and more agitated, scraping his fingers through his hair, letting loose a cloud of black dust. "She was dyin', for god's sake. She didn't have no chance of gettin' better. It would've been a blessin' if she had enough morphine to get addicted, 'cause it would've been enough to stop the pain."

Green paused, pulled a pack of cigarettes and a lighter from his shirt pocket, lit a fresh cigarette with trembling hands.

Tom observed him for a moment, then said, "You hated him."

"Yeah, I hated the son of a bitch. What's that got to do with anything? He's dead and gone now, and I hope he died screamin', I hope he died feelin' the worst pain he ever felt in his sorry life."

"I think he probably did," Tom said.

Green nodded with satisfaction. Tom felt sorry for the guy and hoped to hell he had nothing to do with Hall's death. Green's kids had already lost one parent and shouldn't have to lose the other. "You own a dog, don't you? A big one?"

Green pulled on the cigarette, inhaling deeply, and blew out smoke. "Yeah, a shepherd-lab mix. What about it?"

"The medical examiner says Gordon Hall was killed by one dog, not a pack. And I believe the dog's owner was there. The dog was doing what his owner told him to do."

Green stared at Tom, his face slack with surprise. After a moment he took a deep drag on his cigarette. His words came out on a stream of smoke. "What reason have you got to think that? I heard there wasn't nobody around to see what happened."

"Really? Is that what everybody's saying?" Tom asked. "That there weren't any witnesses?"

Green frowned. "You sayin' there was?"

"I can't give out that information right now," Tom said. "I'd like to stop by your house and take a look at your dog and get a DNA sample. All I need to do is stick a Q-tip in his mouth."

Green's gaze jumped from Tom to Brandon and back. "The hell you will. You leave my dog alone. You can't go on my property without me givin' the okay. And I'm not givin' it. You understand me?"

"What I understand," Tom said, "is that you seem to be afraid of something. What is it you don't want me to find out, Wally?"

Green closed in, pointing a shaking finger at Tom. "You leave my dog alone."

Brandon held up a hand. "Hey, cool it, man. Back off."

"Why don't you hassle that Rasey boy?" Green said. "He's always spoutin' off about how he's gonna get even with Dr. Hall."

"Pete Rasey? What's he got against Gordon Hall?"

Green shook his head. "Some detective you are. The Rasey kid and Hall's girl, they've been goin' at it hot and heavy for a long time now. What I heard, Hall said he'd kill Pete Rasey if he come sniffin' around that girl again, and Pete made some threats right back."

"Are you talking about Beth Hall?" Tom asked.

"They ain't got but one *real* daughter. Now you leave me alone. I got to work. I can't stand around all day talkin' to you."

Green ditched his cigarette, ground it under his boot heel, and stomped off.

Chapter Seven

Rachel climbed into the animal warden's van and dropped to her knees to examine the four cages. She latched each cage door in turn and pushed and pulled, testing their strength. Rachel doubted they could catch as many as four dogs at once, but she wanted to be ready if they got lucky.

"Everything look okay?" Dolan asked when she hopped out onto the parking lot at the animal hospital.

A couple with a white cat in a carrier had paused on their way in to see what was happening. Rachel smiled and lifted a hand in greeting. "I'll be right in."

Looking a little embarrassed to be caught rubbernecking, the couple took their pet into the clinic.

Dolan slammed the rear door of the van shut. "This is gonna take time, you know, getting all of them. We'll be out every night for a while. I'll be honest with you, that pack of lunatics with guns scares the bejeezus out of me. You sure Tom's coming with us tonight?"

"We'll meet you after dinner," Rachel assured him. But how much protection would Tom provide? Ethan Hall and his followers hadn't been swayed by his authority when he confronted them at the Hall house. In the dark, when no one could see his uniform, badge and gun, Tom would be as vulnerable as Rachel and Joe.

◇◇◇

When Tom and Brandon arrived at the Rasey house, Peter Rasey's muscular torso was bent over the engine of a vintage black Thunderbird convertible that sat on the driveway.

"Nice car," Brandon commented. "Seems a little out of place around here."

The small rambler wore a shell of vinyl siding that might have been white when it was new but had long since taken on a gray cast. The front yard consisted mostly of crabgrass and dust, littered with fallen leaves. Weeds poked through cracks on the concrete driveway.

Tom parked the car and he and Brandon got out, slamming their doors. The boy pulled his head out from under the Thunderbird's hood and turned to look at the visitors. His jaw went slack at the sight of them.

"Hey, Pete," Tom called.

The big black dog seemed to come from nowhere, rocketing around Pete's car and down the driveway. Brandon yanked his door open again and stepped behind it. Tom drew his pistol and leaned over the cruiser's hood, the gun leveled at the charging dog.

"Don't shoot him!" Pete yelled. "Bruno! Stop it!"

The dog halted abruptly, ten feet from the cruiser. His body quivering, he issued a low growl. Saliva dripped from one corner of his mouth. He looked like a cross between a rottweiler and a shepherd, with a shepherd's larger ears and long legs and a rottweiler's heavy body and square-jawed face.

"Call him off," Tom told Pete, "and get him tied up."

The dog bared its teeth and raised the volume on its growl.

"*Now!*" Tom ordered. "He comes at us again, we'll shoot to kill."

Scowling at the deputies, the boy stalked down the driveway and grabbed the dog's collar. The animal yelped when Pete yanked him backward. "What do you want?" the boy demanded.

"Get the dog under control, then we'll talk."

Pete mumbled something Tom didn't catch. He dragged the dog toward a maple tree that had a chain looped around it.

Pete attached a hook at the end of the chain to the dog's collar. Returning to his car, he repeated, "What do you want?"

After signaling Brandon to hang back and keep an eye on the dog, Tom moved up the driveway, taking his time. Pete watched him with wary blue eyes. The boy's frayed jeans and old tee shirt bore indelible traces of past grease marks, and Tom guessed these were clothes his mother made him put on when he was working on his car. But with his dark blond hair, perfect features, and toned athlete's body, this kid would look great in rags. He was the kind of boy who attracted droves of girls and always had followers hoping to bask in the glow of his popularity. Tom had trouble imagining him with the bland, quiet Beth Hall.

Tom ignored Pete's twice-asked question and the steady growls from the dog. He circled the Thunderbird, appraising the vehicle. It was a two-door Super Coupe, last made in the early 1990s, with a long, low front end and a sloped roof. The gleaming black paint and black seats were in perfect condition. "This is a great car. You've put a lot of labor into it."

"Yeah, I guess," Pete mumbled.

His run-in with Tom a few months earlier was probably still fresh in the boy's mind. Tom's own blood pressure went up every time he remembered the night Pete harassed Rachel following a raucous community meeting. *I should have locked the punk up for that.*

He forced himself to smile and keep his tone amiable. "It's a good feeling to fix up an old car like this. Now you've really got something special."

One corner of Pete's mouth twitched as if it wanted to broaden into a grin at the compliment. Shrugging again, he said, "My dad says I could probably get a new car for what I've put into this one." He cast a prideful gaze over the Thunderbird and added, "But I got my own special ride here. It's *u-nique.*"

"I'll bet the girls like it, too." A little male bonding might help things along.

Pete's sharp laugh combined disdain and self-assurance. "Oh man, yeah. They go a little crazy over it."

Looking in at the back seat, Tom wondered if Beth Hall had ever gone a little crazy right there. "You got a special girl?"

Pete hesitated, his expression sobering into wariness again. "Why do you want to know that?"

"Just wondering. Is there some reason you don't want to tell me?"

The boy glanced down the driveway at Brandon and back at Tom as if calculating his chances of escape. "Nobody special."

Tom leaned against the car's front fender and crossed his arms. "You've got something going with Beth Hall, don't you?"

Pete winced. His gaze slid toward the dog, and it responded as if summoned, straining against the chain and barking. "Where'd you hear that?"

"It's pretty much common knowledge, isn't it? And everybody seems to know how her dad felt about it."

Pete swung his eyes back to Tom. He opened his mouth to reply, then thought better of it and pivoted toward the house. "Mom!" he yelled, sounding like a scared kid. "Mom, come out here!"

Tom almost laughed.

In a minute Babs Rasey appeared at the screen door, wiping her hands on a dishcloth. When she saw Tom, she pushed open the door. "What's going on?" she asked, coming down the front steps. She was a foot shorter than her son, a handsome rather than a pretty woman, with wavy ash blond hair. She paused beside Pete and asked Tom, "What are you doing out here?"

"I just need to ask your son a few questions."

"About what?"

"His dealings with Gordon Hall."

She frowned at her son. "What dealings with Gordon Hall?"

"He's saying—He's asking—" Pete slammed down the hood of the Thunderbird and grabbed a rag off a fender to wipe his hands. "I don't know what he's talking about."

Folding her arms, Babs Rasey tilted her head to look up at Tom. "You gonna tell us what you're after?"

Her husband, Beck, wasn't around, Tom assumed. If he were, he would have been in Tom's face long before this. "Pete's been seeing the Halls' daughter, Beth, and I heard Dr. Hall didn't approve."

Babs maintained her tight, defensive expression. "You heard old news. That's been over for a while now. And so what, anyway? The man's dead now. Killed by that pack of wild dogs, I heard. Who cares what he thought about anything?"

"The medical examiner has ruled Dr. Hall's death a homicide."

"A homi—You mean a *person* tore out his throat? Well, that's a new one on me." Babs Rasey laughed, shaking her head.

"We believe somebody sicced his dog on Dr. Hall."

Pete ducked his head, hiding his reaction from Tom's scrutiny.

Babs' expression sobered, then twisted into a frown of disgust. "Well, that's pretty cold-blooded. Who would do a thing like that?"

"That's what I'm trying to find out," Tom said. "I'm talking to everybody who had trouble with Gordon Hall."

Pete jerked his head up. He looked scared and ready to bolt. "You accusing *me* of doing it?"

"Now you just hold on a minute, Thomas Bridger," Babs said. She stepped closer to Pete's side. "You've got no right and no reason to come here accusing my son of—of God knows what."

"I'm not accusing him of anything. I just want to ask him some questions. Once I do that, I'll probably be able to rule him out as a suspect, then I can move on. I'd like him to come with me to headquarters—"

"*Mom*," Pete said, his voice rising.

Under the tree, the dog rattled its chain and barked in Tom's direction.

"You're not taking him anywhere," Babs said. "You want to question him, you come back with a warrant. Now get off our property."

"All right, if you want to make it harder on everybody," Tom said. "I'll be back."

She stepped in front of Pete, as if she could protect the muscular young hulk. Behind his mother, the boy's face had gone slack with fright.

Chapter Eight

The Halls' front door opened a crack, and a blue eye peered out over the safety chain. "You're back," Rayanne Stuckey said when she saw Tom, her voice faint with dismay.

"Mrs. Hall around?"

"But you were just here."

"And now, like you said, I'm back. Can I come in?"

"Mrs. Hall told me not to let anybody in. She's scared. And she doesn't want to see anybody that's comin' to sympathize either."

"Well, she's not scared of me, and I'm not here to sympathize. I'm investigating a crime. Open up, Rayanne."

She hesitated a moment longer, then unlatched the door and swung it open. Tom stepped across the threshold into the foyer. "In there." Rayanne waved a hand toward the living room.

He was on his way into the living room when footsteps pounded down the staircase. He swung around to see Beth Hall charging toward him.

"You've got no right!" she screamed. She came to a halt three feet from Tom, hands clenched into fists, her whole body trembling. "Who do you think you are?"

"Beth?" Vicky called from the living room. "What on earth?"

"What's wrong?" Tom asked the girl, although he had a good idea.

Outrage twisted Beth's delicate features into an ugly mask, and her eyes glittered with tears. "You have no right to accuse

Pete of killing my father. It's a lie! You're just a big dumb cop trying to mess up our lives because you don't know how to catch *real* criminals."

"*Beth.*" Vicky stood in the doorway from the living room. "That's enough. Stop this right now."

Soo Jin stood behind Vicky, a derisive smile on her lips as she watched the little drama play out.

"Just calm down," Tom said to Beth. "I don't know what Pete told you, but all I want to do is ask him some questions."

"You called him a murderer!" Tears spilled over and streamed down Beth's cheeks. "Just because you've got that dorky uniform and that stupid badge, you think you can push people around. But it doesn't mean shit, do you hear me?"

Beth shot out a hand, grabbed the badge on his uniform shirt and tried to yank it off. Tom caught her arm and forced her to let go. When he released her, she cradled her arm against her body and howled as if he'd broken it.

"Oh, for pity's sake," Soo Jin said.

"Elizabeth Ann Hall, you stop this nonsense right now," Vicky said. "I am ashamed of you."

The girl plowed into her mother and shoved her with enough force to make her stumble backward. Tom and Soo Jin both darted to Vicky and grabbed her arms before she fell.

When Vicky was steady on her feet, supported by Tom's arm around her waist, Soo Jin marched over to Beth and slapped her face. The loud *pop!* of the blow echoed in the foyer.

"Hey!" Tom said. "That's not necessary."

But Beth was already flinging herself at Soo Jin, hands outstretched to rake fingernails across her face. Soo Jin caught Beth's wrists and held her at arm's length.

"You bitch!" Beth struggled but couldn't free herself from Soo Jin's grip. "You told him about Pete, didn't you? You're always trying to suck up to somebody, you're always trying to tear me down. You're not part of this family, do you hear me? You're just a dirty little bastard somebody found on the street, your own mother didn't want you."

Soo Jin slammed Beth against the wall. Beth wailed and slid down until she sat in a heap, bawling, her face pressed to her knees.

"Oh, dear god," Vicky whispered. She breathed rapidly through bloodless lips. "I don't know how much more I can take."

"Come on and sit down," Tom said. He glanced at Beth to make sure she was going to stay put, then guided Vicky to the living room sofa. Soo Jin followed.

Vicky was weeping by the time she sat down. In the foyer, Beth bellowed like an animal being torn apart. Tom looked back at the girl in amazement. He would never have guessed that quiet little Beth Hall was capable of that much passion and rage. Her relationship with Pete was starting to make sense.

"Tom," Vicky said, pulling his attention back to her, "do you think the Rasey boy had something to do with Gordon's death?"

"I don't have any evidence against anybody at this point." Tom sat in an armchair facing her across the coffee table. Soo Jin sat beside Vicky and rested a hand on her shoulder. "I'm looking into the people who had disputes with your husband, just what I told you I was going to do."

"That business with the Rasey boy was so long ago," Vicky said. "It's been months, and Beth hasn't seen him since then."

Soo Jin snorted. Vicky and Tom both looked at her. "You don't think that's true?" Tom asked.

Soo Jin leaned forward to speak quietly. "They never broke up. They're still seeing each other, and obviously they're still talking."

"Why didn't you tell us?" Vicky said.

"How do you know what's going on?" Tom asked Soo Jin. "You've been away at school."

"I do come home for visits," Soo Jin replied, lifting her chin as if defying him to contradict her. "And I hear Beth on the phone with him, making plans to sneak out—"

"Shut your mouth, you bitch!" Beth yelled from the foyer. She scrambled to her feet and charged toward the living room.

Tom leapt up and caught her as she came through the doorway. "Whoa, whoa." He gripped her shoulders. "Settle down."

"Get your hands off me! You don't have any right to touch me." Beth twisted her shoulders and Tom released her. Instead of going after Soo Jin, she subsided into tears, gasping out her words. "You can't believe all those lies. Everybody's trying to come between us."

"Will you talk to me about it?" Tom asked. "Give me your side of the story?"

Beth raised her head and threw a defiant look at her mother and older sister. "Yeah, I'll tell you the truth. Then you'll see how stupid it is to blame Pete for anything."

"Vicky? Is it okay with you if I talk to Beth privately?"

She waved a hand as if she barely had the strength to lift it. "Use the family room."

Tom followed Beth down the corridor. They entered a room dominated by a wall-mounted HDTV that looked about six feet wide. On the other walls hung dozens of framed photos of all the Hall kids at various ages. Tom took an upholstered chair and Beth collapsed onto the brown leather couch, sniffling. He handed her his handkerchief. "You must still be in shock after finding your father that way."

Her head bowed, Beth answered in a shaky whisper, "It was horrible. The way he looked, lying there with—" Her hand went to her throat. Fresh tears filled her eyes. "Poor Daddy."

"Your father was murdered, Beth, and I have to do my job and investigate everybody who had a grievance against him. From what I hear, he didn't approve of you dating Pete Rasey, and they argued about it."

"Pete didn't do anything to my dad! He *wouldn't*."

"Okay, I get that. But I need to know exactly what happened between them."

Slumped on the sofa, Beth stared toward the window as she thought. From somewhere outside, Tom heard the faint, raspy whistle of a white-throated sparrow, a harbinger of winter.

"Mom and Dad never gave Pete a chance," Beth said at last. "All they've ever done is criticize him. They don't like his father or the place his family lives in or him being a football player.

Dad thinks athletes are stupid, so Pete must be stupid to spend his time throwing a ball around."

"How long have you and Pete been dating?"

"We don't *date*. He can't come here and pick me up and take me somewhere for a *date*. We've always had to sneak around."

"All right, how long have you been involved with him?"

"Why do you want to know? Are you going to ask me whether we have sex? You want all the details?"

This girl was trying his patience, but Tom did his best to keep his voice level. "Just answer my question. I've explained why I have to look into this."

Beth was silent a moment, scraping a fingernail back and forth on the sofa arm with enough pressure to leave an indentation in the leather. "A year. I've been *involved* with Pete for a year."

"Have you witnessed any arguments between your father and Pete?"

She nodded. "But it wasn't Pete's fault."

"What happened?"

"We were just hanging out this summer. We drove down to the river, we took some food and had a picnic, and we were just hanging out. My dad tracked us down, and all of a sudden he was just *there*, and he grabbed Pete and started pushing him around and yelling at him and saying he'd kill Pete if he ever came near me again."

"What were you and Pete doing when your father showed up?"

"I *told* you, we were just hanging out."

Tom gave her a long look, his eyebrows raised skeptically.

Beth tried to hold his gaze with the glare of a stubborn child, but after a few seconds she gave up and averted her eyes. "We were making out, okay? Is that what you want to know?"

"Did you both have all your clothes on?"

The girl's face flamed, her smooth pale skin turning blotchy red. Instead of answering the question, she blurted, "Dad had no *right*. Pete *loves* me. Dad had no right to come between us."

"You say he was pushing Pete around? What did Pete do? How did he react?"

"Well, how do you *think*? He had to defend himself. He wasn't going to just *take* it."

"So they had a fistfight? They were hitting each other?"

Beth inhaled a deep breath, expelled it in a huff, and nodded. "They both had bloody noses. It was so stupid. And it was all Dad's fault."

"You said your father threatened Pete. How did Pete react to that?"

She caught her bottom lip in her teeth, clearly reluctant to tell Tom the truth.

"Beth? Did Pete threaten your father too?"

"Neither one of them *meant* it. It was just, you know, guys saying things when they're mad."

She hadn't looked directly at Tom since she began talking about the confrontation. He had a feeling he'd pushed her as far as she was willing to go, and if he forced anything more out of her he couldn't be sure it was the truth. Now that he'd seen another side of her, a depth of rage he would never have imagined, he had to revise his approach. This was a girl with strongly conflicting feelings about her father.

One of the first things Tom had learned years ago as a detective on the Richmond police force was that family members had to be considered suspects in any murder until they were proven innocent. A spouse wanting out of a soured marriage. A kid infuriated by a controlling parent. But until a few minutes ago, he'd been blinded by Beth's usually meek manner. Pete Rasey could have gone after Gordon Hall in retaliation for trying to come between him and Beth, but maybe he hadn't planned the attack alone. If he needed to know exactly when Hall was outside in the dark, vulnerable to a surprise assault, only someone inside the Hall family home could have given him the information.

Someone like Hall's angry daughter.

Chapter Nine

The full moon hung high in the sky when Rachel and Tom set out in his pickup. Rachel felt jittery, not dreading the search and capture so much as what would come afterward. The dogs hadn't been on their own for long, and odds were that most of them could be re-socialized, but those that resisted contact with people… She hated euthanizing healthy animals and didn't want to think about it.

"Are you sure we're going to the best place?" she asked Tom. "Haven't the dogs been seen in a lot of different parts of the county?"

"Yeah, as far as I can tell they aren't sticking to one territory. And they don't seem to be stopped by the river and the creek. We've even had complaints from Rocky Branch District, and a situation's got to be pretty bad out there before anybody invites the cops to handle it."

The mention of Rocky Branch District brought to mind another worry that Rachel couldn't shake. She knew Tom's day had been long and exhausting, and she didn't want to drag him into an argument, but she had to ask. "What happened to the dogs you rescued from fighting operations in Rocky Branch District?"

Tom was silent for a long moment. The dashboard lights cast a faint glow over his strong features, making Rachel think of an Indian warrior or chief. "All of them were put down right away."

"So they weren't rescued. They were killed. And if you find a new dogfighting operation, those dogs will be destroyed too."

"There's nothing else that can be done with them. They aren't like the dogs we're going after now. They've never been pets. They've been trained to be vicious."

Rachel had plenty to say about this attitude, which she considered cruel and ill-informed, but she would leave the discussion for another time. Instead, she asked, "Who did the procedures? Did Joe do it at the shelter?"

"No, actually he refused to. Almost got fired for it, but he stood his ground."

Rachel's generally good opinion of the animal warden took a giant leap toward admiration. "So who did it?"

"Jim Sullivan."

Why am I not surprised? She let it drop, and they rode in silence for a few minutes.

Tom was the first to speak again. "The pack's been showing up on the Atkinson farm every night around this time. Atkinson runs them off, but he doesn't have a gun so he doesn't fire shots to scare them. I think that makes a difference. It might take them a few nights to get the message, but they usually figure out that a gun means it's not worth the risk."

"Mmm." Rachel started chewing a fingernail, realized what she was doing and dropped her hand to her lap. "Is Ethan Hall going to be problem for Holly and me? Will he try to stop us from rehabbing the dogs?"

"I think he's calming down. He saw what was done to Thor. That's proof that a person was behind Dr. Hall's death. I think he'll lose interest in the feral animals and focus on pestering me to move the murder investigation along faster."

Rachel hoped Tom was right, but she didn't have much faith in anybody's willingness to let go of a firmly held misconception. Especially not one that was shared and reinforced by many other people. "I had four calls this afternoon from clients who wanted to talk me out of trying to help those dogs. They were all people whose pets have disappeared, and they actually believe the pack killed their pets and ate them. If they've killed as many other animals as people are claiming, they'll be too fat to run and we won't have any trouble catching them."

Tom laughed. "The foxes are getting a free ride these days. They can take all the chickens and ducks they want, and the dogs'll get the blame."

"Maybe there really is some evil cosmic influence at work." Rachel leaned forward and studied the star-flecked sky. "You can't even see the dog star this time of year, can you? For most of the night, anyway. I think Sirius rises right before dawn. It's up there all day, but we can't see it." The echo of Mrs. Barker's words sent a shiver through her: *There are evil forces at work in Mason County. They surround you, but you are unable to see them.*

"I'm not interested in the position of a star," Tom said. "All I care about is getting those dogs out of the landscape. There's Joe up ahead."

The animal warden's van sat on the shoulder of the narrow county road, its emergency blinkers flashing on and off.

They pulled alongside the van and Rachel powered down her window. Leaning across her, Tom called to Joe, "Follow us over to the Atkinson place."

When they drove up to the farmhouse, Ken Atkinson clomped down his front steps to greet them. "Hey," he said when he reached Tom's truck. "I sure appreciate y'all coming out. Them dogs have been in my hen house three nights in a row. I ain't seen them so far tonight, but I reckon they'll be here."

"Are they killing chickens?" Rachel asked.

"Not yet. I don't give 'em a chance." He ran a roughened hand over buzz-cut gray hair that looked like a remnant of another era. "I hear a ruckus and I run right out. I find eggshells all over the ground. They'd get around to the chickens if I didn't show up fast enough. Go on, you'd better get set up. They've been coming right around this time of the evening."

Tom and Joe drove across the small farm and parked in the deep shadow behind the barn. Joe had the tranquilizer dart gun loaded and ready, aimed out the window of his van toward the hen house.

Half an hour passed. Rachel wondered if they were wasting time that might be better spent driving around looking for the dogs.

"There!" Tom whispered. He pointed. "Look."

They appeared out of the dark, emerging single file into a pool of moonlight between trees. Most of the dogs were small to medium sized, but the leader of the pack was a massive black animal with a deep chest and square muzzle.

"What is that thing?" Tom whispered. "The first one."

"Mixed breed," Rachel said, "but I'm not sure what."

An animal that size, if it had a good set of teeth, could easily rip out a grown man's throat. But Rachel didn't believe an alpha dog would attack alone. He would always be backed up by his followers.

The big dog stopped suddenly, and the others paused one by one, spreading out around him. The leader raised his snout, sniffing the air. He yelped, spun around and took off, the rest of the pack following.

Rachel groaned with disappointment.

"Christ," Tom said. "He spotted us."

"No, he smelled us."

Rachel heard another yelp and saw the shaggy brown dog in the rear of the pack frantically biting at its flank. The other dogs ignored its distress, barreling past it, bumping it as they fled.

"Joe got it with a dart," she said. "It'll go down in a minute." She already had her door open. When the dog dropped she snatched her medical bag from the floor and jumped out. She sprinted toward the dog, her bag banging against her leg. The rest of the pack had vanished.

Rachel dropped to her knees, yanked the dart from the animal's hip, and stuck her stethoscope in her ears. When Tom and Joe ran up, she said, "He's fine. Let's get him in a cage before he comes to."

Joe carried the limp dog to the van with Rachel walking alongside and supporting the animal's head. Saliva dripped from its lolling tongue. Joe slid the dog into the van, then he and Tom climbed in and maneuvered it into one of the cages.

"We gonna try for more tonight?" Joe asked Rachel.

"They're so spooked, I think we're lucky to get one." She pulled a mini flashlight from her jacket pocket and swept the beam over the tranquilized dog. "Let's get him over to Holly's place."

Rachel remained in the van, examining the dog and administering vaccines. It was a male, mixed breed, of medium size. He'd been out here long enough to lose most of his body fat. Under his filthy, matted brown hair, all Rachel felt were bones. "You're safe now," she whispered.

The cheerful BLUE RIDGE SANCTUARY sign, with its paintings of cats and dogs, couldn't dispel the sense of foreboding Rachel felt every time she entered the property, nor did all the new construction that was altering the secluded, tree-ringed clearing around the old McClure mansion. She had lived through a nightmare in that house and the nearby woods. Memories still invaded her dreams and shook her awake in the middle of the night.

When they parked behind the house, Holly and her grandmother, Sarelda Turner, hurried over. Joe flung open the rear door of the van and both women leaned in to see the dog.

"Oh, wow!" Holly said. "I'm so excited! Our first animal. And we've got a place all ready for it."

Mrs. Turner, a slight dark-haired woman with skin the same deep olive as her granddaughter's, announced, "I'm goin' to get this poor thing a good meal." She headed into the house.

Brandon Connolly, out of uniform and dressed in jeans and a sweater, joined Holly. "Hey, Dr. Rachel," he said, offering his hand to help her out of the van.

Bright lights from flood lamps mounted on poles lit up the area behind the house. A row of dog runs, built of chain link fencing, stood on ground once occupied by Pauline McClure's overgrown, abandoned herb and flower garden.

Brandon took Rachel's place inside the van and pushed the dog's cage forward to Tom and Joe. They carried the cage into the first dog run and set it down. Motioning the men out, Rachel opened the cage door and knelt to check the dog's respiration and heartbeat. When the stethoscope touched its chest, the animal lifted his head groggily, and Rachel's ears filled with the magnified sound of a low whine.

"Get out of there now," Tom said. He stepped into the doorway of the run. "I don't want you getting bitten."

"I'm almost done. He's not capable of biting anybody right now." The dog was scared, not hostile, and Rachel saw that as a good sign for his future. Working quickly, she repositioned the stethoscope a few inches to listen to the dog's lungs.

"Come on," Tom said. "This isn't safe."

"Don't worry," Rachel whispered to the dog. She stroked his head, feeling clumps of dirt and tangled hair under her fingers. "You're going to be fine."

The dog's eyes rolled toward her and it dropped its head.

When the door to the run was closed and locked, they all stood watching the dog struggle to his feet, stand on shaky legs for a moment, and sink to his belly. "He'll be back to normal in an hour," she told Holly. "Then he can have something to eat and drink. Don't let your grandmother overfeed him though. He can't—"

A commotion near the house interrupted her. They all turned to look.

"Oh, no," Rachel groaned when she saw three pickups and two SUVs rumbling toward the dog runs. "The vigilantes have arrived."

The vehicles came to a stop and a dozen men piled out, most carrying shotguns and rifles. Ethan Hall, without a weapon, took the lead as the men approached. Tom stepped into his path.

"You got one of them, didn't you?" Ethan demanded. "Where is it? We ought to shoot it right here and now."

"Nobody's shooting anything," Tom said.

"Them dogs are killers!" a man in the group yelled. "We need to get rid of them."

Rachel moved forward to face Ethan. "This is an animal sanctuary. No animals are going to be killed here."

Ethan shook his head. "Do you think people in this county are going to let you keep a pack of dangerous dogs alive?"

"You're all trespassing," Rachel said. "You have no right to come in here waving guns around."

"Ethan," Tom said, "I thought you'd come to your senses. I want to see you at headquarters in the morning. There are things you need to know. But right now, yeah, you're trespassing, and you and your friends are going to get off this property."

"Who's going to make us?" someone called from the back of crowd.

The men pressed forward, forming a wall of angry faces behind Ethan. Rachel took an involuntary step backward, then stopped herself. She didn't want them to see how much they scared her.

"Whatever you're thinking about doing," Tom said, "you'll have to go through me first. You lay one hand on a deputy sheriff and you'll be in jail for the next year. If anybody points a gun at me, I'll take it as a threat, and I'll have to shoot him in self-defense."

"You wouldn't dare," Ethan spat out.

Tom returned the taunt with a calm smile.

Under the cold light of the flood lamps, Tom and Ethan stared at each other. After a silence that seemed endless to Rachel, the crowd of men began backing off. She realized she'd been holding her breath and forced herself to let it out slowly, breathe in slowly.

"This isn't over," Ethan said. "We're going ahead with our plans. We'll track down those dogs and kill them all ourselves, if we can't count on our so-called public servants to do it."

"Just keep the law in mind," Tom said. "You can't go on private property without permission, and you can't fire a gun on public land without a permit."

Ethan stalked off, pushing past the other men. They all fell into line behind him, heading back to their vehicles.

When they were driving away, Tom said, "It's not going to be safe for anybody to stay here tonight."

Rachel looked around at Holly and Brandon, Joe and Tom. Holly's grandmother, inside for the past few minutes, came out onto the back porch of the house twenty feet away with a dog bowl in hand. "But if everyone leaves," Rachel said, "the dog's as good as dead."

"Well, I'm not goin' anywhere," Holly said. "I didn't start this place so those stupid people could come in here and kill the animals."

"I'm not goin' anywhere either," her grandmother said.

"I'll stay," Brandon said, placing an arm around Holly's shoulders. "And I'll call a couple of my cousins and get them to come out."

They all agreed to that plan, but Rachel felt a deep uneasiness as she and Tom drove away into the night. She gazed up at the sky, knowing Sirius was hiding just below the horizon. Was Mrs. Barker right? Even when it was out of sight, did the dog star hold Mason County in its sinister spell?

Chapter Ten

Early Friday morning, Soo Jin Hall sat in Tom's office and read the preliminary autopsy report twice without speaking. Her face, devoid of makeup except for vivid red lipstick, had the same shell-shocked expression he'd seen on many people who'd lost loved ones to violence.

She placed the report on his desk. "That's a horrible way for anyone to die."

Tom leaned forward, arms folded on the desktop. In front of him lay the small recorder he'd used to play Gordon Hall's answering machine message for her. "Yes, it is. The medical examiners—Dr. Lauter here, the pathologist in Roanoke—agree that the damage was done by a single dog. I hope you believe that now."

Soo Jin nodded. She was unlike any twenty-one-year-old Tom had ever known. Poised, self-contained, she sat with her spine stiff and straight, not touching the back of the chair. Instead of standard young adult gear, she wore black slacks, a white blouse, and a short black jacket with braid along the front edges and sleeves. Stylish, expensive stuff, all of it. A gold clasp held her ink-black hair at the nape of her neck.

"I'm sure Ethan will believe it too when he sees the evidence," she said.

Tom was glad she'd changed her thinking, because he had a feeling this was the member of the Hall family who was most likely to be honest with him. "Why didn't he come with you? I don't mean to sound cold about this, but Ethan needs to start thinking straight and stop interfering in police business."

"For the moment he's channeling his grief into anger at the dogs and the police. He's devastated by his father's death, but, being a man, he feels compelled to *do* something about it, and he doesn't want anyone to see how much he's hurting."

She'd said *his* father, Tom noted, not *our* father. "Then how do you know what he's feeling?"

Soo Jin stared down at her hands, which rested on top of her purse in her lap. "Last night I couldn't sleep, and I was up and walking around. I saw someone on the patio, sitting in one of the chairs, bent over. At first I was startled and frightened. I thought it was an intruder. Then I realized it was Ethan."

When she paused, Tom prodded, "And?"

Soo Jin shifted in her seat, the first sign of discomfort she'd shown; "I went out, and I discovered he was crying. He got mad at me, he was embarrassed that I'd seen him like that. Then he broke down and started sobbing and said it was too late, now he'd never get closer to his father."

Tom pulled a pen and notebook from a drawer and laid the notebook open on his desk. "They weren't close, then? I know Ethan had a rebellious streak when he was a teenager, but didn't they get past that?"

Bringing her gaze back to Tom, Soo Jin said, "I haven't been at home often the past year, and it's been months since I saw the two of them together. But from what I could tell, I think our father finally accepted Ethan's decision not to become a doctor."

Now Gordon Hall was *our* father. Did she have ambivalent feelings about the man who raised her?

"The important thing to our parents is that Ethan is successful," Soo Jin went on. "He's advancing rapidly in his job. But he felt like he had a lot of lost years to make up for." She dropped her gaze. "Now that's never going to happen."

A strong sense of regret would explain Ethan's overwrought state, Tom thought, as well as his determination to lay the blame on the handiest canine culprits. Tom jotted notes on what Soo Jin had told him.

She fell silent while he wrote. When he looked up at her again, she said, "I hope you're looking for evidence against the Rasey boy."

"You believe he was involved in your father's death?"

"I believe it's possible."

Tom leaned back in his chair and studied her for a moment. She returned his gaze coolly. "If Pete Rasey was responsible for your father's death, do you think Beth would protect him?"

"Of course she would, because you'd never make her believe he was guilty. She's absolutely in thrall to that boy."

Tom almost smiled. *In thrall?* That sounded like something Mrs. Barker would say. "How much do you know about Dr. Hall's confrontation with Pete?"

"Which confrontation? There were several."

Tom raised an eyebrow. "Tell me about them."

"I think their worst clash occurred when he caught them together by the river."

"They'd gone on a picnic, right?"

Her lips curled in an unpleasant smile. "They might have had something to eat, but that wasn't their primary activity that day."

"What do you mean?"

"I'm sure you won't be surprised to hear they were having sex. Their clothes were strewn everywhere, and they were lying on a blanket on the ground. But that wasn't the worst of it. Mother told me the Rasey boy had given Beth some kind of drug, and she was so high, absolutely incoherent, that she didn't seem normal again for several days." Soo Jin shook her head. "The girl was fifteen at the time."

"The girl? Is that how you think of your sister?"

Soo Jin expelled an impatient sigh. "She's not my sister, Captain Bridger. I'm not related to any of them. We're part of the same family, but I've never felt much kinship with the others. Perhaps if I'd lived at home, attended local schools—But for a long time, I was just someone who visited on holidays and during the summer."

"You went to boarding school, right? When did that start?"

"When I was nine. By then it was obvious that public schools didn't meet my needs. My parents found a school that would let me move ahead at a faster pace. If I'd stayed in public school, I would still be in college now instead of my second year of medical school."

"You were a prodigy."

"If you want to put a label on me," Soo Jin said.

"But you missed out on family life, bonding with your siblings."

She didn't have a comeback for that. After a moment of silence, Tom said, "The Halls adopted you when you were a baby, didn't they?"

"I was a year old."

"How did that come about? Were they looking for a child to adopt?"

Her already stiff posture seemed to freeze solid. "They were donating their services at a clinic in Seoul and also providing medical care at an orphanage."

"The one where you were being taken care of?"

The little derisive smile twisted her lips again. "I was living there. Whether I was being taken care of is another question. I don't remember it, but I've been told about it."

"So they adopted you, and you're the second oldest child. You were a Hall before any of the others, except Ethan. Why don't you feel like they're your family?"

She rose abruptly, clutching her handbag to her side, and for a second Tom thought she was going to walk out. But she moved to the window and stood there with the mellow autumn sun falling across her face. Without looking at Tom, she said, "I'm fond of my mother. We have more in common than you might imagine. Did you know that she grew up in foster homes? That she doesn't know anyone in her birth family?"

"No," Tom said. "I'd never heard that." Maybe it explained why the Halls adopted three kids.

"I admired my adoptive father," Soo Jin went on. "And he was proud of the way I've turned out. He never let me forget where I came from and how different my life would be if I hadn't been adopted."

"Jesus. Most kids would have grown up hating him for that."

She turned to face Tom. "You don't understand. He wanted me—he wanted all of us—to appreciate how privileged we are, but he didn't want us to be lazy and take it for granted that we could have anything we wanted." She paused. "I admired his work ethic. He ran the hospital efficiently and according to his own standards."

Tom thought that was a strange thing for a kid to find admirable in her dad. "My mother worked there. She was the nursing supervisor."

Curiosity brought a subtle animation to Soo Jin's rigid features. "Did she enjoy working for him?"

Tom's mother had thought Hall was a son of a bitch. He ignored her question and asked, "What happens to the hospital now?"

"It's held in trust. Mother will administer the trust. And my father's personal will leaves everything to my mother. There's no huge profit for any of us in our father's death, if that's what you're wondering."

"Good to know," Tom said. "To get back to Beth, do you think she would protect Pete Rasey, even if he was responsible for her father's death? Tell me—" He paused. "Do you think Beth is capable of being personally involved?"

Soo Jin received the question with no show of surprise. With her head tilted and a slight frown between her eyes, she seemed to consider the possibility of Beth's complicity in the crime. When she snapped her attention back to Tom, she said, "Yes. It's possible. I believe Pete Rasey could talk her into it. Beth hasn't always been troublesome—that started when she became involved with Pete. Until then, she was always the good girl, who did what she was told. And she certainly benefited by comparison with David. He's been such a headache that he made Beth seem angelic."

David, the mixed race boy, was also adopted, Tom reminded himself. "What's his problem?"

"His problem is his identity." Soo Jin returned to her chair but sat on the edge of the seat, clutching her purse with both hands, as if she might leap up again at any second. "Our parents adopted David when he was eight. He's never been under the illusion that he's their child, in any sense. Marcy was very small when they were adopted, and I'm not sure she remembers their real parents. She doesn't exactly share her thoughts and feelings. I've sometimes wondered if the girl is mildly autistic. It drives our mother to distraction sometimes. Did you know that Marcy was born addicted to meth?"

"Yeah, I heard that." Tom's mother had told him the story of the infant's harrowing first weeks of life in the hospital as she suffered through full-blown withdrawal. But David was the one on Tom's mind now. The boy exuded hostility, and Tom had heard talk about him getting into fights at school. A perfectionist like Gordon Hall wouldn't accept such behavior. And every act of discipline, every critical word, would have increased the boy's emotional turmoil and sense of isolation in a family where he didn't belong. Could David have struck out at his adoptive father? Of course. But could he have engineered the kind of death Hall suffered? David claimed to have been inside the house when Hall was killed. Even if that alibi were disproved, as many alibis were in the end, where did the boy get a killer dog that would follow his commands, and where was that dog now?

Tom tapped his pen on the notebook. "You know, some people would say your parents are saints, adopting three kids, giving them all the advantages. But it doesn't sound like any of you have been happy in the Hall family."

"I didn't say I'm unhappy. I have a very good life. The Halls are the only parents I've ever known, and I've always tried to please them. I wanted them to feel I was worth saving from the orphanage."

Tom figured he might as well coax as much inside information out of her as he could while she was in the mood to spill family secrets. "What about Dr. Hall and Mrs. Hall? Did they have a good marriage? Do you know if they've had any problems in their relationship?"

She leveled a look at him, her mouth curling in a sour little smile. "The spouse is always the first suspect. Isn't that the way the police think?"

"The spouse is also the first person we try to eliminate as a suspect."

"Well, Captain, I can tell you that in all the years I've lived with them I have never heard them raise their voices to each other. They were devoted. She adored him, and he would have done anything for her. It's going to be difficult for her now that he's gone."

"Didn't they ever disagree when one of the kids needed disciplining?"

"Oh, no. She left that up to him. Whatever he thought best, she backed him up. He was furious with Beth for seeing Pete Rasey, so she was, too. When he was disappointed in Ethan, so was she. When he forgave Ethan, she did, too. She's always supported his methods of dealing with David when he acted out. Grounding him, taking away his TV and Internet access and cell phone, that sort of thing."

"No physical discipline?" Tom asked.

"Oh, no. They've never believed in striking children. They believed psychological pressures and denial of privileges were more effective."

"Why are you telling me all this?" Tom asked. "You say you owe everything to the Halls, but you're not painting a flattering picture of them."

"Flattering or unflattering, it's the truth, and you would have heard it all eventually anyway. I want you to get the investigation over with as quickly as you can. I'm saving you time by providing you with information so you can clear the family members and find the real killer."

"Ah. You're trying to help me *clear* the family."

She met his gaze for a heartbeat, her dark eyes cold and blank. Then she gave him a rueful little smile. "I'm giving you the wrong impression, with all this emphasis on the negative. We didn't grow up in a hostile environment. We've been given every advantage. Now I'll let you get back to work."

Soo Jin rose, gave Tom a briskly businesslike handshake, and walked out.

Watching her leave, Tom wondered what was really going on behind her mask of cool reserve and disdain. *Every advantage*, he thought. *Yeah, every advantage except love.* Children raised without love could look perfect on the outside while harboring demons on the inside. Maybe Soo Jin had come here to reinforce his suspicion of Pete Rasey and make sure he saw Beth as a possible accomplice, while deflecting his attention from herself.

Chapter Eleven

Rachel turned into the Halls' driveway and found a man with a shotgun blocking her way. She slammed on the brakes. Her mouth went dry. Had she stumbled into a crime scene? Had someone come to kill the rest of the Hall family?

The stocky, balding man approached her window. Rachel shifted into reverse, ready to flee. Then she recognized the middle-aged man as one of Ethan's followers. One of the men determined to hunt down and kill the feral dogs. Were they having a meeting at the Hall house?

The man rapped on her window.

Reluctant to respond, Rachel stared back at him.

"What do you want here?" the man shouted.

Rachel powered down the window about two inches. "Mrs. Hall is expecting me. I'm here to check on the dog."

The man studied her, his gaze crawling over her face and dropping to her breasts, his smirk making her feel vaguely soiled. Then he straightened and jerked a thumb, giving her permission to move forward.

Rachel stepped on the gas, blowing out a long breath of relief as she left the armed man behind. Now she had to worry about encountering Ethan and putting up with his nastiness and verbal abuse.

Maybe, Rachel thought, Ethan wasn't at home.

No such luck. He answered the front door.

"Your mother's expecting me," Rachel said before he could react to her presence. "Would you tell her I'm here to see Thor, please?"

She expected bluster, or at least a disapproving sneer to remind her that he thought she was crazy for championing the killer dogs. Instead, Ethan looked back at her without expression, his eyes dull and red-rimmed. Had he been crying?

"She's in the sun room with Thor," he said, his voice a low monotone. "I'll show you."

It's finally hit him, Rachel thought as she followed Ethan down the hall. This guy ticked her off in quite a few ways, but she felt a surprising pang of sympathy for him. His father had just been murdered, after all, and in a particularly gruesome way.

Ethan left Rachel at the door to the sun room. The German shepherd, stretched on a big dog bed, raised his head and thumped his tail once when she entered the glass-enclosed space. Potted plants, some soaring toward the roof, gave the air a pleasant woodsy aroma. In the corner where Mrs. Hall sat in a wicker chair, blooming orchids of various sizes crowded several tabletops.

"There's a man on your driveway with a gun," Rachel said. "He didn't want to let me in."

Mrs. Hall sighed. "I'm sorry. We have an alarm system and the house can be locked up like a fortress, but Ethan thinks we need additional protection. So he's paying those men to march around with their rifles." She waved a hand. "They won't bother you again. Thank you for coming out to see Thor."

Rachel looked down at the dog. "So he's been up and moving around, huh? That's a good sign."

"I don't know. He seems so depressed. He used to keep Gordon company when he sat in here reading. I think he came in here hoping—" She broke off and shook her head sadly.

Vicky Hall looked terrible. Her condition had deteriorated visibly in the last twenty-four hours. She was probably due for dialysis and would feel better afterward.

"He's grieving," Rachel said, "and he doesn't understand what's happened." She sat on the stone floor and stroked the dog's head.

"He must have been terrified while he was tied up," Mrs. Hall said. "Do you think he was beaten? Nobody's ever hit him before."

"I didn't find anything to indicate a beating," Rachel said. As far as she could tell, all of Thor's wounds had been inflicted by another dog.

Rachel began her examination and didn't look up when Rayanne Stuckey summoned Mrs. Hall to take a telephone call from the funeral home. She was listening to the dog's heart-beat—back to normal—when something brushed against her arm. Startled, she jerked back.

The Halls' youngest daughter knelt beside her.

"Oh," Rachel said, exhaling, feeling her own heart rate slow from a momentary spike. "Hello. You're Marcy, aren't you?"

The girl nodded, her face solemn. She was a stunning child who looked younger than eleven, with delicate features, huge brown eyes, and curly black hair. Her skin was a lovely, light milk-chocolate shade. Rachel had heard that Marcy and her brother David had a black father who dropped out of their lives long before their birth mother died.

Marcy stroked the dog's head and muzzle, and Thor made soft moaning sounds of pleasure.

"He likes you," Rachel said. "Maybe if you spend lots of time with him, he'll start feeling better. He misses your dad too, just like you do."

Rachel sensed the girl stiffening at the remark, and she wished she hadn't mentioned the father.

Her head bowed, Marcy whispered something.

"I'm sorry," Rachel said. "I didn't hear you."

Marcy raised her head a couple of inches, but Rachel still couldn't make out her words.

Rachel touched her shoulder. The girl's body had gone as rigid as a block of wood. "I'm sorry, sweetie, could you speak a little louder?"

The girl looked directly into Rachel's eyes. She was fright-ened. No, that was too mild a word. Marcy was terrified. She said, "Please help—"

"Marcy!"

Rachel jerked her head around to see David Hall in the doorway, his hands fisted at his sides. Marcy pulled away from Rachel and seemed to shrink, head down and shoulders hunched.

"Stop bothering the doctor," David said. "Come on out of there."

"She isn't bothering me at all," Rachel said. Was everybody in this family crazy? The dog had begun whimpering. "She has a good effect on Thor. I'd like her to spend some time with him."

David ignored her. "Marcy," he said, "come on. Right now."

The girl gave Rachel an imploring look, her eyes wide and swimming with tears. Rachel placed a hand on her shoulder, but Marcy slid away, pushed herself up and walked to her brother, dragging her feet as if she faced a dreaded punishment. David grabbed her arm and pulled her out of the room.

"Wait a minute!" Rachel scrambled to her feet and hurried after them. David was marching Marcy down the hall toward the stairs. "I asked you to wait!"

At the foot of the stairs, David finally paused and turned. His face, as striking as his sister's, twisted in an ugly sneer. "You don't give me orders, lady."

"What are you doing to this child?" Rachel demanded. She caught up with them and reached out to Marcy.

David yanked the girl backward so hard Marcy stumbled and lost her balance. David forced her upright. "Leave us alone," he said to Rachel. "You ain't got nothin' to do with us."

Vicky Hall reappeared, emerging from her husband's home office. "What's going on? David? Marcy? What are you up to?"

Marcy whimpered but didn't speak.

"We ain't doin' nothin'," David said.

Mrs. Hall winced. "Oh, David, your grammar. You know better than that."

The boy glared at her but didn't answer.

Rachel had no idea what was happening here, and she told herself it was none of her business. But the despair on little Marcy's face tore at her heart.

"Go to your rooms," Mrs. Hall said. "I don't want to hear another peep out of either of you."

They climbed the stairs, David dragging his sister along by the arm. When she fell behind, he jerked her hard and she almost fell forward onto the steps. Rachel watched, baffled and helpless.

"Those two," Mrs. Hall said with a shake of her head. "Sometimes I think they were the worst mistake we ever made. They're such *beautiful* children, they look like angels. But appearances can certainly be deceiving. Now, how is Thor?"

"He'll be fine," Rachel murmured. Her gaze followed Marcy and David up the steps.

At the top, as they turned to the left, Marcy looked down and her eyes connected with Rachel's. The girl opened her mouth. Although she made no sound, Rachel was certain her lips formed a silent plea: *Help me.*

Chapter Twelve

"I don't want you getting involved with that family." Tom shook a little more salt on his chicken salad sandwich. He and Rachel occupied a secluded corner booth at the Mountaineer, sharing a quick lunch before they both got back to work. Glancing around to make sure no one was eavesdropping, he added, "It's not your responsibility to fix every problem you see."

"I'm not saying I want to fix it." Rachel dropped her unfinished sandwich onto her plate and pushed it aside. "I want *you* to fix it."

Tom laughed in spite of his effort to maintain a disapproving scowl. "I'm not even sure what's wrong, if anything is."

"Oh, something's wrong, all right." Rachel leaned over the table and whispered, "That poor girl is scared to death. I know she's afraid of her brother, but I believe there's more to it—whatever *it* is—than her relationship with David. You should look into it."

"She has a mother, Rachel."

"But her mother's part of the problem! Mrs. Hall is wrapped up in her own grief, and she seems to care more about the dog than her children. I don't think it's just a response to her husband's death. If you saw the way she acts toward them—"

"I have seen it."

"Then you know she's not going to be any help to Marcy. She talks about Marcy and David as if they're exotic plants that need too much care. I doubt there's a single person in that house Marcy can count on."

Tom bit into his sandwich. Rachel was probably right about Marcy feeling isolated in the Hall family, and about Vicky Hall's lack of interest in the girl. But what the hell was going on with David? "Are you sure you didn't misread the situation? Her father was murdered night before last, and she saw his body. She's upset, and she might also be afraid the killer's coming back for the rest of the family."

Rachel shook her head. "No. I'm positive she was reacting to David. And Mrs. Hall's not going to step in. She saw David drag Marcy up the stairs, but all she did was complain about both of them being too much trouble."

The waitress, a woman of about sixty who already seemed worn out at midday, appeared to top off their coffee. Watching the steaming liquid flow into the mugs, Tom thought about what Soo Jin had told him that morning in his office. She'd painted a picture of a household where none of the kids felt comfortable. After the waitress walked away, Tom said, "I remember when they adopted those two. I was living in Richmond, but I heard the whole story from my mother. She was furious about it."

"Furious that they were adopting the kids? Why?" Rachel sipped her coffee.

Tom scanned the room for eavesdroppers again. The economy had been so bad that fewer and fewer customers came to the Mountaineer for lunch. Under the hanging wagon wheels that served as lighting fixtures, people sat in just four other booths, and they seemed too engrossed in their own conversations to listen in on him and Rachel.

"Mom got along with Hall because she had to," Tom told Rachel, "but she never liked him. She thought he was a phony, a hypocrite. I was here for a visit around that time, and she talked the whole weekend about what the Halls were doing."

"That sounds sinister. What bothered your mother so much?"

"Oh, man. I'm crazy to be telling you any of this. I don't want you involved."

"If you stop now, I'm going to kick you," Rachel said. "I want to know the background on those kids."

Tom sighed, hesitated, then continued. "Mom felt the same way you do—David and Marcy were pretty little things Vicky Hall wanted to own but she didn't care much about them as people. She thought they were beautiful, she wanted them, and her husband made sure she got them."

"After their mother died, right?"

"Yeah, but the Halls were trying to get them even before that. There were rumors going around that they offered Jewel Riggs a lot of money for them."

"What? They tried to *buy* them?" Rachel's voice rose in outrage, and Tom made a hushing motion with his hands.

"Let me tell you the whole story. David and Marcy's mother—Jewel—was an addict. She was in rehab a couple of times, but she couldn't stay clean. Even after Marcy was born addicted, Jewel couldn't straighten herself out and do what was right for the kids. She kept landing in the emergency room, usually with David and Marcy in tow."

"God, how awful," Rachel said. Tom saw tears moisten her eyes, but in a second she'd blinked them away. "Is that where Mrs. Hall first saw Marcy and David? At the hospital?"

"Yeah. Vicky was the ER administrator. She got Social Services involved, and the kids were taken away from Jewel a couple of times, but she got them back when she was clean again. Then the Halls got the idea of adopting them—rescuing them—and they started pressuring Jewel to give up her parental rights."

"Didn't their father have anything to say about it?"

"Raymond wasn't around at the time. He was never really in the picture. They never got married—her parents were dead set against her marrying a black man—and he was in and out of Jewel's life because he couldn't find work here. As far as I know, he never supported the kids."

"But their mother wouldn't give them to the Halls, not even for money?"

"No. Both times after she was in rehab she tried to stay clean and take care of them. But in the end she died of an overdose. Then the Halls went to court to get the kids."

"What about their relatives? Grandparents?"

"Jake and Maddy Riggs kept the kids when Jewel was in rehab," Tom said, "but they didn't want them because they were half black."

"Oh, gee, that's nice." Rachel drummed her fingers on the table as a complex mix of anger, sorrow, and pity played across her face.

"Believe me, if you knew them, you wouldn't want the kids to be with them." *I'm going to regret telling her all this,* Tom thought. Rachel would jump right into the Hall family's mess if he didn't stop her. And he was seldom able to stop her from doing anything. "Their uncle was at the Hall house yesterday. Leo Riggs. He was with Ethan at the shelter last night, too."

"That lowlife is their uncle?"

"Yeah, and he was totally in favor of the adoption. From what I heard, he thought the kids really lucked out when the Halls adopted them." *And Leo lucked out too.* Tom had heard that the Halls provided the money to set up Leo's car repair shop at the time of the adoption. Tom's mother had always contended that the Riggses sold the kids to the Halls.

"So," Rachel said, "the Halls went to a lot of trouble to take two kids away from their biological family, maybe for very good reasons, but then they refused to give them the love they deserved. I will never understand why people do things like that."

Tom wondered if Rachel was thinking of the Halls or her own family. Marcy had struck a chord with her, and she probably saw herself in the child. He hated the thought of her old wounds being opened up again. If the Halls' dog hadn't been injured, Rachel would never have become involved. "I can't explain it," he said. "Don't let this eat away at you. Try to put it out of your mind. Okay?"

She didn't answer, and Tom supposed that was the right response to his suggestion that she do the impossible.

He dropped his napkin on the table and motioned for the waitress to bring the check. "Whatever's going on in that family, it'll have to wait. I need to get back to the hospital and talk to some more of Hall's employees, but first I want to follow up on the dogfighting angle. If Hall's dog was being held by somebody in a dogfighting operation, that's the key to finding his killer."

Tom handed the waitress a couple of bills, telling her to keep the change. "Be careful out in Rocky Branch District this afternoon," he told Rachel. "I'll have a deputy out there to look after you and Holly. I'd like to get through the rest of the day without worrying about you every minute."

The dog they had captured the night before cringed in a corner of the enclosure when Rachel stooped next to the chain link fence. Holly hung back. Rachel was afraid the dog would feel threatened if both of them came close.

"Hey, boy," she murmured. She stuck a sausage-flavored treat through the fence. "Look what I've got for you."

The animal's nose twitched as he picked up the strong aroma. Rachel found the smell revolting, but dogs loved the stuff.

"Wouldn't you like to have this?" she coaxed.

Drool leaked from the dog's mouth and plopped on the ground. He swallowed and inched closer, his eyes never leaving the enticing morsel in Rachel's fingers.

"Come on, boy, come on over here and you can have it."

A couple more steps. A high-pitched whine rose from his throat. When Rachel shifted slightly on her haunches, the dog jumped away again, hitting the fence behind him.

"Okay, sweetie," Rachel crooned, "that's enough for one day. You can have it. Come and get it."

She dropped the treat through the fence and shuffled backward two or three feet. She didn't want to spook him by suddenly rising to her full height.

The dog's eyes shifted between Rachel and the treat on the ground and back again. Then he sprang forward, snatched the treat, and bolted for the doghouse at the rear of the enclosure. After he was safely hidden away, Rachel heard him munching noisily.

"Poor thing," Holly said. They turned and walked back toward Rachel's Range Rover. "He must be so lonesome and scared without all the other dogs."

"We have to break their bond as a pack," Rachel said, "and help them bond with people again. That connection is still there. We just have to bring it to the surface."

"I know you're right. I just—" Holly's eyes filled with tears. "I feel so sorry for them. People have been so mean to them, I don't know why they'd ever trust any of us again."

Rachel touched her shoulder. "They will, Holly. We have to work with them and be patient. You need to be tough to do this kind of work." She looked around, assessing the progress that had been made on construction. "We can only bring in as many dogs as you have room for."

A dozen fenced dog runs, each with a covered section and a doghouse, stood ready for use. Behind them, a long shelter was being built to house dogs in cold weather, but only the framing and one wall had gone up so far. Rachel had asked for a one-day break in construction noise for the sake of the frightened dog, and the men were busy nearby, digging holes for the concrete footings of additional fenced enclosures.

"We'll keep some in the house if we have to," Holly said. "Just get all of them in here so we can take care of them."

But would the dogs be safe here? "My big concern right now is security," Rachel said. "Are you sure the guys your grandmother's hiring will be reliable?"

Holly's nod was emphatic. "They know they'd better be, or they'll have to answer to Grandma. They won't let that crazy bunch get in here again."

Rachel didn't like putting the shelter's security in the hands of men from Rocky Branch District, but Holly's grandmother knew everyone in that area and was probably a good judge of who could be trusted. With a few phone calls this morning she had rounded up a full crew of men who wanted the work and could start today. They weren't professionals, though, and Rachel worried that someone would get hurt unnecessarily. But what alternative did they have on short notice? Every animal Rachel and Joe Dolan brought to the shelter would increase the chances of an attack on the place. The dogs and the people who cared for them would be in greater danger with every day—and night—that passed.

Chapter Thirteen

"Oh, man, look at that!" Brandon exclaimed, peering at the house through the cruiser's windshield. "A real log cabin. I've never seen one before."

At the end of the steep gravel road, Tom pulled into the clearing in front of the house and killed the engine. "Some people out in the big wide world believe all of us hillbillies live in log cabins."

"I wouldn't mind it," Brandon said. "That is one cool house."

"It might be a little cooler in the winter than you're used to. Speaking literally." Burt Morgan's cabin perched halfway up a mountainside that wasn't served by electric or gas lines.

When Tom and Brandon stepped out of the car, two big mutts scrambled from under the porch, barking and growling. Tom's hand went to his gun.

Morgan banged open his screen door, yelling, "Rambo! Bullet! Back off!"

The dogs stopped instantly. Whining, they retreated a few feet, but they never took their eyes off Tom and Brandon.

"Lay down, fleabags," Morgan commanded.

The dogs flopped onto their bellies.

"Hey, Burt," Tom said. He kept a wary eye on the dogs. "How have you been?"

"Like you give a shit," Morgan replied, his tone almost amiable. He was in his late fifties, with close-cropped gray hair and a basketball of a belly under a brown flannel shirt. He jammed one fist into the pocket of his loose khaki pants. His other hand held a cigarette. "What can I do for you, Captain?"

Tom moved closer to the house. The dogs, apparently reassured by their owner's acceptance of the visitors, lost interest in him and laid their heads on their paws. Brandon stayed in the background, scouting the property. The small clearing was just big enough for Morgan's house, a wood shed next to it, and parking space for several vehicles. Tom had parked his cruiser next to Morgan's old pickup. On the other side of the truck sat a blue Civic, several years old but shiny and spotless.

Tom rested one booted foot against the bottom step. Drawing on his cigarette, Morgan squinted down at him from the porch.

"I just wanted to check in with you," Tom said. "See how you're doing."

"Uh huh. You Bridgers have always had a real strong interest in my welfare. What the hell's that kid lookin' for?" Morgan gestured toward Brandon. Ash dropped from his cigarette in a shower of sparks.

Tom glanced at Brandon, who had been prowling along the edge of the clearing, scanning the woods. "He's just admiring the scenery. Those two the only dogs you've got here?"

"Only dogs I've got *anywhere*. I'm stayin' out of the fights, if that's what you're snoopin' around about. I don't even go to 'em anymore. Lost my taste for it. But don't go thankin' yourself for that." Morgan jerked a thumb back toward the house. "It was Sylvia's doing."

Tom shifted his gaze to the door and saw a plump, matronly blond woman standing behind the screen door. The owner of the Civic, no doubt. Sylvia was part of the Stuckey clan, a coal miner's widow who worked the dinner shift at the Mountaineer.

"Yeah, I know you cleaned up your act," Tom said. "But there's always somebody waiting to step in. It was quiet for a while, but I think the fights are going on again. A lot of people's pet dogs have been disappearing, and now Gordon Hall's been killed by a dog."

Morgan frowned. "You tyin' that to the fights? I heard it was that wild pack that took Hall out."

"The medical examiner says he was attacked by one dog. You know the rest of a pack wouldn't stand by and watch."

"Naw," Morgan murmured. "That wouldn't happen. Damn. And what's this about people's pets disappearin'? What's that got to do with the fights?"

"I think it's a real possibility that pet dogs are being stolen and used as bait to train the fighters." Tom saw something in Morgan's face, a dawning outrage, that made him think he'd stumbled onto a way to get his help. "Most of them are children's pets."

Morgan shook his head, scowling. "Man, that is low. I never woulda stooped to somethin' like that. A kid's pet, anybody's pet, that's off-limits."

"Well," Tom said, "not everybody has your standards. I need to put a stop to it, Burt. And I need your help. I'll understand if you're scared of these guys—"

"I never said I was scared of anybody. I'm sure as hell not afraid of scum that'd steal pets away from kids. Goddamn idiots is what they sound like, don't know what the hell they're doin'." Morgan punctuated his statement by spitting at the ground. "I hope you catch the sons of bitches."

"Do you know who's organizing the fights now?"

"No idea. Like I said, I steer clear these days."

"But nobody would be surprised if you started taking an interest in betting now and then."

"You're right about that. No matter how you turn yourself around, nobody believes it. They're always just waitin' for you to slip back into old habits." Morgan shook his head. "Syl's the only person that's ever had any faith in me. Gettin' together with her's the smartest move I ever made."

"Will you keep your eyes and ears open, and let me know if you learn anything that could lead me to the organizers? If you find out where and when a fight's taking place, that's all I'd need. I might be able to arrange a reward for you. It wouldn't be a lot, but—"

"Now just hold on," Morgan said. "I'm not takin' any money from the cops. I do what I want to do, I'm not up for sale."

"I hear you," Tom said. "But I need your help. I don't think we have any time to waste if we want to get those kids' pets back to them alive." He extracted a business card from an inside pocket of his uniform jacket. "Call me if you hear something. Anytime, day or night."

Morgan looked at the card in Tom's hand for a long time, his mouth screwed up. Tom was afraid he was about to back away from their tentative deal. But at last Morgan reached for the card, stuck it into his pants pocket. Without speaking again, he turned to go back into his log house. At the door, though, he paused and looked around at Tom. "You know you're messing in some dangerous business here?"

"Yeah, I know," Tom said.

"Well, good luck to you, buddy. You're gonna need it."

Chapter Fourteen

She hated this place.

By the time Rachel turned into the school parking lot, she felt the back of her neck tightening with tension and a sick knot forming in her stomach.

"Oh, my gosh," Holly said, smiling as she took in the crowd of about fifty people already waiting with their dogs outside the gymnasium. "We got a lot of customers today."

They would be here for hours, Rachel thought, and the knot jerked tighter.

Climbing out of her Range Rover, she forced herself to pull in a deep breath of fresh air. The weather was perfect, with that rare combination of warmth and crispness that came only in autumn, and the mountains themselves seem to sway as a breeze rippled through the gaudy leaves on the trees. Sometimes even Rocky Branch District could be beautiful if she looked in the right direction.

Rachel and Holly carried boxes of rabies vaccine, syringes and needles, rabies certificates and tags into the gym, and the waiting people trooped in, struggling to keep their sniffing, yapping animals apart.

Tom had sent one of the older deputies, a man named Don Jones, to make sure Rachel and Holly were safe. While they set up their supplies on the big table the school had provided, Deputy Jones herded the crowd into a straight line, exchanged greetings with men and women he knew, patted a few of the dogs. Several people called hello to Holly, and she gave each a smile and a wave.

This part of the county was home to Holly, where she'd spent her entire life until she'd taken a job at the animal hospital, but Rachel saw it as a dark and threatening place filled with unpredictable people she would never understand. Anytime she began to feel comfortable in Mason County, as if she might fit in here after all, a trip to Rocky Branch District could destroy that assurance and remind her she would always be an outsider.

This school, in particular, gave her the creeps. A couple of months ago, following a contentious community meeting, Pete Rasey and his friends had surrounded her in the parking lot, taunting and threatening her until Tom stepped in. That experience almost made her abandon everything and run all the way back home to McLean. If she had a choice, she would never set foot in the school again, but the county had chosen this venue for the rabies clinic, she was here to administer vaccine provided by the state and county, and she couldn't refuse to perform a public service in the area that needed it most.

She smoothed the front of her white lab coat, forced a smile and motioned for the line to move forward.

The first few dogs were little mutts with exuberant personalities. Rachel vaccinated them and gave each a quick exam. Two dogs had the inevitable accidents, squatting to relieve themselves on the polished gym floor, sending their mortified owners running to the restroom for paper towels to clean up the messes. The nervous dogs scratched and shook themselves, and within minutes a cloud of hairs floated in the sunbeams slanting through the high windows. Somehow the familiar sight of anxious dogs shedding like crazy in the presence of a vet made Rachel feel more comfortable.

Holly filled out paperwork and handed over certificates and new tags to the owners. A tiny dog that looked like a cross between a Chihuahua and a Jack Russell licked Rachel's face like an ice cream cone before his embarrassed owner restrained him. She was laughing and wiping dog spit off her cheek when a young man in a Washington Nationals baseball cap stepped forward, tugging a large black and tan dog by a leash. Behind a leather muzzle, the animal growled and bared its teeth.

"He ain't exactly glad to be here," the young man said.

"I can see that." Rachel recognized German shepherd in the animal's rough coat, Doberman in its elongated head and slender build. "Do you have a problem with him biting?"

"Nope. Don't want no problem, neither. I keep him muzzled when I take him anywhere away from home. It's hard on him, comin' in here. He hates other dogs. But he needs his shot. We got rabid coons out where we live."

While its owner gave Holly the information she needed to fill in the rabies certificate, the muzzled dog snarled and lunged at a puppy behind him. The puppy's elderly owner snatched up her floppy-eared little pet and backed away with it. "My lord in heaven," the woman exclaimed, "can't you keep that thing under control?"

"Sorry, Miz Adams. He gets all wound up—"

The dog lunged again.

"Buddy! Cool it!" The owner gripped the leash with both hands to prevent the animal from breaking free.

Imagining a dog-and-human riot in the making, Rachel filled a syringe with rabies vaccine and stepped around the table. "Let's get this done so you can take him home."

"He don't like needles," the owner said.

"I've never known a dog that did." The only difference was in how many of her fingers they tried to take off in retaliation. "This has to go in his flank. Hold onto him."

The owner knelt, the leash in one hand, and wrapped both arms around the dog's shoulders. "Be still now, Buddy. Be a good boy for me."

The dog's growls escalated as he watched Rachel's movements. When she stepped behind him, out of his sight, he howled and thrashed. He sent his owner flying and turned on Rachel. Holly yelped. The people behind them scattered, and every dog in the place started barking and howling.

Rachel grabbed the leash. The dog tried to bite her arm through his muzzle. The owner, still on his knees, retrieved the leash and clamped both arms around the dog, trying to hold him still.

Over the racket in the room, Rachel heard a man's voice behind her. "Need some help?"

Rachel spun around to find Dr. Jim Sullivan looking back at her with a smirk on his face. She was surprised, but more than that, she was damned glad to see him. "Help him hold the dog," she said, "so I can get the vaccine in."

"No problem." Sullivan approached the snarling animal without evident fear, slipped an arm around its neck, and yanked it back in a firm choke hold. "Do it," he told Rachel.

She jabbed the needle into the dog's flank and emptied the syringe. The owner snatched the tag and certificate from Holly and dragged his unhappy pet toward the door, the dog's nails scraping the shiny gym floor. The other dogs didn't quiet down until the two were gone.

Rachel blew out a breath. "Well, that was fun," she said to Sullivan. "What are you doing here, by the way?"

"Oh, I just happened to be close by on a call and thought you could use some help with the rabies clinic."

Close by on a call? Sullivan didn't treat any animals in this part of the county. There wasn't a farm within ten miles of the school. But Rachel didn't have time to question him. The deputy had started shooing everybody back into line. Tugging her white coat to straighten it, she returned to the table. "I'm glad you showed up when you did," she told Sullivan. "Thank you."

"I'll stick around if you can use an extra pair of hands," Sullivan said.

His affable tone sounded so forced that Rachel stared at him for a moment, trying to figure out what his real mood might be and why he was trying to hide it. Sullivan avoided her gaze, making a show of checking out the supplies on the table. Rachel picked up a syringe and vaccine vial. "Okay, sure. I'd appreciate the help."

Rachel put aside the question of Sullivan's out-of-character behavior and turned her attention to the elderly woman whose puppy had been frightened by the big dog.

Joining Rachel behind the table, Sullivan began his own stream of brief exams and vaccinations. He did the work conscientiously, but he seemed to be watching the door, as if expecting someone to come in, something to happen. She couldn't imagine what he was looking for. The deputy was supposed to protect Rachel and Holly, but she had the weird feeling Sullivan was there for the same reason.

Rachel almost laughed at the thought.

What was Sullivan's real reason for being there? Trying to get back in her good graces? Another laughable thought. He didn't give a damn whether she was annoyed with him or not. So why did he show up, behaving so politely, being so helpful? So phony? What was he up to?

Chapter Fifteen

Was a single staff member at Tri-County General Hospital mourning the death of Gordon Hall? From the receptionist who greeted Tom in the lobby to the white-coated doctors and nurses in scrubs who walked the halls and clustered at nursing stations, no one seemed grief-stricken because the hospital's owner had been murdered. Tom felt their eyes following him, though, taking in his uniform, badge, and gun. Conversation halted when he approached and resumed in whispers after he passed.

He rode the elevator to the second floor. Walking past patient rooms, breathing in the odors of cleaning products and alcohol mingled with the faint stench of vomit, he wondered, as he had a million times, how his mother ever got used to working here. Anne Bridger had been a warm, cheerful woman who filled their home with the scents of baking and fresh flowers. Her deep desire to help others had brought her here every day, to work among the sick and injured and dying and to take orders from an officious ass named Gordon Hall.

Tom still thought of this place as Mason County General Hospital, the name it had before Hall launched an effort to draw patients from neighboring counties. Most people still used the old name. It was a different place now, though. Hall had to be given credit for taking over a failing hospital in a dilapidated building and turning it into a modern health care facility.

Pushing through a swinging door, Tom entered a section of offices. Jonelle Cruise, the nursing director, worked in a corner room at the far end of the corridor. He rapped on the partially open door to draw her attention from the file she was reading.

"Hey, Tommy, come on in," she said, removing her reading glasses. "Close the door, please." A plump woman in her fifties, she had short brown hair streaked with gray. Over her blue blouse she wore a pink lab coat.

"I haven't been here since everything was moved around." Tom sat in the chair facing her desk. Motioning at a stack of cardboard file boxes against one wall, he added, "I guess you're still getting settled."

Jonelle sighed and shook her head. "I still don't have any file cabinets. I'm a creature of habit. I don't see the point of moving everybody from one floor to another, into identical space. But I guess Gordon had his reasons."

"Nobody on the staff seems too broken up about their boss being murdered."

Jonelle picked up her glasses, folded and unfolded the earpieces, then laid them down again. "I'm sure you heard plenty about Gordon from your mother when she had this job."

"Yeah, I did. He was an s.o.b. to work for, wasn't he?"

Sighing, Jonelle sat back in her chair. "I have to be discreet, Tom. I can't afford to lose my job."

"I understand that, and whatever you say is confidential." If she knew anything that could make her a valuable witness, his promise of confidentiality was meaningless, but Tom's immediate concern was getting information from her. "You work all over the hospital. You probably hear everything that goes on. If somebody had a grievance against Hall, I need to look into it."

She folded her arms in a self-protective gesture and hesitated before answering. "Gordon wasn't always…polite when he delivered criticism and suggestions."

Tom didn't respond. He waited, knowing his patience would be rewarded if she felt compelled to fill the expanding silence with words.

"Gordon was—" She broke off, sat forward and clasped her hands on the desktop. She seemed to be debating with herself, and Tom gave her the time she needed. When she spoke again, both her words and tone had a new harshness. "He could be absolutely brutal sometimes. And he had a habit of firing people on the spot if he didn't like something they did. I can't count the number of times I've had to talk him into reinstating nurses and aides. I didn't always succeed. Your mother handled him better than I did."

"What kind of things did he fire people for?"

"Well, with support staff it could be something like an aide not collecting the meal trays as promptly as Gordon liked. He hated walking past rooms and seeing the remains of meals waiting to be picked up."

"Was anybody fired recently?" Tom pulled his notebook and pen from his shirt pocket.

Jonelle eyed the pad and pen warily before continuing. "He fired an aide about two weeks ago. That was over a closed door. Gordon had an obsession about leaving doors to the patient rooms open at all times. I don't know why, but that was his rule."

"Mom thought he was afraid of lawsuits," Tom said. "Something happening to a patient behind a closed door and the staff not realizing it in time."

"Well, in this case a staff member was *with* the patient, so it made no sense at all. Christie was giving a woman a sponge bath, and she drew the curtain around the bed, but the patient wanted the door closed too. Gordon fired Christie for respecting the patient's desire for privacy instead of following his rules."

"How did she take it?"

"Oh, she was furious at first, but she's about to get married to a boy who works in Blacksburg and she was planning to quit and start a family right away. I told her I'd give her a good reference anytime she wanted one, so in the end being let go didn't matter to her."

Tom tapped his pen on the pad. "Do you remember any incident in the last year that was more serious than that? Any conflict between Hall and the staff that caused a lot of bad feeling?"

"Well, there was the business about Mrs. Green. I'm sure you know about that. Her husband's been telling everybody who'll listen that this hospital tortured her. But the nursing staff did the best we could to ease her suffering. It was Gordon who wanted to withhold the drugs, and one of my best nurses lost her job for going against his orders. I couldn't get her reinstated, either."

"Who was this?"

"Phoebe James. I'm sure you know her. She was a friend of your mother's."

Tom nodded and wrote down the name. "I've lost touch with her, I'm afraid," he said. "Where's she working now?"

"Nowhere. Not as a nurse, I mean. Gordon blacklisted her. He made sure no other hospital in the state would hire her. She's clerking at the supermarket. Just an incredible waste, in my opinion."

Tom jotted notes, then looked up at Jonelle. "Maybe now that Hall's out of the way, things will change."

"Out of the way? My goodness, Tom, what a way to put it. But I wouldn't mind some changes around here."

"You think Brian Stevens has a lock on the top job?"

"He's in charge for the time being. But who knows what's going to happen? Vicky Hall owns the hospital now, I guess, but she's so sick I can't see her coming in here and trying to run it. I doubt she has the business savvy, in any case."

"If Stevens gets the job, maybe you'll get your filing cabinets."

She smiled, a flash of beautiful teeth that erased years from her face. "Actually, Brian's promised to get them in here next week."

"There's something else I wanted to ask you about," Tom said. "Do you remember when the Halls adopted their two youngest kids, David and Marcy?"

Jonelle's smile vanished and a flush spread over her cheeks. "I can't tell you anything about Gordon and Vicky's private lives. I don't know a thing about any of their children."

Intrigued by her reaction, Tom studied her for a moment before asking, "David and Marcy's real mother was a patient here several times, wasn't she? Isn't that how the Halls first met her—and the kids?"

Jonelle shook her head. "I really can't tell you anything about that, Tommy."

Tom tried to meet her eyes, but she avoided the contact. "What's wrong? Why is that such a prickly subject?"

"It isn't. It's just—I don't know anything about their family life, their children. I don't *want* to know, and I don't feel comfortable talking about it."

"Jonelle—"

"Tom, please. I have to get back to work."

"All right. Okay." Tom got to his feet. "Thank you for talking to me."

She wouldn't look at him now, but lowered her head and concentrated on shuffling through papers in the file on her desk.

At the door Tom paused and looked back at her. Of all the people he knew, she was the last he would have expected to hide anything from him, but that was exactly what she was doing.

Brian Stevens, acting director of the hospital, hustled toward his office as Tom turned a corner and fell in after him. A thin, gangly man with brown hair and dark-rimmed glasses, Stevens looked from behind like a boy dressed in somebody else's too-big suit.

When Stevens stopped at his office door, Tom said, "Mr. Stevens? Can I talk to you?"

Stevens gave a strangled gasp of surprise and spun around. "Good lord, you startled me."

"Sorry. Didn't mean to sneak up on you."

Stevens touched a hand to his head in the sort of gesture Tom associated with women concerned that their hair was mussed. "I wondered if you'd be back to see me."

They had spoken briefly when Tom came to the hospital to secure Dr. Hall's office before it was searched. "Can we talk in your office?"

Stevens looked as if he'd rather take a flying leap into a vat of boiling oil. "Yes, of course."

Seated in yet another chair facing another standard-issue metal desk, Tom said, "Do you think you'll be taking over as director permanently?"

"You'll have to ask Mrs. Hall about that. It's her decision."

"She's in pretty bad health," Tom said. "Is she capable of stepping in and running this place? And what happens when she dies?"

Stevens spread his hands on the desktop and stared at them. After a moment he said, "It's not something I enjoy thinking about, but of course I've wondered about it. Somebody has to look to the future of the hospital. The facility needs a permanent director."

"If not you, then maybe the Halls' son?" Tom suggested. "Ethan?"

Stevens flinched as if he'd been slapped.

Tom waited, but Stevens didn't explain his reaction. Tom asked, "Do you think Ethan is capable of running the hospital?"

Stevens twisted his lips in an odd grimace and took a long time to answer. "Let's say I would have some reservations if that happened. He's very young, for one thing."

"Dr. Hall was disappointed in Ethan, wasn't he? Because he dropped out of med school? Do you know if they'd patched things up, or was their relationship still pretty rocky?"

"Do I have to answer these questions?"

"Yes, if you want to help me solve Gordon Hall's murder."

"Are you implying that Ethan is a suspect in his father's death?"

"I'm not implying anything. I'm gathering information."

Stevens rubbed a hand over his mouth. "I'm not comfortable gossiping about the family."

"I'm not interested in broadcasting what you tell me," Tom said. "But I need as much information about Hall as I can get. The more personal the information is, the more it will help me."

Stevens still looked dubious. He slumped back in his chair, fingers laced over his belt buckle, and swiveled left and right.

"All right." He sighed. "Gordon never got over his disappointment in Ethan. He told me the boy was rebellious in his teens. It didn't sound like anything unusual to me, but Gordon was a real control fr—" He broke off before he got the whole phrase out.

"A control freak?' Tom offered.

"Well, yes."

"He must have hit the roof when Ethan flunked out of medical school."

"Oh, he didn't flunk out. In fact, Ethan did well enough that he could have completed medical school and gone on to become a doctor."

"Really? Most people think Ethan spent his time partying and couldn't keep up his grades."

"Not true. That was what made it so hard for Gordon to accept." Stevens spoke eagerly now, clearly pleased to be correcting Tom's misconceptions. "Abandoning his studies was Ethan's choice."

"If he realized medicine wasn't for him," Tom said, "and he wanted to get out before he wasted any more time and money, was that such a bad thing?"

"But he made a big speech about deciding he didn't want to be a Gordon Hall clone. Gordon was convinced Ethan planned it from the start, got into medical school and attended for a year to prove he could do it, and do it well, but with no intention of following his father's career path. Gordon was crushed, not to mention furious. He wanted the boy to be his heir, to work here and take over the hospital when he retired."

Tom could barely imagine the depth of anger and contempt necessary to dream up and carry out such a plan. Not many people had the patience to give up a year of their lives just to hurt a controlling parent. "Dr. Hall must have been happy about his oldest daughter deciding to study medicine."

"The Korean girl they adopted? Yes, she's smart and Gordon thinks—thought—she'll make a good doctor, but it's not the same. Gordon was proud of her as if she were an investment that did well. But she's not his blood kin. She's not his son."

"So were Gordon and Ethan still on the outs lately?"

Stevens took off his glasses and rubbed at his eyes. They were bloodshot, Tom noticed, as if he hadn't slept the night before. "I didn't say that. In fact, I think they were on better terms than they had been in a long time. I guess Gordon was making peace with his disappointment."

"I see." That matched the story Tom had heard from Soo Jin.

"Is there anything else, Captain?" Stevens asked. "I've got a million things to catch up on."

"Just one thing. Were you working here when the Halls adopted their two youngest children?"

"No, that was before my time." Stevens didn't seem troubled by the subject the way Jonelle had been. "I came on board a while after that. All I know about the adoption is what I've heard."

"And what have you heard?"

"Well, nothing, except that they adopted two children whose mother died. It seemed a decent thing to do."

Yeah, Tom thought. So why was Jonelle Cruise so rattled by the mention of it?

Chapter Sixteen

As Rachel emerged from her Range Rover, Tom's eight-year-old nephew Simon hurtled down the steps of his grandparents' house and across the yard toward her with the kind of energy generated only by kids and rockets. She braced for the hit, but he nearly knocked her off-balance when he flung himself into her arms.

"Hey, whoa, take it easy," she pleaded, laughing. She returned his ferocious hug and kissed the top of his head. Being a boy, he might not let her do that much longer, and she intended to take advantage of the privilege while it was still allowed. When she ruffled his thick black hair, exactly like Tom's, she felt the surprising sting of tears. She loved this little boy so much. If she ever had a child—

"Billy Bob!" Simon pulled out of Rachel's embrace and stretched upward for the handle of the Range Rover's rear door. The bulldog stood up in the back seat, raking a paw against the glass, demanding release.

Rachel opened the door and the dog tumbled out. After a hug from Simon and a few licks on the face from Billy Bob, the two took off, streaking toward a big pile of red and yellow leaves.

Rachel walked across the grass to join Darla Duncan, Simon's grandmother, on the front porch. A tall, thin woman in her fifties who usually dressed in shirts and jeans, Darla had the same plain vanilla looks as her husband, Deputy Grady Duncan, and a stranger would never have guessed either was related to the little boy with the striking appearance. Simon, with his olive skin and thick black hair, looked like his Melungeon relatives in the Bridger family.

"Hey, hon," Darla said, raising a coffee mug in greeting. The mug probably contained green tea. Darla had been on an antioxidant kick recently and drank the stuff all day.

"Thanks for keeping Billy Bob this weekend," Rachel said as she mounted the steps. "We're both going to be so busy he wouldn't get much play time with us."

"He's a treat. We love having—Oh, no!" Darla burst out laughing when the two little dervishes in the yard plopped into the pile of leaves together and scattered them everywhere. "Well, there goes a whole afternoon of raking."

The bulldog rolled ecstatically on his back while Simon showered him with leaves. Smiling at the two of them, Rachel said, "Sometimes I think Tom should just let Billy Bob live here. Even with Simon in school during the day, he'd probably enjoy being with you more than being stuck at the Sheriff's Department."

"Oh, that dog just worships Tom. He wouldn't want to be separated from him for long. Besides, Simon wears him out. He'll be happy to go back to a quieter life when the weekend's over. Want some green tea?"

"No, thanks. I can't stay." Rachel detested the vile stuff and had to restrain herself from scolding Darla about the amount of caffeine she was ingesting.

"Anyway," Darla went on, "with everything that's going on now, all those pet dogs disappearing right out of their yards, and that wild dog pack roaming loose, maybe he's safer surrounded by cops all day."

"Are you worried about having him here?" Rachel asked.

"No, I'll watch out for him. I won't put him outdoors alone, day or night. Lord, if anything happened to Billy Bob, Tom would kill me."

And it would break Simon's heart, Rachel thought. She watched the boy and the dog playing in the late afternoon sunlight. It was hard to believe this happy child had endured so much loss in his short life, but Rachel had seen how quickly his buoyant mood could turn to despair when any part of his carefully constructed little world was threatened. Simon had lost both his parents and both his Bridger grandparents in the same road accident. Only Tom and Simon had survived. Although he'd been so young that he didn't remember the crash, he was aware of how much was missing from his life. Rachel doubted that Tom, who had been driving when the accident occurred, would ever stop blaming himself.

Darla broke into Rachel's thoughts. "The county fair starts next weekend. Let's all go together if the guys wrap up the Hall case by then."

"You and I can take Simon if Tom and Grady have to work."

"Yeah, that'll be fun." A second later Darla frowned and shook her head. "Lord, it's awful what happened to Dr. Hall. I didn't know him, and I hear he was a real s.o.b., but just thinking about the way he died—" She shuddered. "I sure hope it doesn't turn out somebody in the family was behind it. I've been married to a cop so long that's the first thing that comes to mind when anybody's murdered, that it was the husband or wife or one of their kids."

"The Halls are a strange bunch of people," Rachel murmured. Pity pierced her heart when she thought of Marcy, a scared little girl who seemed utterly alone in an alien place. Like Simon, she had already endured more loss than any child should experience, and she didn't have the kind of loving home and family Simon had to protect and nurture her. What would happen to Marcy if Dr. Hall's death ended up ripping that family apart?

Tom flipped through *Field & Stream* at the end of the grocery aisle, keeping an eye on Phoebe James while she rang up a big grocery order for a chattering dark-haired woman. Her face blank, Phoebe grabbed and scanned automatically, shoving items down to the elderly man working as a bagger. Tom counted four frozen pizzas, six loaves of white bread, ten pounds of baking potatoes, four gallons of milk, big bags of apples and oranges. "Teenage boys are bottomless pits," the customer said. She added with a laugh, "We could have a swimming pool and a new car every year if we didn't have boys to feed."

Phoebe didn't respond, but Tom chuckled, remembering his own mother's astonishment at how fast he and his older brother Chris could empty the refrigerator.

Phoebe read out the customer's total in a voice flat with weariness. Tom hadn't seen her in a while, and he didn't remember her as this slump-shouldered, sad-eyed woman with gray showing at the roots of her dark hair and deep lines framing her mouth. Against the purple of her store smock, her face looked colorless.

The manager, Russ Tandler, sidled up to Tom and whispered, "Is something wrong? What are you doing here? You're not shopping."

"Just waiting to talk to Mrs. James," Tom said. "Routine stuff, nothing to get excited about."

Tandler, a small man around forty with scalp already showing through thin brown hair, squinted as if he detected something a lot more sinister than Tom was revealing. "Is she in some kind of trouble?"

His voice was too loud and attracted the attention of customers in the express lane. An elderly woman with blue-tinted hair stared with frank curiosity. Phoebe James still hadn't noticed Tom's presence.

"No, she's not in trouble, Russ," Tom said. "Take it easy. When she finishes this order, will you give her a break for a few minutes so I can talk to her? Then I'll get out of your way."

Muttering under his breath, Tandler cut through an unused checkout lane to reach Phoebe James. He leaned close and whispered to her.

Only then did she shift her gaze, searching for Tom. When she made eye contact, he raised a hand in greeting. She responded with a frown that deepened the crease between her brows.

After she handed the customer her receipt, Phoebe approached Tom with a puzzled look. "What is this—No, wait," she said.

"Don't tell me until we're out of earshot. Russ said we can talk in his office, but I'd rather not."

She led Tom to the rear of the store and through a swinging door into the warehouse. They passed three male employees cutting open cartons of canned goods and emerged onto the loading dock. A delivery man was hauling boxes of vegetables from a refrigerated truck.

"This way," Phoebe said over her shoulder to Tom.

She descended a set of wooden steps from the dock to the concrete-paved loading area. The steps wobbled under Tom's weight. When they reached a bench pushed against a dilapidated fence on the opposite side of the pavement, Phoebe seemed satisfied that they had put enough distance between them and her boss.

Tom motioned for Phoebe to sit on the bench, but she crossed her arms and remained standing.

"What's this about?" she asked. "Something to do with Dr. Hall getting killed? I don't know anything about that, Tommy. I haven't got a blessed thing to tell you."

"I'm just trying to get a handle on what Hall's life was like, who liked him, who had a grudge—"

"A grudge?" Her lips curved in a bitter smile. "You mean like somebody he fired who might have wanted to kill him over it?"

"I'm not accusing you of anything." Along with her appearance, her personality seemed to have changed. Tom's mother had enjoyed Phoebe's sense of humor and upbeat outlook." If you haven't done anything, you don't have any reason not to talk to me."

To his surprise, her chin began to tremble and tears filled her eyes. Covering her face with her hands, she blurted, "But I thought about it! I was mad enough to kill him, and—oh, god forgive me, when I heard he was dead I was *glad*."

"Come on, sit down." Tom gently steered her to the bench.

She dropped onto it and leaned forward, arms wrapping her waist, as she wept. "The way he died, it was so awful," she gasped between sobs. "I never thought I could be glad about something so awful."

Tom sat beside her. The delivery guy paused on the loading dock, a box marked BROCCOLI in his hands, to stare across at them. Tom gave him a look that told him to mind his own business, and he went back to work.

"I don't think you're the only one who's glad Gordon Hall's gone," Tom told Phoebe. "A lot of people despised him."

Raising her head, she tugged a wad of tissues from a pocket of her smock and blotted her face. A fleck of tissue caught on her lip and she picked it off with a fingertip. "My husband's been cut back to half-time at the lumber mill, and I don't make enough here to keep a dog alive." Her voice broke on a sob. "We might lose our house, Tom. Our *home.*"

"God, I'm sorry to hear that." He laid a hand on her shoulder, feeling the ridiculous inadequacy of the gesture. "But maybe now you can get your nursing job back."

She sniffled and looked at him. "You think so? You don't think *she* would stand in the way?"

"Who? Mrs. Hall?"

"Well, she owns the hospital now, doesn't she?"

"Have you had problems with Mrs. Hall?" Tom expected Tandler to interrupt any minute and tell Phoebe to get back to work. He hoped she would pull herself together enough to give him some answers before that happened. "Is there any reason she wouldn't want you back at the hospital?"

"She'd never go against him. He fired me, and I don't think she'd give me back my job, not even with him dead."

"He let you go because you gave extra pain medication to Naomi Green, is that right?"

A fresh spate of tears poured from her eyes. "Oh, that poor woman. She was in agony. I couldn't stand by without doing a thing to help her. She was dying. It was crazy not to give her some relief."

"What was Hall's objection to giving dying patients pain-killers?"

"He enjoyed seeing people suffer." Her tear-streaked face twisted in a scowl. "I'm convinced of it."

"Do you think Wally Green hated him enough to kill him?"

She pulled in a breath and squeezed her eyes shut as if trying to calm herself. "He wouldn't have done it, because he has children to think of. He wouldn't take a chance on being sent to prison and leaving them without either of their parents." She flicked a glance at Tom. "He talked about doing it, though."

"Oh?" This was more than Tom had hoped for, and the prospect of more revelations stirred up a buzz of excitement in his blood. "What did he say, exactly?"

"I don't want to get him in trouble." Phoebe's knee jiggled as she tapped her foot, but she seemed to realize what she doing and stopped the nervous movement abruptly. "Wally was just blowing off steam. That's all it was, Tom."

"Okay, I believe you. But I need to know what he said."

She looked so miserable that Tom wished he could let it go. But he couldn't.

"Wally almost went out of his mind watching her suffer," she said. A loud *thunk* from inside the vegetable delivery truck made her flinch. "She wasn't even Dr. Hall's patient, but he controlled how much narcotic medication patients received. Other doctors couldn't do anything about it if they wanted to keep their hospital privileges."

Another group of people who probably detested Hall, Tom thought. "How did you happen to be talking to Wally about it?"

"He begged me to help her, to give her something for the pain. He told me he wanted to kill Dr. Hall, but of course I just put it down to the stress he was under. The next time she was due for morphine, I gave her a larger dose, and she was able to sleep comfortably for the first time in weeks."

"How did Hall find out about it?"

"I had to put it on her chart. I couldn't give a narcotic and not account for it. So I knew he'd find out sooner or later. It turned out to be sooner. He stopped by Naomi's room that very night and saw how well she was resting, and he read her chart and started asking questions. I asked him to lift the restrictions and allow her own doctor to help her die in peace. I told him it was the decent thing to do. He fired me on the spot."

"So Wally told you before his wife died that he felt like killing Hall? Did he say anything after she died?"

Phoebe hesitated again. A cool breeze swept through the loading area, lifting a discarded chocolate bar wrapper and blowing it against her left foot. She kicked it away with the toe of her nurse's shoe.

"Tell me about it, Phoebe," Tom said quietly.

She threw up her hands. "All right, all right. I've gone this far, I might as well. Wally was completely crushed when Naomi died. He came to see me and said he was sorry I'd lost my job for trying to help her. He sat in my living room and cried his heart out for an hour. He said he wished he could torture Gordon Hall, make him die slowly and painfully the way Naomi did. But he was just venting. By the time he left he was saying that all he really wanted was an acknowledgment from Dr. Hall that he'd allowed her to suffer unnecessarily."

But that acknowledgment had never come. Green could have worked himself into a rage again and taken revenge on his wife's tormentor. "Phoebe," Tom said, "if you—"

"You planning to come back to work?" Russ Tandler yelled from the loading dock. "I need you on the register right now."

Phoebe jumped up. "I've got to go."

"Wait a minute."

But she was gone, hustling into the store, leaving him with a lot of unanswered questions.

Chapter Seventeen

Tom leaned in to examine the autopsy photos Dr. Gretchen Lauter pinned on the bulletin board in the conference room. Brandon and Dennis Murray crowded in beside him to take a look. With the blood washed away, the ragged hole where Gordon Hall's throat had been was unmistakably the work of an animal. In one photo, Hall's spinal cord showed through the opening.

"Oh, man," Brandon said, a hand over his mouth. He stepped back from the stark display.

"You okay?" Tom asked. "You can leave if you—"

"No. No, sir." Brandon squared his shoulders and drew a deep breath. But he didn't look at the photos again.

Tom didn't have to worry about Dennis, who seemed as inured to violent scenes as Tom was, even though he lacked Tom's advantage of having worked murder cases in Richmond. His face impassive, Dennis pored over the pictures of Hall.

As Tom studied the photos, his mind filled with images of a black dog knocking Hall to the ground, sinking its teeth into his throat, gouging out flesh and esophagus, severing arteries. Arterial spray coated the grass as far away as twenty feet. Crime scene techs had found Hall's thyroid gland near the body, but not so much as a shred of skin and muscle. Tom assumed the dog had swallowed all of it.

He asked Gretchen, "Do you still believe that only one dog attacked him?"

"I'm positive." An expression of mingled pity and sorrow flickered over her face, but she went on in a brisk, impersonal tone. "We might find out more about the breed when the DNA results come back, but that's going to take a while."

"We already know it's big, with rough black hair, and somebody trained it to be damned vicious. Dogs don't get that way on their own." Tom turned from the pictures and pulled out a chair at the conference table. The others followed. Tom and Gretchen sat side by side, with Dennis and Brandon facing them across the table.

"Have you found any connection between the attack on Gordon and dogfighting?" Gretchen asked. "Aside from what was done to his dog?"

"No." Tom rubbed his tired eyes. He'd give anything to go home to Rachel, have a real dinner, and fall into bed. But he would eat fast food, Rachel would be out most of the evening chasing dogs, and he had at least one more stop to make before he could quit for the day. "We don't have much of anything yet. Dennis and a couple of the other guys have been checking up on people who've been involved in dogfighting before, but nothing useful's turned up."

"Three of them are in jail for other stuff," Dennis told Dr. Lauter, "and the rest have pretty strong alibis for the night Hall was killed."

Tom shuffled the papers in front of him and pulled out a report. "The tape I took off Hall's dog had a couple of fingerprints on it, but they don't match anything in our local database. Whoever put the tape on Thor has never been printed in Mason County for any reason, and that rules out most of the locals who've been involved in dogfighting. We sent the prints to the state to see if they turn up anything."

"How'd you track down the dogfighting operations before?" Brandon asked. He'd only been a deputy for a couple of years and had never been involved in a raid.

"Tips," Tom said. "People coming to us with information. And that's probably what we'll have to rely on this time.

Somebody will come forward, or we'll get something through our informant. Meanwhile, we'll keep poking around and try to find out where it's going on."

"Well, if Gordon's death is connected to dogfighting," Dr. Lauter said, "wouldn't that rule out family members? And people from work who had a grudge against him?"

Tom shook his head. "We can't make that kind of assumption. Like I said, we don't know enough yet. For now, everybody in the family is a suspect, along with everybody who had a grievance with him."

"Not Mrs. Hall, though," Brandon protested, leaning forward on his elbows. "You don't think she could have set it up, do you?"

"It doesn't seem likely, but we could be surprised before it's over. We've already verified where everybody in the family was at the time of the murder, but that's no proof of innocence. We need to keep looking at the whole family. Beth and her boyfriend, Pete Rasey—that's a classic setup for trouble. A girl from a rich family gets involved with a boy from the wrong side of the tracks, the dad comes down hard on them, orders them to stay away from each other. The kids lash out and the dad ends up dead. And there's something going on with David, the younger boy. I want to find out what it is."

"The Halls give a whole new meaning to the term dysfunctional family," Dennis said. He pushed his glasses firmly against the bridge of his nose. "They're quite a crew. Real interesting history."

"Gordon came from a family of prominent physicians," Gretchen said.

"Yeah," Dennis said, "and he inherited a lot of money, so he could afford to go off and do charity work in Korea after med school. I guess he didn't have any loans to pay off."

"Ethan was born in Korea, wasn't he?"

"Yep," Dennis said, "and they adopted Soo Jin out of an orphanage before they came back to the States. Dr. Hall had a private practice in Boston until his mother died and left him even more of the family money, then he looked around for a hospital to buy. He had his own ideas about how a hospital ought to be run, and he wanted to be the one in charge. That's how they ended up here. Everybody I've talked to says the same thing—Dr. and Mrs. Hall had a real close marriage, devoted to each other, but he was strict with the kids. Not abusive, nobody'll say that. Just strict. Always expected a lot from them."

"Even if someone in the family wanted to kill him," Gretchen said, "why would they choose this method? Setting up a dog attack? It seems so convoluted. Wouldn't shooting or stabbing make more sense? That's the normal pattern with family murders."

"Good questions," Tom said. "And we don't have any answers. Here's the situation the way I see it. Hall was killed by a dog. From what I heard on the answering machine tape, somebody was with that dog and didn't try to stop the attack. It sounded like it was somebody Hall knew. Hall's dog disappeared and later turned up with his muzzle taped and rope around his neck and one of his back legs. He didn't run off after Hall was attacked, he was taken and held somewhere."

"That doesn't necessarily mean dogfighters took him," Gretchen said.

"No, it doesn't. But I've seen it before—dogs muzzled so they can't bite, and tied up and hobbled so they can't run or fight back. I've seen that done to bait dogs, the ones that are used to train the fighters."

"And we've had all those pet dogs disappearing out of their yards," Dennis put in.

"Yeah," Tom said. "That's something new. The dogfighting operations we've broken up before got their bait dogs in other ways. It's possible the pets are being stolen for some other reason, but my instincts are telling me all this is tied together."

Gretchen smiled at him. "You father used to say that, and when John Bridger's instincts pointed in one direction or other, everybody was wise to follow. He was always right."

"I've never known Tom to be wrong," Dennis said.

Tom barked a laugh. "Thanks for the vote of confidence. Now I'll feel like a total idiot if I'm way off-base here."

Brandon asked, "What're the legendary Bridger instincts saying about the feral dogs? If they didn't attack Hall, are they part of this in any way?"

"God, I hope not," Tom said. "Rachel's got her heart set on saving them all."

"If we could find out where they hole up during the day," Brandon said, "Rachel and Joe Dolan might be able to get all of them at one time."

"As far as I know, nobody's ever seen them in broad daylight," Tom said. "I don't like Rachel out there trying to track them down at night, with Ethan's buddies roaming around with guns, but I don't see any other way to do it."

"Well, don't worry about her tonight," Brandon said. "I'll make sure nothing happens to her."

"Thanks, Bran." Giving responsibility for Rachel's safety to somebody else was damned hard, something Tom had to force himself into, but he knew Brandon was rock-solid dependable. Tom had too much work that couldn't be put off. He couldn't spend his evening chasing down the feral dogs.

◇◇◇

Cicero, Rachel's parrot, landed on her shoulder, shook his gray feathers, and said, "Love you. Love you."

"Aw, sweetie, I love you too." Beyond the window, dusk was fading into night. Brandon and Joe Dolan would arrive shortly to pick her up for another dog hunt. Rachel had downed a quick dinner of soup and sandwich, fed Frank and played with him for a few minutes, and now she had to give Cicero some concentrated attention to make up for her prolonged absences. She slipped her fingertips under his neck feathers and scratched him gently. "I'm sorry I have to leave you."

The last thing she wanted to do was go out there in the dark again.

Mrs. Barker's words snaked back into her mind. *I implore you to take every precaution. There are evil forces at work in Mason County. They surround you, but you are unable to see them.*

Rachel couldn't cope with unseen forces. She had enough trouble dealing with the ones that were clearly visible.

Leo Riggs was about to lower the roll-down door on the service bay when Tom pulled into the lot at Leo's All-Auto Service & Repair outside of Mountainview. Caught in the glare of Tom's headlights, Leo squinted and shaded his eyes with one hand.

"Hey, Leo." Tom lifted a hand in greeting. "Got a minute? I need to talk to you."

Jamming his fists into the pockets of his greasy overalls, Leo said, "Yeah, sure. This about Dr. Hall? Anything I can do to help."

"Are you going out with that gang looking for the dog pack tonight?" Tom asked.

Leo's shoulders twitched in a quick shrug. "Naw, I think I'll skip it. I mean, you made a lot of sense, what you said about lettin' the authorities take care of the problem. Ethan's havin' second thoughts too, and the only reason I was goin' along was because I feel like I owe the family."

Silently Tom surveyed the business property. It stood on a quarter acre of cleared land at the base of a mountain, with a padlocked chain link enclosure protecting cars left overnight, a service bay with four hydraulic lifts, an attached office, and a gas pump out front.

"The Halls helped you get set up here, didn't they?"

"Well, yeah, they invested. But they knew their money wasn't gonna be wasted. I know what I'm doin' with cars. I can handle all of them, old and new." Leo withdrew his hands from his pockets and gestured at the building. "Hey, you mind if I finish closin' up while we're talkin'?"

"No, not at all," Tom said.

Leo pulled down the service area door and padlocked it. Tom followed him into the office.

Tom hadn't been here before, and he was surprised to find the interior spotless, the countertop clear, the tile floor shining, even the maps in a wall rack perfectly aligned. A faint fragrance of lemon air freshener hung in the air. Proud of the place, Tom thought, watching Leo open the register.

"Gotta make a run to the bank and drop this off before I head home," Leo said. He pulled out some of the cash, counted it, noted the amount on a bank slip, and placed it in a night deposit envelope. He began the same process with checks.

Tom leaned his elbows on the counter. "Is that why you agreed to let the Halls have your sister's kids? Because they gave you the money to start your business?"

"Now, wait a minute." Leo paused, several checks in one hand. "It's not like I took money for the kids. I wouldn't do that. I wanted David and Marcy to have a good life. Dr. Hall and Mrs. Hall, I could see how much they could give them."

Everything except love, Tom thought.

"My mama and daddy," Leo went on, "well, you probably know how they felt about the kids havin' a, you know, a black daddy." He began noting the amount of the checks on the deposit slip, but quickly abandoned the multitasking effort and gave his full attention to Tom. "It's pretty sad, them feelin' that way about their own blood kin, but they're set in their ways, and they're gettin' old too. I hate to say it, but they wouldn't have done right by those kids."

"You never thought about raising them yourself?"

"Lord, no. What would I do with two young'uns? They needed a real family. It was the right thing to do, you know?"

The profitable thing to do. "The Halls started trying to adopt David and Marcy before your sister died, didn't they?"

"Well, yeah, they did, but that was a hard thing for Jewel to get her mind around. She knew she wasn't the best mom, with all her problems, not bein' able to stay clean. But they were her kids, her blood, you know? It was hard for her to think they might be better off with somebody else."

"Hadn't she been clean for a while before she died?"

Leo laid the checks on the counter, placed a hand over them. "Yeah, that made it even worse. We all thought she had it licked. She was workin' regular and all, supportin' herself and the kids.

She loved them. But all it takes is one step in the wrong direction, you know? Then she was gone."

"Did the Halls come to you right after Jewel died about adopting David and Marcy?"

Licking his lips, Leo let his gaze wander the room and took a moment to answer. "Pretty soon after, yeah. They wanted to take the kids, get 'em out from underfoot, you know, while we made arrangements and had the funeral."

"So you gave the children to the Halls immediately?"

"Well, I didn't see any cause not to."

"Did they go to their mother's funeral?" Tom asked.

"Naw. Kids don't belong at a funeral."

Tom stepped over to a chart on the wall, studied the list of recommended maintenance work. "How long after your sister died did the Halls invest in your business?"

"Oh… I don't rightly recall."

Tom looked around at him. "You don't recall when you started your business? Most people wouldn't forget something like that."

"Well, I guess it wasn't too long after Jewel died." Leo started entering check amounts on the deposit slip again, keeping his head down.

Tom moved closer. "How did David and Marcy feel about moving to a new home right after losing their mother?"

"Marcy was so little I doubt she knew what was goin' on," Leo said without looking up. "David seemed okay with it. They've been real happy with the Halls."

"David seems a little antisocial," Tom said. "Like he's holding a grudge against the world."

"Aw, you know how teenagers are. They're all like that." Leo scribbled numbers and slid each recorded check into the deposit envelope.

"You spend much time with them?" Tom asked.

"Naw. No point in it. They got a new family now. I don't interfere."

"What I've heard is that the Halls didn't want you anywhere near your sister's kids."

Leo paused, his jaw working. "Well," he said after a moment, "they've got a right. The kids are Halls now, under the law."

"Do you think David misses his real mother?"

Leo expelled an impatient huff. "Man, I don't know. What are you gettin' at?"

"Dr. Hall was pretty strict with all the kids. Maybe David hasn't been happy about that."

"Now wait a minute." Leo frowned. "Are you claimin' the boy had somethin' to do with Hall gettin' killed?"

"What do you think? Is David capable of it?"

Leo folded the deposit slip into the envelope, licked the flap, and pressed it closed. When he spoke again, he sounded less interested in the subject of his nephew's capacity for violence. "Hell, I don't know. I don't see how he could, though. Set up somebody to get killed, I mean. He's just a kid."

"Do you know anybody else who hated Hall enough to do it?" Tom asked. "Do you know anybody with a dog mean enough to kill a grown man?"

"Nope. Not a one. Can't help you."

Tom watched Leo silently for a moment, wondering if the vibe he was getting was simple nervousness under police questioning or something more. Leo had plenty of reason to be grateful to the Halls, and no reason Tom could see to want Gordon Hall dead. David and Marcy might not be thriving in the Hall family, but Tom didn't detect any sign that their biological uncle was interested in their happiness.

One thing Tom was sure of, though: If dogfights were being held in the county, Leo was likely to know about it, at least secondhand. He lived in that level of society. But would he be honest if Tom asked him a straightforward question? Not a chance. And he might let something slip to the wrong people about the kind of questions Tom was asking.

A line of sweat had appeared on Leo's upper lip, and he swiped it off with the back of one hand. "Anything else I can help you with, Captain?"

"Not right now," Tom said. "If you hear anything that might be helpful, give me a call, will you?"

"Oh, you bet. I'll let you know right away."

Sure you will, Tom thought, heading back to his cruiser.

Chapter Eighteen

"At this rate, it'll take forever to get them all," Rachel told Tom. She stripped off her denim jacket, stabbed a coat hanger into its sleeves, and hooked it over the rack in the hall closet. "I'm glad we caught one more, but we need to find out where they're hiding during the day."

"They could be holed up anywhere in the county," Tom said. "Let's hope we'll get lucky and somebody will spot them."

"Hope the *dogs* get lucky." Rachel struck off down the hall for the kitchen, with Frank at her side.

The night's work had been frustrating, as she and Joe and Brandon chased down reported sightings on four different farms, only to be told each time that they had just missed the dogs. When they finally caught up with the pack, Joe's van spooked them and he was lucky to get off one shot from the tranquilizer gun. Another scruffy, emaciated mongrel now occupied a run at Holly's sanctuary.

Rachel grabbed a glass from a cabinet and filled it with tap water. When Tom followed her into the room, she said, "You should see the poor animal we caught tonight. He's starving. He was very happy to get a meal when we got him to the sanctuary, and he wasn't shy. He was begging for attention. They haven't all gone wild."

Tom leaned against the counter next to her. "I'm glad Ethan's pals didn't show themselves."

"That doesn't mean they weren't out there somewhere." With Mrs. Barker's warning in her mind, Rachel had been jittery the entire time, scouring the shadows for men with weapons, braced for the blast of gunfire. Now her head throbbed, and the pain and tension stiffened her neck and shoulders. Setting aside her glass, she kneaded one shoulder.

Tom nudged her to turn around, and he pressed his thumbs into the muscles of her neck. "You're all knotted up. I wish it didn't get to you this way."

"I can't help it. Oh, that feels good." Rachel inclined her head and tried to relax as Tom's strong, warm fingers kneaded and stroked her neck and shoulders. "I've made up my mind to rescue those animals, and I want to get on with it."

"You can't save the whole world, Rachel. You'll drive yourself crazy trying."

She sighed. He was right. Why did she do this to herself, again and again? Why did she leap in and try to solve every problem, right every injustice she stumbled across? "Sometimes I envy people who just don't give a damn," she said. "I wish I didn't care so much."

Tom pulled her back against him. "That's what I love most about you. How much you care."

"Oh, really?" Grinning, she twisted to look up at him. "You could've fooled me. You're always telling me to back off."

"It's what I love about you, but it also keeps me awake at night, worrying." He gave her a quick kiss. "Why don't you take a hot shower, then let me work on those tight muscles some more?"

"Sounds heavenly." Rachel was on her way out of the room when the kitchen wall phone rang. She paused in the doorway, waiting while Tom answered. It was too late in the evening for an inconsequential call. She felt the same clutch of apprehension she always experienced when the phone rang at night. It was never good news.

Tom frowned, listening. "All right," he said at last. "I'm on my way." He dropped the phone onto its hook.

"Oh, no," Rachel groaned. "What is it?"

"That was Dennis. Soo Jin Hall's had a serious car accident."

◇◇◇

Tom stood on the brink of a ravine with Sergeant Dennis Murray and Deputy Kevin Blackwood and watched two young paramedics make the slow ascent with Soo Jin Hall strapped to a stretcher between them. Fifty feet below, her black BMW tilted toward the right with its front end slammed against a massive poplar tree, the left rear turn signal blinking. The medics had left the driver's door open and the interior light burning, The silence of the night was broken only by the sound of pebbles, dislodged by the medics' boots, rolling down the side of the ravine.

Kevin and Dennis had set up portable flood lamps and pointed their vehicles' headlights toward the scene from opposite sides to give the medics more light. The nearly full moon, high in the sky, added a cold, shadow-filled illumination to the ravine and the surrounding mountains.

"How long has it been?" Tom asked.

"More than an hour since I spotted the crash," Kevin said. "I was just driving along on patrol and saw the guard rail knocked over, then I saw the car lights down there. I went down and looked in at her, but I couldn't see much because of the airbag. Just black hair, and blood on the window. She wasn't moving. I didn't know whose car it was until I ran the plates."

"The medics got here before I did," Dennis said, "and it's taken them all this time to get her out of the car. That's a pretty bad angle to work with."

The paramedics crested the incline and stepped over the flattened guard rail, balancing the stretcher between them without jostling it. They had immobilized Soo Jin's head in a bulky brace with straps across her chin and forehead. Several straps held her body in place. Blood covered the left side of her face and matted her black hair.

Tom strode alongside as they moved toward the open ambulance. "Has she come to at all?"

"No, sir," a paramedic with ginger hair answered. "Unconscious the whole time. Her vitals are pretty weak."

They hoisted her into the ambulance. The second medic climbed in with her and was cracking open a treatment kit as the ginger-haired man closed the door. He jogged around to the driver's side, and a minute later they sped off toward Mountainview.

"Any idea what caused this?" Tom asked Dennis and Kevin. The car had gone off the road at a sharp curve. A mountain rose on one side, the ravine opened up on the other. The metal guard rail had proven useless against the weight and speed of the vehicle. Tom switched on his Maglite and swept it over the skid marks where the BMW had veered off the pavement. "We're less than a mile from the Halls' house. Soo Jin must know every inch of this road. Why would she go off it tonight?"

"Maybe she'd been drinking?" Kevin suggested.

"I don't think it was an accident," Dennis said.

"Aw, Christ. Why?"

"Come on down and I'll show you." Dennis switched on his flashlight.

Leaving Kevin behind, they picked their way down the slope, using the path the car had gouged through the brush. Tom's boots slid over scraped-bare earth, caught on protruding roots, collided with half-buried stones.

Beside the tilted car, Tom followed the beam of Dennis' light and immediately realized what had happened. Both the rear tires were halfway to flat. "What the hell? Two flats at once?"

"Not just two. All four." Dennis swung his flashlight beam over the front tires. "Coming around this bend, her tires didn't have enough pressure to maintain traction. And off she went."

"Jesus," Tom said. "She must have noticed the car didn't feel right. Maybe she was trying to make it all the way home. Could she have hit something on the road? I came the same direction she did, and I didn't notice any debris that could puncture all four tires like this."

"I didn't either. I've checked my own tires to make sure I didn't run over anything, but I didn't see any sign of it."

They stood in silence, staring at the car. From somewhere in the distance, Tom heard the deep, booming *hoo-hoo hoooo hoo-hoo* of a great horned owl.

The only explanation for this accident that came to him added a whole new level of complexity to the events of the last couple of days. "So we could be talking about sabotage. Maybe attempted murder."

"Looks like it," Dennis said.

"Let's go back up." Tom's work here was done. A state police accident reconstruction team would arrive soon to take charge of the scene.

When they reached the road again, Tom said, "We'll have to find out where she went tonight, where her car might have been parked when it was tampered with."

"Pretty amateurish kind of tampering," Dennis said. "Letting the air out of the tires."

"It did the job."

"You suppose it's got something to do with her father's murder?" Kevin asked.

Tom gave Kevin a look. "What do you think?"

Rachel showered, wondering the whole time how seriously Soo Jin Hall was hurt and how much more tragedy would strike the Hall family. Vicky Hall appeared to be seriously ill, not strong enough to endure much more. But did she really care about Soo Jin? Did that adopted child mean as little to her as Marcy and David did?

Toweling her hair dry, Rachel thought of timid little Marcy and her silent plea. *Help me.* Rachel was certain she hadn't misunderstood. The child was terrified. Rachel couldn't get rid of the image of David pulling Marcy up the stairs, his hand clamped around her thin arm. What was going on in that family?

"Stop obsessing," she told herself. Right now all she wanted to do was put the Halls out of her mind, put the dog pack out of her mind, and spend some time with her cat.

She went downstairs to the den, settled on the couch with Frank on her lap, and began brushing him. Cicero slept in his covered cage by the window. The parrot developed anxiety if he didn't get enough of her attention, and he didn't seem to accept Tom as a substitute. With the weekend coming up, Rachel decided to give Cicero some special attention, maybe a gentle shower with a spray bottle and a teaching session to work on his vocabulary.

Frank purred on her lap. The old house creaked in a breeze, making Rachel suddenly aware of the silence and her isolation and vulnerability on Tom's little farm. *You are not invincible,* Mrs. Barker had said. *There are evil forces at work...*

Rachel shuddered and told herself to forget Mrs. Barker's melodrama. She couldn't let herself be spooked by a self-styled psychic.

The crash of glass in another room made her jerk and drop the brush. Frank bolted off her lap and dived under the couch.

What on earth? As Rachel rose, another crash sounded.

She ran to the door, but pulled up short, stopped by fear. Where had the sound come from? Was somebody breaking in? Was somebody already in the house?

Automatically she reached for her cell phone, which she always clipped to her shirt pocket. But she was in a robe, and her phone was upstairs. No phone in the den. The closest was— where? The kitchen? Tom's home office?

She was wasting time. She had to do something.

Then she smelled it. Smoke.

"Oh, god, no." The terror of fire blotted out her fear of an intruder. She ran, following the odor. In the living room door-way, she halted, mouth agape. Glass shards littered the floor under the broken window. Orange and yellow flames ate their way up the drapes.

Rachel shot into the darkened kitchen, grabbed the fire extin-guisher from a hook inside the door, and ran back to the living room. She yanked out the pin and aimed at the flames, swinging the extinguisher back and forth as it spewed out a white chemical.

Smoke and fumes gagged her and stung her eyes. In the kitchen, the smoke alarm went off, its high-pitched whine assaulting her ears. In the den, Cicero screeched, "Rachel! Rachel!"

When the fire was out, the drapes hanging in ragged black threads, Rachel dropped the extinguisher and tried to catch her breath and calm her pounding heart. Her gasps pulled smoke into her lungs and set off a wracking cough.

With tears streaming from her irritated eyes, she ran to the kitchen, grabbed the broom from the cupboard and jabbed at the red light on the smoke alarm until it fell silent. She shut the kitchen door to keep more smoke from drifting in. Now only moonlight lit the room, but when her hand found the light switch she hesitated.

Somebody had thrown—what? a Molotov cocktail?—into the house. That person might still be outside, and she didn't want to show herself in the kitchen window. She fumbled for the wall phone by the back door and ran her fingertips over the keypad, picking out 911.

Chapter Nineteen

No point in hanging around the hospital, Tom knew. Soo Jin wouldn't be talking to him anytime soon—if she ever talked to anybody again. He sent Dennis to the hospital to wait for news, left the accident scene to the state police, and headed over to see Vicky Hall, hoping he would be the first to tell her about the crash.

At the entrance to the Halls' driveway, under the glare of a newly installed security light, a bulky guy with a shotgun stepped in front of Tom's cruiser and raised a hand to stop him.

"You've gotta be kidding me," Tom muttered. He powered down the window and stuck his head out. "What the hell do you think you're doing?"

Tom couldn't put a name to the face, but he'd seen the man in that gang of idiots on the Halls' patio. The man was tall and beefy, with thinning dark hair slicked back behind his ears, and he balanced the butt of his shotgun on a sizable paunch. He pointed the gun directly at Tom. "I'm following orders," he said. "I'm not supposed to let anybody but family in."

"Get out of my way," Tom said. "This is police business. And if you don't want a taste of real trouble, you'll stop pointing that weapon in a cop's face."

"I've got my orders." The man jutted his chin and squared his shoulders, but he swung the barrel of the shotgun upward and to the side. "No visitors, Ethan said."

Tom unsnapped his seat belt and flung open the door. With one hand resting on the butt of his holstered pistol, he strode over to the man. He thrust his face close enough to make the guy take a quick step backward. "I want you to pay attention, because I'm not going to repeat myself. I don't know who stuck you out here and made you think you can stand in the way of a police officer—"

"Ethan hired—"

"Shut up. I told you to listen. You're going to get out of my way, and you're going to do it right now, with no backtalk. Now *move.*"

He moved.

Tom slid behind the wheel again, slammed his door, and drove on, ignoring the flashing dashboard light warning that his seat belt wasn't buckled.

It was almost midnight, but most of the house's windows were lit up, and Tom guessed he was too late. The hospital had already notified Vicky about Soo Jin's accident.

Again Tom wondered why the girl had gone out tonight and where she had been.

Ethan answered the door with a somber expression. Before Tom could speak, Ethan said, "We've already heard."

He stepped back, opening the door wider to let Tom enter.

"I'd like to speak to your mother," Tom said when he was in the foyer. "It won't take long."

To his surprise, Ethan didn't argue. "She's upstairs with Rayanne. You'll have to go up. I don't think she ought to try to come down, she shouldn't be on the stairs. I'll just go ahead of you and let her know, so she can put on a robe or whatever."

Tom followed Ethan up the broad staircase. In the hallway at the top, David and Marcy stood side by side against the wall as if waiting for instructions. David wore jeans and a tee shirt, but Marcy had on a robe, with striped pajama legs showing below it. Her bunny slippers still bore smudges of her father's blood, now dried to a rusty brown.

While Ethan tapped on the door and entered the bedroom, Tom studied David and Marcy. With his shoulders hunched and fists jammed into his jeans pockets, David stared sullenly at the floor, ignoring Tom. Marcy stood as rigid as a piece of furniture, arms pressed flat against her sides. For a second her eyes flicked up and met Tom's, but she immediately lowered her lids again.

How did Marcy and David survive in this household? Tom suspected that David would be a problem for the Sheriff's Department before long. Although he hadn't been in trouble before, he gave off the bad vibes of a kid who was holding back enough rage to blow his life apart. His sister Marcy's sad history showed in her tense body and empty face. Was Rachel right in believing the girl was scared of her brother? Or was Marcy constantly terrified of being judged and punished by everyone around her?

Tom could easily see how appealing this child would be to Rachel's kind heart. What he'd learned of Rachel's childhood from her hesitant, wrenching confidences told him she and a child like Marcy had a lot in common. In Tom's view, that was good reason for Rachel to steer clear. She would bring a world of trouble on herself if she got tangled up in this family's mess.

Ethan emerged from the bedroom and told Tom, "You can go in."

Tom stepped into a room that stretched from the front of the house to the back, with one end used as a bedroom and the other as a sitting room complete with sofa, chairs, tables, and widescreen TV.

Vicky sat up in a kingsize bed, with Rayanne Stuckey tugging the collar of a fluffy blue robe up around her chin. A coverlet lay over Vicky's legs. To Tom she seemed even smaller, more shrunken, than before, the outlines of her gaunt body barely detectable inside the folds of fabric. Gray skin stretched tight over sharp cheekbones, and her eyes swam with tears.

Tom paused inside the door. He heard it snick shut behind him. "I'm sorry about your daughter."

"They told me she's critical," Vicky said in a whisper. Rayanne kept a hand on her shoulder. "One of the ER nurses is going to call me with updates. Ethan doesn't want me to go in to be with her, but if I don't and she…" Her voice trailed off to nothing.

"We'll be looking into the accident," Tom said, "trying to figure out what happened. Where had she been? What time did she go out?"

Vicky's shoulders rose and fell in a shrug, and the effort of the movement seemed to exhaust her. She sank farther back against her pillows. "I didn't even know she'd gone out."

Tom moved closer, and Vicky gestured at the chair beside the bed. Rayanne retreated to a spot by the dresser.

Sitting, Tom said, "Would she have gone out to see friends?"

"No." Vicky's head swiveled slowly on the pillow so she could look at him. "Soo doesn't have any friends here. Not that I've been aware of. She never went to school here, and she never spends much time at home."

Tom recalled Soo Jin sitting in his office, rigid and self-contained, her spine never touching the back of the chair, talking about being abandoned in a Seoul orphanage and growing up at a distance from her adoptive family. He wondered if she'd ever found anyone to connect with. For a young woman with so much intelligence and inner strength, hers seemed a bleak existence.

Tom decided not to tell Vicky, for the moment, that Soo's crash was the result of tampering. She looked as if she couldn't take another piece of bad news tonight. The stress of the past few days might well kill this woman. Then what would happen to David and Marcy? For that matter, what would happen to Beth? Tom couldn't imagine Ethan taking over the role of parent to all of them.

"I'll let you get some rest." Tom rose. Knowing how trite it sounded, but at a loss for anything else to say, he added, "I hope Soo Jin will be all right."

He motioned for Rayanne to follow him. Outside the door, Rayanne said, "I can't leave her alone for long. She's in real bad shape."

"You don't usually work at night, do you?"

"No, but somebody's gotta take care of her." She threw a scornful look at Ethan, who leaned against a wall a few feet away, arms folded, head down. In a second the flash of emotion vanished, and Rayanne's face became a bland mask again. The good servant.

"Do you have any idea where Soo Jin went tonight?" Tom asked.

"Lord, no. She'd never tell me anything."

"When did she leave?"

"I don't know that, either."

"Where was her car parked today?" The tires could have been tampered with before she left the property, not while she was gone.

"In the garage, I guess, if it wasn't out front. I don't really notice things like that. Is something... It was an accident, wasn't it?"

Ignoring the question, Tom said, "Thanks. You can get back to her now."

When Rayanne was back inside the bedroom, Tom asked Ethan, "How about you? Do you know what time Soo Jin left the house tonight?"

"What the hell does it matter?" Ethan's attitude and posture mirrored the glum-faced David a few feet farther along the hall.

"It matters," Tom said. "Do you know?"

David said, "Eight o'clock. That's when she left."

Tom swung around to look at the boy. Marcy remained in her stiff posture next to her brother. "You're sure about that?"

"I *said* it, didn't I? I saw her drive off."

"Do you know where she went?"

"Of course he doesn't," Ethan snapped. "How would he know anything?"

Tom studied Ethan for a moment, wondering why he cared enough about this to be irritated. He turned back to the boy. "David? Do you know where she went?"

Casting a wary glance at Ethan, David answered, "Don't know and don't care."

Tom pulled in a breath and released it slowly, trying not to lose patience. "Is anyone from the family going to the hospital tonight?" he asked Ethan.

"Mom can't go," Ethan said without looking up. "She's not strong enough."

"I know that, but how about you?"

Now Ethan's head came up and his eyes widened as if he were surprised by the question. "Me? Why would I go?"

"Because she's your sister, Ethan." What was wrong with these people?

Ethan rolled his eyes.

Tom wanted to shake him until that damned juvenile sulkiness fell away and Ethan started acting like an adult human being. "I guess Beth wouldn't be interested in going, after the row they had. Where is Beth, anyway?"

"How should I know?" Ethan sounded like an irritated twelve-year-old. "I don't keep track of everybody. She's probably in her room."

"No, she's not," David said.

Tom gave the boy his attention again.

"She snuck out, I saw her," David went on. "She's probably out somewhere with Pete Rasey."

"Aw, crap," Ethan said. "I told Ellis not to let her out. Mom's going to have a hissy fit."

"There's plenty of ways to get out," David said, his lips twisted in a sneer. "You don't have to go out the front."

"Is Ellis that goon out there with a gun?" Tom asked. "Are you saying you hired somebody to keep your sister from leaving the house?"

"No. For god's sake. I hired him to protect us."

"Why do you think the family needs protection?"

"Because of what happened to Dad."

"I thought you believed the wild dogs killed your father," Tom said. "So you've changed your mind? You believe he was murdered?"

Ethan ran the tip of his tongue over his lips. "Yeah. Yeah, I believe he was murdered."

Well, hallelujah. "All right then, but you keep your friend Ellis under control. He pointed a gun at me when I drove up. Pointing a gun at a police officer is a good way to get himself shot."

Ethan winced. "I'll talk to him."

"You ought to be worrying about where Beth is. She's a minor, she's not in the best company, and she's not necessarily safe."

Ethan didn't bother to answer.

Tom shook his head. He'd had enough of this family. He wished he could go home to Rachel instead of spending half the night trying to figure out what happened to Soo Jin. "Well, I guess somebody from the hospital will let your mother know how Soo Jin is doing."

He was on his way down the stairs when his cell phone rang in his shirt pocket. He dug it out and answered.

Gail, the night dispatcher, told him, "Captain, you need to get home. Dr. Goddard says somebody tried to burn down your house."

Chapter Twenty

Score one for the psychic, Rachel thought. Mrs. Barker wouldn't be the least bit surprised that this house was now a crime scene.

Rachel sat on the stairs, reduced to an observer while the deputies and fire chief went about their work. She had shut Frank and Cicero in the den to keep them out of the way, and every now and then a piteous yowl issued from behind the closed door, followed by a screech.

A lurid kaleidoscope of red and blue spilled through the open front door from the flashing light bars atop Sheriff's Department cruisers. Four deputies bustled in and out, and the fire chief gathered glass shards in the living room and deposited them in brown paper evidence bags.

Rachel's heart rate had slowed, but when she held out her hands she saw they still trembled. The night air blowing into the house chilled her, even after she'd changed into jeans and a sweatshirt. Leaning her head against the stair railing, she closed her eyes and willed the tension that gripped her to let go and drain away. The dispatcher had located Tom, and he was on his way home. All of this would seem less threatening when he was here.

But she couldn't shake off the horrifying reality of what had happened. Somebody had set fire to the house with her in it. If she'd been asleep, if Tom had been home and they'd both been asleep—

Was this my fault? Did I bring this on by trying to save the dogs?

But what else, in good conscience, could she do? She couldn't leave the fate of the animals to cretins like that. Dealing with Tom's reaction was what she dreaded. It didn't take much to kick him into super-protective mode, and he drove her crazy when he took that I-know-what's-best-for-you attitude.

Footfalls pounded up the front steps and across the porch. She opened her eyes as Tom barreled through the front door. He caught Rachel in his arms before she was fully on her feet.

"Are you all right?"

"Yes, I'm fine, I'm not hurt." For a moment she clung to him, soaking up his warmth and strength, feeling safe again. Then she glanced toward the living room, where the fire chief now stood on a ladder to take down the damaged drapes. "That window's going to need some work, though."

"I don't care about the damned window, I care about you," Tom said. He kissed the top of her head.

She might as well put it into words before he did. Moving out of his embrace, she said, "I suppose this happened because I'm trying to rescue—"

"No." Tom shook his head. "I think it was a message for me." He stepped over to the living room doorway. "Nobody but an idiot would do something like this at a cop's house, and I know exactly which idiot to look at first."

"Who?" Rachel followed him. "And why do you think it was aimed at you? You weren't even here, your department car wasn't here."

"This is how a coward would do it. If you get hurt, it hurts me, too."

"Who do you think is responsible?"

"I'd rather not say right now."

"Don't you think I have a right to—" Rachel stopped herself. "Okay. I understand. I just hope you'll be able to prove it and arrest him, whoever he is."

In the living room, the fire chief had taken down both drapery panels and laid them over the top of the ladder. The odors of burnt cotton fabric and fire extinguisher chemicals still hung in the air, despite the draft through the shattered window.

"Stay where you are," the chief said from the ladder. "I'll show you what we've got."

He backed down off the ladder. Dressed in a rumpled plaid shirt and baggy khakis, he looked like he'd thrown on whatever was handy after being roused from a sound sleep.

From a cardboard box he pulled out a sealed plastic bag containing a brick. "This was probably used just to make sure the window broke and there was an opening. Then this came in." He swapped the first bag for one that held a beer bottle. "Gasoline was the accelerant, I'd say, with a burning rag as a wick. Instead of exploding like an amateur might expect it to, most of the gas splashed out. See the pattern here?"

He pointed to the draperies. Ragged swaths edged with black marked the uneven burns on the fabric.

"But here's where the bottle landed." With the toe of his boot he indicated the black patch on the rug in front of the window. The red fire extinguisher still lay where Rachel had dropped it.

For a second she was back in that moment, her heart thudding, her throat dry with terror, swinging the extinguisher back and forth.

"Jesus Christ." Tom slid an arm around Rachel's shoulders and pulled her closer. "Thank god you were still up when it happened."

"Oh, my gosh!" Holly's exclamation from the doorway made Rachel and Tom turn. Holly had come in with Brandon, and she rushed forward and threw her arms around Rachel, forcing Tom to let go of her. "Are you all right? I just about fainted when I heard your house was on fire."

"I'm fine. You didn't have to come over so late." Rachel blinked back tears and extricated herself from Holly's fierce hug.

"I couldn't keep her from coming to make sure you're okay," Brandon said. With a grim expression on his young face, he surveyed the burned drapes and carpet, the smashed window. He asked Tom, "What do you think about this, Captain?"

"It probably has something to do with the Hall case."

"I still think it might have been intended for me." Rachel couldn't let go of the idea that the gang they'd encountered at the Hall house and the sanctuary had come after her tonight.

"Because of the dogs?" Holly asked.

Brandon's professional demeanor vanished in an instant, giving way to wide-eyed alarm. "Then they might come after Holly too."

"Well, I got news for them," Holly said. "We're not quittin'. We're not gonna give up and just let people shoot those poor creatures." But her voice wavered when she asked Rachel, "We're not, are we? You won't quit, will you?"

"Of course not." Rachel glanced at Tom, hoping he wouldn't argue.

But he wasn't looking at her. He seemed in the grip of his own dark thoughts. The rigid set of his jaw sharpened the angles of his face, and the cold anger she saw building in his eyes made her suddenly afraid of what he would do, not to her but to some unknown enemy.

◇◇◇

Tom and Brandon walked into the yard, out of the women's hearing range. Pausing next to his cruiser, Tom said, "Whoever did this, I don't think they'll stop with one brick and one bottle of gas through a window. If they want to do some real damage, they'll try again. I have to get on top of it before anything else happens."

"You think it's somebody who's mad about the dog pack?"

"Could be. But it also could have been the guy who set his dog on Gordon Hall. If Hall's death is connected somehow to the dogfighting, this might have been a warning to back off."

"They've gotta know we've been nosing around," Brandon said. "You can't keep something like that quiet for two minutes in this county."

"There's another possibility, though. Beth Hall and Pete Rasey. They both think they've got reason to hate me. Beth left home without permission tonight, and nobody in the family knows for sure where she went, but they said she's in the habit of sneaking out to see Pete. I'm going to track him down right now and see what he has to say."

"Okay, I'll go with you."

"No, I want you to stay here with Rachel, just to be on the safe side."

Brandon's face fell, but he didn't argue.

"Don't say anything to Rachel about Pete," Tom told him. "She's still afraid of him because of what happened at that meeting at the Rocky Branch school, and I don't want her to know he set this fire until I've got proof."

When Tom went back inside and told Rachel he had to leave for a while, she simply nodded, didn't ask questions.

Holly, however, was never one to restrain her curiosity. "What's so important that you gotta leave right now?"

"I can't talk about it. I need to get moving. Brandon's going to stay here until I get back."

"And I'm stayin' too." Holly moved closer to Rachel and threw an accusing look at Tom. "She ought not to be by herself after gettin' a shock like this."

No, she shouldn't be, Tom thought. Rachel was too quiet, too calm, and that probably meant she was scared to death.

He put an arm around her shoulders and whispered, "I'm sorry. I wouldn't leave if it wasn't important. I'll be back as soon as I can."

"I understand," she said. "Be careful, wherever you're going. Come back in one piece, okay?" She tried a short laugh but didn't quite carry it off.

She was afraid for his safety, Tom realized then, not her own.

Pete's car wasn't in the driveway. Tom parked on the road near the Rasey house, cut his engine, and waited. Twenty minutes later, he saw headlights approaching from the opposite direction. Near the house, the headlights suddenly went out. Illuminated by the moon, the black Thunderbird rolled slowly into the

Raseys' driveway. Pete was trying to get back into the house without waking his parents.

Without turning on his own headlights, Tom started his engine and moved the cruiser to the bottom of the driveway, blocking it. Pete climbed out of the Thunderbird, caught sight of Tom getting out of the police car, and paused with one hand still on his open door.

Tom was walking up the driveway when the front door of the house banged open and Beck Rasey charged out. Standing under the dim porch light in a tee shirt and boxer shorts, he shouted at his son, "Where the hell have you been? I told you to get back here by nine o'clock. I swear, if you've been sneaking around with that Hall girl again, I'm gonna kill you with my bare hands."

"*Dad.*" Pete pointed at Tom.

"Evening, Beck," Tom said, with a little wave of his hand. "I was just about to ask your son the same question. Where have you been, Pete?"

"What the hell business is it of yours?" Beck stomped down the steps in his slippers and hustled over to Pete, reaching him the same time Tom did. Side by side, they looked like a before-and-after illustration of how a handsome young athlete might end up if he let himself go. "This is family. Keep your damned nose out of it, Bridger."

"I need to know where Pete was tonight." When he looked at Pete, the boy's gaze connected with his for a second before jumping away. "Were you anywhere near my place?"

"What?" Beck said. "What are you talking about? What are you accusing him of?"

His father might be startled and defensive, but Pete didn't seem surprised by Tom's question. Jamming his fists into his jeans pockets, he hunched his shoulders and fixed his gaze on the ground. In that moment, Tom was certain Pete had thrown the brick and firebomb into his house. For now, though, he didn't have a shred of proof.

"Pete knows what happened tonight," Tom said.

Beck poked his son's shoulder. "What have you been up to?"

The boy jerked back from his father's touch. "Nothing! I didn't do anything. He's just winding you up."

Beck rounded on Tom. "I want to know what this is all about."

"Somebody set my house on fire tonight."

Beck's mouth dropped open. His expression wavered between incredulity and outrage. "And you think my kid was responsible?"

Tom didn't answer, but kept his eyes on Pete, pinning him with a stare that seemed to make the boy shrink back inside himself.

"Where's your evidence?" Beck demanded. "You don't have any, do you? And you're not gonna find any, because my boy didn't do squat to your precious house. So you've got no right coming on my property throwing around blame. Now get on out of here."

Tom held his ground for a moment more, long enough for Pete to dare eye contact again. Silently, Tom sent him a message. *I'll get you for this, you little punk.*

Chapter Twenty-one

As if I'm going to sleep tonight. I may never sleep again.

After sitting up until nearly three waiting for Tom's return, Rachel grew tired of Holly and Brandon fussing over her and urging her to rest. She climbed the stairs, changed back into her nightgown, and settled on the bed with Frank curled up at her feet. Although she felt safe with Brandon there, she was certain she wouldn't be able to sleep until Tom came home.

She awoke to see sunlight streaming through the windows. She sat up with a jolt. Where was Tom?

The sheet and pillow on his side of the bed looked rumpled as if he'd slept there. Thank god. If he'd been home, he must be all right. But she hadn't been aware of him coming to bed or getting up again.

Pulling on her robe as she went, she walked down the hall to the bathroom. Tom stood at the sink, wearing his uniform pants and a tee shirt, running an electric shaver over his chin.

She went to him and wrapped her arms around his waist, pressing her face into his neck. Safe and sound, no gunshot wound, no bruises. "Why didn't you wake me up when you came in?"

He hugged her with his free arm, the razor still buzzing in his other hand. "You needed your sleep."

"I wish you'd woken me up. I wanted to hear—" Rachel broke off to yawn.

Tom laughed. "You've made my point for me." He switched off his razor and lifted her chin with a finger so he could kiss her.

"Where did you go?" she asked. "Do you know who started the fire?"

"I've got a suspect. I don't have any proof."

"Who?" Rachel moved away and leaned against the door jamb.

He hesitated, silent as he stowed the razor in the medicine cabinet.

"Tell me," she said. "I have a right to know who's trying to hurt me. Hurt us."

"Just let me handle it. And I will handle it, don't worry."

What was he protecting her from this time? "Isn't it better for me to know—"

"A guy's coming to replace the glass in the window. He'll be here in the next hour. Do you mind dealing with him? He'll send a bill."

Okay, she'd have to worm it out of him, maybe over breakfast. This was Saturday. They'd formed the habit of long, leisurely breakfasts on the weekend. But this wasn't a normal Saturday. "You're going to have something to eat before you leave, aren't you?"

"I'll grab something somewhere. I have to get back to work." He pulled a fresh uniform shirt from a hook on the back of the door. "There's a lot going on with the Halls."

Only then did Rachel remember that the oldest Hall daughter had been in an accident the night before. "How's Soo Jin?"

Buttoning his shirt, Tom said, "She's still unconscious. The airbag deployed, but that didn't stop her from getting a head injury."

"Oh no. Is she paralyzed?"

"They can't tell at this point." He stuffed his shirt into his pants and gave her another quick kiss. "I've got to go. We'll talk later. I know you'll want to go check on the dogs, but don't go out there by yourself. Get Joe Dolan to go with you. Everybody along this road will keep an eye out today and make sure nothing happens."

She could argue with him about Joe, but what would be the point? He was right, after all. She needed protection. If anybody tried to attack her, Joe could shoot him with a tranquilizer dart. She almost smiled at the thought.

Tom brushed past her. On his way down the stairs, he called back, "I've already fed Frank, and I gave Cicero some fresh seeds and water and let him out of his cage."

A minute later she heard the front door open and close.

Rachel walked back to the bedroom, acutely aware that she was now alone, but telling herself it was ridiculous to feel as if Tom had abandoned her. She'd never been the clinging type, and she despised the impulse in herself. "What do you want him to do?" she asked herself as she opened the closet door. "Stay home and hold your hand instead of finding out who set our house on fire?"

She paused, her hand on the shirt she meant to wear. *Our house?* Was she thinking of it that way now?

She pulled the shirt off its hanger, grabbed a clean pair of jeans, and began changing. *Our house.* For weeks she'd felt like a visitor here, an intruder at times. Everywhere she looked, she saw reminders that this house had belonged to Tom's parents, and in spirit it still did, even if Tom's name was on the deed. Everything in it had been chosen by Tom's mother. Some of the rooms had flowered wallpaper that made Rachel wince every time she looked at it, and nothing had been painted in at least a decade. But it had never occurred to Rachel to suggest changes. What right did she have? She was a pretender, playing house with Tom, letting him believe they had a future together when she wasn't sure she believed it herself.

Tom was halfway to town when he got the call. The display on his cell said it came from a public phone.

"Hey, buddy, I got somethin' for you."

For a second the voice didn't register. When it did, Tom yanked the steering wheel to the right and pulled off the road. "Burt? Hey. What is it?"

"I heard there's gonna be a fight tonight."

"Great. Where?" Tom fumbled in his shirt pocket for a pad and pen and flipped open the pad on the passenger seat.

"You know that place called Ladyslipper Hollow?"

"Yeah." Tom wrote down the name. "That's a wetland. How can they do anything in there?"

"That's not the place. You go about two miles past there, maybe a little less, and look for a dirt road on the left. It's hard to see. It's more like a trail or a path than a road. You get on that and keep goin' and you'll find the spot. It'll probably start around nine-thirty or ten."

"Where did you—"

The line went dead.

Tom thought about trying to get Morgan back on the phone, but decided against it. He'd told Tom all he was willing to tell him. Morgan didn't have a phone line at his cabin, and Tom doubted he owned a cell phone, so he'd probably had to go into town to make the call from a public place. He wouldn't take a chance on prolonging the conversation and being overheard.

Tom pressed a speed-dial button and waited until he connected with Dennis at headquarters. "You're there early on a Saturday," Tom said. "Your whole family must be hating me about now."

"They're getting used to it," Dennis said.

"I'm afraid I'm going to keep you busy tonight, too," Tom said. "I got a tip on the location for the dogfights, and we'll need to have a team out there tonight."

"Hey, that's great. I'm ready when you are."

"You got anything from the State Police about Soo Jin's car?"

"The report just came in, with some pictures."

"I'll be there in a few minutes."

When Tom reached headquarters, Dennis had four eight-by-ten close-ups of the tires on Soo Jin's car pinned to the bulletin board in the conference room. Brandon joined Dennis and Tom in studying them.

The photos showed thin slices between the treads on all four tires.

"Man," Brandon said, "that's vicious. Somebody definitely wanted to hurt that girl."

"It could have been vandalism," Dennis said. "Somebody just wanting to give her four flat tires."

"I wish we had some idea of when it happened," Tom said. "How long would it take for the tires to go flat with the car moving? If the damage was done while she was out last night, they wouldn't have lost so much air by the time she headed home. Maybe it was done earlier, before she went out."

"Somebody at the house did it?" Brandon said. "Maybe somebody in the family?"

"Yeah," Tom said. "That's exactly what I think."

Soo Jin could have been killed if the car had rolled all the way over or blown up. She might die yet. Murder usually involved strong emotions, and Soo Jin didn't seem to inspire that kind of feeling in anybody except her adopted sister Beth. Tom had seen the kind of rage Beth was capable of. He wouldn't be surprised if she'd plotted against Soo Jin. Beth could easily have tampered with the tires while the car sat outside the house.

Maybe yesterday had been payback day for both Beth and her boyfriend Pete.

Chapter Twenty-two

The little brown mutt with his ribs poking out didn't look like he could terrorize a whole county. He didn't look as if he wanted to, either. He scampered to the front of the cage, tail wagging, when he saw Rachel approach with Holly and her grandmother, Sarelda Turner. Standing up against the chain link fencing, he bounced and yipped.

Rachel poked a couple of fingers through the fence and scratched the dog's head. "Hey there," she said. "Have you forgiven us for putting you in a cage?"

"That poor little thing's just starved for attention," Mrs. Turner said.

"And starved for good food too," Holly added. "Look at him. He's skin and bones."

The floppy-eared mutt looked as if his filthy, wavy coat had been draped over a skeleton. "He's so small that the other dogs probably never let him get much to eat," Rachel said. Standing, she smiled at Mrs. Turner. "I have a feeling you'll fatten him up."

"You know, I've kind of took a fancy to this one," Mrs. Turner said. "He's real good-natured. I bet he'd get along with my dogs like a charm."

"Let's make sure he's healthy first. Let him settle in today and I'll examine him thoroughly tomorrow. But you can pamper him all you want to in the meantime." Rachel checked her watch for the fourth or fifth time since leaving the house. This was her first stop, and she still had to check on the Halls' dog. Every minute she was away, she worried about somebody showing up at the farm, setting the place on fire or doing other major damage. The neighbors might check on the place and watch the road for strange cars, but the distance between the farms would make it easy for somebody to slip past. Billy Bob was safe with the Duncans, but Frank and Cicero were inside the house with no one to protect them.

Stop it, Rachel told herself. She was worrying too much. If Tom thought the house and the animals were safe, she shouldn't be concerned either.

Still, she wanted to finish up here, make a quick visit to see Thor, and get back home.

She walked over to the first run in the section, where Joe Dolan crouched outside the fence, trying to coax the dog they'd caught two nights before to come closer. The two dogs had been separated because Rachel wanted them to focus on their human caregivers, not each other, but as they captured more members of the pack, this whole line of runs would fill up.

This dog lay resting in a patch of sunshine and didn't respond to Joe's coaxing, but his head was up and his ears cocked, and he was listening. Not friendly, not hostile, simply watchful.

"That's progress," Rachel said.

"Yeah, I think there's hope for this one too."

"He's not gonna be so quick about trustin' people," Mrs. Turner said, as she and Holly joined Rachel and Joe. "But he'll be all right. I've been talkin' to him a lot, and he looks like he's takin' in every word and givin' it a lot of thought."

"You're our dog whisperer," Rachel said. That drew a proud little smile from Mrs. Turner. Holly had been raised by her grandmother after her mother disappeared, and the old woman, who came across as tough and no-nonsense with people, had a deep and tender love for animals that she had passed on to her granddaughter.

"I just hope we'll be allowed to keep them here and work with them," Joe said. "I've been hearing from the county supervisors about this. They think I oughta take the dogs straight to the pound and kill them. There's a lot of people out there that feel the same way."

"That's crazy," Mrs. Turner exclaimed. She gave Rachel a stern look. "Any dogs you bring in here, they're gonna get a second chance. If somebody intends to hurt them, they'll have to get to them over my dead body."

Some might choose to take that route, Rachel thought. "I'm not euthanizing any of them. I'm on their side. Tom and I can probably hold off the supervisors and the sheriff, but I'm seriously worried about somebody getting in here at night."

"We got our protection," Mrs. Turner said. "Round the clock."

"The guys workin' at night don't fall asleep on the job," Holly said. "They're too scared of Grandma. They'd rather tangle with a hungry bobcat than mess with her."

Anybody who would set fire to an occupied house, Rachel thought, probably wouldn't balk at shooting the sanctuary's guards to get past them. She stifled the thought, fervently hoping she was exaggerating the danger. "We'll bring you at least one more dog tonight," she said. "I want to concentrate on catching the alpha dog. That should make it easier to get the rest of them. He's big, and he might be vicious, so you'll have to be especially careful when you get close to him, and take all the precautions when the run needs to be cleaned."

"Oh, don't you worry," Mrs. Turner said, "I expect I can handle him."

That kind of overconfidence, Rachel worried, would get her hurt.

◇◇◇

She felt disturbingly like a damsel in distress who couldn't venture into the world without a man to look after her, but she was glad to have Joe following her in his van. Although he surely had better things to do with his Saturday, he was going to wait for her on the road outside the Halls' house and follow her back to Tom's farm.

At the entrance to the Halls' driveway, the same burly guy who had stopped Rachel before stood on the driveway with one hand up and the other clutching a shotgun. God, these people freaked her out.

She waited while he marched over to her Range Rover, squinted at her as if making sure she was who she was supposed to be. After what seemed a ridiculously long and close scrutiny, he stepped back and waved her on.

"Thank you so much," she muttered. Now she could look forward to an encounter with Ethan at the house.

To her relief, young Marcy answered the door. When she saw Rachel, the girl's blank facade fell away, her eyes brightened, and she almost smiled before some internal restraint put a stop to the show of friendliness. "Hey," she said, her voice barely audible, all emotion wiped from her face.

"Hi, Marcy. It's good to see you again. I'm here to check on Thor."

The girl bobbed her head and opened the door wider to let Rachel in.

As Marcy closed the door, Rachel said, "I was so sorry to hear about your sister's accident. How is she this morning?"

Marcy hunched her shoulders. "I don't know," she murmured. "Nobody told me."

A strange family indeed, Rachel thought. "Could you show me where Thor is? We don't have to bother your mother right now."

Marcy nodded and led Rachel through the living room and out onto the patio, where Thor lay on one of his dog beds, watching squirrels forage among the fallen leaves on the lawn. The girl knelt and stroked his side, prompting a few slow thumps of his tail.

Rachel stooped to scratch Thor's head. "He must be feeling better. Is he eating well and taking his antibiotic?"

"Yes, ma'am." The girl's voice remained a near whisper.

With her brown skin, curly black hair, and long-lashed eyes, Marcy was a beautiful girl, and Rachel longed to see her smile, hear her laugh, see a spark of life in those eyes. This timid, withdrawn child wasn't reacting to her father's death. Rachel felt sure Marcy was like this all the time. Life in the Hall household had drained the spirit from her.

Stay out of it, she could hear Tom say. Rachel turned her attention back to the dog, scratching his neck with one hand while she lifted his lip to check gum color. He was doing well, bouncing back from what must have been a terrifying experience.

Glancing into the empty living room, Rachel wondered where the rest of the family was. This would be a good time to ask Marcy about her plea the last time Rachel had seen her. *Help me.* She was positive that was what the girl said. How could she ignore that?

"Have you been keeping Thor company?" she asked.

"Yes, ma'am. He keeps wanting to come out here." Marcy hesitated, then added, "I think he's waiting for Daddy to come back. But doesn't he know what happened? He saw it. Why does he keep looking?"

She sounded so bewildered that Rachel wanted to pull her into a hug. All she allowed herself to do was place a hand on Marcy's shoulder. This child had seen her father's body immediately after he died. She had seen him lying on the ground with his throat ripped open. "Animals can grieve when they lose someone they love, the same way we do. Give him a lot of attention and make sure he eats well, and he'll probably pull out of it."

For the first time, Marcy lifted her eyes to meet Rachel's. Her voice came out stronger, more urgent. "Why would somebody do a thing like that to another person? I mean, sic a bad dog on him?"

"I don't know, Marcy. I don't understand it either."

"They must have really hated him."

What was she supposed to say to that? *Yeah, I hear your father was a real s.o.b. Plenty of people must be glad he's dead.* She said the only thing she could think of. "The reason doesn't matter. It was wrong. Nobody has a right to do something like to another person."

Marcy didn't respond. She stroked Thor while Rachel checked his wounds and changed his dressings. This was such a peaceful setting, surrounded by woods, with cardinals and wrens singing from the shrubs behind the house, that Rachel could hardly imagine the carnage that had taken place at the bottom of the lawn. How would any of the Halls ever again enjoy a simple walk in the yard, with such a memory intruding?

Marcy murmured something Rachel didn't catch.

Smoothing the last new bandage in place, Rachel glanced up. "I'm sorry, what did you—" She broke off, struck by the change that had come over Marcy.

The girl had gone rigid, her bottom lip trembling, and her gaze seemed to focus inward. For the first time, Rachel saw strong emotions play across Marcy's face, a jumble of bewilderment blending into fear, giving way to—what? Before Rachel's eyes, Marcy's small, beautiful face hardened into a mask of bitterness. Her voice remained quiet, but now it had a cold edge. "He was mean," she said. "He was mean all the time."

Staring at her, Rachel was momentarily at a loss for words. Was she still talking about Gordon Hall? Was the memory of her father stirring up these ugly emotions? "Who, Marcy? Who was mean?"

The girl shot a fearful look at the house. "*Him.*"

"Your father? Dr. Hall?"

Marcy nodded.

What am I doing? Would she make matters worse by coaxing Marcy to confide in her? Did the child have anyone else to talk to? She seemed so alone in the world, and so afraid. Rachel got to her feet. Anybody in the family could overhear them, walk out onto the patio while they were talking. "Let's get Thor out in the yard. He'll feel better with some exercise."

Marcy scrambled up and helped Rachel give Thor a boost onto his feet. With Thor between them, a frail patient who couldn't be rushed, they moved slowly onto the grass.

When they were twenty feet from the house, Rachel said, "Marcy, what did your father do to you? Did he hit you, or... do other things to you?"

She shook her head.

Thank god for that, at least. But there were so many other ways to inflict pain on a child. "Why did you say he was mean?"

As they walked in a slow circle with the dog, Marcy kept glancing at the house as if she expected someone to storm out at any moment. "He said we had bad blood. Our real daddy's blood, and our real mama's. So we couldn't do anything right. He punished David a lot."

"Punished him how?"

She bit her lower lip and hesitated before answering. "He locked him in his room all the time. That night—when Daddy died—he made David go to his room without any dinner, and he locked him in. When everything was happening, after we found Daddy, David heard us all yelling, but he couldn't get out. Beth finally unlocked the door."

Rachel was appalled, and a sudden fresh memory of the fire at Tom's house the night before made her wonder what would have happened to a child in a locked room if the Halls' house were burning. Why would a bedroom have a door that could be locked from the outside?

Now that Dr. Hall was gone, maybe that kind of punishment was over for Marcy's brother, along with the psychological abuse Hall had practiced on both David and Marcy. One thing, though, nagged at Rachel. "Marcy, when I was here yesterday, you said something I didn't understand. I think you said, *Help me.* Am I right?"

Marcy hung her head and mumbled her words. "David wants him and me to go—" She paused and looked back toward the house.

Rachel's gaze followed. David stood on the patio, watching them. How long had he been there?

Marcy's face slammed shut like a door. With a snap of his hand, David summoned her.

Seeing the girl was ready to obey, Rachel said quickly, "Marcy, you can call me anytime you want to talk. Just call the animal hospital number and you'll get through to me. Okay?"

Marcy hesitated, her eyes filled with doubt as she searched Rachel's face. Then she bolted, back to the house and her brother.

Chapter Twenty-three

"I wouldn't have recognized her," Tom said.

He and Brandon stood outside Soo Jin's room in intensive care, looking through a window at the small figure in the bed. Bandages swaddled her head, bruises and swelling distorted her face, and white tape secured a breathing tube to her mouth. Her doctor, a balding and scarecrow thin man named Hurley with a slight stoop that cut a couple of inches off his height, scribbled something on the chart at the foot of her bed.

When the doctor emerged from the room, Tom asked, "Has anybody from the family been in to see her?"

Dr. Hurley responded with a deep sigh. "Not a soul. It saddens me."

"Man, that is cold," Brandon said.

"Have you talked to Mrs. Hall about Soo Jin?" Tom asked.

"Briefly," the doctor said. "She's not well herself, you know, and the stress of Gordon's death—Well, she's nearing the end of her tolerance, I'm afraid. I hope the girl pulls through. Vicky doesn't need another crisis to deal with right now."

Interesting way to put it, Tom thought. He wondered if anybody had the slightest feeling for Soo Jin herself, for the young life that had been brutally interrupted and might come to an early end.

"Has she been conscious at all?" Tom asked. "Has she said anything?"

"Oh, no." Hurley shook his head. "She's been in a coma since she came in."

"But she's still—"

"Yes, yes, there is brain activity. How much damage has been done remains to be seen when she regains consciousness."

"Let me know the minute she does," Tom said. He pulled out his wallet and removed a business card. "Call me. Anytime. Night or day."

For a couple of minutes after the doctor strode away, Tom and Brandon lingered, watching a nurse check the various tubes connected to Soo Jin. Tom had found the girl off-putting, but the sight of her lying helpless and alone in a hospital bed brought a rush of pity and outrage. For the second time in her life, she'd been abandoned by the people who should have loved her.

"What little I've seen of her," Brandon said, "she seemed real chilly. Like she didn't want anybody getting too close. If she was conscious, she probably wouldn't want the Halls hanging around her hospital bed. But I'll bet she never expected one of them to try to kill her."

◇◇◇

Tom turned his cell phone back on as they walked out of the hospital, and it rang immediately. Rachel. "Hey," he said, "what's up? Is everything okay?"

"I just came from seeing the Halls' dog, and I thought you'd want to know something Marcy told me."

"Rachel, I asked you not to get involved—"

"*Listen*, Tom. She told me that Dr. Hall was mean to her and her brother. He didn't hit them, but it sounds as if they got a lot of psychological abuse."

Tom remembered what Soo Jin had told him: *He never let me forget where I came from.*

"And get this," Rachel went on. "Dr. Hall was in the habit of locking David in his room to punish him. David was locked in the night Dr. Hall died. Marcy said Beth let him out later. And I think David's planning to run away and take Marcy with him. I'm so afraid something's going to happen to that little girl."

"Did she say that?" All the Sheriff's Department needed was two of the Hall kids disappearing and triggering an urgent search.

"Not exactly," Rachel admitted. "She didn't have a chance, but she started to say it."

"I'll look into it," Tom said. "I don't want you to get involved."

She didn't answer. That could only mean trouble.

"Rachel? Did you hear me?"

"Of course I heard you."

And you're going to ignore me. He could drive himself crazy just worrying about keeping Rachel safe. "I'll see you at home for dinner."

Walking to the car in the hospital's front lot, Tom told Brandon what Rachel had learned from Marcy.

"So it wasn't David out there with a dog," Brandon said. "And he's just a kid, he couldn't have hired somebody, could he? No matter how much he hated Dr. Hall. They might have given him a lot of stuff, but I'll bet they never let him have much money."

Coming up to the cruiser in the emergency vehicle parking space, Tom said, "I have to admit I'm starting to dread going to that house."

"How are we going to question Beth without getting the whole family in an uproar?"

"I wish to hell I knew. We'll wing it and hope for the best. The last thing I want is for Mrs. Hall to collapse and end up in the hospital along with her daughter."

◇◇◇

This time Ethan's hired guard stepped aside when he saw the cruiser. He lifted a hand in greeting as Tom and Brandon passed. They ignored him.

At the front door, Rayanne told them Vicky Hall was on the patio with Thor. "I just took her out. It's a real nice day, and I thought some sun would do her good." Rayanne walked ahead of them through the foyer and living room, her bleached curls bouncing on her shoulders. Pausing at the patio door, she asked, "Have you heard anything new about Soo Jin?"

"No change," Tom said.

"So she's still unconscious?" Rayanne asked. "She's still not talkin'?"

"Hasn't Mrs. Hall been getting updates from the hospital?"

"Somebody called this mornin', but Mrs. Hall was asleep and Ethan told me not to wake her up. He talked to them. He didn't tell me what they said." Rayanne looked up at Tom, her brow furrowed. She lowered her voice when she spoke again. "Why doesn't anybody go see her?"

"You tell me. You know them better than I do."

Rayanne shook her head. "No. I don't think I'll ever understand what makes this family tick. But I guess I don't need to, long as I get paid on time." She pasted a bright smile on her face and swung open the patio door. "Mrs. Hall, Captain Bridger and Deputy Connolly's here."

Vicky Hall lay on a chaise with a light fleece blanket covering her from waist to feet. Over her blouse she wore a thick, nubbly sweater in a shade of yellow that emphasized the sallow cast of her skin. One arm drooped over the side of the chaise, her hand resting on Thor's back. Rolling her head toward Tom, she looked at him with half-closed eyes that appeared ringed with bruises. Rayanne fussed over her, tucking the blanket closer around her legs.

She was in bad shape, Tom thought, especially considering that she'd had dialysis the day before. She looked worse every time Tom saw her.

"Hello," Vicky said, her voice listless. "Do you have some news?"

"No, I'm afraid not." Tom noticed David near the bottom of the lawn, far from the house, kicking a soccer ball around without enthusiasm. The boy stopped for a second, looked up toward the patio, then went back to what he'd been doing. Tom told Vicky, "We just saw Soo Jin—"

"You did? What did she tell you?"

Tom hesitated. Didn't she know the girl was unconscious? "There hasn't been any change. She's not able to talk yet."

"Oh, that's right." Vicky's head lolled away from him, as if she'd lost interest in what he had to report. "You know, I'm surprised Soo was driving recklessly. It isn't like her. Such a conscientious girl."

Tom let that pass. He wasn't going to tell her everything about Soo Jin's accident until he had to. "If you don't mind, I'd like to ask your children a few questions. Just to clarify some things. Do I have your permission?"

"Of course. Whatever you need to do. I hope Beth will behave in a civilized manner. She's been such a trial the last couple of days, all because of that awful Rasey boy. Gordon could handle her, but I'm not having much luck." Vicky drew in a shuddering breath and let it out. "Oh, I miss him so much. He was my rock. My world."

Tom still had Dennis looking into Vicky's background and her marriage to Hall, but not a scrap of evidence had turned up implicating her in his murder. Looking at her now, Tom dismissed any possibility that she'd been involved. "We'll talk to David first," he said.

As Tom and Brandon walked down the sloping lawn toward him, the boy paused in his halfhearted assault on the soccer ball and pulled himself up straight, arms at his sides with his hands squeezed into fists. His posture reminded Tom of Marcy standing in the upstairs hallway the night before.

"Hey, David," Tom said when they approached.

The boy didn't answer but regarded them with a pinched, suspicious glare.

"We need to ask you a few questions." Tom and Brandon stopped six feet away from the boy, giving him enough space that he wouldn't feel crowded. Even so, David took a step backward. "We need to be sure we're clear about what happened the night Dr. Hall died. We want to get the timing straight. Were you in your room when your mother heard the telephone message your father left?"

"Yeah," David said, his tone guarded. He nudged the soccer ball with the toe of his athletic shoe. "Why does that matter?"

"Like I said, we're just trying to get everything clear. So you were in your room and you heard your mother scream?"

"She didn't scream, she was just yelling. Upset."

"Then Beth and Marcy went out to see what had happened to Dr. Hall? Why didn't you go with them?"

The boy kicked the ball hard enough to bounce it off Brandon's ankles. His bad aim seemed accidental, but instead of apologizing, David glared at Brandon as if the deputy had been at fault. Tom caught Brandon's eye, signaling him to ask the next question.

"You must have wanted to find out what was going on." Brandon picked up the soccer ball and tossed it back to David. The boy caught it, dropped it to the ground, and kept his gaze fixed on it. "I sure would have," Brandon went on. "Was there some reason you didn't go with Beth and Marcy?"

David's head jerked up. "I was locked in, that's why. I couldn't do a fucking thing 'cause *he* locked my fucking door."

"He?" Tom asked. "You mean your father?"

"Stop calling him that! He *wasn't* my father." The boy's voice had risen, but he cast a wary glance at Mrs. Hall on the patio and brought it down to a level she couldn't hear at such a distance. "I don't know what they ever wanted us for. They never acted like we belonged here."

"Why did Dr. Hall lock your door that night?" Brandon asked.

David hesitated, and Tom could see him putting together an answer that avoided the truth. "I talked back to him. He did it all the time. Locked me in to punish me."

"Okay," Tom said. "I want to ask you about something else. Did you see anybody messing around with Soo Jin's car yesterday? Tampering with it?"

The boy's anger instantly vanished, replaced by a blankness so complete it had to be a calculated defense. This, Tom guessed, was the brick wall expression David must have cultivated for dealing with his adoptive father.

"What do you mean, tampering?" David's voice had gone flat.

"Doing something to it. Spending time around it."

David's indifferent shrug seemed forced and self-conscious. "I didn't see anything."

"You're sure Soo Jin left around eight o'clock last night?" Tom asked.

"Yeah. It was—" David broke off, glanced up toward the house again, hesitated as if weighing his words. Tom waited him out. At last David met Tom's eyes, shifted his gaze to Brandon, back to Tom. "She went out right after Ethan did. I think she was following him."

"Oh, really?" Tom said. Finally, something that might be meaningful. "Any idea where Ethan was going?"

"No."

"Did you see which direction he went?"

"Toward town."

"And Soo Jin saw him leave?"

The boy was getting into the story, and he looked more animated than Tom had ever seen him. "Yeah, she was watching from a window, and she went running out and drove off right after him. But he came back around ten—I looked at the clock—and Soo didn't." His voice dropped and trailed off. "By then I guess she'd already..."

"Crashed her car," Tom supplied. If Soo Jin had started back before Ethan, he must have passed by her wrecked car. Had he seen it and driven on? Or was he responsible for the accident? Had he run her off the road?

Tom pulled himself up short. If Soo Jin had continued following him, Ethan would have been in the lead, just as when he'd left, and he might never have been aware of Soo Jin behind him.

Tom thanked the boy, who had already reverted to sulking, and he and Brandon started back up the slope to the house. Brandon had that look he got, bursting at the seams with excitement, when he thought he was onto something significant. Before he could put it into words, Tom said, keeping his voice low, "I know what you're thinking, but let's not jump to conclusions. We don't have any evidence against Ethan."

"But it's suspicious, isn't it?" Brandon asked, matching Tom's near-whisper. "He goes out, she follows him, he comes back and she doesn't. Where did he go?"

"He could have been driving around aimlessly, to get out of the house for a while," Tom said. "This place feels like a pressure cooker to me. I can imagine how it feels to the people living here."

Brandon shook his head. "She thought he was up to something. She wouldn't have followed him if she didn't."

"We'll talk about it later," Tom said. They were close enough to the patio to be overheard. Vicky Hall seemed uninterested in them, but Rayanne watched them like a fox. Stepping onto the patio, Tom asked where to find Beth and Ethan.

"They went off walking in the woods," Rayanne said.

"Together?" Tom asked, unable to hide his surprise.

"Yeah. Darnedest thing, huh?" Rayanne gave a little laugh, but she sobered after a glance at Vicky Hall.

"I'm sure Ethan has his phone with him," Vicky said.

Rather than calling the number she gave him, Tom jotted it in a notebook. "Point us in the right direction."

As they set off toward the trees to the west, Brandon said in an undertone, "Looks like Ethan and Beth have got something to talk about they don't want the rest of the family to hear."

"I don't know what to think," Tom said. "Right now I'd believe almost anything about these people."

They followed a path into the woods, crunching through fallen leaves and shoving aside drooping branches. A gust of wind shook the trees and brought down a shower of red and gold leaves that they had to brush from their hair and shoulders. About a hundred and fifty feet into the woods, Tom heard voices rising and falling in a furious argument.

"You're not having anything else to do with him, and that's final," Ethan said. "I forbid it."

Beth's voice rose to a cry of outrage. "You *forbid* it? You sound just like him! You're not my father, and you're not taking his place."

They were too involved in their fight to realize they weren't alone anymore. Tom and Brandon stopped twenty feet away from them among the trees, watching and listening. Patches of sunlight penetrated the woods, illuminating the brother and sister as if they were on stage but leaving Tom and Brandon in shadow.

"Damn it, you're going to listen to me, and you're going to do what I tell you." Ethan grabbed Beth by the arm, squeezing hard enough to make her yelp and squirm. "That kid is scum, he's nothing but trouble, and he'll drag you down with him. Stay away from him."

"Where do you get off, calling Pete names?" Beth shot back. "After all the things you've done. Drugs and drinking and— Where do you get the right to act like you're *so* much better than Pete?"

"Shut up," Ethan said, his voice carrying a dark warning note.

"You've never been anything but trouble to Mom and Dad. Daddy was *ashamed* of you."

Tom took a step forward, sensing he would have to intervene.

"Just look at you," Beth taunted. Ethan gripped her arm tighter, making her wince, but she went on. "A drug company rep. You're a *salesman*. Even an orphan from Korea's better than you are."

Still holding Beth with one hand, Ethan drew back the other to hit her.

"Stop it, Ethan!" Tom ordered.

Ethan and Beth jerked apart and swung around to stare at the deputies.

"What the hell are you doing, sneaking up on us?" Ethan demanded. He scrubbed the palms of both hands on his slacks, as if drying them. "Can't I talk to my sister without you nosing around?"

"You were doing a little more than talking," Brandon said. "Didn't anybody teach you it's not cool to rough up a girl?"

"I wasn't roughing up—Look, this is none of your business."

"Until we find out the truth about your father's death," Tom said, "everything you do is our business. So you'd better get used to us sticking our noses into every corner of your life."

Ethan's anger dropped away abruptly, replaced by a wary expression. "I didn't have anything to do with my father's death. Are you accusing me? That's crazy."

Tom pressed ahead before Ethan could regain his composure. "What about Soo Jin's accident? Did you witness it? Or did you just see her car after it went off the road?"

Brandon added, "Did you drive on past and leave your sister out there to die?"

Ethan's heavy, rapid breaths sounded loud in the quiet woods. Beads of sweat had popped out on his forehead and upper lip, despite the cool breeze that swept around them. A scarlet oak leaf settled on his shoulder and he got rid of it with a furious swipe. "I wasn't anywhere near the accident."

"You went out right before she did," Tom said. "She headed in the same direction you did. I think she was following you. Did she catch up with you? Did she see something you didn't want her to see?"

"Who said—"

"Where did you go?"

"I don't have to tell you that."

"I'm trying to find out who killed your father," Tom said. "You've done nothing but stand in my way. Why is that, Ethan? Most relatives of murder victims want to help the police any way they can."

Beth listened to the exchange with a smirk on her face.

"You're not asking me to help you," Ethan said. "You're asking me to incriminate myself."

"Oh? Are you saying your activities last night were incriminating?"

"You're twisting everything I say!" Ethan spun away in exasperation, raking both hands through his brown hair.

Beth spoke up in a teasing singsong. "Yeah, where'd you go, Ethan? What are you hiding?"

"Shut up!" Ethan snapped, pivoting to face his sister. "Where the hell were *you* until past midnight? Did you spend the whole evening spreading your legs in the back seat of Pete Rasey's car?"

"You—" Beth lunged at Ethan with fingernails aimed at his face.

Brandon caught her around the waist. "Hey, now, settle down."

"Get your hands off me!" Beth writhed in Brandon's grip.

Brandon held on, wearing an expression of sorely tested patience.

"I'd like to know where you were, too," Tom said to the girl. "Were you with Pete?"

"So what if I was?" She kicked backward, but Brandon shifted his right leg to keep her foot from connecting with his shin.

"Somebody set my house on fire last night," Tom said. "Do you know anything about that?"

"Oh, great," Ethan exclaimed, throwing up his hands. "That's just perfect, you and your muscle-bound boyfriend setting fire to a cop's house. Don't you have any sense at all?"

Beth strained forward, still trying to get at him. "You go to hell!" she screamed. Then she broke down and collapsed in Brandon's arms, sobbing.

"Beth," Tom said, "were you with Pete when he did it?"

"I swear," Ethan said, "if you're mixed up in something like that—"

"Shut up, Ethan," Tom said. "Beth?"

"I didn't *do* anything," she cried.

"If you didn't help Pete," Tom said, "you won't be in trouble."

Tom waited, but Beth had worked herself into a state of near-hysteria, and he knew he wouldn't get anything else out of her. He nodded at Brandon, and Brandon let her go. She charged off, threading her way through the trees and crashing through the undergrowth toward the house.

"Do you really think she helped Pete set your house on fire?" Ethan asked.

"Let's get back to what you were doing last night," Tom said. "You're not helping yourself by refusing to tell me where you went. You're making me damned suspicious."

"All right, all right." Ethan threw up his hands. "I went to see Leo Riggs, okay? I told him to back off and let the dog warden and Dr. Goddard catch the damned dog pack."

Interesting. When Tom saw Riggs earlier in the evening, he already seemed to know that Ethan had changed his mind about tracking down the dogs. "Why didn't you want to tell me that?"

Ethan swiped the back of a hand across his mouth. "I should've just answered your question."

"Did you know Soo Jin was following you?"

"No. I never saw her. I swear."

"Did you see her car after it wrecked?"

"Of course not. I would've called 911 if I had. And I would've stayed there and tried to help her."

For a moment Tom studied Ethan, who stared back at him with a belligerence that had a strong undertone of fear. Maybe it was time to reveal the truth and see whether Ethan was surprised by it. "We believe somebody tried to kill Soo Jin."

Ethan's face went slack. "Kill her? What do you mean? How?"

Tom doubted Ethan was faking that stunned reaction. "Somebody slit her tires. I think it was done at the house, probably sometime yesterday."

Ethan stared into space as if trying to absorb the information. Then he focused on Tom again. "Are you saying you think one of us did it?"

"Is that possible?"

"No. I mean—" Ethan stumbled over his words, and Tom had the impression he couldn't keep up with his thoughts. He ended up saying firmly, "No. Absolutely not. Nobody in the family would've done anything like that."

"Soo Jin and Beth had a pretty bad scene over Pete Rasey."

Ethan took his time responding to that. When he did, all he said was, "Beth's had a hard time of it lately. Because of that boy. I haven't been here, but what I've heard… She's been doing things I never thought she was capable of. It's like he's turned her into a different person."

"What are you saying? Do you think she could have gotten back at Soo Jin by slashing her tires?"

Ethan raised his hands. "Now wait a minute. I'm not accusing my sister of anything. If she did something like that, it would've been vandalism. I mean, wouldn't a kid expect the tires to go flat right away? She wouldn't expect the car to be drivable and dangerous. And how would she know Soo would go out last night anyway?" He added quickly, "I'm not saying I think Beth did it."

First Ethan had seemed committed to total denial. Now he was defending the sister he'd been haranguing a few minutes ago. Tom wondered how he would get any straight answers out of this family. "Do you think David could have done it?" he asked. "Did he have any reason to?"

"Don't expect me to explain what goes on in that kid's head. You'll have to figure it out for yourself. Now I have an appointment with a funeral home about my father's service, so if you don't mind, I'm leaving."

Chapter Twenty-four

Rachel frowned as she pulled in next to Jim Sullivan's van outside the animal hospital. Why was he here again? Just a couple of days before, he'd picked up enough medical supplies to last a month.

Joe Dolan, still acting as her escort, parked his van beside Rachel's Range Rover and waited while she went in to pick up vaccines for the dogs they hoped to capture that night.

Inside, Rachel stopped in the pharmacy room doorway. This time Sullivan was taking bandaging materials, rolls of gauze and surgical tape. He looked like a farmer in his old jeans and plaid shirt, and his battered boots gave off a distinct odor of manure. "Hello again," Rachel said.

"Dr. Goddard," Sullivan answered, without looking her way.

"Did you forget something when you were here the other day?"

One corner of his mouth lifted in a humorless smile. "Obviously."

She moved past him, found the right key on her key ring, and unlocked the vaccine cabinet. "Thanks again for helping out at the rabies clinic," she said. "And for helping us get that big dog under control."

He responded with a grunt. Whatever friendly feeling had led him to assist her the day before had apparently vanished overnight.

"Dr. Sullivan—Jim—you treat some dogs on the farms you visit, don't you?"

"Some, yeah." He stuffed boxes of gauze rolls into his leather bag as if he couldn't get it done and leave fast enough. "No point in people bringing their dogs all the way into town when I'll be stopping by anyway."

"Oh, sure. That's fine with me." Rachel plucked a vial of distemper vaccine from the cabinet. "I was just wondering if any farm dogs have gone missing lately."

He raised his head, frowning, and almost met her eyes. "You mean like the dogs in those notices out front?"

"Yes."

"Not that I know of."

"Good. That's a relief." She turned the key in the cabinet lock. "I was afraid there'd been some disappearances we hadn't heard about."

"Well, like I said, none that I know of." He zipped his case, lifted it off the counter, and turned toward the door.

"One other thing before you go," Rachel said.

Sullivan hesitated before turning back to her. "Yeah?"

"I think it would be a good idea for you to bring all your records in so we can make copies, and in the future I'd like to keep duplicate copies here routinely." He would fight her on this, Rachel was sure. He wouldn't win.

Sullivan looked directly into her eyes now, pinning her with a cold stare. "Why? What brought this on?"

God, the man had an intimidating manner. If Rachel worked for him instead of the other way around, she would avoid contact as much as possible. "It's the proper business procedure. This is my practice, and I'm accountable for every aspect of it. I don't want things going on that I'm not aware of."

"Are you accusing me of something?"

"Of course not. I—"

"If you think I'm incompetent, just say so. You could've gotten rid of me when you bought the place."

Rachel took a moment to breathe deeply. He had good reason for his resentment. It wasn't personal. "I've never said you're incompetent, and I've never thought so, not for a second. Look.

Let's clear the air once and for all. You wanted to buy the clinic. I was an outsider and I ended up with it. If you don't like the way things turned out, I understand. But I own the practice, and I'm legally responsible for what every employee does on the job, whether you're working in the building or outside. So please, bring in your records to be copied, and keep copies of all your future records on file here."

"Yes, *ma'am*." Sullivan pivoted toward the door.

He might walk out on her again, but Rachel wouldn't let him have the last word. "I'm glad we understand each other," she said to his back.

Sometimes, Rachel thought as the door swung shut behind him, she envied her patients the ability to produce a deep growl or a wet hiss.

◇◇◇

The full moon cast a bright silvery glow over the pastures and cornfields as Rachel and Joe Dolan sped past in the county animal control van. Tom rode in a cruiser ahead of them. They would spend at least an hour searching for the dogs, but Tom and Joe had something else going on later in the evening that Tom refused to talk about. Rachel was sure he was planning a raid on a dogfight, and the thought of the violence that might erupt scared her witless.

"We don't really need security, do we?" Joe asked. "If Ethan Hall's told his pals to back off."

"Tom's not sure they have," Rachel said. "Ethan probably didn't tell anybody to set our house on fire, but somebody did. Those people enjoy scaring us too much to stop. They're probably beyond listening to Ethan."

Joe didn't answer, and in the silence Rachel felt sure his thoughts were taking the same track as hers. If anyone wanted to hurt her and Joe, Tom alone wouldn't be much protection.

Back at Tom's farm, every light in the house was burning and several neighbors, including Tom's uncle and a couple of retired deputies, had a poker game going in the living room. The house, at least, was safe for now. But what would they encounter out here on the dark back roads of Mason County?

Relax. Concentrate on the job at hand. What they were doing was necessary, not only for the safety of the feral pack but also for the safety of Mason County's citizens and the local farmers' livestock. The dogs had to be captured.

A couple of sightings had been reported tonight in the southern half of the county, not far from Tom's place. Rachel knew this part of the county better than any other because she had lived out here on the McKendrick horse farm for more than a year before moving in with Tom. Many of the people in this area grew crops and raised livestock for their own use and for sale at the county farmer's market. Some were younger couples who had day jobs and tended their farms on the weekends. Others worked full-time on land their families had owned for generations. It wasn't an easy way to make a living. Losing anything, from eggs to livestock, could create a hardship.

Rachel's cell phone rang, and she dug it out of her shirt pocket. Tom was calling from the car ahead of them. "I just heard from dispatch," he said. "The dogs are on the Buckham farm right now. It's right down the road."

Rachel passed the message to Joe, and he sped up, staying close behind Tom's cruiser.

"The Buckhams have got calves," Joe told her. "They haven't lost any yet, but one of them got its hindquarters torn up pretty bad the last time the dogs came around. Dr. Sullivan had to patch it up."

"Let's go get the alpha dog," Rachel said, sounding more confident than she felt.

"He looks like a real mean son of a bitch."

"That he does." Rachel's mouth had gone dry. Mrs. Turner seemed sure she could handle the dog. She probably could, after he was locked in a cage. Rachel was more concerned about whether she and Joe could get him into that cage.

The Buckhams' small wood frame farmhouse sat close to the road, with rolling hills spread out beyond it in the moonlight, looking like a spot the entire modern world had passed by. At the entrance to the gravel driveway, a tin mailbox on a wooden post leaned to one side.

Even before Joe powered down his window, Rachel heard the dogs baying.

The elderly farmer emerged from the house and hurried over to Joe's van. "You got here in the nick of time. I penned up my cows to keep the calves safe, but those dogs just went right over the fence. Hurry, before they kill one of my calves."

"We'll get rid of them, Mr. Buckham," Joe said.

With Tom leading, they raced past the house toward the pen. The noise rose in volume, dogs baying and yipping, calves bleating, frantic cows bellowing. Joe raised his voice to be heard over the racket pouring in through his open window. "I don't think we have to hide. They're too busy to notice us."

Joe and Tom braked their vehicles twenty feet from the pen. Rachel watched, horrified, as the cows and calves roiled and stumbled, with dogs nipping at their legs and flanks.

Joe lifted the tranquilizer gun from the rack behind their seats. "Getting a shot won't be easy," he said. "I need to get up higher—"

He flung open his door. Dart gun in hand, he mounted the hood of the van. Tom clambered up beside him with a handheld spotlight and focused it on the pen.

Holding her breath, Rachel watched Joe take aim. He released a dart. A split second later a dog yelped, then let out a long howl. "I got him!" Joe yelled. "I got the leader."

In the confusion, Rachel couldn't see which animal Joe had hit.

The other dogs panicked and jumped at the fence, clawing their way over. Joe reloaded, aimed again. A dart caught one of the fleeing dogs in the flank.

In seconds, the rest of the pack vanished, leaving behind the two Joe had darted. Rachel jumped out with her medical case. She sprinted to the nearest dog, the one outside the pen. A medium-sized Lab mix. She touched its chest, confirmed it was breathing, then ran to the gate of the pen.

Tom and Joe went in ahead of her. They herded the cows out of the way while Rachel dropped to her knees beside the leader of the feral pack. He was solid black, filthy from head to tail, undernourished but probably well over a hundred pounds, with a pit bull face and rottweiler body. He breathed in ragged gulps.

Rachel yanked the dart from his flank, then pulled a muzzle from her case and slipped it over the dog's nose and mouth.

His head jerked up. He shook off the muzzle and bared his teeth. A growl sounded deep in his throat.

"Oh my god." Rachel scooted backward. "Joe! He's not under!"

"Rachel!" Tom cried. He ran to her side, grabbed her and pulled her back from the dog.

The animal struggled to his feet, swayed, and lunged. Rachel and Tom jumped out of his path and hit the fence. Trapped. Tom yanked his pistol from his holster.

"Don't shoot him!" Rachel cried. "Joe, dart him again!"

The dog wobbled for a moment, then regained his balance. Snarling, he threw himself at them again, his bared teeth glinting in the moonlight.

Joe fired a dart into his flank. The dog spun, teeth snapping, trying to get at the dart. Within seconds, he dropped to the ground.

The three of them stayed back, watching the animal. The cows complained and bumped into each other.

"Is he really out this time?" Tom asked.

Rachel ran her tongue over her dry lips. She could hear the beat of her pulse in her temples. "I think so." She scooped the muzzle off the ground.

"Be careful," Tom said.

With Tom on one side and Joe on the other, hovering like bodyguards, Rachel knelt and buckled the muzzle onto the dog.

"Get him in the van, and I'll take care of the other one." Rachel jumped to her feet and ran out to the second dog. Sweeping a flashlight beam over it, she realized it was a pregnant female, her abdomen bulging below visible ribs. She had bare patches on her flank and shoulder, and her dirty coat looked thin all over her body. Rachel pulled out the tranquilizer dart and fastened a muzzle in place. "Poor little things," she murmured, laying a hand on the bulge. They would be born malnourished and underdeveloped. In the meantime, they sapped energy from a mother who didn't have it to give.

Rachel rode in the back of the van and administered vaccines to both dogs as Joe sped to the sanctuary. She also drew two vials of blood from the alpha dog for DNA tests. She studied the big male, wondering about his history and what had made him the leader of the pack. Using her flashlight, she found scars on his face, throat, chest and flanks. This dog had been in fights, probably a lot of them, and his wounds had been cleaned and repaired by an expert. Rachel believed she was looking at an escapee from the dogfighting operation.

Chapter Twenty-five

The security lights aimed at the pens cast long shadows over the alpha dog's body. Tom crouched next to Rachel and switched on his Maglite to get a better view of the caged animal. Every part of his body bore the deep scars of a lifetime of fighting to survive. Mud and bits of leaf litter matted his black hair, and he stank of something dead and decaying.

"He looks capable of killing a grown man." He squeezed Rachel's shoulder. "He could have killed you tonight."

Rachel sucked in a breath and stood abruptly. "You had a gun and Joe had the darts. I was perfectly safe."

And scared to death, Tom thought, *like I was.* In his years as a cop, he'd been shot, he'd had a maniac come at him with a knife, he'd gone into places he couldn't expect to come out of in one piece, but nothing matched the pure terror that gripped him when this dog roused from his stupor and went for Rachel.

Tom knew she would never admit how scared she'd been, and she wouldn't want to hear about his fears for her safety. Rising, he said, "His coat's the same color and length as the dog that attacked Hall. But all the evidence is against the whole pack being involved."

"Right," Rachel said. "And a dog that's firmly established as leader of a pack isn't likely to go out alone and attack somebody. Especially not on the command of a human. This isn't the dog that killed Dr. Hall, and the DNA will prove it. I don't want anybody demanding that we destroy an animal just because he *could* have done it."

"I can't promise quick action from the crime lab on the DNA. The state won't give it priority treatment."

Rachel sighed, and Tom watched her go through a mental process that had become familiar to him, setting aside a nagging concern and focusing on the task in front of her. Her ability to do that consistently was one of many traits he admired, regardless of how often she exasperated him.

"I wish we had somewhere to stash this guy where the rest of them couldn't see him, hear him, or smell him," Rachel said. "They're going to react to his presence, and that'll make them harder to handle. I can't take him to the clinic. He'd have the place in an uproar. I have to put my patients first."

Mrs. Turner walked up beside her and peered in at the black dog, wrinkling her nose. "Oo-wee. He's been rollin' in somethin' that died a *long* time ago. I think I oughta get my Bobby out of here so he won't have to deal with any bad influence."

"Who's Bobby?" Tom asked.

"The little brown one, the second one we caught." Rachel said, gesturing toward the other end of the line of enclosures. "Mrs. Turner wants to adopt him."

"Now wait a minute," Tom said. "I don't think it's safe to rush into anything. Wait and make sure you know what the animal's temperament is."

"I've been watchin' him," Mrs. Turner said. "I know his nature. And I know he'd be better off livin' in the house with me than he is out here where that beast—" She flung a hand toward the big black dog. "—can get him all riled up."

"What makes you think your own dogs will accept him?" Tom argued.

She folded her arms and gave him a smug little smile. "They already have. I brought 'em out to visit him. They got along just fine. They was playin' together, best they could with a fence between 'em."

"If you feel confident about him," Rachel said, "I don't see any reason why you can't take him in tonight, but don't turn him loose in the house around your cats."

"You don't have to tell me to look out for my cats. It's a big house. We'll be just fine. And I thought about fleas too, if you're about to bring that up. Holly's makin' him a nice warm bed in the basement right now. We'll give him a bath in the mornin'. I've got a leash all ready to use." Mrs. Turner set off toward the brown dog's enclosure.

Rachel laughed. "I wondered where Holly disappeared to. They didn't have much doubt that I'd give the okay."

"This is dangerous," Tom said. "I can't believe you're going along with it."

"Don't worry. I trust her instincts. She knows what she's doing."

Tom wasn't so sure about Mrs. Turner's instincts. He usually trusted Rachel's judgment about animals, though. If she was okay with this, he should be too. But he would have a hard time watching any of the feral dogs go into people's homes. "I hope you won't let anybody walk off with this one," he said, looking down at the brute in the cage.

"I don't know what he'll turn out to be like," Rachel said. "He's been abused. I think he's been used in dogfights. Look at all those scars. His wounds were treated properly by someone who knew how to do it, but his psychological wounds won't be so easy to deal with. He probably hates people."

"Well, yeah, I'd say he's already proved that to us. Christ, is he coming around already, with all that dope in him?"

The animal began to stir, snuffling and snorting as he tried to lift his head.

"He's pretty amazing," Rachel said, "but with two doses, I think he'll be groggy the rest of the night. Which is just as well. He's not going to be happy about being here."

Tom moved the light over the dog's scars. He'd been ripped open too many times to count. "Yeah, he's a fighter. A veteran. But he's been living with other dogs, hunting with them, cooperating with them to stay alive."

"Fighting is what people forced him to do," Rachel said, "not necessarily what he wanted to do. Do you think he could have escaped from the local operation?"

"Maybe. But he could have been dumped out here too, like the rest of the pack."

"There's a database of DNA from fighting dogs. We might be able to find out what part of the country he came from. That probably won't help your investigation, but it's one more piece of information about the trade in fighting dogs."

Tom shone his light on his watch. "If you're done here, I'll run you home. Joe and I have to get going."

"You're not going to question a suspect with the dog warden along," Rachel said. "So what are you doing tonight?"

"I'd rather not say right now."

He saw the flash of irritation in her face, saw her quickly extinguish it and put on a neutral expression. He knew she wasn't done with the subject, though.

She picked up her medical bag and they started toward his car. Joe Dolan waited, leaning against his van. He and Tom were going to meet Brandon, Dennis, and several other deputies at headquarters and head out as a group to the dogfight.

Mrs. Turner and the mutt she'd named Bobby emerged from his pen as Tom and Rachel approached. She'd fastened a collar and a leash on him, apparently without any trouble. Wagging his tail, the dog strained toward Rachel. Tom tried to grab her and pull her out of harm's way, but she shook off his hand and stooped to pet the animal. Without any fear, she scratched him and let him lick her face. Tom drew a deep breath and reminded himself that she knew animals and he had to trust her judgment.

Mrs. Turner led her charge away and Rachel pulled a tissue from her jeans pocket to wipe dog spit off her cheek. Falling into step with Tom again, she said, "You're going to a dogfight tonight, aren't you? You're staging a raid."

Tom sighed. "Yes," he admitted. "I got a tip on a location. I'm taking a team of deputies and Joe's going to handle the dogs."

They stopped by his car and he opened the passenger door for her. Rachel paused before getting in. "Is it going to be dangerous?"

"Nobody's going to get hurt."

She ducked her head so he couldn't see her face, couldn't tell whether she really believed him. When she looked up at him again, she said, "You should have a vet along. I'll go with you."

"No. Not a chance. I don't want you getting hurt—" He broke off, realizing his mistake.

She nodded. "So it will be dangerous. You don't have to protect me, Tom. I'd rather know the truth. Believe it or not, I can handle it."

"I didn't see any reason to worry you. I've been on these raids before, and nobody's ever been hurt. Nobody'll get hurt tonight."

Rachel gave him a long, steady look. Shadows played across her face as a breeze rustled through the trees and shook loose a shower of leaves. For a moment he thought she was angry. But she set down her bag, moved closer, and wrapped her arms around his waist. As he enclosed her in his arms, she pressed her face to his neck and whispered, "Be careful. Please. I couldn't take it if anything happened to you."

The full harvest moon, high in the sky, made it easier than Tom expected to find the turnoff Burt Morgan had described. He pulled onto the shoulder and braked, and four more cars driven by deputies lined up behind his cruiser. Joe Dolan brought up the rear in his animal control van.

"Man, when he told you it was just a path, he wasn't kidding," Brandon said. Powering down his window, he focused his flashlight on the ground. "I can see tire tracks, though. There's definitely been vehicles going in and out of there."

The plan was to park on the road so their vehicles wouldn't be spotted by anybody attending the dogfight. They would go in on foot. Joe would wait on the road until they needed him.

Silently they all piled out of their cars and gathered at the head of the path. The Blackwood twins, tall blond mirror images, practically vibrated with controlled excitement. Dennis Murray, stolid as always, pushed his chronically slipping glasses up his nose and rested a hand on the butt of his holstered pistol. Grady Duncan, a middle-aged veteran of several dogfighting busts, looked as calm as a man out for an evening stroll.

Tom took the lead going in, shotgun in hand. He hoped they'd be able to go the distance without using their flashlights. With the trees shedding leaves, they didn't have the dense cover the woods would have provided in summer, and one spot of light would be enough to give them away.

They walked without speaking. The woods grew denser, with branches arching over the path and shutting out most of the moonlight. Tom couldn't see his own boots anymore. He stepped on rocks, stumbled on roots. Behind him, he heard quiet swearing every few minutes when somebody hit an obstacle. The last crickets of the season chirped in the leaf litter and somewhere a screech owl let loose its bone-chilling cry.

Where the hell was the place? They'd been walking almost ten minutes. Tom expected to hear raucous cries from the dogfight audience, but the woods remained hushed and peaceful. He'd feel stupid if it turned out Burt was gaming him, sending him on a wild goose chase.

Suddenly the path veered to the right, and there it was, a broad open space in the woods, bathed in moonlight. A circle of wire fencing created a pen in the center. And not a person in sight.

"Damn," Tom said.

Brandon came up behind him. "You suppose they heard we were onto them and called it off?"

"Either that, or this is just one of several spots they use, and tonight they're holding a fight somewhere else."

Switching on his Maglite, Tom moved forward, sweeping the beam over the ground. The trip wouldn't be a total loss if they found evidence that dogfights had taken place here. Empty beer cans and cigarette packs littered the ground around tree stumps.

He walked around the pen, examining the five-foot high fencing and the shallow pit inside. Clinging to the fence wire he found half a dozen tufts of hair, a couple with bloody skin attached, dried and withered. Patches of a darker substance on the dirt looked like dried blood.

"Let's get some bags from the cars and collect everything," Tom told Dennis. "We'll get fingerprints off the trash, and we can compare the dog hair with—"

A shot cracked the air and Tom heard a bullet whiz past his head.

"Get down!" he yelled.

The men dropped to their knees and pulled their weapons.

"Where'd it come from?" Dennis whispered.

"I don't see anything. Hold your fire." His heart galloping, Tom scanned the woods for movement. Nothing. But he and his men were exposed, easy targets.

Another shot rang out, and Tom heard the slug slam into a tree behind him. The shooter was right in front of them but they couldn't see him among the trees.

"Captain? Return fire?" Brandon urged. He had his pistol in both hands, aimed toward the woods.

"Hold on," Tom ordered.

The third shot made him jump. It hit the ground two feet in front of him, inside the fence, and sent a shower of dust into the air. It came from a different position, to their left. Was it only one person, moving around? Or were there more, spread out in the woods and just waiting to open up on them with a volley of shots?

The path that offered escape was twenty-five, thirty feet away. If more than one shooter lurked in the woods, they could all be killed before they made it. And if they stayed here, firing back at an invisible, moving target while they crouched in the open with only a wire fence as a shield, they would certainly be killed.

They didn't have any choice. Tom raised his shotgun. "When I fire, I want all of you to get out of here," he whispered.

"Captain," Brandon protested, "you can't stay—"

"Don't argue with me. Do what I tell you."

"Tom," Dennis said, "let's all go. All of us."

"I'll be right behind you." He shouldered his shotgun, balancing it on the edge of the wire fence. "Okay now. Be ready."

He fired into the woods, and the men took off.

An answering shot pinged off the fence a foot from his head.

Tom jumped up, fired again, turned and ran.

Two more shots followed him. A bullet split the bark on a tree and drove splinters into his face.

He ran on through the dark woods, following the other men. The shooting stopped and he couldn't hear anyone behind him, but that didn't mean the deputies were safe. The shooter could be taking a parallel route through the trees.

Tom emerged from the woods breathless and sweating. The other men were getting into their cars. Brandon waited by Tom's cruiser, the passenger door open. Joe's van was already speeding away.

"Get out of here," Tom called out. "Go home."

He slid into his car. "We're going to see Burt Morgan right now," he told Brandon as he started the engine. "That son of a bitch has a lot to answer for."

Chapter Twenty-six

Rachel pushed herself up in bed, flipped her pillow again, and punched it a few times, wishing she could pound away the thoughts that kept her awake. With every wallop she told herself it was a ridiculous notion, but there it sat in her head, like an obnoxious visitor with no intention of leaving. When she'd seen the big dog's neat scars, obviously the result of professional-level care of his wounds, something had clicked in her mind. Now she couldn't get rid of the image of the irascible Dr. Jim Sullivan filling his case with antibiotics and surgical supplies.

She lay down again.

Sullivan was a veterinarian. He had a legitimate use for those supplies. True, he harbored no warm and fuzzy feelings about animals, but Rachel wanted to believe he was an ethical practitioner. How could she suspect him of being connected to dogfighting?

One part of her mind told her she was reacting to his obvious contempt for her as a boss.

Another part of her mind asked how much she really knew about the man.

Next to nothing.

She'd heard something about his son having problems—drugs?—and his wife leaving him, but she couldn't recall any details. Most of the time he operated like a phantom employee, doing his work beyond her sight and supervision, coming in after hours to pick up supplies or drop off the checks and cash clients had paid to him directly. Most of the income from his farm visits arrived in check form through the mail, and his salary was deposited directly to his bank account.

Sullivan had years of experience. He was established as the farm vet everyone called, and he generated a lot of income for the clinic. Rachel had trusted him as a professional. But he could be getting away with murder, for all she knew.

She sat up again, drawing her knees to her chest. At the foot of the bed, Frank emitted a sleepy croak of protest at being disturbed. Even with the curtains drawn, the hastily installed security lights around the outside of the house lit the windows and reminded her that she had to be protected from people who wanted to hurt her. A deputy sat in a cruiser in front of the house, and he would be there until Tom came home.

Where was Tom? What was taking so long?

She told herself that booking the men arrested at the dogfight would take hours. If anything had happened to Tom, someone would have called her by now. If any of the animals needed immediate medical attention, Tom would have called her himself. She had remained dressed and ready to go until midnight, past the time when she might have been summoned, then gone to bed. She might as well have stayed up, though, because she wouldn't sleep until Tom came home.

Maybe the raid tonight would answer a lot of questions. It might lead to the recovery of the stolen pets. The dogs used in the fights would be rescued. Tom might find out whether the leader of the pack was an escapee from the fights, and who had done such an admirable job of stitching up his wounds.

Tom was still in a rage when he hit the cruiser's brakes and killed the engine outside Burt Morgan's log cabin. He didn't see any lights in the house, and only the full moon illuminated the clearing. Burt's truck and his girlfriend's car sat in front of the cabin.

"He's either gone to bed without a care in the world," Tom said, "or he's waiting for us. You know the drill. Let's go."

"He could open fire before we ever make it to the door," Brandon protested.

"All right, stay in the car. I'll handle it."

"No, Captain, I didn't mean—I'm going with you."

They stepped out of the car, drew their pistols, and charged up the steps to the porch. They positioned themselves on either side of the door.

"Burt!" Tom banged on the door. "It's Tom Bridger. Open up!"

He went on hammering with his fist until a faint glow appeared through the uncurtained window on the far side of Brandon's position.

In a moment, the door flew open and Morgan stood there with a battery-operated lantern in one hand, wearing boxer shorts and a tee shirt that barely covered his bulging belly. His two big mutts, Rambo and Bullet, flanked him, growling at Tom. "Shut up," Morgan snapped at the dogs, and they both promptly fell silent and sat on their haunches. "What the hell, Bridger? What time is it?"

"You son of a bitch." Tom pointed a finger in Morgan's grizzled face. "You set us up. Somebody could've been killed out there tonight."

"What?" Morgan's eyes flicked to Tom's pistol. "What are you talkin' about?"

"I trusted you, I gave you a chance to prove yourself, and you set us up for an ambush."

"Hey, now. Whoa, whoa." Morgan raised a hand to stop Tom. "You sayin' somethin' went wrong?"

Another lantern light swam out of the darkness behind Morgan, and Tom saw the man's woman friend, Sylvia, clutching a terry-cloth robe around her plump body as she approached the door.

"Come out here," Tom ordered Morgan. "And shut the door behind you."

"Well, all right, if it'll calm you down any. You gonna put that gun away first, though?"

Satisfied that he and Brandon were in no immediate danger, Tom holstered his weapon. Brandon did the same, but kept one hand on the butt.

Morgan stepped out and pulled the door closed on Sylvia and the dogs. "Now tell me what you're so riled up about. What happened?"

"You know damned well what happened," Tom said. "I took your word for it and took my men out to that spot you directed me to. There was nothing going on, nobody in sight. Then somebody opened fire on us."

"Good God almighty. Anybody get hit?"

"No, thank God, and no thanks to you." Although Morgan sounded genuinely concerned, Tom knew the man was a skilled liar when he had to be. "They were hiding in the woods, waiting for us. At least one person, maybe more. They knew we were coming. Who did you tell, Burt?"

"Look now," Morgan said. "I don't know how to make you believe me, but I didn't rat on you, I didn't pass the word about a raid goin' down."

"You told somebody. How the hell did they know if it didn't come from you?"

"I can't answer that for you. All I can tell you, and I'd swear it on a Bible, is I didn't warn them. Hell, I don't even know who's runnin' the fights this time around. I was just passin' on what I heard about where the fights are goin' on. I promised Syl I was gonna stay out of that life, and I'm keepin' my promise."

Against his better judgment, Tom was beginning to believe Morgan was telling him the truth. "So how were you able to get information about the fights, if you don't even know who's involved?"

"I know plenty of people that go to the fights and bet on them. Don't ask me who they are, 'cause they'd deny it to their dyin' breath if you called 'em on it. You couldn't pin anything on them anyway unless you caught them at it. But they go, and they still try to get me interested. That's how I found out."

"And these friends of yours haven't mentioned who's running the fights?"

Morgan shook his head. "They don't throw around names. They know better."

His anger dissolving into weariness, Tom rubbed the knot of tension at the back of his neck. "Burt, they knew we were coming. It was an ambush. That's the one thing I'm sure of. If it didn't come from you—" Tom looked pointedly at the house.

"Oh, no," Morgan said. "No, sir. Don't you go blamin' Syl for any of this. I'd put my life in that woman's hands. She knows she'd be settin' me up for big trouble if she told people I was helpin' the cops. I never told her exactly what was goin' on anyway."

"I want to talk to her," Tom said.

Morgan sighed, but after a moment he called, "Syl? Could you step outside?"

She opened the door promptly, which told Tom she'd been listening. The two dogs barreled out around her, knocking her off-balance. Holding a lantern in one hand, she grabbed the door frame with the other to steady herself before she stepped onto the porch. "What is it, hon?"

"Captain Bridger's got some questions for you."

She pulled the terrycloth robe tighter around her throat, her gaze darting between Morgan and Tom, then over to Brandon, who stood off to one side. "Questions about what?"

"Have you been telling people about Burt's dealings with me? Telling people he's helping the Sheriff's Department?"

"Lord, no." Her brassy blonde hair was crushed on the right side where she'd been sleeping on it, and she brushed at it self-consciously with her fingers. "That's the last thing I'd be blabbin' about. You think I want to get him shot?" She threw a pleading look at Morgan. "Honey, you don't think I'd do that, do you?"

"Naw, I don't."

They faced Tom, united.

He didn't trust either of them, but he also didn't see any reason for them to lie. Sylvia had no cause to put half a dozen deputies in danger, and Morgan seemed to have genuinely turned his life around with her help.

Yet somebody had alerted the dogfighters that deputies were coming tonight.

"This isn't over," Tom told them. "I'll going to find out who was responsible for what happened tonight, and you'd better hope I don't turn up proof the two of you were involved."

Chapter Twenty-seven

Rachel lay awake, staring at the bedroom ceiling, listening for Tom's car. When all this was over, she decided, she would insist that Tom take down the security lights, or at least promise never to turn them on again. Even blinds and drawn curtains couldn't shut out all the light, and the light kept her awake.

No. Worrying about Tom kept her awake. She sighed and shut her eyes, hoping to rest, if not sleep.

Close to one in the morning, she heard a car door slam outside. She leapt from the bed and looked out the window to see Tom leaning down to talk to the young deputy who'd been parked in front of the house all evening. Tom straightened, thumped the top of the cruiser, and the deputy drove off.

Rachel ran downstairs and opened the front door before Tom reached it.

"Did it go okay?" she asked when he came in. No, it hadn't. His grim expression told her that. Rachel closed the door and slid the bolt in place. "Tom? What's wrong?"

Before answering, he yanked off his gun belt and stashed it on the shelf in the hall closet, then shucked his uniform jacket and hung it up. "There wasn't any dogfight," he said, closing the closet door. "Somebody warned them about the raid."

"Oh no. I was hoping you could put an end to it tonight, rescue all those dogs—" Rachel broke off, realizing she wasn't making the situation any easier for Tom. "But it's just a temporary setback."

"Yeah, we'll put a stop to it one way or another." He flexed his shoulders as if they felt stiff. "I might as well tell you what happened before you hear it from somebody else."

A wave of apprehension flooded through her, but she instantly dismissed it as nonsense. Nothing had happened to Tom. He stood right in front of her, safe and sound. "Tell me what?" she asked.

"Let's talk upstairs," he said. "I need to get ready for bed. I'm dead tired." Placing an arm around her shoulders, he steered her toward the steps.

Holding her impatience in check, Rachel stayed silent as they mounted the stairs together. *He's fine, he's okay, he's home,* she told herself.

Halfway up, Tom said, "First of all, none of us got shot. Nobody was hit."

Rachel gasped and halted on the stairs, grabbing the front of his shirt to make him look at her. "Somebody was shooting at you?"

He nudged her to keep moving up the stairs. "Like I said, nobody got hurt. But somebody was waiting for us. It was an ambush."

Rachel lost her footing and stumbled on the steps. Tom's strong arm circled her waist and kept her from falling. "An ambush? Who? How did they know—"

"I don't have any answers. It was one guy, two maybe, and I don't know who tipped them off."

When they reached the top of the stairs she put her arms around him and buried her face in his shoulder. She didn't think she could speak without letting her terror for him pour out. If it happened this time, she thought, it could happen the next time. And the next time, somebody could be killed. Tom could be killed.

He pulled her close for a tight hug. "It'll be over before long," he said when he let her go. "We'll get them and shut down their operation. We always do. I don't want you worrying about it."

How could she not worry? How could she not fear the worst every time he went out into the night in search of people who wouldn't hesitate to murder him? He worked in a place where almost everybody owned a gun and many people neither respected nor feared the police.

While Tom showered Rachel lay awake, wanting only to lie in his arms and appreciate the miracle of his surviving the ambush. He was doing his job, and living with a cop demanded strength and acceptance of the risks. When she'd moved in with Tom she thought she could handle these violent eruptions in their normally placid lives. Now she wondered if she could ever learn to live this way.

Tom crouched next to the fence around the pit, plucked a tuft of hair, skin and dried blood from the wire, and deposited it in a plastic bag. His boot prints from the night before still showed in the dirt, and being in the same spot brought back the memory of darkness and fear and a bullet whizzing by inches from his head.

He stood when he heard a vehicle approaching. What the hell? He'd given the order that everybody had to come to the clearing on foot to avoid destroying evidence at the dogfighting site. Around him, half a dozen deputies combed the ground for tufts of dog hair and any trash that might yield a fingerprint.

The new arrival was Sheriff Willingham in his personal car. He stopped at the end of the dirt road without entering the clearing. Swearing under his breath, Tom strode toward the vehicle. What was Willingham doing here? He wasn't physically capable of joining the search for evidence, and he'd slow them down if he started throwing out nonsensical orders. But Tom knew better than to tell the sheriff he shouldn't have bothered coming. He held the car door open while Willingham struggled out, his movements slow and clumsy, the effort bringing beads of sweat to his forehead.

He emerged from his car with a cane in hand, a concession to weakness that surprised Tom. His gray suit, white shirt, and tie meant he'd come straight from church. A tall, big-boned man, he'd lost so much weight in the past year that the jacket seemed to swallow his upper body, and Tom could see that only a tightly notched belt held the loose trousers up. He leaned on the cane, taking in the scene. "This is county land, you know. This patch was cleared and used for dogfights about fifteen years ago. Looks like somebody's been here lately and cut down the brush again."

The clearing looked bigger to Tom in the bright light of Sunday morning, and he estimated that close to twenty vehicles could park around the fringes. "This can't be the only spot they use," Tom said, "but they've used it recently." He held up the plastic bag containing bloody dog hair and skin.

"I'm surprised they didn't get in here and clean up every scrap of evidence before you could get back out," Willingham said. "Damned amateurs."

"They've been smart enough to keep their operation quiet for months," Tom said. "I knew the drug trade was getting back in full swing, but I thought that was our only problem. I didn't even suspect we had another dogfighting operation in the county until I saw what happened to Gordon Hall's dog."

"I wouldn't be surprised if the same people are behind the drug dealing and the dogfights." The sheriff heaved a sigh that made him sound personally burdened by all the evils of the world. "I came out to bring you some news. I tried to raise you on your cell phone, but I guess you can't get a signal."

Tom's first thought was that something had happened at the house. *Rachel.* He had a sudden sensation of falling, spinning through space, although he hadn't moved. He opened his suddenly dry mouth to ask, "What is it?"

"You don't have to look like the world's coming to an end. It's good news. Soo Jin Hall came out of her coma about an hour ago."

Relief swept through Tom, leaving him breathless. Rachel was safe. It took a few seconds for the full meaning of the news to sink in. "Is she talking? Has she said anything about—"

"No, no," the sheriff said. "They still have to get the tube out of her throat and see if she can breathe on her own. It'll be a while before she can talk, and the doctor says she's not likely to remember the accident."

"But she can tell us who might have cut her tires, and she can tell us why she was following Ethan. Is anybody in the family with her?"

"No, she's by herself," the sheriff said. "Listen, do you really believe that dog you caught last night was a fighter that got loose?"

Tom refocused his attention. "Seems likely."

"Well, then," the sheriff said, "it makes sense to me that he could be the dog that killed Hall."

Not this again, Tom thought. "I don't think he would have been out at night without his pack." He went on, cutting off the sheriff when the old man tried to interrupt. "We've got DNA off Hall's body, in any case. We'll prove one way or another whether the dog we caught was responsible. Until then, we have to keep looking into the people who might have wanted Hall dead."

The sheriff's sour expression told Tom he hadn't taken well to his chief deputy shutting down his argument. After a moment, Willingham said, "And just who are you looking at? You don't think Vicky Hall's got anything to do with it, I hope."

"No, we've pretty much ruled her out. All the evidence is that they had a solid relationship."

"Somebody at the hospital holding a grudge?"

"Plenty of them detested Hall, but Dennis and I have both been questioning people, and we haven't found anybody who would have gone so far as to turn a killer dog on him. Or anybody who has access to a killer dog, for that matter. Phoebe James and her husband—"

"Oh, come on now," the sheriff scoffed.

"I was about to say, they've got motive, but no connection we can find to anybody with a dog like that. We've taken a hard look at Wally Green, checked out his movements, the people he associates with. Same situation. And he's been so loudmouthed about hating Hall, he'd be crazy to act on it. He was the first person I questioned, with good reason. But I don't think he was involved."

"What about the rest of Hall's family?" Willingham asked. "That oldest boy of his has been nothing but trouble most of his life. I've heard tales about him and Gordon having screaming matches."

"Something's going on with Ethan," Tom said, "but I don't know what yet. Something made Soo Jin follow him the night she had her accident. And I think Beth Hall was with Pete Rasey when he firebombed my house—"

"When are you gonna throw that punk in jail? He's overdue."

"I have to wait until I have the evidence," Tom said.

"Then see that you get it. Save us a lot of trouble out of him in the future." Willingham straightened, preparing to leave. Before he got into his car, he added, "I still believe you might already have that killer dog in a pen. I have a high regard for Dr. Goddard, you know that, but trying to rescue all those wild dogs is a damned fool thing to do."

As the sheriff turned his car and drove back through the woods, Tom wasn't thinking about the dogs or the murder case. Looking up at the clear blue sky through a stark maze of tree branches, he thought of Soo Jin, who had begun life as an unwanted baby, lying in a hospital twenty-one years later without a single loved one present to rejoice when she regained consciousness.

Chapter Twenty-eight

The big black dog bared his teeth and threw himself at the fence like a battering ram. Instinctively Rachel jumped backward, pulling Holly and Joe Dolan with her.

"Like you predicted," Joe said, "he's not real happy to be here."

Drooling and snarling, the dog backed up and flung himself at the fence around his pen again, rattling the chain link.

"He can't get over," Rachel said, eyeing the top of the fence, six feet high. "And the footings are solid, right? He can't knock it down."

"He can't dig out either," Holly said. "That fence is sunk two feet deep in concrete, just like Joe told us to do."

"Even if he can't get out, he's going to hurt himself if he keeps this up."

Rachel didn't believe the dog had ever been anyone's pet. He'd been used in fights—and seeing his scars in daylight, she was positive his wounds had been treated by a professional. Should she tell Tom what she suspected about Jim Sullivan? She had no proof of anything. The dog could have been a fighter somewhere else and might have no connection to the local operation. If Tom started asking Sullivan questions, he might quit in a huff and she would lose the clinic's only farm vet. No, she would keep quiet for now, and figure out a way to prove or disprove her suspicions on her own before involving Tom.

The dog banged against the fence.

"Has he been eating?" Rachel asked.

"Oh, yeah," Holly said. She pointed to a large aluminum dish just inside the front of the pen. The dish was empty, licked clean. "We put it in when he was asleep, then we got out of the way so he couldn't see us. He ate every bit and had a real long drink."

Unable to get at them, the dog started barking. At the other end of the line of pens, the first mutt they'd captured began to whine in response to its former leader.

Rachel raised her voice to be heard over the racket. "We can't leave him here, not if we're going to bring in more dogs. It's bad for them and it's bad for him. He's overstimulated. He needs a quiet place without a lot of people around."

"I can isolate him at the pound," Joe said, "but I'll have to tranquilize him to move him. I hate to do it again this soon after—"

Rachel's cell phone rang. She dug it out of her shirt pocket and moved away from the barking dog to answer. Tom was calling. "Hi," she said, "what's up?"

"The dogs are out running around," Tom said. "The department's had half a dozen reports this morning about sightings in the same area. You and Joe need to get out there. I'll meet you."

◇◇◇

With Rachel in the passenger seat, Joe sped north in the animal control van, between mountains blanketed with fall foliage. This could be it, Rachel thought, their chance to get all the dogs at once and bring them to a safe place.

"Indian Mountain's out this way," Joe said when they'd been on the road for twenty minutes. "Isn't that where—"

"Yes," Rachel cut him off. "That's why I didn't want to tell Holly and her grandmother what part of the county we're headed for."

Although she appreciated its beauty, Rachel would always think of this area of Mason County the same way she thought of the McClure house, as a place where horrific things had happened. On top of Indian Mountain, the bones of Holly's aunt,

Pauline McClure, were uncovered by a crew clearing trees and brush for construction of an outsider's country retreat. Another discovery in a cave at the base of the mountain had changed Holly's life forever. The wealthy man who owned the mountain had decided he didn't want to spend time there after all, and he was still trying to sell it nine months later.

"There's Tom," Rachel said.

He was leaning against his cruiser at the side of the road. When Joe pulled in behind the police car, Tom walked back to talk to them. "It's damned hard to keep in touch out here," he said, "with the mountains breaking up the signals. The last I heard, the dogs were on a farm near here. They got into the hen house, looking for eggs, and the farmer ran them off. We'll see them if we keep moving around."

"I've got the darts and the cages," Joe said. "Let's roll."

Guided by spotty radio reports full of static, they drove from one farm to another. Nearly an hour passed before they caught sight of the dogs, trotting across a field through the brown stubs of corn plants. Tom, in the lead, slowed to keep pace with the dogs, and Joe stayed close behind the cruiser.

Rachel watched the animals with Joe's binoculars. "Ten of them left," she said. "They're all emaciated."

"Oh, man, it ticks me off when I think about anybody dumping dogs out here instead of taking them to a shelter. What the hell's wrong with people?"

"Maybe they think they're giving the animals a chance to live," Rachel said. "But out here on their own, they'll starve to death."

Joe didn't answer but his hands tightened on the steering wheel, and Rachel could hear his teeth grinding.

The dogs, frightened by the vehicles, picked up speed and sprinted through fallow fields. The animals ranged from small to medium sized, all of them mutts. A few showed traces of recognizable breeds in their head or body shapes, but nothing about them was special. Disposable dogs, Rachel thought, the kind that would be difficult to find new homes for once they got past the cute puppy stage.

"They can't keep running like this," Rachel said. "They're in such bad shape, I'm amazed they've lasted this long."

"Shit!" Joe exclaimed. "Look at that!"

Jolted, Rachel took her eyes off the dogs and looked up ahead, where Joe pointed. An old SUV had stopped on the road in the other lane, and four men piled out of it. All of them carried shotguns.

Tom's car lurched to a stop with a screech of tires. Joe pulled up behind the cruiser. Tom threw open his door and jumped out, drawing his gun.

The four men ignored Tom and lined up along the road, aiming their shotguns at the fleeing dogs.

"Oh god," Rachel moaned. She couldn't sit still while this happened. She reached for the door handle.

"Oh no you don't." Joe grabbed her arm. "You stay right where you are. Let Tom handle this."

Rachel watched, hands clamped over her mouth, as Tom took a stance on the road, raised his gun, and shouted at the men. They all looked around but didn't lower their weapons. One of the men, Rachel saw, was Ellis, the goon who'd stopped her at the Hall property. Joe powered down his window in time for them to hear Ellis yell at Tom, "We're takin' care of this once and for all. Stay out of our way, Bridger."

"Get back in your car and get out of here," Tom said.

"Go to hell," Ellis said.

"I'll shoot that damned gun out of your hands if I have to. You might lose a few fingers."

"You wouldn't dare," Ellis sneered.

"I never make a threat unless I'm ready to back it up."

In the silence that followed, nobody moved. Tom kept his weapon trained on the four men. They stared back at him with their shotguns raised.

Rachel's lungs burned from lack of air. She gulped in a breath.

"Joe?" Tom called without looking around.

Joe leaned out his window. "Yeah, Captain?"

"Follow the dogs. Don't lose them. I'll catch up with you."

"No!" Rachel cried. "We can't leave Tom here alone!"

"He knows what he's doing," Joe said.

Rachel's heart banged in her chest as Joe pulled the van around the cruiser and drove on past the men. She twisted in her seat to keep Tom in sight.

"There's a patch of woods up ahead," Joe said. "If the dogs go in there, we'll lose them."

She couldn't look at the dogs. She couldn't take her eyes off Tom.

Joe checked the rearview mirror. "Looks like he got through to them."

The men were climbing back into the SUV. Rachel thought she might faint with relief. "Oh, thank god," she gasped.

"What did you expect?" Joe asked. "Those guys know we saw them. We could identify every one of them. They wouldn't have let us go if they planned to shoot Tom."

"My head knows that," Rachel said, her heart still racing, her mouth dust-dry, "but they scared the hell out of me anyway." *Calm down, calm down, he's safe,* she told herself.

"Watch the dogs," Joe said. "We don't want to lose them."

She faced forward and made herself focus on the pack of animals streaking toward the woods.

They had left the farms behind and entered an area where trees and brush crowded the pavement, leaving no clear space on either side for the dogs to run. Rachel expected them to vanish into the woods. But suddenly they veered onto the road in the path of the van. Joe slammed on his brakes, throwing Rachel forward against her seat belt.

The dogs ran on the road for half a mile. Glancing in the rearview mirror, Rachel saw Tom's cruiser close behind the van. Their energy drained, their tongues lolling, the dogs now moved at little more than a trot. Joe and Tom slowed their vehicles to stay with them.

We're killing these poor animals, Rachel thought. The dogs were using up their pitifully low reserves of energy and strength.

Abruptly the whole pack cut to the left. Then they were gone.

Joe braked, and Rachel jumped out. "Where did they go?" she called to Tom, who had stopped behind the van. "Where are they?"

Getting out of the cruiser, Tom pointed across the road.

Rachel's gaze followed, and she realized with a start where they were. Indian Mountain loomed before them.

"Do you see it?" Tom said. He pointed to an opening at the base of the mountain, a narrow hole no more than three feet high and wide that was visible only because the leaves had dropped from the wild bushes around it. Beyond the opening, Rachel saw nothing but darkness.

"Is that the cave—"

"Yeah," Tom said. "Where we found her."

Her. Holly's mother, or at least part of her. Rachel shuddered. "The dogs are living in there?"

"Looks like it. They went straight for it. They could hole up here during the day and nobody would ever bother them."

"Well," Joe said, "we need to bother them now. Y'all got any ideas about how to get them out of there?"

Tom shook his head. "Joe, a dogcatcher's supposed to know these things."

"Well, heck, I never had to get a whole pack of dogs out of a cave before. Cut me some slack, will you?"

"I think we're all about to have a learning experience," Rachel said. "How deep is the cave?"

"About thirty feet," Tom said, "if I remember right. It's low all the way, high enough for a bear to walk in, but not for a man to stand upright."

"Obviously we're not going in after them," Rachel said. "We have to make them come out."

"Any chance we could get some more of your men to help?" Joe asked.

"No. Most of them are still searching the woods at the dogfighting site, and the rest are following up tips about Hall's murder."

"We can do this by ourselves," Rachel said, "but we have to get them out of the cave." She looked at Joe. "Don't you carry food to use as a lure for strays?"

"Yeah, I've got some real stinky stuff dogs always go for when they're hungry," Joe said. "And I've got two big traps we can set up. We can bait the traps and put them at the mouth of the cave. Unless they all try to get at the food at once, we could trap a couple at a time and move them to cages."

"You don't have enough cages for all of them, though," Rachel pointed out. "We'll have to tie some of them up in the van for transport."

"Let's not get ahead of ourselves," Tom said. "I think you ought to plan on coming out here more than once."

"No," Rachel said. "I'm not leaving a single dog out here to get shot. My goal is to get them all, and damn it, that's what we're going to do. I don't want to hear any more talk about giving up, okay?"

"Yes, ma'am. Whatever you say, ma'am."

"And don't make fun of me."

"No, ma'am. Wouldn't think of it, ma'am."

Rachel gave him a grudging grin. "Just watch your attitude, pal, or you'll pay a price at home."

Tom laughed. "All right," he said, "let's do this thing."

They moved their vehicles out of sight down the road. Tom and Joe unfolded the wire traps while Rachel emptied canned food into two bowls.

"Whew," Tom said. "That stuff smells like a dead skunk."

"The worse it stinks, the more they like it," Joe said.

"No more talking," Rachel said. She placed the food inside the cages. "Let them think we're gone."

Moving silently, Joe and Rachel placed the traps in the opening of the cave. The three of them withdrew, hid behind trees across the road, and waited for the sound of the spring-loaded traps to snap shut. Twenty minutes passed. Thirty minutes.

Rachel was beginning to lose hope when she heard the first *clank,* followed immediately by the second. She shot a look at Joe, who grinned back at her. *Yes.*

Stepping out from behind her tree, she saw two dogs the size of beagles circling inside the traps, pawing at the steel mesh.

Tom and Joe ran across the road, snatched up the traps, and raced back to Joe's van. They lifted the traps with the dogs into the back, clambered in after them, and swung the doors shut. A couple of minutes later the doors opened and Tom and Joe jumped out with the empty traps. While Rachel climbed into the van, Joe baited the traps again. He and Tom carried them back to the cave mouth.

Rachel stayed in the van with the two scared dogs. Both of them shrank away from her, but when she poured bottled water through the wire screen into the bowls attached to the inside, the dogs eagerly lapped it up. She refilled the dishes and they drank again. She knew they were hungry, but they were also agitated, and she didn't want to offer them food until they were in pens at the sanctuary and wouldn't have to be moved again.

Forty-five minutes passed before Tom and Joe returned with two more dogs. Now the van's cages were full.

The next two dogs were captured more quickly, and left in the traps. They had to shift gears now.

"We'll have to dart the last four," Rachel said. She sat with her legs hanging out the back of the van.

"You sure you don't want to take these in and come back another time?" Tom asked. "We've been out here a long time."

"No," Rachel said. "Even if nobody shoots them, they might move somewhere else. It could take us forever to find them again."

"Okay, then," Joe said, "let's get ready for some excitement."

They didn't have any more food bowls, and Rachel didn't want to risk reaching into the traps to retrieve the ones they'd used for bait. She improvised, tearing off pieces of a fold-up state map she found in the van. When Joe protested, she said, "I'll buy you a new one, for heaven's sake."

She placed the first scrap of paper inside the opening of the cave, with a spoonful of the smelly canned food on it. She spaced out the rest of the paper, moving farther from the cave and spreading them wide, a dollop of food on each, to give Joe a clear shot with the dart gun.

"You really think this is gonna work?" Joe whispered when they retreated to the woods across the road.

Rachel shrugged. She'd trapped wild animals, but she'd never caught feral dogs before. This was the only way she could think of to get them out in the open.

The dogs in the van remained quiet. They'd all taken water, and as the afternoon had worn on and they calmed down Rachel had given them hard dog biscuits to gnaw on.

She and Tom and Joe settled in to wait, hidden among the trees. Rachel peeked out from behind her tree every few minutes, checking for activity at the cave opening. Fifteen minutes passed, thirty, forty. Then she spotted movement at the mouth of the cave. A dog poked his head out, looked one way, then the other. His tongue swiped his lips. He'd eaten the first bit of food.

A second dog appeared beside the first.

Rachel held her breath.

The first dog ventured farther out, hesitant, pausing again and again to scan his surroundings. The second dog hung back. Behind it, in the shadows, Rachel saw the remaining two.

"Come on, come on," Rachel whispered. "Come and get it."

With its tail tucked between its hind legs, the first dog slunk toward a scrap of paper with food on it. With one more look around, he gulped the food, then jumped back.

Joe raised the dart gun, but Rachel shook her head and held up a hand to stop him. If he darted one dog now, the three timid ones might never emerge. She wanted all four of them out in the open.

Gradually the other three crept from the cave, alert and scared but drawn by the odor of the food. Rachel gave Joe a hand signal.

The first dog was eating when the dart hit him. He jerked at the sting but made no sound, and the other dogs seemed unaware of what had happened.

Joe reloaded quickly.

The second dog yelped when the dart went in and spun around, trying to get at the object dangling from his flank.

The other two shied away, searching for a threat, but they didn't run back into the cave.

The first two dogs wobbled and sank to the ground.

The third dog let out a piercing yowl when the dart hit him. The little black and white mutt with him took off, straight back into the cave.

"Oh, no," Rachel groaned. They waited a couple of minutes, but the fourth dog didn't reappear. They didn't have much time to get the tranquilized animals into the van, muzzled and tied up, before they started coming around. "All right," she said. "Let's get them."

The dogs in cages looked on silently while they lifted the three unconscious animals into the van. Joe fastened collars and tethers to them and Rachel muzzled them.

"What do you want to do about the little runt that's left?" Joe asked.

"I'm going to get him," Rachel said. "I'm not leaving him out here by himself."

"You know, we could leave him some food and water—"

"No. You can take these dogs to the sanctuary, but I'm staying. I don't want to lose sight of him."

"Rachel," Tom said, leaning into the van, "it's one dog. We've got the rest. We did good. Let's all go—"

"I said no. He'll die one way or another if we don't take him in. I'm not leaving without that dog."

Tom sighed. "Okay. Joe, you go on to Holly's place. Rachel and I will stay here."

She felt like kissing him. When she hopped out of the van, she did.

"You are the most willful woman I've ever known," Tom said, but he was smiling. "I'll keep the dart gun. We can put him in the back seat of my car once he goes under. We just have to wait for him to come out again so I can get a shot."

"I'm not sure he will," Rachel said. "He's terrified. All the other dogs disappearing, one by one. He's probably as far back in the cave as he can get."

Rachel placed more food on paper a couple of feet outside the cave entrance, and they waited. As time passed, she began to worry about nightfall. Could they do this in the dark? She glanced at the sky. Overcast, and more clouds rolling in from the west. They wouldn't have the light of the moon tonight.

"I'm going in after him," she told Tom.

"What? Have you lost your mind?"

"I'll take the dart gun. I know how to use it."

"That's not what I'm worried about," Tom said. "I'm not letting you crawl into a cave with a wild dog."

"It's not wild. It's a discarded pet that's scared to death."

"Which makes him dangerous. You know that as well as I do."

She did. But the dog was small, and there was a good chance that a combination of fear and need would make him submissive. "I'm going in there, with or without the dart gun. At least let me borrow your flashlight."

"Oh, for god's sake." Tom raked a hand through his hair. "Rachel—"

"We're wasting time," she said. "Let's get this done."

Tom thought about it, his face working with indecision, irritation. Rachel waited, barely controlling her impatience.

"I've been in that cave," he said at last. "Once you're inside, it's wide enough for two people side by side, but we'll have to crawl. It's not high enough to stand up. You're not claustrophobic, are you?"

She smiled. "Let's get the flashlight."

Chapter Twenty-nine

Tom crawled into the cave first. Rachel followed, wincing as her knees came down on hard little pebbles in the dirt. Tom's flashlight lit the way ahead, but Rachel had to feel along the ground with her hands to avoid protruding rocks. She'd expected the cave to be cold, but it felt no cooler than the outside.

The place reeked of wet dog, unwashed dog, musky male dog.

As they approached the end of the cave, Rachel heard a faint whining. Tom turned the light full on the little dog. The whine turned into a long, mournful cry. The animal pressed against the wall of the cave, its whole body shaking violently.

Rachel came up beside Tom. "It's okay, it's okay," she whispered to the dog. "Tom, he can't see us with the light in his eyes."

Tom swiveled the light between the dog and Rachel. "Be careful," he said, keeping his voice low. "Let me dart him."

"No. We don't need to."

Murmuring to the terrified dog, she crawled forward slowly. A few feet from him, she shifted and sat with her legs crossed. "It's okay," she said. "I won't hurt you. Nobody's going to hurt you."

He cried out again, then lapsed into a loud whine.

"You're all right now," she said. "It's all right."

Rachel talked quietly to the dog for five minutes, afraid all the time that Tom would become impatient and interrupt. But he held the light and didn't interfere.

The dog's whine subsided to a whimper, then he fell silent, his big eyes riveted on Rachel.

Moving slowly, she pulled two dog biscuits from her jeans pocket and held one out to him. She could hear him sniffing. He whimpered and inched closer, staring at the treat. "Come on," she whispered. "You can have it. You must be so hungry. Come on."

The dog looked up at her, back at the biscuit. Rachel murmured to him. He went down on his belly and crawled toward her, whining. He snatched the biscuit from her fingers. After he'd devoured it, she opened her palm to show him the second biscuit. He crawled closer and took it.

When Rachel touched his head he flinched, but he stayed where he was. She stroked his head and talked to him quietly until his tail thumped a couple of times. "Let's go," she said. "Let's go someplace better and have a good dinner. How does that sound?"

He thumped his tail again.

Tom stayed out of the way, and the dog didn't seem to mind his presence. The animal was fixated on Rachel, and she kept his attention by talking to him continuously in a soothing voice. She turned around, and he stayed in front of her, between her arms, as she crawled out of the cave. Outside, he smelled the leftover food and went straight for it, downing it in one gulp.

He didn't resist when Rachel scooped him up and carried him to Tom's car. The size of a Jack Russell, he had curly hair, black except for dirty white on his throat and muzzle. He was starvation thin and felt like an insubstantial ball of fluff in Rachel's arms.

He lay on Rachel's lap in the back seat during the ride to the sanctuary. Stroking and scratching him, she hated the thought of locking him in a pen by himself.

As if sensing her thoughts, Tom said, "Rachel, we can't take this dog in. We've got Billy Bob and Frank and Cicero—"

"Holly might like him."

"They've already got dogs in the house, and they just took in another one."

"Well, like Mrs. Turner said, it's a big house."

"Good god," Tom said, powering down his window as the guard let them through the sanctuary gate. "Listen to that."

The howls and yelps carried all the way from the pens behind the house.

"That's what I was afraid of," Rachel said from the back seat. "I'm sure the alpha dog got them started."

The dog on her lap had begun whining, and when Tom looked around he saw the animal sitting up, eyes wide and ears cocked. Tom closed the window, but when they approached the pens the racket was too loud to be shut out. The dog Rachel held got more worked up by the second. Instead of driving all the way back to the pens, Tom stopped next to the house. "I guess you don't want to add that one to the mix," he said.

"No," Rachel said. "He's scared out of his wits. I'll stay in the car with him. Tell Holly I need to see her, and tell Joe to get the alpha dog out of here right now, or the others will be impossible to handle."

Taking the tranquilizer rifle with him, Tom got out and walked around behind the house. He found Holly and her grandmother going from one pen to another, trying to quiet the barking, howling dogs with treats. The animals ignored the women, paced their enclosures, responded with yelps and howls every time the pack leader barked. Tom pulled Holly aside and sent her to Rachel.

Joe Dolan stood before the alpha dog's pen, watching the animal lunge at the fencing over and over. When he saw Tom, he yelled over the uproar, "It's about time! I needed that an hour ago."

Tom handed over the gun, already loaded with a dart.

"This is gonna take more than one," Joe said. "I'll be right back." He ran toward his van nearby.

The snarling, growling dog turned his attention on Tom. Although Tom knew he was safe, the wild ferocity of the animal as it backed up and hurled itself at the fence stirred a primitive fear in him. The rest of the feral dogs had probably been pets from birth and might be saved, but this brute seemed beyond redemption. The dog had suffered at the hands of people, had likely never known any kindness, and it could be too late to turn him around now. Rachel would be disappointed, but Tom hoped sentiment wouldn't blind her to the truth.

When Joe returned, he thrust the end of the tranquilizer rifle through an opening in the chain link. The dog leapt at it, snapping, and Joe jerked it back just in time to keep him from grabbing it. "Good Lord almighty. Distract him for me, will you?"

Tom walked a few feet away, and the dog followed, snarling at him. Tom crouched, closer to the fence than felt comfortable. If no barrier separated them, he wouldn't dare make eye contact with a hostile animal, but in this case it was the best way to keep its attention. He stared into the dog's eyes, and its fury rose, building to full-blown mania. The dog lunged, pawed at the fence, growled and barked.

The other dogs responded with a chorus of howls.

When the first dart struck home, the alpha dog didn't even notice the prick. And as several minutes passed, he showed only a mild reaction to the tranquilizer, wobbling a little but keeping up the intensity of his attack on Tom.

The second dart got a reaction, a whine that sounded especially pathetic to Tom, coming from an animal whose viciousness was its only defense against a cruel world.

Within a couple of minutes, the dog quieted, swayed, and slowly folded onto his belly in the dirt.

Rachel ran up then. "Is he ready to go? Oh, God, Joe, you had to dart him twice? He's had a lot of that stuff in less than twenty-four hours. We're going to kill him at this rate."

That might be the kindest thing to do, Tom thought, but he kept silent.

Joe muzzled the tranquilized dog and Tom helped him carry the animal to the van and place him in a cage. Rachel checked his heart rate and respiration, pronounced them normal, and locked him in.

She stood with Tom, her face bleak, as they watched Joe drive off to the pound. The other dogs had already begun to calm down. Only a few whines and soft barks broke the quiet.

Tom laid a hand on Rachel's shoulder. "What did you do with the little guy?"

"Holly took him in the house. It was love at first sight. She's going to give him a flea bath right now so he won't have to spend the night in the basement."

"Holly and her grandmother can't make pets of all of them," Tom said. He swept his gaze down the long line of runs, most of them filled now with other people's rejected dogs. And more would come, more abandoned animals tossed onto the roads of Mason County like trash.

When Rachel didn't answer, Tom put an arm around her shoulders. "Hey, come on. Let's go home and wash off the dirt and fleas and god knows what else we've picked up. Then I'll go get Billy Bob. Let's have a nice quiet evening for a change."

Rachel looked up at him. "No work tonight? Nobody to question or hunt down?"

"I just need to make a few phone calls for updates from the other guys."

"But you don't have to go anywhere?"

"I don't have to go anywhere."

He could hope, anyway.

Chapter Thirty

The jangling phone woke Tom from a deep sleep. Groaning, he pulled his arm out from under Rachel's head, checked the time on the bedside clock's LED, and fumbled for the receiver.

"What?" he answered.

"Hey, Tom, it's me, Joe."

"What the hell? It's after two in the morning."

"Yeah, I know, sorry. But I got a situation here."

"A situation?"

Beside Tom, Rachel stirred. "What's happen—" A yawn cut off her question.

Tom pushed himself up and switched on the lamp. Frank blinked from the foot of the bed and Billy Bob groaned in his spot by the door.

"Well," Joe said, "I was kinda worried about this dog, you know, afraid he was gonna hurt himself trying to get loose, and I couldn't sleep for worrying, so I came back over here to the pound to check on him, and it's a good thing I did."

Tom clasped a hand to his forehead and closed his eyes briefly, praying for patience. "Your point, Joe? You've got a point?"

"The lock on the back door was busted, and I walked right in on Pete Rasey trying to get that dog out of his cage with wire cutters."

"What?" Wide awake now, Tom threw off the covers and swung his feet to the floor. "He was trying to steal the dog?"

"Tom?" Rachel sounded alarmed. "Which dog? What's going on?"

Tom waved a hand to hush her. "Is he still there?"

"You bet he is," Joe said. "I held the little bastard at bay with the tranq gun, and I locked him in the kennel. He's making more noise than the dog. Trying to kick the door down."

"Don't let him get loose. I'm on my way."

Tom filled Rachel in while he threw on some clothes. Sitting up in bed with her auburn hair loose around her face, she looked so beautiful that he wanted to forget about the Rasey kid and crawl back into bed.

"It could be a teenage prank," she said.

"Or it could mean Pete's connected to the dogfighting operation." Tom sat on the side of the bed to pull on his boots. "If that dog's an escaped fighter, they probably want him back." He shifted to look at her. "I'm positive it was Pete Rasey that set fire to the house."

"What? Why didn't you tell me? Why haven't you arrested him?"

"I don't have the evidence to make it stick. I was going to say I don't like leaving you here alone, but with Pete out of commission, I doubt there's much danger. If you don't feel safe, though, I want you to go over to my aunt and uncle's house."

"I'll be fine," Rachel said. "Go, go. I really like the thought of Pete Rasey in a jail cell."

When Tom reached the pound, Pete was screaming obscenities and pounding on the locked kennel door, accompanied by the big alpha dog's howls and barks.

Kevin Blackwood, on night patrol, had arrived before Tom and stood in the corridor outside the door, grinning as if he'd never had such a good time. "Man," the young blond deputy said to Tom, "this sure beats riding around in the dark by myself."

Tom laughed. "We need to get you back on day duty." Leaning toward the door, he yelled, "Pete! It's Tom Bridger.

Just settle down. You're coming with me, and you might as well accept that."

"Fuck off, dickface!"

"Okay, if you want to take that attitude." Tom motioned for Joe to unlock the door.

Pete was making so much noise that Tom doubted he heard the key turn in the lock. Tom shoved the door open and sent Pete stumbling backward. Moving fast, Tom and Kevin caught him while he was off-balance, grabbed his arms and jerked them behind his back.

"Get your hands off me!" Pete shouted. He twisted and kicked while Tom fastened cuffs around his wrists. "You goddamn motherfucking shitface—"

"Good lord," Tom said. "What would your mom say if she could hear her little boy right now?"

"Fuck off!"

"Yeah, yeah, I got the message the first time."

Pete kicked backward, connecting with Tom's shin.

Tom yanked the boy's arms back hard, making him yelp. "You assault me again and I'll shackle your ankles and put a gag in your filthy mouth. Now calm down. You hear me?"

Pete quieted, his breath coming in hoarse gasps, and when Tom looked at his face he could have sworn the boy was blinking back tears. Tough guy.

Tom didn't try to get anything out of Pete on the ride to headquarters. He let the boy stew in the back seat, hunched forward because of his cuffed hands, looking like a kid outraged at the unfairness of being caught misbehaving. The bloody excitement of illegal dogfights probably had a lot of appeal for somebody like Pete. Tom hoped to god that trying to free the alpha dog hadn't been a prank, as Rachel suggested, but would provide a solid link back to the fight organizers.

"I'll call your parents when we get to headquarters," Tom said. "They'll probably be surprised to find out you're not in bed asleep."

Pete huffed but said nothing.

Almost an hour later, Tom placed a paper cup of water on the conference room table for the boy. Pete, his wrists cuffed in front now, his face still screwed up with sullen resentment, stared at the cup for a moment. Then he brought his hands up and whacked it sideways. Water sloshed across the tabletop. The cup rolled and fell to the floor.

Tom walked down the hall to the restroom, grabbed a few paper towels, brought them back and tossed them onto the table. "Stop acting like a baby and mop it up," he said. "This table had better be dry when I come back."

◇◇◇

Usually Beck Rasey was the loud one, but this time his wife Babs screamed at Kevin Blackwood. Tom could hear her all the way down the hall. "This is the craziest thing I've ever heard in my life. You expect us to believe our son is out stealing dogs? From the *pound?* Why? That doesn't even make sense."

Looking past her, Kevin threw a pleading look at Tom as he approached.

"He was caught in the act," Tom said.

Babs spun around. Her blond hair stuck out in messy clumps, and she wore bedroom slippers with her jeans and sweatshirt. Beside her, Beck was sleepy-eyed and unshaven. "I don't believe you," she told Tom. "I'm not taking your word for anything."

"Joe Dolan walked in on Pete trying to cut an opening in the dog's cage. I don't know whether he was trying to steal it or set it loose, but either one is illegal. And he resisted arrest."

"I want to hear what my son says."

"Where is he?" Beck asked. "Back there?"

He tried to brush past, but Tom planted a hand on his shoulder. "Hey, whoa. I'll tell you when you can see him."

"He's a minor. You can't question him unless we let you. And we're not letting you."

"Didn't Pete turn eighteen a couple weeks ago?" Tom asked.

Beck didn't reply, but expelled a noisy breath through his nose.

Babs erupted again. "Will you just explain to us why our son would do something so crazy? Huh? Can you tell us that?"

"It's not up to me to explain his behavior," Tom said. "It's up to him. The dog he was trying to let loose is one of the meanest animals I've ever come across. It looks like it's been used in dog-fights, maybe escaped from his handlers. If Pete had let it out of the cage, it would have torn him apart. I don't know what the hell he thought he was doing, unless he's gotten involved in the fights and somebody sent him to get that dog. I need some answers."

"We want to see our son," Babs said. "Now."

"I'll let you see him if you think you can get an explanation out of him."

"I didn't say we want to help you make a case against him," Babs shot back. "I said we want to see our son. And we don't want you in the room."

Tom didn't object to that. He could listen to their conversation over the intercom. He ushered the two of them into the conference room, then stepped into the sheriff's office next to it and jabbed a button on the speaker on the wall. He was just in time to hear a loud *POP!* One of the Raseys had greeted their son with a slap. Babs, Tom guessed.

"What the hell's got into you?" Babs demanded. Her voice sounded scratchy over the old intercom system. "I thought you were in your room asleep, then we get a call from the police."

"*Mom*," Pete protested. "That hurt."

"I'll show you what hurts," Beck yelled. "Don't you have any sense at all? What did you think you were doing? What do you want with a dog from the pound?"

Pete said nothing.

"I asked you a question," Beck said.

Pete remained silent. Tom could picture the sullen expression on the boy's face, having seen it often enough.

"You listen to me," Babs said. "We've put up with as much of this behavior as we intend to. Sneaking out to see that Hall girl, getting up to god knows what. This is the last straw, do you hear me? If I find out you're mixed up in dogfighting, I'm gonna—"

"What?" Pete broke in, suddenly belligerent and challenging. "What're you gonna do? Hit me again? You better watch out, I might hit you back next time."

"You little shit," Beck said. "You hit your mother and that'll be the last thing you ever do on this earth."

"Go to hell, both of you!" Pete yelled.

Then Tom heard a scuffle and the clunk of something hitting the floor. He rushed out of the sheriff's office and threw open the conference room door.

Beck had hauled Pete to his feet, knocking over the chair. Clutching the front of Pete's shirt, Beck slammed his son against the wall. Pete raised his cuffed hands and punched Beck in the face.

"Stop it!" Babs cried.

Tom tried to get between them, but Pete and Beck kept throwing punches at each other around his head. After the third time he narrowly missed getting clobbered, he jabbed both of them in the stomach with his elbows and shoved them apart. "That's enough. Settle down or you'll both spend the rest of the night in jail."

Beck stumbled backward, gasping for breath, a hand to his stomach.

Tom grabbed the chair and set it upright. "Sit down," he told Pete.

The boy slumped into the chair.

"Out, both of you," Tom said to Babs and Beck. They didn't argue. Tom ushered them into the corridor and told them, "Go on home. I'll be in touch with you after the sun comes up. Your boy's going to need a lawyer, so you ought to start looking for one first thing in the morning."

As Tom closed the door on them, Babs looked as if she were about to burst into tears. Tom felt a degree of sympathy for her because he knew that seeing a kid in trouble would be hard on most mothers, but at the same time he held both her and Beck responsible for the boy's behavior. No kid turned into an arrogant jerk all by himself. Pete's attitude was a reflection of the way he was raised. Maybe now, though, the Raseys would stop making excuses for him.

Tom pulled out a chair and sat down across the table from Pete. The boy stared down at his cuffed hands, his face twisted in a scowl.

"How did you know that dog was moved to the pound?" Tom asked.

"Plenty of people knew."

Tom didn't doubt it. The capture of the pack's leader would be a big deal to farmers and anybody else who lived in fear of the roaming dogs. One or more of the guys working at the sanctuary had probably told friends or family, and within a couple of hours the grapevine would have been buzzing with the story.

"So why did you want to turn the dog loose?" Tom asked. "Is that what you were trying to do? Or did you plan on taking it somewhere?"

Pete didn't answer.

"Did somebody ask you to get it out of the pound?" Tom persisted. "Did the guys running the dogfights want to get their champion back?"

Pete's head came up, and Tom knew he'd guessed correctly. Pete needed a few seconds to get his reaction under control and arrange his features into a sullen mask again. "I don't know what you're talking about."

Without changing his tone, Tom asked, "How involved are you in the fights? You enjoy that kind of thing? Seeing animals tear each other apart? You ever take Beth Hall to a dogfight?"

Pete's face blazed red, and he opened his mouth to speak. He changed his mind, clamped his mouth shut, and dropped his gaze.

Tom had seen enough in Pete's reaction to know that Beth might be the way to break down the boy's defenses. "She's an odd girl," Tom said. "Not what she seems to be."

"You don't even know her," Pete spat out.

"Well, not the way you do." Tom paused. "Her father thought you were a bad influence on her. He thought you corrupted his little girl."

Pete snorted. "Well, he's not here to boss her around anymore, is he?"

"Sounds like you're glad he's dead."

Pete leaned forward over the table. "Yeah, I'm glad the son of a bitch is dead. He got what he deserved."

"Did you have something to do with it?"

"Just because I'm glad he's dead doesn't mean I killed him."

"How does Beth feel about it?"

"What do you think? He was always on her case about something—"

"About you, mostly," Tom said.

"About *everything.* He thought that Korean girl they adopted was perfect. He was always telling Beth she oughta be more like Soo Jin."

"I can see how that would get under Beth's skin. Did you know somebody slit Soo Jin's tires and deliberately caused her accident? Maybe somebody in the family."

Pete opened his mouth, but shut it again as if realizing he'd already said too much.

"Was Beth with you when you set my house on fire?" Tom asked. "Was it her idea? Did she throw the bottle herself?"

"No!" Pete cried. "Stop blaming her. It was my idea, and she never even touched it."

"So she just went along for the fun of it? She watched while you set my house on fire with Dr. Goddard inside?"

Pete's sharp intake of breath sounded loud in the closed room. "I didn't say I—"

"Yes, you did," Tom said.

Pete slumped lower in the chair. "Dad says you shouldn't ever talk to the cops without a lawyer. And I'm not going to. I'm done."

Chapter Thirty-one

"If you're sure Pete Rasey was the one who caused the fire," Rachel said over breakfast Monday morning, "I guess I don't need anybody playing bodyguard anymore."

"Yeah, I think you're okay with Pete in jail." Tom filled her coffee cup, then his own. "But if anything suspicious happens, if you think somebody's following you—"

"I'll yell for help."

Rachel let a few minutes pass in silence as Tom ate his eggs and she finished her shredded wheat and berries. The day had dawned bright and beautiful, and sunlight flooded the farmhouse kitchen. Billy Bob and Frank both lay on their sides on the floor, drowsing and soaking up rays. With the entire feral pack safe and well cared for, Rachel knew she should be in a buoyant mood, enjoying the ordinary pleasure of a real breakfast with Tom. But now that one worry had been dealt with, Marcy had reclaimed her thoughts. She couldn't shake the image of the girl's sad face. How could that lost, lonely child survive emotionally in a family that was falling apart?

"Tom," she said, "I keep thinking about Marcy, and her brother too. What's going to happen to them if Mrs. Hall dies too? Soo Jin's in the hospital, and Ethan doesn't care about those kids."

He hesitated, scraping butter over a slice of toast before he answered. "I don't know. I've wondered about that myself. Losing her husband the way she did would knock anybody for a loop, let alone a woman in her condition. We just have to hope her health will get better after she's past the shock."

"She's not going to recover, Tom. She's being kept alive by dialysis. That means end stage renal failure. *End stage.* And she's not going to get a kidney transplant, not with advanced lupus. The woman is dying."

Tom lifted a forkful of scrambled egg halfway to his mouth, halted and set it down on his plate. "Rachel," he said, sounding to her like an exasperated adult trying to reason with a stubborn child, "this isn't our problem. We can't do anything about it. Those kids are legally Vicky Hall's son and daughter."

"She doesn't *care* about them, don't you get that? They're just ornaments to her, pretty little playthings, and now she's tired of them because they don't behave the way she wants them to. She doesn't love them. She doesn't give a damn about them."

"You can't get involved. You have to back off."

She jumped up, jarring the table and sloshing the coffee from her cup. "You don't understand. But I know what it's like for those kids. I know what it's like to grow up in a house with somebody who's supposed to be your mother but never shows you any love, never does anything but judge you and criticize you and try to make you fit *her* idea of what you ought to be. I can't stand—"

"Rachel, stop." Tom rose and pulled her into his arms. "Don't do this to yourself."

She stood rigid in his arms, but he didn't let her go. After a couple of minutes she felt calmer and stepped away from him. She sat at the table, her head in her hands. "I'm all right. I'm sorry."

He sat across from her and held out a hand. He withdrew it when she didn't respond. *You're going to drive him away,* Rachel told herself, the truth of it cutting like a knife. *He'll give up trying to get through to you.*

"Listen," Tom said, "I'll find out what the situation is. I'll do what I can. One thing Vicky Hall needs is a real nurse taking care of her. I don't think Rayanne Stuckey's capable of judging when she needs emergency care."

Rachel pulled in a deep breath and tried to speak in a level voice, a sane voice. "She doesn't have any health care training, does she? Why is she working there in the first place?"

"I think she was hired as a housekeeper and a driver, but now she seems to be taking care of Vicky full-time. She—" Tom broke off, his mouth still open, and an expression of amazement came over his face. "My god. Why didn't I realize—"

He pushed his chair back from the table and stood.

"Realize what?" Rachel asked, looking up at him. "Tom?"

"Gotta get to headquarters." He gave her a quick kiss. "Come on, Billy Bob. You're with me today."

Then he was out the door with the bulldog on his heels.

Frank jumped into Tom's chair.

"What awful thing's going to happen next?" Rachel wondered aloud.

The cat started eating the leftover scrambled eggs on Tom's plate.

"Burt Morgan's girlfriend is Rayanne Stuckey's cousin." Tom dropped into the chair next to Dennis Murray's desk in the squad room. "The connection was staring us right in the face and we didn't see it."

Dennis considered this for a moment while he sipped coffee from a mug with *World's Best Dad* printed on it. Steam rising from the coffee clouded the bottom halves of his glasses. "So Morgan told Sylvia about the raid, and Sylvia told Rayanne, and Rayanne told—who?"

"Who do you think?" Tom said. "She's living with Leo Riggs."

"So you reckon Riggs is mixed up in the dogfighting?"

"I wouldn't be the least bit surprised," Tom said. "He always seems to be working one angle or another. It's hard to know what's really going on in his head. He strikes me as somebody who's so used to lying he does it automatically, whether it's called for or not."

"But I thought Burt's girlfriend was so set against dogfighting that she made him promise to stay away from it. Why would she want to protect the people doing it?"

"She was probably just confiding in her cousin," Tom said, "worrying aloud about somebody going after Burt for helping the cops. I'll bet she has no idea Leo's involved."

"*If* he's involved," Dennis said.

"Yeah. But this theory feels right to me. We're on the right track. I feel it in my gut."

"What about Hall's death?" Dennis asked. "You think Leo had something to do with that?"

Tom thought for a moment, trying to round up all of Leo's connections to the Halls and his possible grievances. "He claims he's okay with the Halls adopting his sister's kids. And he got a big chunk of money from them to open his garage. But he was quick to tell me he didn't sell Jewel's kids."

"Yeah, right," Dennis said. "It was just a coincidence the Halls were feeling generous about helping out a small businessman around the same time the kids were up for grabs."

Unable to sit still, his nerves thrumming, Tom rose and paced back and forth. "There's no doubt Leo milked the situation for all he could get, but nobody in the Riggs family wanted Jewel's children."

"And their real father and his folks never made any legal claim to them," Dennis said.

Tom stopped and stared out the window, barely seeing the cars in the parking lot, the gaudy leaves that littered the pavement. In his mind he sorted through chunks of information, trying and failing to make them fit together to form a coherent whole. "There's something going on here that we don't know about, maybe something that hasn't even occurred to us."

Dennis laughed. "Isn't that usually the case? Anytime we start out with all the information we need, we don't have much work left to do."

Tom turned back to Dennis. "We need solid proof. I haven't come across anything yet that made me think Leo was involved in dogfighting. If he's got an operation set up somewhere, it's well hidden. And all the history between the Riggs family and the Halls doesn't prove a thing about Gordon Hall's death. A lot of people had bad history with him. The fact that Burt Morgan's girlfriend and Leo's girlfriend are cousins doesn't prove Leo's involved in dogfighting, either. That's a big leap."

"But we've got an awful lot of coincidences involving one guy," Dennis pointed out. "If you ask me, it all points straight at him."

"Yeah, it does. Maybe our guest over at the jail can give us something that'll lead to solid proof."

The jail, located behind the courthouse and adjacent to the sheriff's headquarters, was a short walk away through a connecting passage. When Tom and Dennis opened the door into the jail's entrance lobby, they found Beck Rasey and Beth Hall arguing at the front desk. The jailer, a retired deputy with a completely bald head, flung a hand in Tom's direction and said, "Take it up with the captain or move it outside. I'm not listening to any more of this."

"What are you doing here, Beth?" Tom asked.

"She's trying to get to my son," Beck blurted before the girl could answer. A flush of anger darkened his face. "I don't want her anywhere near him. She's the reason he's acting up in the first place."

"You don't know what you're talking about!" Beth cried. "We *love* each other."

"What do you know about love, little girl? Get back in your fancy car and go back to your fancy house and stay clear of my son."

Beth focused her ire on Tom. "He's here, isn't he? You locked him in a cage like an animal. You had no right. He didn't do anything. It was me, okay? I set your house on fire, not Pete, I swear it. I'll plead guilty if you'll let him go."

Tom frowned at her, wondering what on earth made this girl so willing to throw her life away for the likes of Pete Rasey. "He's not getting out, not for a while, and you're not getting in to see him, so you might as well go home. I'll be over there to talk to you later. Right now, you ought to be with your family. You've lost your father, your sister's been in a serious accident—your mother needs you now."

"Yeah, sure. It'll be the first time she ever needed me." Beth pivoted and marched to the door. Before leaving, she threw a contemptuous glance over her shoulder and said, "For your information, my car's not *fancy*. It's a Camry."

Beck looked like he wanted to go after her and throttle her. Watching the door swing shut, Tom wondered again if Beth had slit Soo Jin's tires in a fit of pique because the older girl insulted Pete. The thought of wading back into the primordial ooze that made up the Hall family relationships wearied him, but he had no choice. He had to get to the bottom of all this.

"Look," Beck said, "Babs and I stayed up the rest of the night figuring out what to do about this mess. Before we get a lawyer involved and he tells Pete not to cooperate—you know that's what a lawyer will tell him—"

"Probably," Tom said. This sounded promising. He waited for Beck to go on.

"I want another chance to talk some sense into him."

"I don't know if it's safe to let you in the same room with him."

"I know, I know." Beck ran a hand over his buzz-cut hair. "I lost my temper. Babs did too. It just took us by surprise. But we decided the best thing for Pete to do is tell you what he knows, if it'll make a difference in the charges you bring against him. If he levels with you, would you give him a break, considering he's never been in trouble before?"

Never been in trouble before? Pete didn't have a record of criminal charges, but he hadn't been an angel either. Technically, though, Beck was right. "Depends on what he tells me," Tom said. "How honest he is."

"If he tells you everything he knows—"

Which he's not likely to do, Tom thought.

"—could you see your way clear to go a little easy on him?"

"Beck, despite what Beth says, your boy set my house on fire while Rachel Goddard was inside. He could have killed her. That's a little hard to overlook."

"I know it is." Beck stood with his hands on his hips, his gaze on the floor. "I don't know if I could, in your shoes."

Tom let a minute pass in silence. He could hear Beck's breathing, in and out, sounding as if he'd just run a couple of miles. At last Tom said, "I'll tell you what. If he gives up the dogfighters, tells me who's running the fights, where the next fight's going to be, and anything else he knows about it, I'll see what I can do to help him. I can't wipe the slate clean. He's going to have to pay a price for what he's done. But if you and Babs want to keep your son out of state prison, I can do that for you—if I'm satisfied with what he gives me."

Beck let out a rush of air and nodded vigorously. "That'd be a load of worry off our minds. I appreciate this, Tom."

"Don't thank me yet. We still have to get Pete to talk."

Chapter Thirty-two

Rachel slowed as she approached the roadside mailbox with the name Sullivan printed on the side. Dr. Jim Sullivan's small frame house, set back from the road about fifty feet, had the slightly run-down air of a place whose owner had recently lost interest in it. The white paint looked in good condition, but a long black streak below the gutter indicated an untended leak. Autumn leaves from several oaks and maples lay deep on the lawn and covered half the roof.

No vehicle in the driveway, no lights on in the house. Sullivan must be out making his farm rounds. Rachel drove on.

What am I doing here? More to the point, how was she going to snoop on Sullivan and find out whether he had a connection to the dogfighting operation? She would have to shadow him night and day to learn anything. *I'm probably just imagining things,* she told herself as she turned onto the road that would take her to the Hall house. *Why would a vet get involved in dogfighting?*

She'd wasted time with her detour past Sullivan's house, and she would have to rush through her visit to Thor, but she hoped she'd get a chance to see Marcy while she was there. Were the kids back in school yet, or were they being kept at home until after Gordon Hall's funeral? Rachel wondered if anybody was running the Hall household now. Vicky Hall was in no condition to do it. Were the kids fending for themselves?

A glum-faced Ethan let her into the house without so much as a perfunctory greeting.

Standing in the foyer with no idea where to go next, Rachel asked, "Where is Thor?"

"Dad's office," Ethan said, hooking a thumb toward the back of the house. He started up the stairs.

"Ethan, wait." When he stopped and looked down at her, Rachel asked, "I'd like to speak to your mother. Could she—"

"No," Rayanne said from behind Rachel.

Startled, Rachel turned to find the woman no more than three feet away. She hadn't heard Rayanne approach. Stepping back to a more comfortable distance, Rachel addressed Ethan again. "I'd like to speak to your mother about Thor's care. Would you let her know, please?"

"She's not seein' any company," Rayanne said.

Rachel looked from Rayanne to Ethan, her brows raised quizzically.

Clutching the stair railing with a white-knuckled hand, Ethan didn't respond with the decisiveness Rachel expected. As Mrs. Hall's adult son, he should be the one acting on her behalf, but he looked at his mother's employee as if she were in charge.

Rachel stepped closer to him. "Ethan, is your mother all right?"

"She's got people takin' good care of her," Rayanne said. "It's not anything for you to worry about." She moved forward as if trying to get between Rachel and Ethan, but Rachel stood too close to the stairs for Rayanne to edge her way in.

"I'll tell her you want to talk to her," Ethan said. He mounted the stairs without looking back.

Two red spots burned on Rayanne's cheeks as she watched Ethan go, and her pinched mouth showed her displeasure.

Rachel took advantage of Rayanne's distraction to head down the hallway toward the office. She heard Rayanne's footfalls behind her but didn't look back. Once in the office, she shut the door without bothering to check whether she was closing it in Rayanne's face.

Thor, stretched out on his bed, lifted his head and thumped his tail as Rachel approached. At one end of the sofa sat Marcy, her legs tucked under her, so unobtrusive that Rachel hadn't noticed her at first.

"Hi," Marcy said in a whisper. Her gaze met Rachel's for a second before darting away.

"Hi. How are you, Marcy?"

"We're gonna have a funeral."

Rachel stooped and scratched Thor's ears. "Are you staying out of school until then?"

"Yeah, I guess. I've been studying, though. I don't want to get way behind."

"Good for you. I'm sure you'll be glad you did that." Opening her bag, Rachel debated how deeply she could pry into what was going on in this household. She had a feeling Rayanne was listening at the door, and anything Rachel said to Marcy could be used to cause an unpleasant scene.

They didn't speak while Rachel examined Thor's wounds and changed the dressing on his neck. When she was finished, she sat on the couch next to Marcy. "He's healing very well. I don't think we have to worry about him." Dropping her voice, she asked, "Is there anything you want to tell me about?"

The girl hesitated, chewing her lip and picking at the seam of her jeans leg.

Rachel spoke in a whisper. "What is it, Marcy?"

"David says our mom's gonna die. This mom, I mean." Marcy's voice was so faint that Rachel had to lean within inches to catch her words.

"David doesn't know that for sure. Nobody does." Rachel clasped one of Marcy's hands. "But I know you're scared. I don't blame you."

"He says when she dies we'll go live with our real dad, because nobody here wants us." Marcy screwed up her face in an effort to hold back tears. "David remembers him but I don't. Our real daddy. He never wanted us before. What if he's mean to us?"

"Oh, sweetheart." Rachel slipped an arm around the girl's shoulders.

Marcy slumped against her, tears spilling over. "She's so sick. It's like she's not here anymore."

"I know she's ill, and your father's death was a terrible shock to her, but she can come through this. Life will get back to normal." She was lying to the child, she didn't believe a word of what she was telling Marcy, but what else could she say? That nothing would ever be normal again? What was normal for these people, anyway?

The door flew open and Rayanne stood there, her freckled face mottled with anger. "There you are," she said, pinning Marcy with stern eyes. "Why are you hiding in here? You have to try on that dress for the funeral."

Marcy rose obediently. Rachel had to restrain an urge to grab her, hold onto her.

"Are you ready to leave now?" Rayanne asked Rachel.

Rachel stood. "After I talk to Mrs. Hall."

"I told you she's not seein' company."

Rachel started to speak but held back when she heard the click of footsteps in the hall. Ethan appeared behind Rayanne in the doorway. "Dr. Goddard," he said, "I'll take you up to see my mother if you're ready. I'll have to ask you not to mention Soo Jin, though. It upsets her."

If Vicky Hall was in that fragile a state, Rachel thought, she should be in a hospital.

"*Ethan*," Rayanne said, "she doesn't want—"

"It's all right. She wants to see Dr. Goddard."

Rayanne crossed her arms over her chest. "You're just wearin' her out."

Rachel collected her bag and squeezed past Rayanne, who didn't budge to get out of the doorway. Why did they put up with this woman? Rachel wouldn't have kept her as an employee for five minutes.

They mounted the stairs, Rayanne on their heels. At the top, Rayanne scurried around Rachel and Ethan to one of the closed doors on the right side of the landing. "I have to be with her in case she needs anything."

"If she does, I'll take care of it," Ethan said.

But Rayanne had already opened the door to enter the room.

Rachel followed Ethan inside. With the draperies still closed, the big room was dark except for a pool of light cast by one bedside lamp. In the middle of the king-sized bed, Vicky Hall slumped against a mound of pillows, most of her body concealed by a puffy comforter. Rayanne positioned herself like a sentry by the head of the bed, arms folded, eyes fixed on Rachel.

"Good morning, Mrs. Hall," Rachel said from just inside the doorway.

"How is Thor doing?" Mrs. Hall asked in a whisper.

"Very well," Rachel said. She moved closer to get a better look and try to assess the woman's condition. In the shadowy light she looked like a cadaver propped up in bed. "I'm sure he'll make a full recovery."

Mrs. Hall's faint smile, barely visible to Rachel, came and went in a second. "Gordon loved that old dog so much. We have to take good care of him. That's what Gordon would want."

And what about taking care of your children? Would he want that? Aloud, Rachel said, "I'm sure Thor has a few more good years left."

Mrs. Hall drew in an audible breath and released it as a shuddering sigh. "Yes, a few more years…"

She seemed on the verge of drifting into unconsciousness, and alarm pushed Rachel toward the bed. "Mrs. Hall? Are you all right?"

"She's fine," Rayanne said, placing a hand on Mrs. Hall's shoulder.

"I'm not so sure about that." Rachel lifted the woman's limp hand and felt for her pulse. A regular rhythm, but weak and rapid.

"What are you doing?" Rayanne demanded.

Rachel ignored her and spoke to Ethan, who waited by the door. "Your mother needs to be in the hospital."

"Who are you to decide?" Rayanne protested. "You're an *animal* doctor!"

Hesitating, Ethan looked from Rachel to Rayanne to his mother. "She's going in for dialysis in a little while."

"That's right," Rayanne said. "A *real* doctor can check her out."

"Good," Rachel said. "I'm glad to hear that. But I wouldn't delay it even by an hour. She needs to go right now."

"She has her regular appointment time," Rayanne said.

"She goes in three times a week at the same time," Ethan said.

"What…" Mrs. Hall murmured. Her eyes remained closed. "What's… wrong?"

"See, now you've upset her," Rayanne said. "Ethan, I need to start getting her dressed."

"Right, right," he said. "Dr. Goddard, if that's all—"

Rachel walked out because she had no choice, but she wasn't going to let this drop. Something was going on here that had to be stopped.

In the hallway, she found Marcy with her back pressed against a wall, as if trying to make herself invisible. Rachel wanted to look confident and reassuring for the girl, but her expression felt more like a grimace on her face. "Your mom's going to the hospital for her treatment. She'll feel better afterward."

Marcy, her head bowed, whispered something.

"I'm sorry, sweetie, I didn't hear you." Rachel leaned closer.

Marcy kept her head down, but this time Rachel heard what she said. "She doesn't feel better afterward. She used to, but now she always feels worse."

Ethan stared into space as if he'd totally detached himself from what was happening. *Dear god,* Rachel thought, *this is a madhouse.*

Shifting her bag from one hand to the other, Rachel surreptitiously drew one of her business cards from an outer pocket. The card had her cell phone number on it as well as the animal hospital number. She slipped it into Marcy's hand at the same time she leaned close enough to speak without Ethan overhearing. "Remember what I said. You can call me anytime you need help."

Rachel got out of the house as fast as she could, and when she was outside, in her car, she called Tom's cell phone. Straight to voice mail. He must have turned it off. She left a message. then called the sheriff's department and asked where Tom was. At the jail, she was told, talking to a prisoner. "Tell him to call me as quickly as he can," Rachel said. "It's important."

Chapter Thirty-three

A few hours behind bars had done wonders for Pete Rasey's attitude. No more backtalk. No more profanity. Resentment simmered in the boy's eyes, but he didn't give voice to it. He waited silently, his gaze skittering between his father and Tom while the jailer opened the cell door.

"You're not being released," Tom said. "We're just going back over to headquarters to talk some more. Hold out your hands."

Pete looked as if he might burst into tears, but he stuck out his hands and let Tom snap the cuffs onto his wrists. Head down, he shuffled between Tom and Beck along the passageway between the jail and the Sheriff's Department. At one point, Beck reached out to pat his son's back, a gesture that made Tom hopeful for a good outcome.

He ushered Pete and Beck into the conference room. "I'll let you two talk," he said. "I'll be back shortly."

He closed the door on them, then joined Dennis and Brandon at the intercom in the sheriff's office next door.

For a while, Tom couldn't make out anything they said to each other. Tom pictured them with their heads together, Beck talking in a low, urgent tone. A couple of times Pete broke in with, "But, Dad—" and Beck silenced him with an order to be quiet and listen.

Tom waited half an hour, the time he and Beck had agreed on. He rapped on the door before entering. Pete slumped forward, his cuffed hands resting on the table. Beck, sitting next to his son, told Tom, "I think I've managed to talk some sense into him. Pete? Tell the captain what he wants to know."

When Pete raised his head, he looked like a terrified child. "They'll kill me," he said. "I'm not kidding. They'll *kill* me."

Tom pulled out a chair and sat down across from Pete and Beck. He placed a small tape recorder, already running, on the table. "Who's *they?*"

Pete stared at the recorder, then threw a pleading look at his father.

"You gotta tell him," Beck said. "Think about yourself now."

"I *am* thinking about myself. I told you, they'll kill me if I talk."

"Sounds like real nice people you're mixed up with," Tom said. "How long have you been working for them?"

Dropping his chin, Pete mumbled, "All summer."

"Doing what, exactly?"

"Different stuff. Finding dogs."

"Finding dogs?" Tom asked. "What do you mean?"

"Tell him," Beck ordered.

Pete hesitated, but at last he said, without meeting Tom's eyes, "Dogs for training. You know, to teach the fighting dogs."

"Bait, you mean," Tom said.

Pete nodded.

"Where did you get these bait dogs?"

Pete mumbled something, his chin so low it almost touched his chest.

"What was that?" Tom asked. "I didn't hear you."

Pete drew in a deep breath, let it out, and spoke clearly. "Out of people's yards."

"You stole people's pet dogs out of their yards?"

Pete nodded.

"I need to hear you say it," Tom told him.

Clearing his throat, Pete spoke directly at the recorder. "I stole dogs out of people's yards."

"Did you get paid?"

Pete nodded. "Yeah. Fifty bucks for every one I brought in."

The price of a conscience, Tom thought, was depressingly low these days. He bit back the things he wanted to say, the shaming lecture about breaking the hearts of kids and older people whose only company was a pet, the cruelty of throwing a pampered pet into a situation where it would be torn apart. He wasn't sure this boy was capable of shame in any conventional sense. He cared what his parents thought, though, and Tom had to rely on that. He probably cared what Beth Hall thought too.

"Who did you turn the dogs over to?" Tom asked.

The question made Pete squirm in his chair. He shifted around, leaned forward, slumped back again. "You're gonna get me killed," he protested, but weakly, knowing his argument was already lost.

Beck slapped him on the shoulder. "You want to stay out of prison, you'd better tell him."

"All right, all right," Pete said. Tears welled in his eyes. "I stole dogs for Leo Riggs."

Finally, Tom thought, they were getting somewhere. "What did Leo Riggs tell you the dogs would be used for?"

"I told you already—" He winced when Beck whacked him on the back of the head. "All right, all right. Leo told me they used the dogs I stole to train fighters."

"Did you go to the dogfights?" Tom asked.

Pete nodded.

"Out loud," Tom said.

"Yeah, I went."

"Did you do any work at the fights?"

"Sometimes. Handling dogs."

"Did you see Leo Riggs at the fights?" Tom asked.

"Yeah. He was in charge. He took the bets. Handled the money."

"Who else worked for him?"

Pete named Ellis, the guy who'd lately been acting as a guard at the Hall house, and a couple of others Tom knew by sight.

"When's the next fight? And where?"

"Tonight." Pete gave Tom directions to the spot. "That's why Leo wanted that dog out of the pound. He wanted to use it in the fight."

"So Leo asked you to get the black dog out of the pound?"

Nodding, Pete said, "Yeah, that's his dog. It got loose a while ago. That's his toughest fighter, and he wanted it back."

"Does Leo have any dogs trained to attack people?"

Screwing up his face, blinking back tears, Pete appealed to his father. "Dad, he's gonna come after me, he'll kill me for this."

Beck leaned closer and spoke into his son's face. "And if you don't tell the captain everything you know, you won't have to worry about Leo, 'cause I'll kill you myself."

In that moment, when Pete realized how alone he was, what a corner he'd backed himself into, Tom almost felt sorry for him. Almost. He repeated, "Does Leo have a dog that's trained to attack people?"

"Yeah. I think it's a brother to the one in the pound. I never saw it, though. I just heard about it."

"What do you know about Dr. Hall's death, Pete?"

"Nothing," he said, his eyes beseeching. "I swear I don't know a thing. I didn't have anything to do with it, I swear."

Tom sat back, watching the boy and tapping his fingers on the table as he thought. There was one more piece of information he wanted. Sitting forward again, he asked, "Where does Leo keep the dogs?"

Pete shook his head. "I don't know. I'm not lying, I really don't. When I turned over dogs to him, I just met him along the road wherever he told me to. I never got to see the place where he keeps the fighters."

Rachel was saying goodbye to a client and her pissed off Siamese cat when the front desk receptionist, Shannon, caught her eye. Holding up the telephone receiver, Shannon mouthed, "Captain Bridger."

Cutting short her parting exchange with the client, Rachel ran around the corner from the front desk to her office. She snatched up her desk telephone and punched the blinking button. "Tom?"

"What's up?"

"I went out to the Hall house this morning to see Thor, and I was shocked at Mrs. Hall's condition. She's barely alive, she ought to be in the hospital—"

"She has dialysis at the hospital. If the nurses thought she needed to be admitted—"

"I know, I know." Was Tom going to brush off her concerns again? "But I feel like something awful's about to happen. And those kids are caught in the middle of it. Can't you intervene somehow? At least talk to Mrs. Hall's doctor?"

"I'm on my way over to the Hall house now," Tom said. "I've got some new information that might give us a break in the case. I'll fill you in later. But I'll see what I can do for Vicky Hall."

Rachel wanted to know what he'd found out—from who? Pete Rasey?—but right now she couldn't delay him for a second. "Okay, go. I'll talk to you later."

She hung up, enormously relieved that Tom was looking into the situation at the Hall house, and that he'd scored some kind of breakthrough in the investigation. But she couldn't shake loose the dread that had taken root inside her, a sick fear that the killing wasn't over yet.

Chapter Thirty-four

When Tom entered Soo Jin's room she was sitting up in bed, looking like hell but wide awake and breathing without a respirator.

"Hey," he said, stopping at the foot of her bed. "How are you doing?"

Her swollen lips twisted in a wry lopsided grin. Her voice came out low and hoarse. "I can feel all my toes and fingers. I guess I'll live."

"I won't make you talk a lot," Tom said. "I know your throat's sore from the tube. I just wanted to ask if you remember the accident."

"No," she rasped. "All I know is that I wanted to find out where Ethan was going."

"Do you remember that part? Where he went?"

"To see Leo Riggs."

Tom nodded. He started to ask another question, but she interrupted.

"Listen. I have to tell you—" A wracking cough cut off her words.

Tom went to the bedside table, poured a glass of water, and held it while she sipped. "Don't try to talk if it hurts," he said, putting the glass down.

She grabbed his arm, her grip surprisingly strong. "I have to tell you," she said again. "I believe that woman is trying to kill my mother."

For a second Tom was too startled to speak. Suddenly a lot of things made sense. He was sure he knew the answer, but he asked anyway because he wanted to hear Soo Jin say it aloud. "What woman?"

In her dark eyes, circled by bruises, he saw rage mingled with desperate fear. "Rayanne," she said. "I think Rayanne is poisoning my mother."

Ellis was there again, standing guard with his shotgun at the bottom of the Halls' driveway. This time Tom saw the guy not as a nuisance but as a sinister presence hovering around a family that was imploding, like a hunter waiting for the weak and wounded to become easy prey.

Ellis worked for Leo Riggs. Like Rayanne, he was in a position to keep Leo informed about what was going on in the Hall household.

After their previous clashes, Tom doubted Ellis would expect a friendly greeting. Tom nodded indifferently as he passed the man. He'd have Ellis and his boss Leo in jail tonight if Pete's information could be trusted. He wanted to catch Leo at a dog-fight, and in the meantime he didn't want to say or do anything to tip Leo off that the cops were on to him.

At the door, Tom pushed past Ethan into the house without waiting to be invited. "I need to see your mother."

"Why is everybody so determined to bother my mother today?" Ethan said. "Rayanne's getting her dressed to go in for dialysis. Leave her alone."

"I'll wait here until she comes down." Tom stood at the bottom of the stairs and folded his arms.

Ethan wiped the back of his hand across his upper lip. "What do you need to talk to her about? Can I help you?"

"No." Tom couldn't risk asking Ethan about Gordon Hall's recent contacts with Leo, or whether Hall knew about the dog-fights. Ethan couldn't be trusted to keep his mouth shut about this turn in the investigation.

"All right," Ethan said, "if you want to wait, then go ahead and wait." He drew a breath, released it in a sigh. Dark circles under his eyes spoke of sleepless nights. He'd missed a spot on his left cheek with his razor, leaving a little patch of day-old whiskers near his jaw line.

"Have you decided when you'll have the services for your father?" Tom asked.

"Thursday."

"Are you leaving after that? Going back to work?"

"I don't know." Ethan poked his fists into his pants pockets and stared at the floor. "I don't think I can leave Mom for a while. I'm not sure she can cope with—with everything. A lot of decisions have to be made."

"That's true," Tom said. "Is she—"

He broke off when he heard voices from above. Rayanne stood at the top of the stairs, holding Vicky Hall by one arm. Beth had both her arms around her mother. "She can't get down the stairs," Beth protested. "She'll fall. Are you trying to kill her or something?"

Her face ashen, Vicky sagged against Beth.

"I know how to take care of her," Rayanne said. "It's my job. Now she needs to go to dialysis. Let go of her and get out of the way."

"Hold it," Tom said. "Ethan, come on." Tom took the stairs two at a time, Ethan behind him.

"We'll do just fine if everybody'll stay out of the way," Rayanne said. "We need to get goin' now."

When Tom reached Vicky Hall he was shocked by her appearance. She looked barely conscious, and he was sure she would collapse if Rayanne and Beth weren't holding her up.

"She needs an ambulance," Tom said. "I'm calling 911."

"We don't need an ambulance!" Rayanne exclaimed. "I'll take her in the car like I always do."

"You're not taking her anywhere." Tom reached into his shirt pocket for his cell phone.

"I'll call," Ethan said. He pulled his phone from his pants pocket and punched in the number. He issued quick, clear instructions to the emergency dispatcher.

"Let's get her back on the bed," Tom said. "Ethan, help me." He nudged Rayanne to make her step aside, but she remained planted where she was. He gave her a little shove. "Move. Now."

Rayanne stomped down the stairs and disappeared.

Vicky was so out of it that she couldn't take a single step on her own. Tom lifted her and carried her back to her bedroom. She weighed no more than a child.

As he laid her on the bed, her eyelids fluttered and she mumbled, "Gordie? Is that you?"

Looking down at her gaunt, colorless face, Tom wondered how everyone around her could have watched her deteriorate so quickly without becoming alarmed. He was as guilty as the rest, blaming her condition on her husband's death until Rachel forced him to give the situation a fresh look. He would insist that Vicky's blood be tested before dialysis removed any toxins.

Beth dropped to her knees beside the bed and clasped her mother's hand. "Mommy? I'm here, Mommy. Please, please…" She buried her face in the rumpled comforter.

Ethan stood at the foot of the bed, watching his mother with a stunned expression. "I didn't realize how bad she was. I swear I didn't."

Tom grabbed his arm and pulled him toward the door. "I want to talk to you before the ambulance gets here."

In the hallway they encountered David and Marcy. The boy's usual belligerence was firmly in place, but his wide, moist eyes betrayed fear and confusion. Marcy pressed a fist to her mouth as tears ran silently down her cheeks.

"Kids," Tom said, "why don't you wait downstairs? An ambulance is coming to take your mother to the hospital."

"Is she going to die?" Marcy asked, her voice a faint whimper.

"I hope not," Tom said. "Wait downstairs, okay?"

They set off down the steps, and Tom motioned for Ethan to move farther away from his mother's open bedroom door.

Although Ethan looked as if he wanted to argue or resist, after a brief hesitation he walked a few feet down the hall, Tom following.

"Have you talked to her doctor about her condition?" Tom asked.

Ethan frowned, puzzled. "No. Should I?"

Jesus Christ, Tom thought. Did the woman have to die in front of her son before it would occur to Ethan that she might need medical help? "Yeah, I believe you should. You should have let him know she was going downhill so fast. Now she's reached a crisis point. Don't expect her to be back home anytime soon." *If ever.*

"Oh, shit, she'll hate being in the hospital."

"Not if it saves her life."

"But the nurses in the dialysis center have been seeing her," Ethan said. "If she's all that sick, why didn't they do something?"

"She hasn't been to dialysis since Friday," Tom said. "She hasn't been anywhere but this house. You should have kept an eye on her condition."

"Rayanne takes care of her." Ethan leaned against the wall, rubbing his eyes.

"Why isn't somebody better qualified looking after your mother?"

"All Mom needs," Ethan said, "is somebody to drive her to dialysis and do things for her at home. I don't know what you mean by better qualified. Why would she need anybody with special training?"

"How did Rayanne get this job?"

Ethan shrugged. "Don't ask me. I wasn't around when she was hired."

"How much do you know about her?"

"Why would I know anything about her?"

"Seems to me you'd want some information about a woman who's in the house all day and into the night."

Beth spoke up before Ethan could answer. From the doorway of her mother's room, she said, "Soo Jin accused her of stealing."

Tom looked at the girl. "Come over here. Stealing what?"

"She doesn't know what he's talking about," Ethan said.

Ignoring him, Tom asked Beth, "What did Soo Jin think Rayanne stole?"

Beth folded her arms and hunched her shoulders as if she were suddenly chilled. Tears still swam in her eyes. "Money, and some other stuff she could sell. Silverware and stuff."

"She's just making this up," Ethan told Tom.

"I am *not,*" Beth shot back. "I heard them. I heard Soo call her a thief. She said she was going to tell on her and get Mom to fire her."

"Don't listen to this," Ethan said. "My sister is a chronic liar."

"Don't you dare call me a liar." Beth started toward Ethan.

"Hey, whoa." Tom grabbed Beth's arm and got between her and Ethan. "Cool it, both of you."

Beth's lower lip trembled and tears spilled down her cheeks as she suddenly abandoned the argument. "When's the ambulance getting here? Mom can't seem to stay awake."

"It'll be here in a few minutes. Go back in there with her."

When Beth was gone, Tom asked Ethan, "Are you aware of anything missing from the house? Anything that could have been stolen?"

"I don't know. I don't count the silverware. And I told you, you can't take Beth's word for it."

And if Beth hadn't made it up? Was Rayanne the one who had slashed Soo Jin's tires? Tom was already reasonably sure that Sylvia, Burt Morgan's girlfriend, had told her cousin Rayanne about the planned raid on the dogfight, and Rayanne had passed the information on to Leo. Had Rayanne also tried to kill Soo Jin? Was Ethan showing a natural resistance to an unpleasant truth, or did he have some reason to protect Rayanne?

Tom wanted to keep at him until he got some answers, but he could hear the ambulance siren in the distance, faint but coming closer. He only had a couple more minutes here. He turned to the question that mattered most to Rachel. "What's going to happen to these kids if your mother dies? Beth and David and Marcy."

"My mother's not dying. She's going to be fine. You're exaggerating everything—"

"Listen to me. Your mother is being kept alive by dialysis. Your father's death seems to have pushed her over the edge—"

"That's not true!" Ethan spun away from Tom and bumped a knee against the leg of a console table. "Shit." He grabbed his knee and squeezed his eyes shut.

Tom waited, and listened to the ambulance siren growing louder by the second.

After clutching his knee and grimacing for a few seconds, Ethan took a deep breath. "My mother is not dying," he said again, his voice still tremulous. "Once the funeral's behind us, she'll be better."

"Do you really think she'll be okay without your father? They were very close, she leaned on him—"

"She'll learn to lean on me."

"That's not the same thing."

Ethan's certainty dissolved as quickly as it had appeared. "Oh, shit, what a mess," he groaned, covering his face with his hands.

"Somebody's going to have to make a decision about David and Marcy's future, if your mother can't take care of them."

"That's our family's business. It's not something for you to get involved in."

Beth rushed out of her mother's bedroom. "The ambulance is coming up the driveway."

Chapter Thirty-five

Rachel had never met the tall black man, but she knew who he was the instant she opened the door. His skin was darker, but his features, especially his large, beautiful eyes, were strikingly like those of his son David and his daughter Marcy.

Before she could find her voice, Tom came up behind her. "Hey, Raymond," he said. "I didn't know you were back in the county. What can I do for you?"

"Hey, Tom," the man said. "I just got here a while ago. Drove down from Richmond. Sorry to bother you at home, but I need to talk to you."

"Come on in," Tom said. He reached over Rachel's head and pushed the door open all the way.

"Yes, please," she said. She gave Tom a pointed look: *An introduction might be good at this point.*

"Rachel, this is Raymond Porter. Raymond, this is Dr. Goddard."

"Hello," she said.

He nodded to Rachel without meeting her eyes.

She couldn't stop staring at him. He was around Tom's age, early to mid-thirties, and had the same kind of lean athletic build. Rachel could imagine them on a basketball court together as teenagers.

He stepped inside but halted just inside the door, hands in his jacket pockets. "Am I interrupting your dinner?"

"No, no, we've finished dinner," Rachel said. "Come into the living room."

He seemed uneasy, and he sat down hesitantly, as if he doubted the wisdom of being there at all.

Questions swarmed in Rachel's mind as she sat on the couch across from him. *Are you here for your children? Do you want them? Do you care about them at all?*

"What can I do for you?" Tom sat beside Rachel. "And what brings you back home?"

Raymond clasped his hands between his knees and stared down at them for a moment before answering. "I've been hearing all this stuff—Dr. Hall getting killed, his daughter having a bad accident, and just a little while ago my cousin Rhonda that works at the hospital told me Mrs. Hall's real bad off. Rhonda said she might die. Is that true?"

"She's been hospitalized in serious condition," Tom said.

Rachel watched Raymond, taking in every flicker of emotion on his face, every tense angle of his posture. What she saw was a man in turmoil, a man who felt helpless.

"What's happening to David and Marcy?" Raymond asked. "Who's looking after them, making sure they're okay?"

"The Halls' daughter Beth promised me she'd take care of them," Tom said. "She's sixteen. She told me she'll do the cooking and make sure everybody gets their meals on time."

Raymond nodded, but the information didn't seem to relieve his concern. "But what's going to happen if Mrs. Hall dies?"

"I don't know."

Rachel waited for Tom to say more, but he didn't. Why didn't he ask about Raymond's plans? Was the man here to take David and Marcy away from the Hall family? Before she could stop herself, she blurted, "David told Marcy that he's going to run away and find you. He wants to take Marcy with him. He thinks they're going to live with you."

Raymond looked dumbstruck, staring openmouthed at Rachel.

"Are you in touch with David?" Tom asked.

"No. No, I've steered clear. I thought that was the best thing for everybody." Raymond shook his head. "Why would David even think something like that?"

"Maybe their uncle Leo offered to help them find you," Tom said.

A harsh laugh burst from Raymond. "Leo hates my guts. He always said—" He broke off, shaking his head. "Hell, what does it matter? It's too late now."

"Why didn't you take them when their mother died?' Rachel asked. "Why did you let the Halls have them?"

"Rachel," Tom said, the one word conveying shock and disapproval.

"It's a fair question," Raymond said. He kept his gaze on his clenched hands as he went on. "The Halls already had them before I even knew what was going on. Leo said he'd fight me if I tried to take them. He'd make sure everybody thought I was a drug addict and wasn't fit. I didn't think I could fight the Halls, anyway. They had money; Dr. Hall was head of the hospital. I couldn't win."

"Did you even try?" Rachel asked. "Did you see a lawyer about it?"

"Yeah, I did. He said the same thing. With my history, I didn't stand a chance against the Halls. Funny thing is, by the time Jewel died I had myself straightened out. I never got hooked bad, the way she did. I was getting my life together. I'd been talking to Jewel on the phone a lot, talking about her and the kids leaving here, coming to live with me. I thought she was finally clean. Then—" He spread his hands helplessly. "All of a sudden she was dead. I haven't seen our kids since before she died."

"Wait a minute," Rachel said. "Did you ever sign a document relinquishing your parental rights?"

"No, I didn't. And I never would have."

"Then the adoption wasn't—"

"I'll try to keep you informed about what's happening," Tom broke in. He got to his feet, signaling an end to the conversation.

"Tom," Rachel protested.

He ignored her and asked Raymond, "Are you staying with your folks?"

Raymond nodded. Rising slowly, he looked weary and disappointed. "All right. I guess that's the most I can expect."

"I want you to stay away from the Halls' house," Tom said. "And from the Riggs family."

"Don't worry," Raymond said, moving toward the door. "I can't imagine any two places I'd be less welcome."

After seeing Raymond out, Tom turned to Rachel, a hand up to stop the torrent of words ready to spill out of her. "I know you want to talk about this, but I've got to get going. My men are waiting for me at headquarters." He pulled her into his arms. "We'll talk later, okay?"

"Yes. Okay," Rachel said, her voice muffled as she pressed her face against his shoulder. For a few minutes she'd been able to forget where he was going tonight. Now it hit her again, and brought a flood of paralyzing fear. She held onto Tom, knowing he had to leave, not wanting to let him go out into the night. "Be careful," she said. "Please, please don't get hurt."

He kissed her forehead and gently pushed her away. "Don't worry about things that probably won't happen. I just hope this isn't another false lead. I'll call you if any of the dogs need treatment right away."

When he was gone, Rachel leaned against the closed door and listened to his cruiser start up and drive away. She would be trapped in a state of pure terror until she heard the raid had gone smoothly. After the ambush on Saturday night, she couldn't believe a raid on a dogfight was a routine operation with little risk. Even with Pete Rasey locked up, unable to communicate with the people in the dogfighting ring, Rachel worried that they had somehow found out about the raid and would be lying in wait for the deputies. Somebody could get killed tonight.

Chapter Thirty-six

"Oh, man," Brandon said, "I don't mind admitting I'm nervous about this." He rode with Tom, leading a caravan of eight Sheriff's Department cars with Joe Dolan bringing up the rear in his animal control van.

"There's no way Pete could have got a message to Leo," Tom said. "They don't know we're coming." What he said was true, he believed it, but reason couldn't dissolve the knot of dread in his gut.

Before setting out, the deputies had gathered at headquarters and donned bulletproof vests. They hadn't bothered with vests last time, and it was pure dumb luck that nobody had been killed. Acknowledgment that they might need the protection had upped the tension among them to an almost palpable level.

They drove deep into Rocky Branch District, the most sparsely populated section of the county, where their headlights cut through a darkness rarely relieved by the lights from houses. Heavy cloud cover hid the moon and stars.

Tom slowed, worried about missing the turnoff. "Is that it?"

Brandon leaned forward to squint through the windshield. "Could be. Oh, yeah, there's that little reflector Pete said to look for."

Another dirt track through dense woods. Tom braked and stared into the black hole he and his men had to enter. This time they would drive in, to prevent anybody from escaping and to give themselves another layer of protection if somebody opened fire. The track wasn't wide enough for them to turn their cars around, though. If they had to flee, they would have to do it by driving in reverse. Not a thought Tom wanted to dwell on.

"They might see us coming," Brandon said, "with most of the leaves off the trees."

"Remember they're inside a building, a shed with no windows." Tom had made Pete describe it in detail so the deputies would know what they were dealing with. "Pete said he's never seen anybody acting as a lookout. They seem pretty sure they won't get caught. But now that they know we're after them, we can't assume anything."

Tom turned onto the dirt track. He could hear Brandon's rapid, shallow breaths.

He switched off his headlights, and in the rearview mirror he saw them blink off on every car, one by one. Only the running lights allowed them to see each other and stay on track in the inky darkness.

Half a mile in, Tom saw lights up ahead through the trees. "Looks like lanterns on poles," he said. "You see any men?"

"No," Brandon said. "But there's plenty of cars parked in there. "

"We'll go the rest of the way on foot." Tom shifted into park and killed the engine. The deputies behind him did the same.

Silently they emerged from their vehicles and closed the doors without a sound. Only Joe would stay behind with his vehicle. Tom drew his pistol. Everybody had extra handcuffs, metal and plastic, attached to their equipment belts. They were as ready as they would ever be.

Tom gave a short, low whistle, his signal to follow him in. Moving forward, he raised his weapon. Behind him, he heard the deputies' boot soles scuffing through dry leaves as they picked their way along the dark path.

As they got closer, Tom heard men shouting encouragement and curses, groaning in disappointment. When he entered the clearing, he crouched behind one of the parked cars and motioned for the other men to get down too. He wanted to watch and listen for a few minutes and get some idea of what they might encounter. The "shed" Pete had described was a good-sized building, maybe forty by thirty feet. No windows. Tin roof. It wasn't built for human habitation and had probably been constructed specifically for the dogfights. Battery-operated camp lanterns hung on hooks outside the door and in several places around the clearing, probably to make parking easier.

Tom estimated twenty vehicles in the clearing, some of them older trucks and cars, some newer, more expensive cars. These exhibitions of animals tearing each other apart attracted men from the lowest to the highest levels of society. Tom had heard that some spectators would drive a hundred miles or more to gamble on a fight.

A sudden howl made Tom jump. It took him a second to place the sound. It was coming from inside a big van parked next to the building's door. Another dog joined in. The dogs waiting their turn were getting worked up by the noise of the crowd inside.

Tom waited to see if anybody would come out to silence or check on the dogs in the van. When nobody did, he stood and motioned to his team. He drew in a deep breath and, heart suddenly racing, charged toward the shed. He slammed a booted foot into the door, knocking it open, and ran inside with his gun raised and ready. The other deputies piled in behind him.

Curses and shouts of alarm rose from the men in the room. Several made for the door, but they ran into a barricade of deputies with drawn pistols. Cigarette smoke clouded the air, and the only light came from the lanterns hanging above the fighting pit.

"Face the wall!" Tom yelled. "Now! Put your hands up and keep them where we can see them."

The deputies shoved men against the walls and started patting them down.

"Cuff everybody," Tom said. "We're taking all of them in."

That was greeted with a chorus of groans. "Aw, come on," one man protested. "Don't the cops have anything better to do than keep people from having fun?"

"Shut up, all of you," Tom said. Scanning the room, he realized with a stab of disappointment that the one man he wanted wasn't there.

Brandon, frisking the big man named Ellis, called out to Tom from the far side of the room. "Hey, Captain!" He held up a pistol. "This guy was carrying."

Tom edged past lined-up men to reach Brandon and Ellis. "You in charge tonight?" he asked Ellis.

"I don't know what you're talking about, Captain."

"Yeah, and I guess you didn't notice what was going on here." Tom looked down into the depression in the dirt floor, where two pit bulls had backed away from each other, distracted by all the activity among the people in the room. One dog's cheek dripped blood from a torn flap of skin. The other dog cowered against the side of the pit, alternately staring up at the people and licking at a gash in its side. The fight, Tom guessed, hadn't been underway long before the deputies broke in.

Ellis hadn't responded to Tom's remark. Tom demanded, "Where's Leo?"

"How would I know? He don't tell me his plans."

"You work for him. Did he send you over here tonight because he was afraid to show up himself?"

"I told you, I don't know what you're talking about."

Turning away from the man, Tom said, "All right, guys, let's get these jokers back to the jail and get them booked."

As the deputies moved the men out one by one, Joe Dolan pushed past them into the building and over to the wire fencing around the pit. "These dogs need a vet," he told Tom.

"Rachel's standing by for a call. Did you check on the dogs in the van?"

"Yeah, there's eight of them in there, in cages. If I can get these two back in there, one of your men could drive the whole lot of them to the pound."

"Hey, Bran," Tom called to Brandon, who was shoving Ellis toward the door, "I think you'll find the keys to that van outside in your guy's pocket. Lock him in the back of my car, then come help us get these two dogs into the van."

While the deputies shoved the protesting men into police cars, Joe darted the injured dogs. When they were under, Tom and Joe pushed aside the makeshift gate in the fencing, dropped into the pit and lifted out the tranquilized dogs.

When the animals were in the van and the door was closed, Brandon asked Tom, "Why do you suppose Leo didn't show up?"

"He's a coward and doesn't want to take a risk," Tom said. "He's probably been home with his girlfriend all evening so he can claim he doesn't have anything to do with the fight. After we get these guys to jail and the dogs to the pound, we'll go looking for Leo."

◇◇◇

Accompanied by Brandon, Tom pulled into the gravel driveway behind Rayanne's yellow Volkswagen Bug. No lights burned in Leo's little house. Was Leo even here? Tom didn't see his car anywhere, but it could be parked behind the house.

They got out and quietly pushed their doors closed. Brandon headed toward the back, his pistol drawn, and Tom walked across the grass to the front door. As he mounted the three wooden steps to the porch, a creak made him stop and hold his breath. No reaction from inside. The floorboards on the porch also creaked under his weight, and he moved quickly to press his back against the house next to the front door. His gun in one hand, he balled the other into a fist and reached sideways to pound on the door.

He waited a few seconds, but no lights came on inside and no one appeared. He banged on the door again and called out, "Leo! Open up! It's Tom Bridger."

If Riggs was inside and wanted to run, this was the moment when he would do it. Tom knew Brandon was ready for him at the rear door.

A light came on in the house and spilled through the window to Tom's right. After a moment he heard a bolt slide back. The front door opened and Rayanne Stuckey blinked at him through the screen door.

"What do you want?" she asked, pushing a mass of blond curls off her face with both hands. She wore a long tee shirt and fuzzy blue slippers.

"I need to see Leo." Tom faced the door but stayed off to one side to keep out of the line of fire if Leo started shooting from inside.

"He's not here." Rayanne yawned, covering her mouth with a hand. "He said he might not be home tonight."

"Where is he?"

"I don't know. He didn't tell me."

"He stays gone all night and doesn't tell you where he is?"

"That's right." Rayanne folded her arms over her chest, catching enough of the tee shirt to make it ride up and expose a hint of red panties.

"Mind if I come in and make sure of that?" Tom asked.

"Yeah, I do mind. Look, you don't see his car, do you? He's not here. What do you want him for, anyway?"

"I think you know."

"I'm not a mind reader."

"How often do you talk to your cousin Sylvia?"

A sharp inhalation gave away her surprise, although her expression remained obstinate. "What business is that of yours?" Without giving him a chance to answer, she went on, "You know, I didn't like the way you talked to me at the Halls' house. Like I'm some kind of ignorant little hick."

Tom didn't respond, but waited to hear what else she might say.

"And your girlfriend's just as bad," she went on. "Acting like she can order me around."

"We're both worried about Mrs. Hall. She's in bad shape."

"You think I don't know that? You think her kids don't know it? She's got family, and she's got me. You don't have to go pokin' your nose in. And your animal doctor friend oughta stick to dogs and cats."

"Tell me something," Tom said. "How did you get along with Soo Jinn?"

Rayanne's eyes narrowed. "What are you talkin' about now? I'm gettin' cold standin' here listenin' to you."

"Did you like her?"

"Nobody liked her. Why would I? She treated me like something nasty she stepped in."

That wasn't hard to imagine. "I hear she accused you of stealing from the Halls."

"She accused me of a lot of things," Rayanne said, her voice turning haughty, "but none of it's true."

"Must be hard for somebody like you, working in a place with so many expensive things sitting around. Jewelry, silver—"

"Somebody like me?" she broke in. "What's that crack supposed to mean?"

"We'll talk about this again," Tom said. "Right now, if you know where Leo is, you'd better tell me. If he's in the house—"

"Oh, for god's sake, come on in and look if that'll get rid of you faster." She pushed the screen door open.

Tom kept his gun in hand as he entered.

The interior smelled faintly of popcorn and butter. A snack before bedtime, maybe. The living room was so bare it was hard to believe anybody lived here. No magazines, no books, none of the clutter of daily life. The kitchen and bathroom were spotless, without so much as a potholder or a shampoo bottle in sight. The obsessively clean, spare look of the place reminded Tom of Leo's business office at his garage. In the bedroom, a kingsize bed took up so much space that the chest of drawers had been moved out into the short hallway. Only one side of the bed was rumpled.

Tom walked through every room and checked out the dirt-floor cellar to satisfy himself that Leo wasn't lurking anywhere. In the kitchen, he rapped on the locked back door and called out, "Hey, Bran, he's not here. Go on back to the car."

As they drove away in the cruiser, Brandon said, "Maybe the guys had better luck at his mom and dad's place."

Tom had sent two deputies to the home of Leo's parents at the same time he and Brandon had come to Leo's house. "I doubt it. If he's gone into hiding, that's too obvious a place. My guess is that he's hunkered down wherever he keeps his fighters."

When they found Leo Riggs, Tom believed, they would also find the dog that had torn out Gordon Hall's throat.

Chapter Thirty-seven

At three in the morning, Rachel drew the final stitch into a firm knot and clipped the thread. The unconscious pit bull on the operating table breathed evenly, at peace for the moment.

After examining the two fighters' injuries at the pound, she had asked Joe to move them to the animal hospital, where she had all the supplies she needed for surgical repair of wounds. She worked without the assistance of a tech, in an eerily silent clinic that would be bustling with people and animals in a few hours.

Like the other dog whose wounds she had treated, this one was so thin that Rachel easily lifted him and carried him to a cage. After arranging him in a comfortable position and adjusting his IV, she stroked the dog's head, something she might not be able to do when he was awake. While she was working on them, she could stay focused and keep her emotions in check. But she felt the rage building in her, and if she gave in to it she'd be ready to kill somebody.

When she walked out to the reception area, she found Tom, not Joe, leaning against the front desk.

"Hey," he said. "Joe wanted to get back to the pound. How are the patients doing?"

"They'll be all right. Their biggest problem is that they're seriously malnourished."

"Fighters are kept lean and hungry," Tom said. "Makes them meaner."

"If they get plenty to eat and they're treated well, we might be able to save most of them."

"Rachel, come on," Tom said. "Who's going to want these dogs?"

"We can't just assume that nobody will want them. We have to give them a chance." Tom squeezed her shoulder, an acknowledgment of her feelings that annoyed her because it felt like condescension. She pulled away from his touch. "They're not going to be put down. I'll go to court to stop it if I have to."

Tom opened his mouth to say something but apparently thought better of it.

"I'm staying here for a while to keep an eye on them," she said. "I'll be okay. Nobody can get in unless I open the door from the inside. What are you going to do next?"

"We need to find the base for the fighting operation. Pete Rasey's never seen where the dogs are kept, but he says Leo has about twenty fighting dogs right now, so we only picked up half of them tonight."

"What about the stolen pets?" Rachel asked, her gaze shifting beyond Tom to the lost-dog posters on the waiting room walls.

"Pete thinks some of them are still alive because Leo told him he had all he needed for a while. But we have to find Leo before he destroys all the evidence."

Rachel pictured Riggs shooting dogs, strangling them, bashing in their heads, dumping them into a burial pit. A shudder moved through her. "What did Pete say about the one we caught, the alpha male? Was he trained to attack people, like his litter mate?"

"That one was used in fights. The other dog's the one we're after. I think if we can find it we'll be able to match it to the DNA we got off Hall's body."

"And that makes Leo Riggs guilty of murder under the law?" Rachel asked.

"As surely as if he'd used a gun to kill Gordon Hall. His weapon just happened to be a dog. I hope we can—" Tom broke off when his cell phone bleated from his jacket pocket. He fished it out, answered and listened. "Aw, god, no," he groaned. "All right. I'll leave right now."

Rachel went cold inside. "What's happened?"

Tom stuck his phone back in his pocket. "Beck Rasey's dead. Killed by a dog, just like Gordon Hall."

Babs Rasey screamed again and again. She was on the front porch, barefoot and wearing only a nightgown, and one of the Blackwood twins was trying to hold her back as she struggled to get to her husband.

Beck lay spread-eagle in the yard at the bottom of the front steps. The other Blackwood twin—Keith, Tom guessed as he walked up the driveway—stood a few feet away from the body. Gretchen Lauter hadn't arrived yet.

Keith flicked his flashlight beam over the driveway pavement ahead of Tom. "Watch out there, Captain. Blood."

Tom unhooked his flashlight from his equipment belt, switched it on, and swept the light across the driveway. Arterial spray, at least fifteen feet from the body, was soaking into the cracks in the concrete. He stepped onto the grass and picked out a path that didn't require him to walk in blood.

Crouching beside Beck, he examined the wound. Beck's throat, like Hall's, had been torn out all the way down to the spinal cord. Shifting the light, Tom saw a few scratches on Beck's bare chest where his terrycloth robe had fallen open. Blood soaked the robe.

Babs Rasey went on screaming.

Tom walked up the front steps, his ears ringing from her high-pitched cries. He hoped to god she had seen something, heard something. "Babs," he said, keeping his voice calm, "do you have any idea who did this?"

"Yes, god damn it!" she yelled. "I saw him! Leo Riggs, that filthy piece of trash. He turned that monster dog on Beck. He killed him, Tom, he killed Beck." She sagged, and Kevin Blackwood had to grab her around the waist to keep her on her feet.

Ah, god, Tom thought. Leo probably knew Pete Rasey was in jail, and it didn't take much brain power to figure out that the boy had given up the time and location of the dogfight. Leo couldn't get to Pete—yet—so he'd killed Beck instead. "Tell me exactly what happened," Tom said to Babs.

She choked out the words between sobs. "He walked right up to our door and knocked, and he got Beck outside and turned that dog on him. Oh, god, Beck never should've made Pete talk to you."

With her husband lying dead in the yard, Tom wasn't going to argue the point with her. All he could do now was promise to keep her son safely locked up until they caught Leo. They would have to protect Babs too. Why hadn't Leo killed her? Why did he leave a witness behind? "Did Leo threaten you?" he asked. "How did you get rid of him?"

"I shot him, that's how!" She gestured toward the shotgun leaning against the wall next to the front door. "I tied to shoot the dog too, but he got out of range."

"Are you sure you hit Leo?"

"Oh, yeah, I know for damned sure I hit him. I was close, and I got him right in the belly." In the space of a few seconds, her grief morphed into dry-eyed fury. "I shot that son of a bitch and he took off running like the coward he is."

Chapter Thirty-eight

"I need your help this morning," Rachel told Jim Sullivan on the phone. She'd called at six a.m., but as a farm vet he was used to early hours, and she doubted she would wake him. He'd answered on the first ring. "Could you reschedule any appointments you have so you can come with me?"

"Come with you where?" He sounded wary. "Help you with what?"

"The deputies rescued some dogs last night in a raid on a dogfight." Rachel waited to see if Sullivan would react to that. He remained silent. "I patched up two of them, and they're at the clinic now. I need to examine the others at the pound. I'd like you to help me."

A short silence, then, "I've got my own work to do."

"I'm sure nobody will mind if you reschedule."

"Why are you asking me? Why can't somebody else help you?"

"Because these are aggressive animals and I need someone who won't be afraid of them."

"Look, I don't think so."

"Dr. Sullivan—Jim—the clinic has a contract with the county to provide medical care to animals at the pound. This is part of our job."

"I'm just saying one of the other vets can go with you."

Rachel could give him a direct order, but that wouldn't go over well. Softening her voice, she said, "You know how young and inexperienced they are. You're the only vet on the staff I can trust with these dogs. I'll feel a lot more confident if you're there with me."

He didn't answer.

Okay, I'll take that as a yes. "Would you meet me at the pound? Say, within the hour? If we work fast, maybe you'll only be a little late for your appointments and you won't have to reschedule anything for another day."

Rachel heard him sigh. She waited.

"All right," he said. "I'll be there."

Yes! She was determined to put her doubts about Sullivan to rest—or prove she'd been right all along.

Tom wasn't surprised to see Sheriff Willingham pulling into the parking lot at headquarters ahead of him. The sheriff's phone had probably started ringing before daybreak.

Tom parked in his reserved space next to the sheriff's and got out. He walked over and held the door as Willingham struggled out of his vehicle. Before the sheriff could speak, Tom said, "We released most of them after booking, but they'll have to show up in court. I'm not letting any of then off, no matter who they are."

Willingham sighed and shook his head. "I've seen it before, but I'll never stop being shocked that respectable men would be part of that nasty business. No real man takes pleasure in animals being forced to hurt each other. Make them pay a price for it."

"I'm glad you see it that way." Tom was a little surprised the sheriff wasn't making exceptions for a couple of his political supporters who'd been arrested at the dogfight.

"I was wrong about those abandoned dogs," Willingham said. "I'm glad y'all got them rounded up—good job, quick and thorough—and I don't mind admitting I was an ass for thinking they killed Gordon Hall."

The sheriff was full of surprises today. "That's done with now," Tom said. "We've got bigger problems to tackle. The guys are inside waiting for me—"

"Hold on a minute." The sheriff leaned on his cane. "You know, if you plan to campaign for sheriff, you'll get some trouble from people you've run afoul of. You've got principles. Not everybody appreciates that."

For a moment Tom was too confused to respond. "I'm not running for any office. You're the sheriff. I'm not planning to oppose you."

"I've been meaning to talk to you about that." Willingham placed a hand on his shoulder. Tom had the feeling he was about to hear momentous news, but he didn't want to imagine what it might be.

"You know how much your dad meant to me," Willingham said.

"Yes, sir," Tom said. He was a little alarmed by the quaver in Willingham's voice. "He thought a lot of you too. He was always telling Chris and me stories about the two of you in Vietnam. Mom didn't want to hear about it, but we ate it up."

Willingham nodded, blinking rapidly. Did the old man actually have tears in his eyes?

"Well, I've watched you turn into a fine man too," Willingham said, "as smart and honest and dependable as John was. A fine law enforcement officer."

What was this leading up to? While the sheriff kept him out here in the parking lot, deputies waited inside for him to prepare them for a dangerous manhunt. "Sir—"

Willingham hushed him with a motion of one hand. "I won't be running for reelection, Tom. My health is just too bad, I'm not serving the county the way a sheriff ought to. I hope you'll run for the office next year. I'll give you my full backing."

Tom was dumbfounded. He'd known the sheriff's health was failing, he'd known that eventually Willingham would have to step down, but he'd never considered what that might mean for his own future. And he didn't have time to think about it now. "Sir, I—I don't know what to say."

"One piece of advice, though," Willingham said. "You know folks around here are pretty conservative. So before you announce you're going to run, you and Dr. Goddard need to get married."

◇◇◇

A few minutes later, Tom addressed the dozen deputies assembled around the conference room table. The sheriff sat in a chair against a wall and kept silent. "If Leo's wounded," Tom said, "and we have to assume he is, then he'll need help, but he's not likely to show up in the ER. If he's not at his parents' place, they'll know where he is. Before we head out there, we have to be sure what we're up against. They could all open fire on us."

"Even his mom?" Brandon asked with a grin.

"Maddy Riggs isn't some harmless little old lady, believe me. She might not give a damn about her half-black grandkids, but she'll protect her son any way she has to. And she's a great shot."

"So how are we going to manage this?' Dennis asked. "They're up on the side of a mountain, and with most of the leaves down, they can see anything that's coming their way."

"We're not going to try sneaking up on them. We're not going up on foot. That's too dangerous." Tom had a sudden sharp memory of another time, less than a year before, when he and Brandon had approached a suspect's cabin in the woods and he'd ended up with a bullet in his arm. "We'll be safer in our vehicles. But be careful. I don't want to break bad news to anybody's family today."

◇◇◇

Rachel paced the small parking area in front of the county pound, checking her watch every couple of minutes. She was early, Sullivan wasn't late yet. But would he show up at all? How would she, as his boss, deal with him if he didn't come?

She was so close to believing he would stand her up that the sight of his mud-covered van coming down the road startled her. She rushed to her Range Rover, snatched her medical bag from the passenger seat, and waited at the building's door as if she'd just arrived.

Looking grim, Sullivan joined her with his bag in hand and pulled open the door. He didn't speak and he didn't make eye contact. If he didn't want to talk, fine. Rachel hadn't summoned him here to chat with him.

"Hey, docs," Joe Dolan said when they entered the small front office of the building. This early in the morning no one was working behind the counter that served as a reception desk. Joe waved them toward the door into the kennel. "They've all had breakfast and they seem pretty calm. I guess they're used to being in cages."

Rachel detected no trace of emotion on Sullivan's face. He seemed distant, as if his mind were elsewhere. He followed Joe and Rachel into the kennel.

Cages at floor level lined the bright room. In one big cage, four brown puppies slept in a pile, their plump bellies rising and falling with every breath. Joe kept the place immaculate, and usually when Rachel came here the only smell she detected was that of clean dog hair. Today she smelled urine and feces. All eight of the pit bulls, in individual cages against one wall, shrank back, trying to hide as the three people approached.

Rachel kept her voice quiet to avoid alarming the dogs further. "I'd like to get blood samples from them," she told Sullivan, "but that'll have to wait. Examining them and giving them vaccines is probably all we can get done today."

Sullivan finally broke his silence. "Blood samples? For what?"

"For the national database of fighting dogs. It can help police track a dog's origin."

Sullivan frowned, his face pinched, but he didn't respond.

Rachel crouched by the first cage. The dog inside looked half-grown, more of a pup than an adult. It watched Rachel with wary eyes from a bed that took up a third of the cage. "I can't believe an animal this young was going to be forced to fight," she said.

Sullivan, standing above her, said nothing.

"Hey, there," Rachel crooned to the dog. "We're not going to hurt you. You're safe now."

The dog cocked his ears forward. When he made eye contact with Rachel, he whimpered softly.

Rachel pulled a bag of dog treats from her bag and offered one of the sausage-like snacks through the mesh on the cage door. "Want a treat? It smells good, doesn't it? Come on now, you can have it."

"Let me try." Sullivan crouched beside her.

Startled by his abrupt willingness, she said, "Oh. Okay, sure."

Sullivan took the treat. "Move off a little, would you? Both of you."

Rachel and Joe stepped back, against the wall. Rachel wasn't sure what she expected. She didn't know what it would take to prove her theory that Sullivan had treated these dogs before.

Sullivan offered the treat to the dog. "Here you go, boy. Come and get it."

The dog began to wag his tail. After a moment he stood and crept toward the mesh that separated him from the man. He took the treat from Sullivan's fingers and stood in place, chewing, his eyes locked on Sullivan. His tail wagged faster.

This one knows him, Rachel thought. She felt queasy, revolted, at the same time she was grateful to see evidence that Sullivan had treated the dogs kindly.

"He wants another one," Sullivan said.

Rachel pulled out another fake sausage and handed it to Sullivan. This time, after downing the treat, the dog allowed Sullivan to poke a couple of fingers through the mesh and scratch his head.

Moving slowly, Sullivan unlatched the door and reached in to pet the dog. After a minute, he gently scooped up the animal. Rachel expected the dog to react to being handled, struggle and perhaps try to bite Sullivan, but the animal remained calm.

"In here," Joe said, opening a door into another room.

Sullivan carried the young pit bull to a steel table and set him down. Rachel followed with Sullivan's bag and her own. She stood back to watch Sullivan examine the dog. The animal didn't seem to mind the vet's hands on him, and when Sullivan stuck the needle into his flanks, the dog barely flinched.

"All right," Sullivan said to Joe. "Why don't you let him out in one of the runs for a potty break and I'll get the next one."

"You're so good with them," Rachel said. "I'll let you handle them, and I'll step in if you need help."

"Whatever," Sullivan said.

The other seven dogs, adults with scars from past fights, seemed equally unconcerned about Sullivan handling them. They were all big but underweight, and he carried them easily.

When he closed the last cage, Rachel said, "Let's take a look at the alpha dog we caught with the pack."

"You don't need me for that," Sullivan said. He was already stashing his stethoscope in his medical bag.

"Yes, I do," she said, leaving no room for argument.

Sullivan's sigh was audible. "After you."

Joe led them into the room where the alpha dog had been isolated to keep him from whipping the others into a frenzy. At the sight of Rachel and Joe, the animal leapt to its feet, snarling.

"Aw, now," Joe said, "is that any way to act after I gave you that good breakfast?"

Rachel stepped closer to the cage. The dog bared his teeth and growled.

"I haven't been able to clean his cage yet," Joe said. "I'm afraid he'll go nuts if I try to shift him to a clean one."

Looking around, Rachel saw that Sullivan had stopped just inside the room. "Come here and help me, please," she said.

"What are you planning to do?" Sullivan asked. "Didn't you have the good sense to vaccinate him when he was unconscious?"

"Of course I did. I just want to get a closer look at him."

Shaking his head, Sullivan said, "Don't let him out of the cage. You don't know what you're dealing with here."

"Oh? What am I dealing with?"

"You can *see* that." He gestured at the dog.

But the animal was no longer growling and snarling. He'd fallen silent, his gaze fixed on Sullivan. He looked a little puzzled, and—what? expectant? He whined softly.

And this one knows him too, Rachel thought. The dog might not have seen Sullivan for weeks or months, but he remembered the vet.

She dared to say it. "You've seen all these dogs before, haven't you? And they have some kind of positive association with you."

"That's crazy. How would I know any of them?"

"You've been taking care of them."

"Good lord," Joe Dolan exclaimed, staring at Sullivan as if the light had suddenly switched on in his head.

"What?" Sullivan shot a look at Dolan, then Rachel. "What are you two blathering about?"

"You take care of the fighting dogs when they're hurt," Rachel said, knowing she could be totally off-base but betting that she wasn't. "You're the only person who's ever been kind to them."

"You've lost your mind, you know that? I'm done here." Sullivan wheeled around and almost ran from the room.

He was out of the building, with Rachel right behind him, when he stopped abruptly and rounded on her. Leaning down, he said in a gruff whisper, "You don't know what you're sticking your nose into. Back off. For your own good. Just back off."

"No. I want some answers. What's going on? How did you get involved with dogfighting?"

"You're making wild guesses—"

"Do you enjoy it? Do you watch them tear each other apart, then patch them up afterwards?"

"No!" Sullivan shook his head. "You don't understand."

"Then make me understand! Tell me how a vet gets involved in dogfighting."

"I've got work to do." Sullivan turned away and yanked open the door of his van.

Rachel grabbed his arm, her fingers bunching the fabric of his khaki jacket. "Don't you dare try to blow me off. I want an answer. Why on earth are you working for a dogfighting operation? What do you get out of it? Do you need extra money that badly?"

For a second his eyes met Rachel's, then he jerked his head sideways and stared into the distance, his face contorted by anger mixed with shame. "It's not money. I wouldn't take money for something like that. It's filthy work, it's disgusting, it's…" He shook his head as if he'd run out of words.

"Then why?" Rachel demanded.

He bowed his head. She waited.

He cleared his throat before he spoke, but his voice was hoarse with emotion. "My son. You know about him?"

Rachel frowned. "Your son who's in rehab? You only have one, don't you?"

Sullivan nodded. "You raise a kid, you pour everything you've got into him—" He paused, blinked, cleared his throat again. "Then he does something stupid and it's all gone. It's all for nothing."

Rachel placed a hand on Sullivan's arm and was encouraged when he let it stay. In a quiet voice, she asked, "What happened to your son, Jim?"

He shrugged helplessly. "What happens to a lot of kids? Drugs. He thought it was fun to get high. They set him up to get to me. They got him hooked on meth, they gave him anything he wanted, said they'd run a tab for him, he could pay when he got the money. More and more and more, until he owed them a small fortune. Then all of a sudden they wanted their money."

"Why didn't you turn them in? Tell the police?"

"They threatened my son. Threatened my wife and me. They wouldn't take our money to pay off our son's debt. Leo Riggs wanted me to make it up in services, tending to the dogs that got hurt."

"But still, you could have—"

"Don't you understand? These people are dangerous. They mean what they say. I threatened to turn them in, and our son just disappeared one night. We searched for two nights and days and couldn't find him. We were scared to death he was lying dead in a ditch somewhere. Then Leo called and said if I'd take care of his dogs, our boy would be home within the hour. My wife was going crazy. Hysterical. I would've agreed to anything. And I agreed to that. We got our son into rehab, and my wife left so she could be close to him. I started taking care of the dogs. Now Leo won't let me stop. He'll kill me if I do. I'm lucky he didn't kill me when I let the Halls' dog go after—"

Rachel's cell phone rang and he broke off.

"Damn it." She yanked the device from her shirt pocket. "I'm sorry, just let me get rid of whoever—" She glanced at the screen for the caller's ID. Marcy Hall. "Oh. It's—I'm sorry, I—"

"Take it," Sullivan said. "I need to get going."

"No, wait." Rachel grabbed his arm and held on. "Just wait a minute, please. Don't go."

Sullivan heaved a weary sigh and stayed where he was.

Still gripping his arm, Rachel punched a button to answer the call. "Marcy? Is something wrong?"

She could barely hear the girl's whisper. She caught a few words. "…David… Uncle Leo called…"

"What? Marcy, I can hardly hear you. Wait—" Rachel adjusted the volume on her phone. "Where are you? What's wrong? Tell me again."

With the volume turned up, she could make out what the girl was whispering. "Our Uncle Leo called David and told him our real daddy wanted him to get us and bring us to him. David made me come. But I don't think he's taking us to our daddy. He's acting crazy, and he's *bleeding.* I'm scared, Dr. Goddard."

Rachel felt like she'd been kicked in the stomach, and for a moment she couldn't catch her breath and speak. "Marcy, are you—You're with Leo now?"

"I told Leo I had to pee, and I was afraid I might pee in his nice clean car, so he let me out and I came back here in the bushes. He doesn't know I have a phone."

Rachel told herself to stay calm. She had to sound calm for Marcy's sake. "Where are you right now?"

"Out on Bald Knob Road," Marcy whispered, "where it meets Kirby Road."

Suddenly Rachel heard a man's voice in the background. "Come on, girl! What's takin' you so damned long?"

"It's him, I have to go," Marcy said in a rush. "Please, Dr. Goddard, please find us and help us."

The phone went dead.

"Oh, no," Rachel moaned.

"What is it?" Sullivan asked, suddenly brusque and business-like again.

"Leo Riggs has Marcy and David Hall." She stared at the phone in her trembling hand as if it might come to life again. "He told them he's taking them to their real father."

"Taking them to their real father?" Sullivan said, incredulous. "Like hell he is. He thinks their father's nigger trash, if you'll excuse the expression."

"I know that!" Rachel cried. Terror rose in her, a drowning flood. "What's he going to do with them? He's wounded, anyway. How can he even—"

"Wounded?" Sullivan said. "What do you mean?"

"Haven't you heard? He took his attack dog to the Rasey house last night and killed Beck Rasey—"

"Aw, shit."

"—and Mrs. Rasey shot him. He's wounded and the police are looking for him. What does he want with two kids? What's he going to do with them?"

Sullivan's face had gone ashen. "We've got to stop this. Where are they?"

"On Knob Hill Road where it meets Kirby."

"That's close to where he keeps the dogs. Call Tom Bridger and tell him to go out to Leo's parents' place. He keeps the dogs in the woods out beyond their house." Sullivan opened the door of his van. "I'm going out there."

"You're not leaving me here," Rachel said. "I'm going with you."

"No, you'll just get hurt."

"I'm going with you," Rachel said. Before Sullivan could stop her, she jogged around the van and climbed into the pas-senger seat.

Chapter Thirty-nine

"Oh, for god's sake, I can't get through to Tom's cell phone," Rachel slapped her phone against the armrest.

"You keep banging that thing around and you won't be able to get through to anybody," Jim Sullivan said.

"This place drives me crazy. One minute you're in the twenty-first century and the next you're totally cut off. We don't have time for this. Maybe I can get through to dispatch."

Rachel tried twice. No luck. She wanted to pitch her useless phone out the window. "It's these damned mountains blocking the signals. Are we going to be riding in a valley the whole way?"

"Just hang on a bit," Sullivan said.

Five minutes later the van emerged from between mountains onto a stretch of road with open land on one side. Rachel tried Tom's phone but still couldn't get through. Next she called the Sheriff's Department dispatcher, and this time she got a connection. "Oh, thank god, thank god." When she had the dispatcher on the line she repeated Sullivan's detailed directions to the spot where Tom should meet them.

"I'll pass it on the minute I get in touch with him, Dr. Goddard," the dispatcher said.

"Where is he?" Rachel asked. "Where was he headed?"

"Well, ma'am, I'm sorry, but a dispatcher's not really at liberty to give out that information. Maybe if you called somebody you know in the department—"

"Okay, okay, just find Tom," Rachel said. "Find him *now*. And tell somebody else what's going on, any officers you can reach. Call the sheriff. They've got to help those kids before Leo Riggs—" Before he did what? She swallowed hard. "He could kill those children. Do you understand?"

"Yes, ma'am, I do understand. I'll pass it on."

Rachel punched the button to end the call.

"Leo probably thinks he'll be safe as long as he's got those kids as hostages," Sullivan said. He leaned forward over the steering wheel as if trying to make the van move faster. "God knows what he's planning to do."

"If he hasn't had any medical treatment, he's probably in a lot of pain," Rachel said. "He won't be thinking clearly." Leo might have reached his hideout by now, with David and Marcy in tow. What would he do in his fury and frustration when he realized he couldn't get away, that taking the kids wouldn't protect him from the police? Rachel imagined Marcy cringing in terror as she realized what was happening to her and her brother.

Why didn't I do something to help her when I had the chance? Why did I let Tom stop me?

◇◇◇

Tom braked at the foot of the slope and looked up at the little stone house where Leo's parents lived. Smoke curled from the chimney.

He studied the lay of the land, assessing the danger to his men. This wasn't a mountain so much as a series of gentle, tree-covered slopes with a few nearly flat patches of ground. The house and several outbuildings rested on the first of those plateaus a hundred feet above the road. Anyone in the house could look directly down the unpaved road and see any vehicles headed upward.

Next to the roadside mailbox a wooden sign about three feet wide warned *Private Property NO TRESPASSING* in hand-painted letters.

Tom turned onto the narrow dirt road and started the climb, with the other cruisers close behind.

They were halfway up when two gaunt figures emerged from the house. Leo's parents took up positions on their front porch, side by side with shotguns aimed at the approaching deputies.

Tom's throat tightened. A bloody scenario sprang up in his mind, playing out as vividly as a movie on the screen. Whatever happened, they were on their own. They couldn't get through to the dispatcher on their car radios from out here. Cell phones wouldn't work. Half the county's police force was on this job, and they couldn't call for backup if they ran into trouble.

"They'd be crazy to open fire on all of us," Brandon said. The tremor in his voice betrayed his fear.

"Get your weapon ready," Tom said. "We need a show of force."

Brandon unsnapped his holster and slid out his pistol.

"Bridger's not coming," Sullivan said. He tapped his fist on the steering wheel in a rapid rhythm.

Rachel grabbed his arm. "If you don't stop doing that, I can't be responsible for my actions."

Sullivan had parked his van at the bottom of a dirt path that seemed to be nothing more than a hiking trail. When Rachel looked closely, she saw tire tracks, probably made when rain had reduced the ground to mud. The trail curved out of sight among the trees, and even with most of the leaves down she saw no buildings or activity up on the hillside. They'd been sitting here for twenty minutes.

"The dispatcher will find him," Rachel said. "He'll come." But how long could she wait, knowing that every minute counted, that Marcy and David could be in mortal danger?

Having stopped his relentless tapping, Sullivan now had a white-knuckle grip on the steering wheel. "If he doesn't show up in a few minutes, I'm going to leave you here and go up there."

"You're not leaving me anywhere," Rachel said.

"Look," Sullivan said, "Leo won't feel threatened if I show up. I'll pretend I don't know about the raid, I'll say I came to take care of the dogs that fought last—Oh, shit." His eyes fastened on something beyond Rachel.

Rachel turned in her seat to look out the window and found herself face to face with Leo Riggs.

"I don't see Leo's car," Brandon said.

"Doesn't mean he's not here." Tom parked in front of the house, and the other seven cruisers pulled in around his, one by one.

In perfectly matched movements, Jake and Maddy Riggs followed the deputies with their shotguns.

Tom got out of his car. Using the door as a shield, he rested his arms on its top edge with his gun trained on the couple. Brandon and the other deputies did the same.

"Can't you boys read signs?" Jake Riggs demanded. "This is private property. What the hell do you think you're doin'?"

The man stood with his feet apart, braced to fire, but Tom thought he saw beads of sweat on Jake's brow and nearly bald head. He wasn't as confident as he wanted the deputies to believe.

"Lower your weapons and lay them on the floor," Tom said. "You ought to know better than to point a gun at this many uniforms."

"This is our land," Maddy Riggs said, her pale bony face pinched with anger. She kept her weapon aimed at Tom. "You're the one that's got no right to be pointin' a gun."

"We're looking for Leo," Tom said. "We know he's been shot. Just let us take him, and we'll get him right to the hospital."

Maddy snorted. "Yeah, you'll make sure he gets treatment—so you can stick him in a prison cell. Or on death row, more likely."

"That's for the courts to decide down the road," Tom said. "It's got nothing to do with what's happening here and now. I'm going to ask you one more time to lay down your guns."

They exchanged a look, then stared back at Tom, their faces hostile and implacable.

Tom shifted his gun, aiming straight at Maddy. He figured she was likely to be the more trigger-happy of the two. If anything was going to go wrong, it would be now, with rage and fear brewing behind those obstinate faces. A band of tension squeezed Tom's chest. "I won't wait much longer," he said.

Jake and Maddy exchanged another look, nervous this time, edgy.

"Do it," Tom said. "Now."

They held on for another stubborn moment, their eyes darting from one deputy to another. Slowly, their faces belligerent, they lowered their shotguns. Hatred glittered in their eyes.

"Lay them down," Tom said.

Again they resisted his order for a few silent seconds before placing the shotguns on the porch floor.

The band around Tom's chest loosened a little, but they weren't out of danger. If Leo was around, maybe watching all this, he'd be waiting for the right time to fire his own gun. He would see the protective vest. He would aim for Tom's head.

"Where's Leo?"

"He ain't in our house," Maddy said. "Go on, tear the place apart if it makes you feel like a big tough lawman. You won't find him in there."

But Leo was nearby, Tom felt certain. Somebody would have to stay with Jake and Maddy while the rest of the men spread out, searched the outbuildings. They were not leaving here without Leo Riggs in custody.

Rachel swallowed a scream. Sullivan grabbed her arm and yanked her toward him. In the next instant she heard something whack against her window, then shards of safety glass flew into the van, showering her lap, her seat, the floor. When she dared to look around, she saw Leo Riggs, his face contorted with rage, slamming a crowbar against the remnants of the window.

Sullivan fumbled with the key in the ignition, turned it.

Get us out of here, Rachel thought. But they couldn't leave Marcy and David. They couldn't run and leave those children behind.

The muzzle of a gun appeared inches from her face. "You're both comin' with me," Leo said.

Chapter Forty

Tom left the protection of his car door and moved closer to the house, his gun still raised. "Where is he?" he demanded.

Jake and Maddy Riggs looked back at him with sullen eyes.

Tom mounted the cinderblock steps. "Is he hiding in one of those sheds out back? Or does he have another hideout around here? You'd damned well better tell me right now. I'm losing patience with the two of you."

"Leave us alone!" Maddy launched herself at Tom and pummeled his shoulder and chest with her fists.

He raised his gun out of her reach and tried to fend her off with his free hand.

In another second the porch overflowed with deputies, and it took four of them to drag Maddy Riggs away from Tom.

Tom turned his attention back to Jake, who had taken advantage of the ruckus to retreat a few feet. He was leaning down, a hand stretched toward one of the shotguns.

Tom grabbed his arm and yanked him upright. "Somebody get these damned guns out of the way," he said. As Brandon scooped them up, Tom shoved Jake against the front of the house. "Is Leo hiding out back?"

Jake maintained his show of bravado for a few more seconds, but staring into the barrel of Tom's pistol brought him around. "He's got a camp up the hill. Close to the top."

"Shut up!" his wife screamed at him.

"Is that where he keeps the dogs?" Tom asked.

"Yeah," Jake said.

"Shut your damned mouth!" Maddy yelled.

"You want us both to get killed?" Jake shouted back. "I'm not aimin' to die today, woman."

Maddy let loose a stream of curses.

"Get these two cuffed and out of the way," Tom told the other deputies. "Put them in separate cars."

"I'm cooperatin'," Jake protested. "You got no call to arrest me."

"Your wife's going in for assaulting a police officer," Tom said. "I'm holding you for questioning. I don't have to charge you."

Brandon held Maddy's arms while Dennis cuffed her and recited her rights. She responded by trying to spit at him, but she couldn't get at him and hit a porch post instead. With the help of both the Blackwood twins, Brandon wrestled her down the steps and into the back of a cruiser. Jake was easier, swearing nonstop but putting up no resistance while Tom cuffed him. Dennis led him to another car.

Tom signaled all the deputies to gather round him. "First we're going to check those sheds out back," he said. "Then we'll spread out and go up the hill. If you spot something, don't go in alone. Use your two-way to let the rest of us know, then wait for my order." His own two-way radio was hooked to his equipment belt and turned off. He pressed the button to activate it.

Tom left Dennis to watch Maddy and Jake Riggs. The rest of the deputies followed him. Gun drawn, he moved along the side of the house and peered around the corner. Four weather-beaten sheds dotted the backyard, in no particular order, as if they'd been randomly dropped onto the landscape. The brown shed farthest from the house was about a hundred feet away.

Tom paused to think. If Leo had a camp on the hill, they'd probably find him there. The risk of him opening fire from one of the sheds was slight. But slight risks sometimes led to funerals.

He motioned for the deputies to spread out. On his signal, they charged toward the sheds.

They flung open the doors one by one, prepared to shoot if necessary.

The sheds were crammed full of wood, coal, and a jumble of rusted gardening tools. Leo wasn't there. Tom could see the deputies relaxing, letting go of the tension generated by fear. But they couldn't relax for long.

"All right," he said. "Let's go up this hill and find him."

In the rearview mirror, Rachel saw Leo glowering from the back seat. The cold muzzle of his gun pressed hard into the nape of her neck.

"Drive," he told Sullivan. "You so much as think about crossin' me and I'll blow her brains out."

"Leo—" Sullivan started.

"Get goin'!"

"Do what he says, Jim, please," Rachel said.

Sullivan turned the van onto the dirt track and started up the hill.

They were going where Marcy and David were, Rachel told herself. They would find a way to free the children. She had to hang onto that thought. Flicking another glance at the rearview mirror, she said, "You're hurt. You're bleeding. You need a doctor."

"I got two doctors right here," he said. "You're gonna do what needs to be done."

"For god's sake, Leo," Sullivan said, "you've got a gunshot wound in your abdomen. You need a surgeon, a hospit—"

"We'll do everything we can," Rachel said. "We'll do our best. Right, Jim?"

He locked eyes with her for a second. "Yeah," he said, shifting his gaze back to the road. "We'll do our best."

Tom threaded his way among the trees, scanning the wooded hillside. He glimpsed Brandon and one of the Blackwood twins, hundreds of feet away on either side of him, moving upward. He'd lost sight of the other deputies.

In some places the hill was easy going, in others it became steep and rocky, and he worked up a sweat fighting his way through brush and tangled vines. He paused when he reached a narrow plateau. If Jake was telling the truth about Leo's camp being near the top of the hill, he should be getting close.

Tom saw nothing but woods up ahead. He looked to his right. In a clearing a couple hundred yards away, he spotted a vehicle.

For a crazy second he thought he recognized the old van. Jim Sullivan had driven it out to the Bridger farm often enough over the years when the sheep needed a vet's attention. But Sullivan couldn't be here. Tom moved closer. The van was parked outside a cabin built of raw planks, faded to a dry gray. At the far edge of the clearing stood an aluminum shed that was bigger than the cabin. Leo kept his dogs in there, Tom guessed. Fallen leaves covered the ground, and half a dozen posts dotted the clearing, dog chains dangling from them.

Tom unhooked his two-way radio from his belt and brought it close to his mouth. Speaking barely above a whisper, he told the other men to move in. Hanging the radio back on his belt, he started toward the cabin.

◇◇◇

Rachel and Sullivan stepped into the cabin with Leo's gun at their backs. The interior was dim, with natural light through a single small window, and bare except for a cot in one corner and a wood-burning stove in another. Next to the stove stood a big black dog.

Rachel's first thought was that the animal looked identical to the alpha dog they'd captured. Then she heard the low growl rumbling in its throat and saw the glint of bared teeth. This was Leo's personal dog, Rachel realized with a shock. The dog that had killed Gordon Hall and Beck Rasey. And it wasn't chained or tied up.

"Down!" Leo snapped.

The dog dropped onto its belly.

Rachel released the breath she'd been holding.

"He does what I tell him to," Leo said, easing himself onto the cot. He leaned back, propped against pillows, his gun in one hand. "And if y'all don't do what I tell you to, you'll have to deal with him."

Rachel's throat was so dry she could barely get her words out. "We can't do anything without more light."

"Turn on all the lanterns," Leo said, waving his gun around the room. "There'll be light enough."

Rachel and Sullivan moved around the room, switching on lanterns that hung from chains attached to the ceiling. She never turned her back on the dog, and Sullivan was equally careful. Neither of them went near the lantern hanging directly above the animal.

Rachel tried to keep an eye on the dog as she and Sullivan removed Leo's blood-soaked shirt and peeled off a wad of sodden gauze to expose his wound. Blood dripped from the gauze as Rachel lifted it.

She stared, horrified, at Leo's abdomen. The ragged hole, six inches across, still oozed blood. Dozens of gunshot pellets studded the muscle tissue. How had he survived this long without treatment?

"Fix it," Leo said. He breathed in rough gasps, air whistling through his teeth. His grip on the gun never loosened. "Get that birdshot outta my gut and sew me the fuck up."

This man was going to die, and Rachel didn't care. All she could think about was Marcy, waiting for Rachel to come for her and her brother. *Where are they? What has he done with them?*

Jim Sullivan seemed transfixed by the sight of the wound. "Good god, Leo, if we start digging around in there you won't be able to stand the pain. We have to give you something—"

"The hell you will!"

Leo's sharp tone brought the dog to its feet, nails scrabbling on the wooden floor, its growl turning to a snarl. Rachel went rigid, her breath caught in her throat.

"You're not dopin' me up. You think I'm that stupid?" Leo swiveled his head on the pillow to glare at the agitated dog. "Quiet! Down!"

The dog fell silent and lowered himself to his belly. Rachel breathed again.

Sullivan kept wary eyes on the dog as he spoke to Leo. "We need surgical implements. I've got everything we need in my van. I'll go get—"

"No," Leo said.

"We can't do anything for you without the right instruments and supplies."

"I know you, Sullivan. You wouldn't think twice about takin' off. You'd save your own hide, you wouldn't give a damn about leavin' her behind to get killed."

Rachel didn't want to look at Sullivan. She was afraid to see in his face a confirmation of what Leo had said. She kept her head down and waited.

"But she wouldn't do that to you," Leo said, his voice a weak rasp. "Would you?"

Rachel raised her head. Leo's eyes gleamed with the desperation of a man crazed by pain. Sweat poured off his face. The gun wobbled in his trembling hands. The smallest thing could set him off, make him pull the trigger.

"No," Rachel said. "I wouldn't do that to him or anyone else."

Leo snorted. "A real bleedin' heart. Always wantin' to help. Too stupid to live, that's what I call you."

"Let me get the supplies and instruments," Rachel said. "I won't run, not as long as Dr. Sullivan's in here with you."

Tom edged closer, using trees for cover. He didn't see the other deputies yet. He would watch and wait until they found their way to him.

The door of the cabin opened and Rachel emerged.

"What the hell—" Tom realized he'd spoken aloud, and he clamped his mouth shut. What in god's name was she doing here?

Rachel ran across a carpet of fallen leaves to the van, yanked open the rear door and hoisted herself inside.

He had to get her attention, find out what was happening. Darting from tree to tree, he closed in on the clearing. He could see the cabin's window, so he had to assume that anybody looking out that window might catch sight of him. He pressed against an oak tree, standing sideways to reduce his visibility, and sneaked a look every few seconds. The van had the Mountainview Animal Hospital name, barely visible through a layer of dirt, on the driver's door.

What was Rachel doing in the van? Why was she out here, and why was Jim Sullivan with her?

He heard the slap and rustle of her feet hitting dead leaves. Daring exposure, he poked his head out from behind the tree. Rachel struggled to hold onto a cardboard box with one arm while she closed the van's door.

Tom gave a short, sharp whistle, the whistle he always used to call Billy Bob.

Rachel spun around, scanned the woods, locked eyes with Tom. Her mouth opened, but she made no sound. For a moment she seemed frozen in place. Then she shook her head, a clear warning.

Clutching the box against her chest, she turned and ran back to the cabin. When the door closed behind her, Tom felt as if she'd dropped into an abyss and he was helpless to catch her.

Rachel wanted to torture Leo, make him scream, make him beg for mercy, but the rage inside her didn't direct the movements of her hands. Using forceps she'd retrieved from the van, she picked gunshot pellets out of the gaping wound with the same care she would bring to any procedure. Her gentleness hardly mattered. Without anesthetic, this had to hurt like hell.

Leo's teeth chattered as he tried to grit them against the pain. Jim Sullivan dabbed the wound with gauze again and again, soaking up the blood so Rachel could see what she was doing. In the corner, the dog growled, a constant menacing background noise.

Rachel was aware of Sullivan glancing repeatedly at the animal, and when she looked up what she saw on his face made her go cold inside. Sullivan might be fearless in handling other aggressive dogs, but he was terrified of this one.

Tom was outside. He wouldn't be alone. Other deputies must be out there in the woods around the cabin. They might think they could burst in and overpower Leo, but they couldn't know the dog was in here, ready to attack on Leo's command.

She pressed the forceps into the muscle to get at a deeply imbedded pellet. Leo cried out.

The dog jumped to his feet and snarled.

"Sorry," Rachel said, her eyes on the dog. "I didn't mean to hurt you. That one was hard to get at."

She waited while he relaxed a little and his breathing returned to a rapid but normal rhythm. The dog, too, relaxed and settled down. Rachel went back to work.

After a couple of minutes, she dared to ask, "Where are Marcy and David? Are they here somewhere?"

"None of your damned business," Leo choked out. "Keep workin'."

"I just want to know they're okay."

Leo pushed himself up with one arm and leveled the gun at her. "Shut up and keep workin'."

Where the hell were the other guys? What was taking them so long to find him? Tom checked the sky to orient himself, then spoke quietly into his two-way radio. "The camp is on the southeast slope. Repeat, move southeast. I need backup."

One voice answered, "Roger, Captain." Brandon.

He couldn't just stand here behind a tree and wait. He needed to know what was happening in that cabin. Moving sideways, tree to tree, he worked his way into a spot that wouldn't be visible from the cabin's single front window. He broke away from his tree cover and sprinted to the side of the cabin. Dropping down, he duck-walked around to the front. He crouched directly under the window and listened for voices from inside.

"We have to use clamps," Sullivan told Rachel, keeping his voice low. But he was watching the dog. The animal moved about restlessly in its corner, as if waiting for Leo's command to release him from an invisible cage. "We can't close this with sutures."

"Stop whisperin'," Leo said. "I know you're plottin' against me. You can just forget about your little plans. You cross me and you'll end up like Hall and Rasey."

"We're just trying to decide how to close the wound," Rachel said. "It's going to hurt, no matter what we do."

"Just get on with it!" he bellowed.

The dog snarled and took a couple of steps toward them.

"Please don't shout," Rachel pleaded. "Try to stay quiet." *You're upsetting your dog,* she almost said, and she had a wild urge to laugh at the innocuous sound of it.

"Stop yappin' and do your goddamn job!" Leo pointed his pistol at the ceiling and fired.

Rachel cried out and stumbled backward into Sullivan.

The door banged open and Tom charged in.

The dog lunged. It slammed into Tom's side and knocked him to the floor. His gun flew out of his hands.

"Leo, stop the dog!" Rachel screamed. "Call him off!"

Leo's answer was a cackling laugh.

Tom rolled on the floor, the dog on top of him and tearing at his jacket.

Rachel threw herself at the animal, gripped its ears and pulled. The dog ignored her and ripped a sleeve off Tom's jacket.

Where was Tom's gun? Rachel searched frantically. There, on the floor against the wall. She dove for it.

"Good boy," Leo called to the dog. "Good boy."

Rachel focused on Tom's gun and was barely aware of Sullivan struggling with Leo. She heard Leo cry out in pain. The blast of another gunshot filled the room.

"Rachel!" Tom cried. He'd pulled his body into a tight knot, one arm over his head. The other reached toward Rachel.

She scrambled toward him on her knees, the gun in one hand. Could she shoot the dog? Could she do it without hitting Tom?

"Give it to me," Tom yelled. "Rachel, give me the gun!"

She pressed it into his hand.

The dog sank its teeth into Tom's other arm. Tom raised the pistol and shot the animal between the eyes.

The next few seconds passed in a blur of movement. The dog dropped to the floor. Tom rolled onto his knees and pushed himself to his feet. All Rachel saw as she jumped up was Tom's torn and bleeding arm.

Tom turned the gun on Leo. Only then did Rachel realize Leo could have shot them both, still might shoot them—if he had his gun. But the pistol was in Jim Sullivan's hand now, and he held it out to Tom.

Leo moaned. He lay on the cot, a hand to his shoulder, blood from a fresh wound seeping through his fingers.

"Jim," Rachel said, "did you—"

"It was him or me," Sullivan said. His face had drained of color and he looked stunned, unbelieving. "Him or me."

"You did good," Tom gasped.

"Tom, you need a doctor," Rachel said. "You have to get to the hospital. But we need to find Marcy and David—"

"Marcy and David? What are you talking about?"

"Didn't the dispatcher—She must not have—Leo took Marcy and David, he brought them up here, at least we thought he did."

"They've got to be here somewhere," Sullivan said. He rubbed at his eyes as if trying to wake himself from a daze.

In three strides, Tom crossed the room to Leo. "Where are those kids?"

Leo laughed, a ragged noise filled with contempt and anger and pain.

Tom brought a knee down on Leo's open wound. Leo screamed. "Answer me, you goddamned piece of shit. Where are they?"

"Out back—dog shed—Get off me, get off me!"

Rachel raced out the door. Deputies were running out of the woods from every direction. "Help Tom!" she yelled, but she didn't slow down.

The sheet metal shed stood at the edge of the clearing. Rachel wrenched open the door and saw only darkness inside. She heard the rustle of animals moving about. "Marcy! It's Dr. Goddard. Are you in there?"

A muffled cry answered her.

Suddenly Brandon was beside Rachel, switching on a flashlight. "Hold on, let's check it out before we go in."

When Brandon shone the light into the shed, Rachel leaned forward along with him to see what they were facing. Cages lined the walls. A few were empty. Pit bulls stared back from others.

The muffled cry came again, and another joined it.

Rachel and Brandon rushed inside and fell to their knees in front of two cages that held Marcy and David. Bound and gagged, scared out of their wits, but alive.

The Blackwood twins entered the cabin with weapons drawn. "Everything's under control." Tom tried to ignore the searing pain in his arm, the blood flowing from his wounds. "Get this son of a bitch on his feet."

Leo moaned and swore as Kevin and Keith hauled him upright.

"You're under arrest for the murders of Gordon Hall and—"

"He deserved it!" Leo yelled. "That son of a bitch killed my sister so he could get her kids for his wife."

"What the hell are you talking about?" Tom said.

Leo looked up at Tom with fevered eyes. "The great Dr. Hall murdered my sister, right there in his damned hospital."

"Yeah, sure, Leo. So you sold the kids to him, then waited nine years to kill him?"

Leo gave his hideous laugh again. "You think you're so damned smart. You don't know the half of it yet. You don't know who paid me to get rid of Hall."

Chapter Forty-one

The sound of Tom's footsteps on the tile floor echoed in his ears, loud and intrusive, as he walked down the hushed corridor of the intensive care unit. His wounded left arm throbbed in time to his footfalls. In the glass-walled rooms he passed, patients lay quietly dying or struggling to hang onto life, with tubes measuring out nourishment and pain relief and monitors tracking every faltering heartbeat. At the far end of the corridor Vicky Hall was fighting her own battle.

Tom felt as if he'd come to deliver the final blow for Vicky. He was about to destroy what was left of her family.

He found Beth Hall sitting on the floor outside Vicky's room, her back against the wall. For one white-hot moment Tom wanted to drag the girl to her feet and shake the breath out of her. He wanted to make her answer for her stupidity. *Do you have any idea what happened to Marcy and David today?* Would she give a damn?

The moment passed. Marcy and David were safe in temporary foster care while the sheriff himself pulled strings to get their real grandparents declared their guardians. Leo Riggs had died on the operating table and Rayanne was being held on suspicion of drugging Vicky. Beth turned out to be relatively blameless in this mess, and she had a hard enough time ahead, with a lot of fast growing up to do. Tom didn't need the satisfaction of ripping into her. Instead, he asked, "How's your mother doing?"

Beth looked up at him with tear-reddened eyes. "She's a little better now, but she's in really bad shape."

Tom looked through the glass at the frail figure lying in bed with an IV tube in one arm and a cannula delivering oxygen through her nose. At the foot of the bed stood Ethan, unshaven and rumpled, his shoulders slumped with exhaustion.

"Soo Jin!" Beth exclaimed. She scrambled to her feet.

Tom turned to see Soo Jin coming down the hall in a wheelchair pushed by a young blond nurse. An IV bag hung from a stand attached to the chair.

"She wants to see her mother," the nurse said when they reached Tom and Beth. "The doctor okayed it. But not for long. She needs to get back in bed."

Beth dropped to her knees beside the wheelchair and grasped one of Soo Jin's hands. "I'm so glad you're all right, I thought you were going to die too." Fresh tears spilled down Beth's cheeks. "I'm sorry I was so nasty to you. Please don't leave me alone. Please."

Soo Jin laid her free hand on the girl's head. The IV tube trailed from the back of her hand. "You're not alone, Beth. Let's go in and see Mother."

"Just two at a time," the young nurse said.

"I've got business with Ethan," Tom said. "He'll be leaving."

"Leaving?" Beth said. She pushed herself to her feet. "Why?"

"I'll explain later." Tom tapped lightly on the glass. When Ethan's eyes met Tom's his face went slack as realization flooded in. He'd probably heard that Leo Riggs had been arrested, that he was here in the hospital undergoing surgery. Ethan knew what was coming. He'd simply been waiting for Tom to uncover the truth.

Tom motioned for him to come out. Ethan went to his mother and kissed her forehead. He looked down at his mother for one long, last moment before he walked out of the room to face Tom. He didn't seem surprised to see Soo Jin in the hall in her wheelchair.

Beth cocked her head. "What's going on?"

"Go in with Mom," Ethan said.

"But—"

"Beth," Soo Jin said, taking the girl's hand, "come with me."

For a second Soo Jin's eyes met Tom's, and he realized that somehow she understood what was happening.

Tom held the door open for them. Doubtful and reluctant, still looking back at Tom and Ethan, Beth followed her sister into their mother's room.

Tom watched panic building in Ethan as he clenched and unclenched his fists and his gaze darted around without lighting anywhere.

"Come on," Tom said, gripping Ethan's arm. "It's time to go."

At headquarters, Tom sat across the conference room table and waited while Ethan laid his head on his folded arms and sobbed. "I'm sorry, I'm so sorry," he moaned.

A tape recorder lay on the table between them, but Tom hadn't turned it on yet. Ethan had been pouring out his misery in tears for almost twenty minutes. Watching him, Tom wondered how this kid—in almost every way except age, he was still just a kid—could possibly survive in prison.

When Ethan's sobs subsided to faint gasps and he raised his head, Tom switched on the recorder and recited the date and his and Ethan's names. "Why did you do it, Ethan?" he asked. "How did you ever get hooked up with Leo, and why would you hire him to do something like that to your father?"

"I didn't know he was going to use a dog. I didn't know it was going to be..." His voice trailed off and he hung his head.

"So killing your father with a gun or a knife would have been okay?" Tom asked. "Your only regret is the murder method Leo used?"

Ethan buried his face in his hands.

"You've cried enough." Tom reached across the table and tore Ethan's hands away from his face. "It's time for you to own up to what you've done. Tell me why you wanted your father dead."

"You don't understand what it was like."

"Okay, tell me what it was like. Tell me your story."

"Nothing I ever did was good enough for him," Ethan choked out.

Jesus Christ, Tom thought. Had Ethan ever made it past the emotional age of ten? "So you hated him."

"No!" Ethan cried. "I loved him. He was my dad. But my whole life, he made me feel like I was never going to measure up. All of us, we were…" He searched for a word. "We were just *projects* to him, like the hospital was. He was proud of Soo Jin, as if she was something he created. And Marcy and David, he liked the thought of rescuing them and making them into something better, so he could get the credit. I think Mom wanted them because she thought they were cute. Like pets. Beth and me, we didn't mean much to them either. And Soo was the only one who turned out the way they wanted."

Tom's mother had seen past the facade of the Hall family, and Rachel had picked up on the truth in just a few brief encounters with the Halls. Part of the truth, anyway. A lot more might remain to be uncovered. "Leo claims your father killed Marcy and David's real mother so he could get the kids for your mother," Tom said. "Do you think that's true?"

Ethan shook his head. "I don't know. But I can tell you, it wouldn't surprise me. He thought there were some people who didn't deserve to be helped. He thought drug addicts ought to be allowed to kill themselves with overdoses, nobody should try to help them get clean. He called them garbage. He said the world would be better off if we got rid of the garbage."

"How did you get involved with Leo?" Tom asked.

"He came after me," Ethan said. "He sought me out. And he played me, he made me feel like he was the only one who understood what I was going through. He really got off on getting me to do things behind Dad's back, things Dad would've hated. He gave me drugs, he paid me to sell drugs at school."

Tom interrupted. "You're saying Leo's been dealing drugs since you were in high school?"

Ethan nodded. "He was working for the Shacklefords. Then when you arrested them back in January, he just took over and kept the business going."

All this time, Tom thought, *and I didn't have a damned clue. Some sheriff material I am.* "Are you still part of it?"

"Yeah. I've been a courier ever since I moved to Florida. And Dad found out. It was my own stupidity—It was almost like I wanted him to find out, you know? I didn't, not consciously, but I brought stuff into the house the last time I visited, it's like I set myself up to get caught."

"You told him you were working for Leo?" Tom asked.

"Yeah." Ethan sniffled and wiped his nose with the back of his hand. "He said he'd rather see me in prison than know I was living that way."

"But he didn't turn you in," Tom pointed out. "You or Leo."

"He was trying to decide how to handle it. He went to see Leo, he cut off the money—he'd been giving Leo money regularly. Dad didn't know he had money coming in from dealing, and he thought Leo needed help to keep the garage going. When he found out about the drugs, he cut off the money supply and said he was going to make Leo pay for what he was doing."

It was all clear to Tom now, the whole pathetic mess. Hall had no idea how much danger he'd put himself in by voicing his threat. The man's massive ego probably made him feel invulnerable. He thought he could continue with his life while he kept his son and a lunatic like Leo waiting to learn whether he was going to expose them.

"It was Leo's idea to kill him, not mine," Ethan said, "I swear it was."

"But you thought it was a good idea," Tom said.

Ethan's eyes, hot with shame, met Tom's briefly. "He said he'd do it, but wanted money. He wanted ten thousand up front, and more after it was over. I didn't know he was going to use a dog. I didn't have any idea. Once it was done, he had this hold over me; he was in charge. His girlfriend was already working in the house, and she was telling him every move I made. Then he sent his friends to the house with guns, and I had to act like I wanted them there guarding the place. They were there to scare me. To remind me I had to go along with the plan."

"So Leo wanted your father out of the way because he blamed your father for his sister Jewel's death, and also because he was afraid of being turned in for drug dealing."

Ethan nodded. "But that wasn't all. After he killed my dad, he wanted to get rid of my mother too. He figured if they were both out of the way, I'd get control of all the money and they could bleed me dry."

"Has Rayanne been drugging your mother? I asked for a tox screen before she had dialysis. When the results come back, are they going to show something in her blood that shouldn't be there?"

"Yes. I don't know exactly what it was, but she was giving Mom a tranquilizer or something, and I couldn't stop her. I tried, I swear I did."

"Who slashed Soo Jin's tires? Did Leo make you do that?"

"No! That was Rayanne too. She told me she did it. Soo was asking a lot of questions. She's smart, smarter than I'll ever be, and she was figuring it all out. Rayanne was scared of her. If I hadn't gone out to see Leo that night, Soo wouldn't have gone out either, and the accident wouldn't have happened. But Rayanne and Leo would've found another way to kill her." He covered his face with his hands.

"Ethan," Tom said, "do you admit that you paid Leo Riggs to kill your father?"

"Yes," Ethan said, his voice hardly more than a whisper behind his hands.

"Say it. Clearly."

He dropped his hands. "I paid Leo Riggs to kill my father."

Chapter Forty-two

One week later

Rachel watched Marcy's reflection in the mirror as the girl filled the dresser drawers with her underwear and sweaters. She was transferring everything she owned, all the clothes and books and toys she'd accumulated as a member of the Hall family, into a small bedroom at her grandparents' house, but her expressionless face offered no clue to her feelings about this monumental change in her life.

A burst of laughter came from the kitchen down the hall, and Marcy paused as if listening. Rachel heard David's voice, then Raymond's. Marcy had chosen not to join the rest of the family in a snack, and Rachel had followed her to the bedroom to help her unpack and keep her from being alone.

"Let's sit down and talk for a minute," Rachel said. She stepped around the big box they'd been emptying and sat on the bed.

Obediently, Marcy left a dresser drawer standing open and came to sit beside Rachel.

"Your grandparents put a lot of time into fixing up this room for you," Rachel said. "Your grandmother made the curtains herself."

"They're pretty. It's a nice room." But Marcy wasn't looking at the blue walls and curtains, the new throw rug and bedspread. She sat with her head down, her hands clasped in her lap.

"Do you understand everything that's happening?" Rachel asked. "Did the judge explain it clearly enough?"

"He said David and I are going to live here until our real dad gets custody. He said that Mother and Daddy—I mean—"

"I know who you mean, sweetie."

"He said they didn't do the adoption the way the law says they're supposed to."

"They didn't have your real dad's permission to take you."

Marcy was silent a moment, her body perfectly still. Rachel had never seen a child who could hold herself as still as Marcy did, like a rabbit afraid of catching a predator's eye. When she spoke again, her voice was so soft Rachel had to ask her to repeat what she'd said.

"Is Mother going to die?"

In that quiet question Rachel heard a sadness and longing that broke her heart. Vicky Hall, whatever her flaws, was the only mother Marcy remembered, and now she'd vanished from the girl's life. "Mrs. Hall is very sick," Rachel said. "Rayanne made her condition worse by giving her sedatives that her body couldn't handle. She's better now, but I won't lie to you, I don't think we can expect her to live much longer."

Marcy nodded as if accepting this. "But Soo Jin's okay?"

"She's recovering. She'll look after Beth."

"They don't like each other."

"They'll have to learn to get along," Rachel said. "They'll be the only ones left to inherit the hospital. They might end up as business partners, although I'll admit that's hard to imagine."

Rachel saw a flicker of amusement on Marcy's face and felt like whooping in triumph. The numbness was wearing off. Maybe Marcy was ready to start connecting with the world around her.

"Don't worry about anybody else," Rachel said. "You need to concentrate on settling in and getting to know your grandparents and your father. I hope you realize how happy they are to have you and David here."

"They seem nice."

"They're good people, Marcy. I know you don't remember them, but they remember you, and they never stopped loving you."

"David's happy now."

"And I hope you will be too."

After another silence, Marcy asked, "Who am I now? Is my last name Porter? I'm not Marcy Hall anymore, am I?"

"Oh, sweetheart." Rachel placed an arm around Marcy's shoulders and pulled her close. "The name might change, but you're the same person you always were. So many people care about you and want you to be happy. I know it's a big adjustment—it's a *huge* adjustment—but please give your grandparents and father a chance to show you how much they love you."

This had seemed the best outcome to Rachel, and only now was she beginning to see how difficult it would be for Marcy. Her uncle and a man she considered a brother had teamed up to kill the man she thought of as a father, her older sister had almost died, her uncle had locked her and her brother in a cage in a dark shed. She had gone from a white family to a black one, from a cold but comfortingly familiar home to one so different it might as well sit on another planet. The one thing Rachel didn't pity Marcy for was losing the luxuries of the Hall household. Compared to a cold, loveless mansion with all the creature comforts, a humble but loving home was the hands-down winner.

A tap sounded on the open door. "You about ready to go?" Tom asked.

Marcy pulled away from Rachel's embrace as if she'd been caught doing something forbidden. *How can I leave her here?* Rachel thought. She wanted to scoop Marcy up and take her home and be a mother to her.

Crazy thoughts. Crazy feelings. She had to surrender Marcy to her family and allow them to help her heal emotionally.

Rachel hugged the girl again, felt Marcy relax just enough to hug her back. "It's going to be all right," Rachel whispered. "It really is. And you can call me anytime you want to talk. I'll be back to see you again. Lots of times."

She forced herself to let go of Marcy and walk out of the room.

Abel and Lucinda Porter, their son Raymond, and their grandson David sat around a big table in the old-fashioned kitchen. A wonderful sweet aroma filled the room. Mrs. Porter had a cake in the oven, and all the ingredients for chocolate icing sat ready on a counter.

David and his father had been laughing, Rachel realized with a jolt. She wouldn't have thought David was capable of it. He hardly looked like the same boy anymore, with a not-quite-believing-it elation replacing his habitual sullenness. He had what he wanted. He had his father back.

"Is Marcy all right?" Mrs. Porter asked Rachel. "Should I go look in on her?"

"She's putting her things away. I think she just needs a little time to herself."

"Well, then, I'll let her be until dinnertime. I'm cooking up a treat for her. David tells me she can't resist chocolate cake."

"If we don't get out of here," Tom said, "you're going to have me lining up for a piece."

"I can make a chocolate cake," Rachel said. "Let's go home and I'll prove it."

"Dr. Goddard, before you leave—" Raymond stood and held out a hand to Rachel. "I want to thank you for going out to Leo's place to find my children."

She smiled and shook his hand. "I'm glad it's working out for all of you."

After a round of goodbyes and promises to get together again soon, Tom and Rachel took their leave of the reunited Porter family. As they walked out into the chilly autumn afternoon, Tom put an arm around Rachel. "I know this is hard," he said, "but she'll be all right. You believe that, don't you?"

"Yes, I believe that. And sooner or later I'll pull myself together and start acting like I believe it."

They climbed into Tom's pickup truck, which they'd used to cart Marcy and David's belongings from the Hall house. A social worker had brought the children from the temporary foster home to the farm.

Rachel buckled her seat belt. "Did you tell the Porters about the trust fund?"

"No." Tom turned the key in the ignition. "They'll find out from Vicky Hall's lawyer. It won't affect the kids' lives now, anyway. It's for their college educations."

"It's the least Mrs. Hall can do for them, after the way she's treated them."

"Let's be grateful she's giving them up without a fight." Tom drove down the driveway toward the road. "Soo Jin says Vicky's tying up loose ends before she dies."

Rachel expelled a sour laugh. "Loose ends? Is that how she sees two kids she stole from their family?"

"It's over, Rachel." Tom braked at the end of the driveway and reached over to brush her cheek with his palm. "You have to step back now and let it go."

"I know. I'm trying, I really am." She drew a deep, calming breath, let it out. Marcy's plight had struck too close to home for Rachel and dredged up all the emotional turmoil of her own childhood. But she refused to wallow in it, and she had no reason to doubt that Marcy was in good hands.

Tom turned onto the road and they set off toward home. "It all worked out for the best. Leo's gone. He can't hurt the kids anymore. Ethan and Rayanne and Pete are in jail. The dogs are safe—"

"Thank you for not charging Jim Sullivan for working with Leo. He's a good farm vet, and he doesn't deserve to lose his career."

"Leo forced him into it," Tom said. "I don't want to ruin the man's life."

They rode in silence for a few minutes. Rachel watched the hills and fields they passed and couldn't help wondering how many more abandoned dogs would have to be rescued from starvation as winter took hold in the mountains.

"Rachel," Tom said, "will you do something for me?"

"Of course." She turned to him. "What is it?"

Tom reached for her hand. "Will you stop making a face every time you look at my mother's wallpaper and just pick out what you want to replace it, so we can get started?"

Rachel almost laughed, but she stifled the impulse when she realized Tom wasn't laughing. He glanced at her with eyes as solemn as the questions he hadn't spoken aloud. *Can you think of my house as ours, as your home? Will you promise to stay with me?*

For a moment the old panic gripped her, sucked the air from her lungs. She was a pretender, she wasn't who she said she was. She could never forget that she had another life, a shadow life, suspended in time but always waiting to reclaim her. Would she ever stop feeling this loneliness, an ache so deep and familiar that she couldn't imagine its absence? Her life before she met Tom had been so bizarre he couldn't possibly comprehend what she'd been through, however much of the story she shared with him. He seemed to realize that. He hadn't pushed her to tell him every detail. She had almost begun to believe he might love her even though there were dark places in her heart and mind he could never enter.

"Rachel?" he said softly, his hand gripping hers but his gaze fixed on the road ahead. "What do you think?"

"Blue," she said. "Blue paint for the bedroom. I'm not sure yet about the rest. But no more flowered wallpaper. Please."

Tom smiled, a slow sweet smile that crinkled the corners of his eyes and lit up his face. "Let's meet for lunch at the Mountaineer tomorrow. We can stop by the hardware store afterward and pick up some paint samples."

"It's a date." How easy it was to make this huge commitment, she thought, even when she was scared to death she was going to do everything wrong.

To receive a free catalog of Poisoned Pen Press titles, please contact us in one of the following ways:

Phone: 1-800-421-3976
Facsimile: 1-480-949-1707
Email: info@poisonedpenpress.com
Website: www.poisonedpenpress.com

Poisoned Pen Press
6962 E. First Ave. Ste. 103
Scottsdale, AZ 85251